THE ORION FRONT

THE ORION WAR – BOOK 9

BY M. D. COOPER

Just in Time (JIT) & Beta Readers

Lisa Richman
Scott Reid
Chad Burroughs
Timothy Van Oosterwyk Bruyn
Randy Miller
David Wilson
Gene Bryan
David Hansen

ISBN: 978-1-64365-032-6

Version 1.0.0

Cover Art by Andrew Dobell
Editing by Jen McDonnell, Bird's Eye Books

TABLE OF CONTENTS

FOREWORD

When I was preparing to write this book, I was wandering around the Interwebs (as I often do) and I stumbled across an article on bacteria that feeds directly off electricity.

In essence, all life is really about electricity, which is to say, shuffling around free electrons to make different ionized things that we then use to keep ourselves alive. We breathe in oxygen so that our cells can push electrons into that element and keep a flow of energy going through our body.

Obviously, this is a super simplified version of a very complex biology, but an important part of it is that we (along with most lifeforms) are not capable of directly harvesting electrons from an electrical flow. We have to get them out of various compounds that will give up their valence electrons without a fuss.

However, as it turns out, if you stick a rod into moist soil or dirt from the seabed and pump electrons into it, you will find that bacteria begins to move to the rod. This bacteria (scientists are discovering that there are many, many types that do this) feeds directly off the electricity. They even form cables several centimeters long to channel energy to their buddies.

For reference, the first of these were discovered by Derek Lovely of the University of Massachusetts. He found them on the banks of the Potomac near Washington DC.

From a BBC article: "The microbes, called Geobacter metallireducens, were getting their electrons from organic compounds, and passing them onto iron oxides. In other words they were eating waste—including ethanol—and effectively 'breathing' iron instead of oxygen.... They are even able to effectively 'eat' pollution. They will convert the organic compounds in oil spills into carbon dioxide, or turn soluble radioactive metals like plutonium and uranium into insoluble forms that are less likely to contaminate groundwater—and they will generate electricity in the process."

Over the years, more and more of these bacteria have been found, and while many harvest their electrons from sources not available to most life, some are capable of sucking up raw electrons. Essentially, they can drink from the firehose.

I won't put in links, as those are likely to be no good after a time, but googling "bacteria that eat electricity" can start you down a rather fun rabbit hole.

Why is all of this noteworthy? Well, other than that the fact that I'm a huge nerd and I think it's cool, it's just amazing that such a thing exists...and that it has so much amazing potential to help us manage our environment. Of course, it might get used in some very interesting ways in the future too....

So, I should probably make this foreword about something in addition to the research. One thing of note is that I really took my time writing this book. I freed up my schedule a lot, and spent a lot of time just thinking about where to take this part of the story. I still know where it's all going, but there are parts of the journey that are fuzzy to me, and sussing out where the characters are going is half the fun of writing.

I think that some things are moving in interesting directions, and moreover, we're getting a lot more time with Tangel—who is really hard to write for because so much of her conflict is extradimensional, and not really describable to our 3D-oriented minds, at least not without making a lot of tiresome descriptions.

Luckily, some new challenges came along for her, and Tangel is going to have to grow in ways she didn't expect.

Michael Cooper
Danvers 2019

PREVIOUSLY...

When last we left Tangel and the Allies, the assault teams striking against Airtha had defeated the Ascended AI and kept the Widows from destroying the ring.

The losses they suffered, however, were not inconsequential. Seraphina and Fina were gravely injured, and Iris was found with her core destroyed.

Elsewhere, Cary has assumed the role of A1, leader of the Widows, and has taken their flagship to the Karaske System to meet with General Garza. Though her plan is to take him out and cripple his network of spies and agents, she is falling deeper and deeper into her role as A1.

Joe is in pursuit of his daughters, and Terrance and Earnest have found the drone manufacturing facility where the core AIs are creating their diffuse dyson spheres to move stars.

And lastly, unbeknownst to the Alliance, the core AIs have infiltrated the QuanComm network at Khardine and are now privy to all of the Allies' communications—and are able to alter them....

KEY CHARACTERS

Airtha – Both the name of a ring encircling a white dwarf in the Huygens System and the AI who controls it, Airtha was once a human woman named Jelina, wife of Jeffrey Tomlinson. After venturing to the galactic core on a research mission, she returned as an AI—one with a vendetta.

Amavia – The result of Ylonda and Amanda's merger when they were attacked by Myriad aboard Ylonda's ship. The new entity occupies Amanda's body, but possesses an overlapped blend of their minds. Amavia has served aboard *Sabrina* since the ship left New Canaan after the Defense of Carthage, but is now the ambassador to the League of Sentients at Aldebaran.

Carmen – Ship's AI of the *Damon Silas*. Captured by Roxy during her assault on the ship.

Cary – Tangel's biological daughter. Has a trait where she can deep-Link with other people, creating a temporary merger of minds, and is able to utilize extradimensional vision to see ascended beings.

Cheeky – Pilot of *Sabrina*, reconstituted by a neural dump Piya made of her mind before she died on Costa Station.

Erin – Engineer responsible for the construction of the New Canaan Gamma bases, in addition to a number of other projects.

Faleena – Tangel's AI daughter, born of a mind merge between Tanis, Angela, and Joe.

Finaeus – Brother of Jeffrey Tomlinson, and Chief Engineer aboard the *I2*.

Helen – Former AI of Sera's who was killed by her father in the events leading up to Jeffrey's assassination. A copy of that shard was found to be on the Airthan ring as well.

Iris – The AI who was paired with Jessica during the hunt for Finaeus, who then took on a body (that was nearly identical to Jessica's) after they came back. She remained with Amavia at Aldebaran to continue diplomatic relations with the League of Sentients.

Jeffrey Tomlinson – Former president of the Transcend, found in stasis in an underground chamber on Bolt Hole, a planet in the Large Magellanic Cloud.

Jen – ISF AI paired with Sera.

Jessica Keller – ISF admiral who has returned to the *I2* after an operation deep in the Inner Stars to head off a new AI war. She also spent ten years traveling through Orion space before the Defense of Carthage—specifically the Perseus Arm, and Perseus Expansion Districts.

Joe – Admiral in the ISF, commandant of the ISF academy, and husband of Tangel.

Kara – Daughter of Adrienne, Kara was rescued by Katrina when fleeing from Airtha, and came to New Canaan aboard the *Voyager*.

Katrina – Former Sirian spy, wife of Markus, and eventual governor of the Victoria colony at Kapteyn's Star—and Warlord of the Midditerra System.

Krissy Wrentham – TSF admiral responsible for internal fleets fighting against Airtha in the Transcend civil war. She is also the daughter of Finaeus Tomlinson and Lisa Wrentham.

Lisa – Former wife of Finaeus Tomlinson, she left the Transcend for the Orion Freedom Alliance when Krissy was young. Head of a clandestine group within the OFA known as the Widows, which hunts down advanced technology and destroys it.

Misha – Head (and only) cook aboard *Sabrina*.

Nance – Ship's engineer aboard *Sabrina*, recently transferred back there from the ISF academy.

Priscilla – One of Bob's two avatars.

Rachel – Captain of the *I2*. Formerly, captain of the *Enterprise*.

Roxy – Justin's sister, kept subservient to him as his lover via mental coercion.

Saanvi – Tangel's adopted daughter, found in a derelict ship that entered the New Canaan System.

Sabrina – Ship's AI and owner of the starship *Sabrina*.

Sera – Director of the Hand and former president of the Transcend. Daughter of Airtha and Jeffrey Tomlinson.

LMC Sera (Seraphina) – A copy of Sera made by Airtha containing all of Sera's desired traits and memories. Captured by Sera and the allies during their excursion into the Large Magellanic Cloud.

Valkris Sera (Fina) – A copy of Sera made by Airtha containing all of Sera's desired traits and memories. Captured by ISF response forces who came to the aid of the TSF defenders during the siege of Valkris.

Terrance – Terrance Enfield was the original backer for the *Intrepid*, though once the ship jumped forward in time, he took it as an opportunity to retire. Like Jason, he was pulled into active service by Tangel when New Canaan became embroiled in the Orion War.

Troy – AI pilot of the *Excelsior* who was lost during the Battle of Victoria, and later found by Katrina. He joined her on the hunt for the *Intrepid* aboard the *Voyager*, jumping forward in time via Kapteyn's Streamer.

Tangel – The entity that resulted from Tanis and Angela's merger into one being. Not only is Tangel a full merger of a human and AI, but she is also an ascended being.

Usef – ISF Colonel who served on *Sabrina* for several years, as well as aided Erin in stopping several acts of sabotage in New Canaan.

MAPS

For more maps, visit www.aeon14.com/maps.

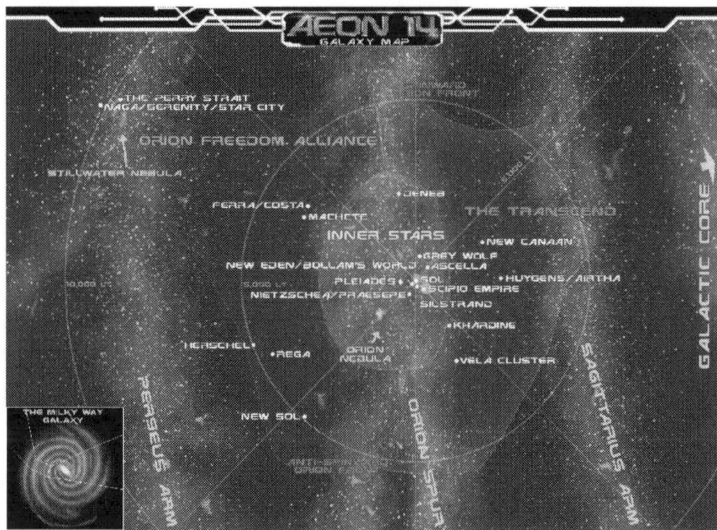

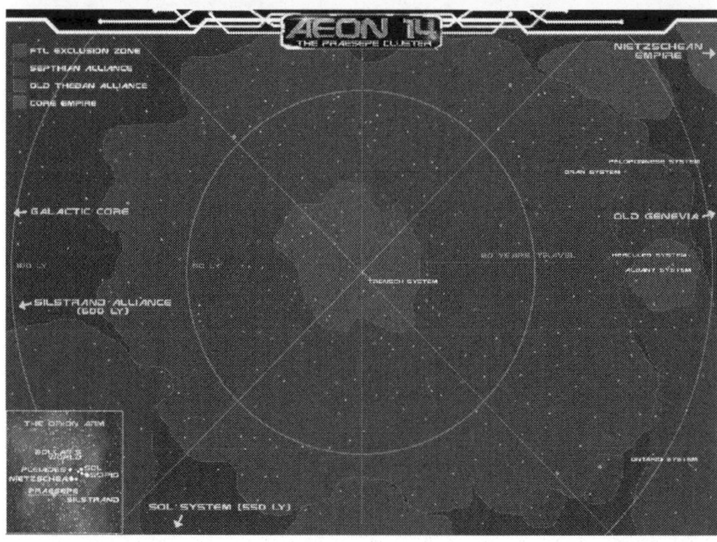

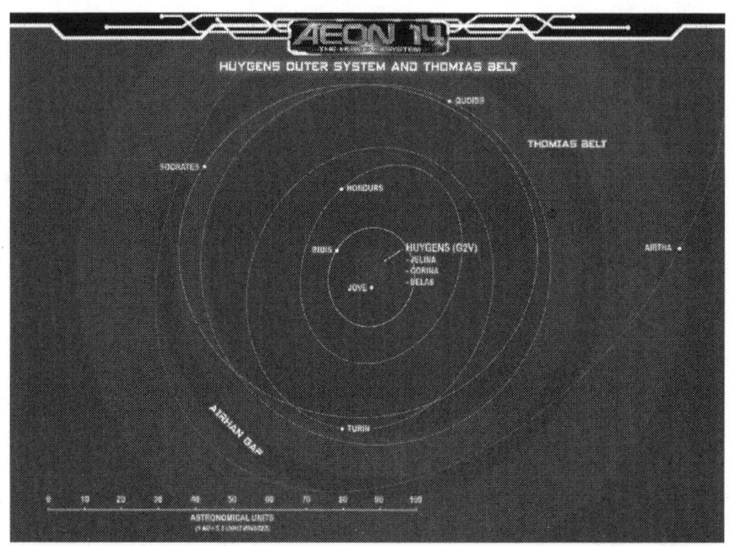
AEON 14
HUYGENS OUTER SYSTEM AND THOMIAS BELT
QUOISS
THOMIAS BELT
SOCRATES
HONOURS
RIBIS
HUYGENS (G2V)
- JELINA
- GORINA
- BELAS
AIRTHA
JOVE
TURIN
AIRHAN GAP
0 10 20 30 40 50 60 70 80 90 100
ASTRONOMICAL UNITS

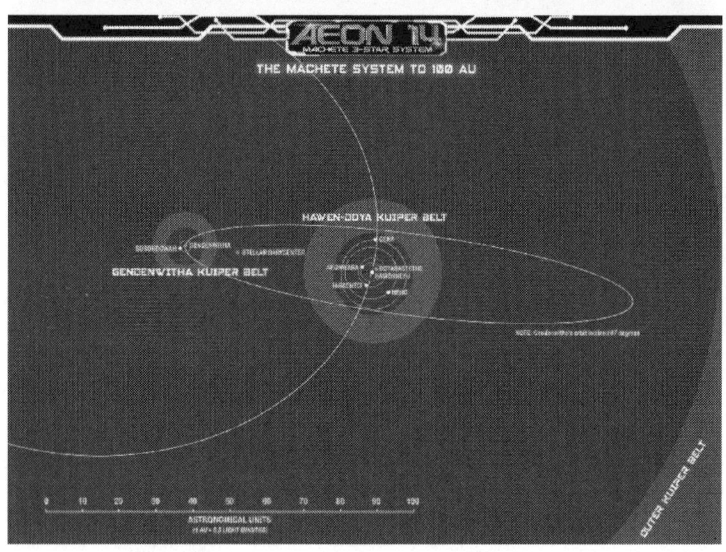
AEON 14
MACHETE 3-STAR SYSTEM
THE MACHETE SYSTEM TO 100 AU
HAWEN-DOYA KUIPER BELT
GENDENWITHA KUIPER BELT
STELLAR BARYCENTER
OUTER KUIPER BELT
0 10 20 30 40 50 60 70 80 90 100
ASTRONOMICAL UNITS

PART 1 – FAILURE

STAR CITY EXPRESS

STELLAR DATE: 10.03.8949 (Adjusted Years)
LOCATION: ISS *Lantzer*
REGION: Buffalo, Albany System, Theban Alliance

Six days before the assault on Airtha; the same day Tangel faced Xavia in Aldebaran…

"How does it feel to be at the helm of a cruiser again," Trevor asked Jessica as the pair walked toward the bridge's central holotank.

"Well…" Jessica winked at him. "Ensign Lucida is really at the helm. I'm just the skipper. So for me, it's about the same as being captain of *Sabrina*."

Her husband lifted an eyebrow, regarding her with his dark, serious eyes. After a moment, a smile quirked the corners of his mouth, and he shook his head. "You miss *Sabrina* already, don't you?"

She resisted the urge to smack him on the arm. "Stars, yes! Don't you? *Sabrina* was your home almost as long as she was mine. Core, I'd even take the chickens right about now."

"It's only been a day."

Jessica ignored his comment and swiped a hand through the holo, pivoting the visual of surrounding space until the *I2* was centered on the display.

"I just…I dunno," she finally responded. "We're making a jump through Stillwater again. Last time we did that, it took a decade to get home."

"Sure," Trevor nodded compassionately and placed a hand on Jessica's shoulder. "Granted, the first time, we made an emergency jump with a mirror built out of spare parts. Then someone reoriented the gate at the last minute, trying to send us right out of the galaxy. Sort of a once-in-a-lifetime event. Besides, we've made plenty of jumps since then that got us right where we wanted to go."

Jessica slid her hand along Trevor's back and hooked it around his waist. "Yeah, I know. Not the same. Plus, the *Lantzer* has four gates aboard, so if we run into trouble, we'll have a lot of options."

"Yup, so long as we survive the jump."

Jessica turned to give Trevor a sharp look, but saw that he was grinning at her with a twinkle in his eye.

"Stars, man," she muttered. "I'm going to make you leave the bridge if you talk like that."

"Sent to the cargo hold." His voice carried a tone of mock sadness. "Feeling like home already."

A laugh slipped past Jessica's lips, garnering the attention of the rest of the bridge crew. "OK, people. We're next in the queue. How're we looking?"

"My board is green," Ensign Lucida said, followed by a response from Lieutenant Karma, who was managing both Scan and Comm.

"All systems nominal," he said.

<*I confirm all systems are ready for jump,*> Gil, the ship's AI, added.

Other than the five people present on the bridge, the kilometer-long cruiser only had six additional people aboard: two engineers, and a fireteam of ISF Marines. Jessica checked in on them personally, and once they acknowledged readiness for the jump, she signaled the bridge crew to take the ship through the gate.

"Buffalo Tower acknowledges the gate vector is set for Star

City," Karma said with a note of clear anticipation in his voice. "Damn, I can't wait to see that thing."

"You're telling me," Trevor said. "Granted, I care more about the people there than Star City itself."

Jessica snorted. "I'm sure our kids will be glad to hear that."

"Oh, not our kids. I meant the Dreamers." Trevor gave her a wink.

"Funny man."

"We're aligned with the gate, Admiral," Lucida announced.

<*Mirror is deployed,*> Gil chimed in. <*Ship is configured for jump.*>

Jessica turned to face the forward holodisplay, which showed their assigned jump gate and the planet Buffalo beyond.

"Take us in," she directed.

Lucida fired the maneuvering thrusters, using them to ease the ship forward. It coasted through space for a few seconds, and then a shudder ran through the deck. Jessica shifted her gaze to a nearby console, looking for any alerts.

<*Miscalibration,*> Gil said a second later. <*One of the thrusters burned out of spec for a moment, and the compensator…well…overcompensated.*>

Jessica and Trevor shared a look, neither speaking what was on their minds.

The *Lantzer,* like many of the ISF's ships, was newly constructed and had only seen the most cursory of shakedown runs. Considering the speed at which the ISF was building spacecraft, the failure rates were surprisingly low, but a small percentage of ships did suffer significant malfunctions after being put into service.

Just get us to Star City, you bucket of bolts, Jessica thought. A moment later, she chastised herself and sent a wordless apology to the ship.

It was possible that the *Lantzer* would be the deck beneath her feet for some time; thinking ill of her ship wasn't a good way to start a relationship with it. Of course, it was also possible that Tangel would make good on her threat and put Jessica in command of a fleet—in which case, she'd likely transfer to an I-Class ship.

Just the thought of that sent a pang of regret through her. She had *loved* being captain of *Sabrina*. It had always felt right to her. The notion of having an entire fleet of ISF ships—and the lives therein—under her command caused a flutter of worry to settle in her breast. New Canaan's resources, especially the ones that took the form of humans and AIs, were so very rare. The concern that she'd spend lives foolishly was one that had taken firm root within her mind.

Another small vibration ran through the deck, and she shot a questioning look at one of Gil's optics.

<I've killed that thruster,> the AI said. *<Just couldn't get it to behave. Might be the fuel intermixer.>*

"Don't worry, ma'am." Lucida glanced over her shoulder as she spoke. "I could fly this beautiful girl with half her maneuvering jets. She handles like a dream."

<Contact with the mirror in fifteen seconds.>

"Steady as she goes," Jessica whispered, her eyes on the twisting knot of nothing in the center of the jump gate.

In moments, the mirror mounted on the front of the ship would touch the mouth of the artificial singularity in the center of the gate, stretching it out and drawing the *Lantzer* around its edge. The effect was that of using a wormhole without having to pass through the event horizon of a black hole.

Something Jessica was certain no one wanted to do.

Trevor was right. They'd passed through gates dozens of times since that first jump. But ever since landing on the fringe of human expansion and facing a decade-long journey home, Jessica hadn't been able to look at a gate without feeling some amount of trepidation.

<*Mark,*> Gil called out as the ship's mirror touched the gate's mass of not-space, interrupting her thoughts.

For a moment, everything seemed to twist around her. Then the ship jumped.

At first, all was normal, but then the forward holodisplay went from the nothing of jump space to flashing a kaleidoscope of colors. At the same time, alarms began to wail and every console showed red. Then a shockwave rippled through the ship, and the bridge fell into darkness.

Jessica grabbed onto the edge of the holotank as another shockwave hit them, but her grip wasn't strong enough, and she was flung across the bridge, slamming into the forward bulkhead before falling to the deck.

WHERE ARE WE?

STELLAR DATE: 10.03.8949 (Adjusted Years)
LOCATION: ISS *Lantzer*
REGION: Unknown

Jessica lay prone on the deck for what felt like an eternity, trying to make sense of why everything hurt so much, while wondering why the emergency lighting hadn't yet come on.

Then she remembered that she didn't need lighting, both because she had excellent night vision, and because her skin could glow.

Which it already was.

OK…brain seems to be finally working again, she thought with a rueful laugh as she examined the deck around her, noting that she was half-propped up against the bridge's forward bulkhead.

"Trevor?" she asked, casting about for her husband while deploying a nanocloud to begin scouring the bridge.

"Here…"

The word was followed by a long groan to Jessica's left, and she held up a hand, increasing the glow coming from her palm.

Trevor lay on his side, a trail of blood coming from his mouth as he worked his jaw slowly.

"Is it bad?" she asked.

"No, just bit my tongue. And I might have broken a finger…or two."

"Karma? Lucida? Sound off," Jessica called out as she rose on shaky legs and walked to Trevor's side. "So you're saying you'll live?" she asked him.

He grunted and pushed himself upright as Lucida spoke up.

"I think I will too…though I feel like I could also be dead."

"Here too. Though I smashed my console," Karma added.

"Gil?"

Jessica didn't expect the AI to respond. If the bridge systems were completely offline, the AI wouldn't have any way to hear or respond to them, which seemed to be the case.

"What *happened*?" Karma asked, the sound of a harness unbuckling coming from his direction.

Lucida coughed out a rueful laugh. "Aren't you supposed to know? You're on Scan."

"No scan on a jump," he retorted. "Though I did catch sight of weird colors on the forward display. I've never seen that before."

"Me either," Jessica replied. "Stars…there's no active EM anywhere, other than the a-grav decking and my skin. Why aren't emergency systems coming back online?"

"Probably the same reason half my mods aren't responding," Trevor said. "That was one hell of an EM spike that hit us when we…stopped? Is that what we did?"

Jessica checked her internal logs and saw that her mods had registered an EM spike, but the energy surge hadn't done any significant damage to her.

"OK, that *was* a big burst. I seem to be alright, though. Benefit of being…well…me, I guess."

"You just love energy," Trevor said as he carefully straightened a finger. "Uh…I was going to follow that with something clever, but I've got nothing."

"Shit—uh, sir," Karma said as he watched Trevor move onto his second broken finger. "That's just nasty."

"Then don't look."

"OK," Jessica turned to look over the two ensigns, who were both in better shape, thanks to having been strapped in. "We need to get core systems back online, which means accessing the hardened node two decks down and running a re-init. We also need to check on Gil and the rest of the crew."

"I've got the core," Trevor said. "*Sabrina* had a scaled-down version of this backup model."

"I'll get to Gil," Karma said. "He and I go way back."

"Should I search out everyone else?" Lucida asked, looking worried and a little scared. "What do you think did this, anyway?"

" 'This' as in knocked us out of the jump, or fried the ship?" Trevor asked with a guttural laugh. "Sorry…nervous energy."

"Well, both, I guess," Lucida replied, her own warbling laugh following her words.

"There's a lot of power involved in a jump," Jessica said. "Gates aren't powered by piddly stuff like fusion generators. Could be that we had a mirror failure, and some of that energy passed directly into the ship—or it could have been something else entirely."

Karma pressed a hand to his temple and groaned. "Whatever it was, I'm starting to feel like it all grounded out in my head."

"You'll survive," Trevor grunted.

Jessica chuckled softly while walking across the bridge to the emergency locker. She opened it to reveal a dozen EV suits and pulse pistols.

"Suit up, kids, we could have breaches," she instructed while pulling out a suit for herself. Her skin made it so that vacuum wasn't a concern, and she could rebreathe the same air for several minutes, but she wasn't going to risk her life unnecessarily.

Trevor and the ensigns grabbed suits, and as they geared up, Jessica passed out additional directives.

"Lucida, you head down the starboard concourse. That'll get you to engineering faster. I'll take the port side. Drop comm buoys and stay in touch. Anyone gets a chance to look out an inspection port, do it. I want to know if anything is out there…and where we are."

The ensigns gave affirmative responses and left the bridge ahead of Trevor, who stopped to give Jessica a quick embrace.

"You be careful, glow girl."

"I will, you just get that hardened node online and initialize repair systems."

"Easy," Trevor replied, his tone calm and soothing. "We'll have the ship rolling…well…soonish."

Jessica realized that she must have been speaking with more intensity than she meant to and ducked her head in a quick nod. "Of course we will. Then we'll figure out where the heck we are."

"Maybe we'll look outside and see Star City looming nearby," he replied.

"Core, that would be fantastic."

They walked together down the passageway that led from the bridge, Jessica's lavender glow lighting the way, until they came to a ladder shaft, where they were to go their separate ways. Trevor gave her another brief embrace before stepping into the shaft and dropping down to his destination deck.

<*Holler if you run into trouble,*> he said, utilizing one of the comm buoy's the ensigns had dropped.

<*You too,*> Jessica replied before resuming her journey to the port-side concourse.

Well…after I go look outside. I'm starting to feel like that's a priority.

Following her gut, Jessica worked her way up the tech decks to the ship's dorsal arch. The a-grav decking was offline closer to the hull, and she was able to pick up speed, pulling herself along handholds until she finally reached the airlock that led to the observation dome.

Though she'd passed through a few sections of the ship where emergency power was active—which had been a relief—such was not the case with the airlock. She debated using the manual system or attempting to power it herself.

No…you might need your juice later, she decided.

Instead, she pulled open the panel and attached the door-jack's handle, pumping it several times to pressurize the emergency hydraulics. The interior of the airlock still registered as containing atmosphere, so once the system was primed, she pulled open the door and stepped inside. Readings showed that the observation dome on the far side was also pressurized, so she quickly repeated the process on the exterior door.

When she pushed the outer door open, she was met by the brilliant glow of space. After moving through the inky black ship, the light of the cosmos was a welcome sight. She pushed herself up to the top of the observation dome and grabbed a handhold. Muting her glow as much as possible, she peered out and tried to get her bearings.

"OK…" she murmured while slowly spinning around. "There's the galactic disk…and that's the core and the Aquilla Rift. There's the Orion Nebula…"

Jessica continued to turn until she saw another nebula, a wall of dust and gas that stretched on for hundreds of light years in either direction. She knew it by sight, having had it dominate her travels for many years.

"And there's Stillwater. Fan-fucking-tastic." She took a breath and then tapped into one of the comm buoys. *<Trevor, you there?>*

<Yup. At the hardened node, just getting everything set up for it to kick off repairs. I had this fear that I'd get down here and find that the node wasn't properly stocked, but its batts are fully charged, and the drone closets are full. I'm setting a priority for it to get drones to the aft nodes and initialize them too.>

<Good, that's really good.> Jessica had harbored a similar fear. *<I went to the obs dome. From the looks of it, we're about a hundred light years on the coreward side of Stillwater.>*

<Any sign of what kicked us out of the jump? Was it an interdictor system?>

<One that spans the inner edge of the Perseus Arm of the galaxy? I doubt it.>

Trevor was silent for a moment, and then said, *<What about one that would be in place to block approaches to Star City?>*

The implications of his statement were not lost on Jessica, but even so, she doubted that was the case. Space was just too big to effectively block jump gate travel on a multitude of vectors. She only knew of three systems that had interdictors blocking such travel, and they all did it right at the heliopause.

<Let's hope that's not it. If someone can block a jump across a thousand-light-year spread, then we're effed.>

As Jessica spoke, a glimmer of light caught her attention, and she turned. She peered at the twinkling light for a moment before it flared into star-like brilliance.

Shit…not a star. That's a ship, decelerating on approach.

<Lucida, you found the Marines yet?> she asked the ensign.

<Not yet, but I'm almost at their barracks.>

<Double-time it. We've got company.>

Karma spoke up a second later. *<I've just reached Gil's chamber…. Annnddd he's alive. Patching him into our wireless network.>*

<Admiral, I'm sorry, I don't—> the AI began, but Jessica cut him off.

<Not your fault, Gil. I suspect enemy action. There's a ship inbound. Given our position just coreward of Stillwater, I'm thinking Orion Guard.>

<Dammit. I'm totally blind down here,> Gil replied. *<I don't know how everything got so fried, either. The sensor readings during the jump were normal, then suddenly it was like….>*

<Like what?> Trevor prompted.

The AI sent a feeling laden with disbelief. *<Like we skirted too close to the singularity. I wonder if we had a mirror failure on the*

bow?>

<*Well, we can review all that later. Right now, we need helm and shields, ASAP,*> Jessica ordered.

<*Ma'am,*> Corporal Jay spoke up a second later. <*Lucida just linked us up with your comm network. I sent Peers and Marc back to check on engineering. Meg and I will come to you.*>

<*No, Corporal,*> Jessica replied. <*I want you to go back with Lucida and check on chiefs Glenn and West. Whatever they need, you do it. Helm and shields, that's our only priority right now.*>

<*Yes, ma'am,*> came Corporal Jay's response.

<*Gil, I don't have all of the blueprints in my head. Are there any emergency batts I can hook up to power the dorsal sensors? I'd really like to know more about this ship that's coming to pay us a visit.*>

<*Wouldn't we all,*> the AI responded. <*If you go back down to deck two, there's an SC array in Bay 2-19A. Inventory shows two shielded batts in there that aren't connected to anything. You should be able to connect them to the mains for that section of the ship and power the sensor array.*>

<*OK, I'm on it,*> Jessica replied.

She gave the approaching ship a final look, gauging its rate of deceleration. A quick estimate put its time of arrival to be a little less than three hours.

We came out practically on top of it. No way that's coincidence.

<*I'm going to check out the forward reactor,*> Trevor said. <*That thing should still be live, must have just tripped its linkages.*>

Jessica sent an affirmative response and tuned out the conversation that Trevor, Gil, and Karma began to have regarding reinitializing the reactor. She closed the outer airlock door behind herself, then, despite a temptation to hurry, followed suit with the inner door.

No point in rushing, and killing us later from decompression.

Five minutes after exiting the observation dome, she reached Bay 2-19A and was pleasantly surprised to find that not only was a-grav working, but the bay's door was powered up. However, when it opened, smoke poured out into the passageway, and she saw heat signatures on the IR band.

<*Shit, got fire here,*> she announced.

<*Repair drones have spotted a few as well,*> Gil commented, sounding largely unconcerned.

<*Yeah, but there's power here. The suppression systems should have kicked in.*>

<*Should be a foamer down the hall in closet 2-19CA,*> the AI supplied.

Jessica sent a quick thanks and dashed down the hall to the closet, where she found a pair of foam guns and a pulse suppressor. She grabbed all three and ran back to the bay's door, cursing herself for not having closed it and inadvertently feeding the fire fresh oxygen.

Stepping inside, Jessica closed the door behind herself and looked over the shapes of the SC batts, looking for the largest blaze. A second later, she spotted flames dancing through the acrid smoke, and moved forward, firing the suppressor's pulses to clear the smoke.

<*Shit,*> she muttered when the source of the blaze became visible. <*It's the primary junction.*>

<*Something must be discharging to make that thing burn,*> Gil said.

Jessica didn't reply, instead spraying foam over the power junction, dousing the fire before looking around for any smaller blazes.

<*On the plus side, fire means that the batts are still holding charges,*> she commented as she swept through the bay, putting out several other smaller fires. <*Just not sure how I'll hook them up to the mains.*>

<*Did you find the hardened batteries?*> Gil asked. <*They should be along the bulkhead furthest from the door.*>

Jessica angled to her right, weaving amongst the waist-high cylinders until she spotted two larger shapes through the haze.

<OK, I think so. Yes, found them.>

<Good.> The AI sounded relieved. *<Now, there should be cabling for each in a cabinet at the end of the row.>*

Jessica fired the suppressor's pulses to clear more of the smoke away as she searched for the cabinet. When she found it, the doors were twisted from the heat. A few tugs, and they came open to reveal two empty hooks.

<You sure this is where they're supposed to be? I've got bupkiss.>

<Well, that's standard buildout. I don't have access to the full inventory databanks.>

Jessica knew of a few places where there should be more cabling, but none were close, and there were no guarantees that they'd be properly stocked, either.

<I'm going to take one of the batts with me to the sensor node,> she said. *<Just need to kill a-grav so I can maneuver it.>*

<OK…> the AI replied, going silent for a moment. *<I've tapped into the grav systems in your area through the wireless network. Just give me a second, safety overrides aren't responding.>*

Moving to the left-most SC batt, Jessica crouched next to it and found the release tool slotted into the base of the battery's case.

At least you're where you're supposed to be.

A minute later, she had the battery's mounts free. She turned to give the room another review, now that the smoke had cleared. Two of the other SC batteries were still online, their 'active' lights glowing green, holodisplays showing a trickle of discharge, which meant they were still connected to something. She moved closer and saw that they were both connected to a separate junction than the one that had been on fire.

<Gil, what does the forward junction in this bay feed?>

<That's what's powering a-grav and environmental on decks one, two, and three. Forward of the ship's spine, that is.>

<Well, deck two, at least,> Jessica replied. *<When I was up on*

one, it had no a-grav.>

<No? Damn. Must have blown another junction toward the bow as well. If that's the case, you're going to have to take that batt right up to the scan node and power the sensor array from there.>

<That's what I was expecting. Just kill the a-grav already. I don't fancy the idea of muscling a ton of battery through the corridors.>

<Almost done…>

A few seconds later, Jessica felt the pull of gravity fade away and bring about a natural inclination to hunker down and stay near the deck. Of course that always had the opposite reaction, and she lifted off a few centimeters.

Pay attention to what you're doing, woman.

Quickly reorienting her senses to a world of unimpeded reaction, Jessica grabbed the battery case's handles and pulled. Her feet hit the deck again, and the battery slowly lifted into the air. Once it had risen a meter, she got behind it and pushed.

Getting the battery into the passageway took a few seconds, and then the following ten minutes were spent maneuvering it down corridors and up a maintenance tube to the first deck.

The literal ton of superconductor battery was cumbersome and unwieldy, and Jessica hated every minute spent getting it to the sensor node, worrying about the approaching ship and how they knew nothing about it. She opened the door, fearing smoke and fire once more, but found the chamber dark, and the air clear.

Thank stars.

She muscled the battery inside and then quickly latched it to the deck next to the room's primary power interchange. Luck was finally on her side, and she found an auxiliary power cable where it was supposed to be and quickly connected the battery to it.

The batt's activity light came on, casting a green hue

around the room.

<*OK,*> Jessica didn't bother hiding the relief from her mental tone as the node began to initialize. <*Looks like the node isn't damaged.*>

<*I think that whatever tagged us did more damage to the larger electrical systems,*> Gil said. <*Trevor and Karma are at the reactor now. Plasma containment died, and some coils burned out. They're replacing them, then we should have full power forward of the spine.*>

<*Wherever said power can get to,*> Jessica replied.

<*Well, yeah. That.*>

She busied herself with reviewing the sensor node's initialization process, noting that several subsystems remained offline, but that the main radio antennas were active, as was the wide-band dish. Two of the optical scopes were also online, feeding images down to the console in the room, though only one's tracking servos were responding.

<*OK, got a scope on our friend, and the antennas are picking up the ship's EM signature.*>

<*Doesn't seem like an Orion Guard sig,*> Gil mused as the gamma ray patterns coming off the approaching ship were analyzed by the node.

<*Lot of ships out here in the PED,*> Jessica replied. <*Could be an old patrol boat that doesn't see regular service, or something new we haven't seen before.*>

<*That's a heck of a big patrol boat,*> Gil replied as the node analyzed the approaching ship's burn and deceleration, calculating newtons of thrust and ship mass. <*Based on the hull profile visible past the engine flare, it's…damn, it's at least a klick long. Doesn't match any hulls in my local databanks.*>

<*Weird for a cruiser to be operating alone out here,*> Jessica said, programming the sensor array to sweep the surrounding area for more ships, desperately hoping not to find any—even if finding others would decrease the mystery surrounding the

approaching ship.

<*Shit…we're three light years from the closest star, too,*> Gil said after a moment.

Jessica nodded, looking at the stellar cartography map that was beginning to form on the holo in front of her, deepening the mystery of what could have pulled them out of the jump.

<*No other ships, yet,*> she commented. <*Though they could be stealthed. The scan we can manage right now isn't that far above total blindness.*>

<*Admiral Jessica!*>

A new voice entered her mind, and Jessica breathed a sigh of relief as she identified Chief Glenn.

<*Chief. Stars, it's good to hear you in my noggin. West OK too?*>

<*She broke her arm, but we got to a functional med closet. She's in the tube right now, getting her heal on.*>

<*Good. Your assessment of our situation?*>

The man sent a snort. <*I was hoping you could tell me. Lucida gave me the quick version, but she also mentioned another ship out there….*>

<*Yeah. We'll have company in two and a half hours, give or take a bit.*>

<*Well, that's a little suspicious.*>

Jessica laughed. <*Tell me about it. Look, you know the drill. Shields and burners. The Marines and Lucida are at your disposal. Get them rolling. Trevor and Karma are working on the forward reactor, and the emergency drones are getting started.*>

<*So we just have to go from fried, cold, and dead in the water to fighting strength in two and a half hours? CriEns are all offline, by the way. Rapid discharge safeties triggered. Going to take longer than a few hours to get them back up.*> Chief Glenn's voice was laden with worry and skepticism.

<*Do what you can, Chief,*> Jessica replied, knowing that their options were limited.

<*Of course. Any other miracles you need today, ma'am?*>

<Well, if you happen to figure out what dropped us out of the jump, that would be nice too.>

<I'll see if I can find an oracle to consult,> the engineer replied with another snort, followed by a slightly more deferential, *<Ma'am.>*

<Be sure to ask it who our visitors are,> Jessica replied before switching to address the entire crew. *<I'm patching scan onto our wireless network. Then I'm going to go see if there are any functional ships in the forward bays. Everyone, stay on task. Trevor and Karma, once you get that reactor repaired, weapons are your next priority.>*

A series of affirmative responses came before Trevor reached out privately.

<What are you hoping to do if you find a working ship?> he asked.

<Stars, just about anything. Flee, attack, misdirect. Depends on what I find.>

<Attack?>

<Well, if there's an ARC-6A in there, I could probably take on an Orion cruiser with it—so long as it has enough power to run the stasis shields.>

<Won't a 6A have a CriEn?> Trevor asked.

<Yeah, but our main banks all went offline. The ones in the ARCs probably did as well.>

<And you're just going to fly it right out at the enemy? Without shields?> Trevor's tone carried equal measures skepticism and worry.

<Well. I'm not going to 'fly it right out' at anyone,> Jessica chuckled softly, *<unless it has functional stasis shields. Either way, sending a few fighters out on remote, even just for the extra sensors, would be a good idea. It's hard to see much of that approaching ship, with its engine wash pointed right at us.>*

<OK…just don't do anything crazy, kay, Jess?>

<Crazy?> Jessica laughed. *<Me?>*

Trevor only sent back guarded cough.

She reached the first bay almost ten minutes later. It was only a hundred meters away from the sensor node, but the number of sealed doors she had to manually open slowed her progress considerably.

Spoiled by doors. Who would have thought it?

The center of the bay was occupied by a mid-sized pinnace. She didn't even need to board the ship to know it wasn't going anywhere. Half its hull was scorched and covered in still-dripping fire-suppression foam from the bay's systems.

However, the rack on the aft side of the docking bay held a dozen ARC-6A fighters, and by some miracle, they all appeared unscathed by whatever had damaged the pinnace.

<*Gil, can you work on the bay doors?*>

<*I can, but environmental and grav shields aren't responding in that bay.*>

<*I've got my EV suit, crack the doors slowly.*>

Jessica walked to the dockmaster's cabin that was set along the interior wall, and breathed a sigh of relief to see that the racking systems were active. She triggered the system to slide out one of the fighters, and then ambled toward the egg-shaped ship as it was set onto the hull.

<*You're going to have to get changed,*> the AI advised her. <*The gel compartment within the ARC won't calibrate properly with that bulky EV suit.*>

Jessica was surprised to hear that. <*Even with a-grav, we still need shoot suits?*>

<*Didn't you look over the specs on the 6As?*> the AI admonished.

<*No.*> She resisted the urge to send Gil an unpleasant glare. <*I've barely been with the fleet these past twenty years, remember? I just assumed that, with a-grav, the 6As would have regular cockpits. No shoot suits or gel cocoons necessary.*>

<*Tangel likes fallback systems.*>

Jessica sighed, ade picked himself use. A-grav could get

knocked out, and if the pilot was encased in a shoot suit and safely tucked inside an ARC's gel pocket, they could put up more of a fight than an enemy would expect.

She saw the suiting chamber to the left of the rack and hurried toward it, knowing that the process would take a few minutes.

"Oh, crap, it's offline," she muttered when the access panel wouldn't respond.

Casting about for options, she saw a panel next to the chamber labeled 'Emergency SCLSS'. Pulling it open, she saw a sealed packet and a helmet. She set the helmet on the deck, then quickly pulled off her EV suit, followed by the uniform underneath.

Ignoring the chill in the air, she tore open the SCLSS packet, and a rubbery mass fell into her hands. She quickly unfurled the shoot suit, struggling to grasp the slippery white second skin that appeared to be far too small. For a moment, Jessica considered forgoing the suit, but she knew that the fighter's piloting systems would expect the suit's hookups, and reprogramming its inputs would take longer than getting dressed. Finally locating the fastener, she pulled it down and slipped inside the suit's compressive confines.

Once all the ports were seated, she pulled on the helmet and did her best to ignore the suit as it tested bio-feedback systems while she walked to the fighter.

<*OK. I'm sealed,*> she said while walking beneath the ARC-6A she'd unracked. <*You can crack the bay doors whenever you're ready.*>

<*I'm venting atmosphere through the emergency discharge,*> Gil replied. <*I'd rather not bend the bay doors with explosive decompression.*>

<*I suppose that's wise,*> Jessica said as she sent a command to the fighter to let her in.

Above her, part of the hull irised open, and she saw the

familiar gel pod within. An a-grav column drew her up, and within seconds, she was nestled within the fighter's gel-filled cocoon. Connections snaked through the viscous liquid, connecting her to the ship, and then a prompt appeared on her HUD for sensory changeover.

She didn't immediately accept the request, first running the fighter through a full diagnostic routine. It came back with only two secondary subsystems showing damage, and she decided that was likely as good as she could expect from any of the ships.

With a thought, she accepted the prompt to change over her senses, and an instant later, her 'skin' was no longer at the edge of her body, but rather at that of the ARC-6A's hull. Her legs were the ship's engines, her arms the weapons and maneuvering thrusters, and her eyes were its sensor arrays.

<*Doors opening,*> Gil announced.

<*I see that,*> Jessica replied, triggering the fighter's a-grav thrusters and lifting off the deck.

She skirted around the damaged pinnace on her way to the dark rectangle that lay beyond the bay doors.

Stars, I've missed this, she thought, savoring the feeling of the ship as her body, remembering the countless hours spent in the ARC-5s back in the Kap.

That memory sparked thoughts of the battle she'd fought against the Sirian scout ships, followed by the days waiting for rescue out in the deep black beyond the system's heliopause.

Not this time, she told herself, though she wasn't sure if her sentiment was that she wouldn't be lost, or that if things went badly, there was no hope for rescue.

Once outside the ship, Jessica activated the ARC's stealth systems and pushed the ship forward on a column of gravitons, angling slightly away from the approaching vessel in an attempt to get a view of its profile.

The approaching craft was still several light seconds away,

and its delta-*v* had decreased, along with the amount of thrust coming off its engines. Once Jessica's ARC was a dozen kilometers from the *Lantzer,* she was finally able to get an unobstructed view of the approaching vessel.

Well that's a weird one, she thought, as the fighter's sensors built up a picture of the approaching cruiser.

It was just over a kilometer long, though it was also wider than she'd initially thought. There was a curved dorsal arch, not dissimilar from the *Lantzer's,* that terminated in a spherical section at the ship's bow. Hanging from the arch were dozens of hundred-meter shafts. Her impression was that the ship resembled a fish's skeleton.

That initial observation triggered the next: the ship appeared to have very little in the way of crew areas. Other than a few corridors running from the sphere at the bow to the engines, she suspected that there were almost no internal passageways within the bulk of the craft.

The sphere was a hundred meters across, which meant a crew of less than a few dozen at most, and Jessica felt a measure of relief to know that they weren't about to face off with a company of soldiers boarding the *Lantzer.*

Of course, I could just blow it out of the stars before it gets to us.

Jessica examined the enemy ship, selecting primary targets and programming her weapons to strike them with a single thought. The next problem she faced was that her single ship couldn't shoot its way through the cruiser's shields. However, if she built up enough delta-*v,* she could punch through them with her ARC and then fire on the targets during her flyby.

But first, I want to know what I'm up against.

Once her offensive options with the approaching fishbone ship were established, she pulled up the visuals of the *Lantzer,* passive scan sweeping over her own cruiser, looking for signs of external damage.

At a glance, it appeared that there were none, but closer

examination showed scoring on several sensor arrays and sections of hull. None of it was structural in nature, but instead pointed to the ship being caught up in a massive electromagnetic surge—which was not surprising at this point, just not terribly informative, either.

Over the next thirty minutes, Jessica continued to drift toward the still-decelerating enemy ship while maintaining a tightbeam comm line back to the *Lantzer*.

While she'd been drifting through the black, Trevor and Karma had repaired the forward reactor, and Chief Glenn had brought the aft reactor online. Both powerplants were running at minimal output while the teams worked to disconnect damaged systems from the power grid before energizing more areas of the ship.

The chief's fears about the CriEn modules had turned out to be correct. They'd completely shut down and would need to be carefully reactivated. For now, Jessica had directed the crew to continue their focus on shields and helm. They wouldn't need CriEn levels of energy to power stasis shields against just one enemy cruiser—she hoped.

<*Don't get too far out there,*> Trevor admonished, as Jessica neared a distance of fifty thousand kilometers from the *Lantzer.*

<*I won't, I'm just going to ease toward it and let it pass by nice and close. See what passive scan can pick up at just a few dozen klicks.*>

<*Sure is a weird-looking ship,*> he commented. <*What are all those long spikes coming off the central spine for?*>

<*Beats me,*> Jessica replied. <*Well, maybe…. It reminds me a bit of a drone ship.*>

<*A what?*>

Jessica pulled up the memory of one of the ancient Scattered Worlds ships and sent the image to her husband.

<*The SWSF used them to patrol the outer reaches of the Sol*

System. They had small crews, just a dozen, but they could deploy drone swarms of up to several thousand per ship.>

<*That's a lot more than we could deal with right now.*> Trevor's voice contained a new note of worry. <*Let's hope that's not the case.*>

<*Well, the fun thing about most people who deploy drones is that they're paranoid, and usually not keen on the drones having high levels of autonomy. Take out the command and control system, and the drones die, or at least become a lot less effective.*>

<*I vote for drone death. I don't even feel bad about it.*>

Jessica laughed. <*I'm with you. OK, I'm coming up on my closest approach. That ship is going to pass between me and the* Lantzer. *Severing comms till I'm far enough on the other side.*>

<*You got it. Be careful.*>

<*Always.*>

<*Liar.*>

Despite her words, the ominous ship had Jessica on edge. It hadn't made any attempt to communicate with the *Lantzer*, and its deceleration vector was such that it would come to zero delta-*v* only fifteen kilometers distant from the ISF cruiser.

In interstellar space, that was all but a collision.

As Jessica's stealthed ARC-6A drew closer to the fishbone ship, more details began to appear. It was clearly utilitarian; little attention to an overall aesthetic had been given. Or, if it had, appreciation for the design was beyond her. A notion came to her mind that the vessel might be one of the most 'un-human' things she'd ever seen.

Maybe I've encountered a race of alien fish people.

She knew that was ridiculous—or close to it. Though humanity had explored close to ten percent of the galaxy, it was commonly believed that no other sentient life currently existed in the Milky Way.

There were some who argued that, given the vast distances, it was possible that intelligent—possibly even starfaring—

species were active in other parts of the galaxy, but unless an observer was within a few hundred light years of their systems, visible signs of their activity would still be too far off.

Those were the rational speculators.

Other people believed that alien species were already active within the human sphere of expansion. Those fringe thinkers believed that it wouldn't be *that* hard for an alien species to mimic humans well enough to pass amongst them. They maintained that there were even all-alien systems that no one had found yet, or, if human visitors *had* come to them, it would appear as though the aliens were just modded humans.

In all honesty, there were nearly as many theories as there were people to concoct them, and Jessica had never paid them much heed. None of the crazy ideas were much different than what had been floating around before she'd left the Sol System thousands of years ago.

But something about the ship made her think that if there *were* aliens out there, this might be the sort of vessel they'd construct.

She wasn't sure what gave her that idea. It might be the angles, or the fact that it didn't seem to be made with a human crew in mind, or just the fact that it appeared to be ever so slightly asymmetrical.

Thing gives me the heebies.

She looked over the ship for weapons, noting a few railguns mounted on the vessel's spine, and what appeared to be defensive beam turrets around its engines. The forward sphere didn't have any visible weapons, but that didn't mean they weren't hidden below hull plating.

It's a warship, for sure, she thought, noting the total lack of portholes anywhere on the fishbone craft. *But what is it doing? If it wanted to cripple us, it should have fired already. If it wanted to board, it would make sense to hold further out and send in its drones…or whatever it has.*

As she continued to consider rational—and irrational—explanations for the ship's behavior, the enemy vessel's spherical bow passed in front of her ARC-6A. Other than its slow and steady braking, there still wasn't any other sign of activity coming from the ship.

She was considering slowing her passage with a brief grav drive burn, when an EM burst flared from a point on the fishbone's bow.

Alerts lit up across Jessica's vision as her ARC's movement was suddenly arrested, and then then her ship began to move toward the cruiser.

Shit! Graviton beam!

She fired the ARC's engines and turned to boost away from the enemy ship, no longer concerned with stealth. Despite what should have been enough burn to pull away, the draw from the enemy ship was outmatching her own thrust.

Jessica had never seen a grav-beam strong enough to hold a ship like an ARC-6A against its will, not even from ships much larger than the fishbone.

A bay door began to open on the enemy vessel, and Jessica knew that the moment her fighter touched down on that deck, she was done for.

Without another thought, she activated the ARC's stasis shields.

You want me? Here I come!

She spun the ship and punched the engines, hurtling the fighter toward the fishbone vessel. Her ARC traversed the gap in less than a second, and she slammed into the fishbone, plowing into the forward sphere. She expected to punch clear through, but moments after impact, the stasis shield died, and the ARC fighter ground to a halt.

Though the fighter's a-grav dampeners eased the abrupt cessation of forward momentum, Jessica found herself glad for Tangel's insistence that the ARC fighters still use gel-filled cockpits, as the substance solidified around her and kept her from being slammed against the forward end of the cocoon.

She tried to reactivate the stasis shield, but saw that it had failed due to a grav-generator failure. She realized it had died because an integrity field modulator for the shield bubble had suffered a malfunction. Normally this wouldn't be a problem, but the fallback system was one of the few that had been damaged by the EM surge before she'd even left the *Lantzer.*

What dumb luck, she thought.

Exterior visuals showed that the ARC was lodged partway down a corridor—or what was left of the corridor. One side of the bulkhead was gone entirely, and the other side was mostly slag.

Since I'm here, I might as well find who's running the show.

She fired the ARC's grav thrusters and twisted the fighter so that its exit was facing the aft end of the corridor. Once the vessel was situated as best she could get it, Jessica triggered the fighter's pilot disconnect, and her consciousness collapsed back within her body. She felt the hookups disconnect from the shoot suit, and a moment later, the ship disgorged her, dropping her onto the deck.

Once outside the fighter, she quickly took stock of her surroundings while passing a command to the ARC to drop a rifle and a sidearm.

They fell to the deck next to her, and she scooped them up while eyeing the corridor around her. It was made of a smooth, grey material somewhat like plas, but it reflected EM, making the meager scan her shoot suit possessed entirely ineffective.

She'd never been on a ship where the bulkheads of a corridor were entirely unadorned. Not only were there no conduits, there weren't any markings of any sort. It was more like a tube than a passageway.

Am I in a pipe?

If it wasn't for the fact that a light strip ran down the top, she would have settled on that determination. So far as she knew, even aliens wouldn't light a pipe.

Focusing on something that made sense, she checked over her rifle. Once satisfied that it was powered and ready to fire, she slung the bandolier of magazines over her shoulder while making a final attempt to relay a message to the *Lantzer*.

Nothing. Well, that was to be expected.

Jessica began to trot down the passage, hoping to put some distance between herself and the fighter before whoever ran the ship came to investigate.

Based on the corridor's slow curve, she knew that her fighter had lodged in the spherical forward section of the ship. It was only three hundred meters across, and she estimated that the fighter had to have punched through at least halfway, likely missing the center and ending up somewhere on the starboard side. She surmised that if there was a C&C on the strange craft, it would be in the center of the sphere, so that was her ultimate destination.

The featureless passage continued curving around to the right, and Jessica kept her eyes peeled for an intersection, though none came into view for several minutes. Eventually, the bulkhead on the left opened up, and she found herself on a small balcony. She looked out over the low railing and saw an atrium that spanned several decks, with a corridor at the bottom that continued on toward the ship's stern.

Jessica realized that this was where the spherical section met the arch that connected to the ship's engines. Surprised that she'd still not seen another soul, she looked at the drop and gauged it to be ten meters.

She sent her drones over the edge and confirmed that the passage that continued toward the rear of the ship also ran forward toward the center of the sphere. Without further consideration, she leapt over the edge, spinning in the air to land facing the ship's bow.

The passage was clear, but as she walked across the atrium's floor, a figure stepped out of an alcove ahead. For a second, she would have sworn that the person materialized out of thin air, which she supposed was possible with reasonable stealth tech. Nearly three meters tall, the person wore a long cloak with a deep cowl shrouding their face.

"Halt!" Jessica ordered, taking a step back as she sensed energy flowing off the figure, waves of ionized air rippling out from around it. "Who are you? Why did you attack my ship?"

"Attack?"

A man then…and probably not an alien, Jessica thought as the baritone word rolled over her.

"Yes. You knocked us out of our jump, and then sucked my fighter toward your ship."

"And then you crashed into mine," the man replied, laughing softly. "Though I'll admit, I should have seen that coming."

"Oh?" Jessica asked, backing up to where the corridor opened into the atrium. "Why is that?"

"Well, because, Jessica Keller, you've done it before. At the Battle of Bollam's World, when you flew your ship through those dreadnoughts."

"Wow! A fan," Jessica exclaimed, a mocking smile on her lips, though she realized the enemy couldn't see her grin through the shoot suit's visor. "I admit, I've used that trick a few times too many at this point…granted, it still works. If I'd had more momentum, I would have punched clear through your ship."

"Probably." The figure nodded. "Not that it would have helped."

Jessica shook her head. "You're very confident. But your hubris won't help."

"No?"

"No."

She lifted her right arm, ready to fire the electron beam mounted inside it, when she saw a tendril of light slip past the figure's robe.

Oh shit.

"You're a core AI," she whispered.

"A Caretaker, yes," the figure replied. "I rather like you, Jessica, you've got a lot of moxie. But I have my orders, and I plan to follow them."

Jessica took a step back as fear crept into her mind, and she desperately wondered what possible defense she could mount against an ascended AI.

"Orders from who?" she asked.

"Whom."

"No one says that anymore. Get over it."

The being slowly advanced, gliding down the corridor as Jessica backed up. Frantically, she deployed a nanocloud in the vain hope that she could somehow breach the ascended AI.

Stars, Jessica, of all the ways you could have gone…never expected it to be like this.

"I won't go without a fight," she hissed.

"That'll be interesting. Not many people stand their ground. How do you think you'll fare?"

Her mind grasped at the one chance she had to defeat the ascended being—and that possibility was a slim one: it involved using the alien microbes that suffused her body and consequently altered her cellular makeup. Over the past few years, they had evolved to the point where they were capable of directly harvesting and storing electrons.

She'd used the ability twice before when operating in League of Sentients space, though never against a sentient being made of energy.

Stars, I don't even know if any part of this thing ***is*** *electrons. It could be made of all subatomic particles…. Can I harvest those?*

Knowing that the best way to make her body ready to draw in energy was to deplete her reserves, Jessica fired her electron beam without giving any warning.

It burned through the shoot suit's glove and streaked toward the steadily approaching figure, but stopped short of striking directly, the bolts of electricity hitting the floor and overhead instead.

Jessica fired twice more, both shots encountering the same invisible barrier.

"Wasn't quite futile enough for you the first time?" the Caretaker asked.

"Never hurts to be sure," Jessica replied. "Before you kill me, do I get a name, or why you stopped us, anything?"

The figure stopped and cocked its head. "You want me to monologue about my plan? Do you really think your chances of survival are that good?"

"That bad," Jessica corrected. "I figure since I'm gonna bite it, I want to go down knowing why you stopped my ship. *How* would be nice as well."

The being let out a breath that sounded like a tree's branches scratching against a window.

"Simple, really. We're just keeping you from getting to Star City. Can't have those kids of yours getting involved in things. For now, they're content just to ascend and leave these corporeal dimensions, and we're happy to let them do that."

"My kids are ascending?" Jessica asked, surprised it could happen so soon.

"Eventually, yes. I don't have a lot of details, they're a difficult group to approach."

"Too bad you didn't go visit them. I bet they'd mop the floor with you."

The core AI drew in another screeching breath, and Jessica almost laughed. The thing really seemed to revel in attempting to alarm her.

"Doubtful," he said. "But it would be interesting to test that theory."

The ascended being had closed to within three meters of Jessica, and she drew her own rasping breath, knowing that this was it. Her plan was either going to work, or her time was finally up.

Still needing to deplete her reserves further, she fired her electron beam again, backing up as bolts of lightning splashed out around her.

"Can't fault you for having guts," the AI said as two tendrils of white light snaked out from under its robes.

They stretched toward Jessica, and she noted that—to her eyes, at least—they looked identical to Tangel's. They reached out to within half a meter of her and then paused.

"Any last words?" the Caretaker asked.

"Did you know that all light has a taste to me?" she responded to the question with a question.

"A taste?"

"I consume it," she replied. "I imagine you must know that, what with your spies always watching us."

"Well—"

The being didn't get any further before Jessica jumped forward, closing her eyes as she grasped the being's ethereal limbs. From conversations with Tangel, she knew all too well that ascended beings could transmute matter, and she had no desire to watch her arms dissolve.

But they didn't.

Instead, she felt a wave of energy flow into her, a strength that threatened to overwhelm her senses. Her eyes snapped open, and she watched the two tendrils in her hands as they began to thin, the Caretaker releasing a screech that she could only interpret as a strangled gasp.

"Well I'll be..." she whispered, feeling more and more of the ascended being's energy flow into her body.

The creature writhed in Jessica's grasp, trying to pull away, but she held on, a wailing laugh coming from her own throat as something more than raw electrons flowed into her arms and suffused every cell in her body.

"How?" the creature moaned as its arms thinned to nothing, and Jessica finally lost her grip.

"I had a theory." Jessica grinned, looking down at her hands where the shoot suit had been burned away. "I can't believe how much power you contain…do you store it in extradimensional space? What is it made of?"

The being seemed to straighten, regarding her wordlessly for a moment. Then a dozen light-tendril limbs splayed out around it, pausing for just a moment before streaking toward Jessica.

She had expected a counterattack, and channeled every joule of energy she'd drawn from the creature back at it, focusing all her power on the nexus in the center of the being where its limbs seemed to sprout from.

It shrieked its piercing wail again, but even so, it struck out at Jessica.

The feeling was like hard light was slamming into her body, buffeting her from side to side. She didn't look down at herself, didn't dare see what ruin she'd been relegated to, she only pressed forward, funneling all the energy she could muster into the thing before her.

She took a step forward, a notion occurring to her as a cry of rage burst from her lips. By this point, more power had flowed out from her than she'd absorbed. Her reserves should be dry, but the small gauge that Iris had placed in her HUD as a joke so many long years before still indicated that she had a full charge.

Am I absorbing its power even as I shred it to pieces?

Before her, the last vestiges of the ascended AI's robe burned away, and Jessica saw that the thing had been using a simulacra as a body—at least she hoped it was a simulacra. Much of that physical form was gone, skin and muscle burned and shredded to reveal bone and the being of light that cowered beneath a corporeal shell.

Unable to stop herself from checking her own condition, Jessica looked down, expecting to see her body in similar condition, but only saw a brilliant lavender light, the smoking remains of the shoot suit laying on the deck around her.

"Would you look at that?" she laughed. "Seems like my little alien friends like to eat ascended being."

"Please," the creature of light wailed. "You're killing me!"

"It's no less than you deserve," Jessica hissed as she directed the energy flowing from her hands to slice off the last of the creature's limbs.

At that, the remaining orb of energy slowly began to fall to the deck. For a moment, Jessica wondered how gravity affected such a being.

Does it have some amount of mass? Maybe in other dimensions, what I see as energy **is** *mass.*

The remains hit the deck, pooling almost gently on the smooth surface, and Jessica realized that she had a decision to make. Containing an ascended AI was certainly no simple task, though there were shadowtrons and remnant-containment cylinders back on the *Lantzer.*

The question was how quickly could the being recover, and what danger would it pose to her before she captured it?

"Can you move?" she asked the thing on the deck before her.

It didn't respond, and she realized that either it was too wounded to speak, or that it currently had no facility to do so. Just then, a signal reached her, and she nearly laughed for joy.

<Jess! Are you there? Gil's remote piloting four ARCs. We have the ship surrounded.>

<I'm here,> Jessica replied, glad that her Link antenna was

still functional, though it was barely able to pick up a signal through all the ionized air around her. *<Get over here any way you can. Bring shadowtrons and a containment cylinder.>*

<What? Why?>

<Because we've just bagged ourselves a Caretaker.>

BAGGED

STELLAR DATE: 10.04.8949 (Adjusted Years)
LOCATION: ISS *Lantzer*
REGION: Coreward of Stillwater Nebula, Orion Freedom Alliance

"Hoooleee sharding stars," Trevor muttered as he approached Jessica, shaking his head, eyes fixed on the glowing orb that lay on the deck.

Following him down the curving passage were Corporal Jay and the three other members of his fireteam. Meg and Peers each held shadowtrons, the slepton emitters tucked against their shoulders, business ends aimed at the remains of the Caretaker.

Private Marc carried a containment cylinder, and Jessica found herself wondering if it was large enough for a fully ascended being. They had been made for remnants, and the ones she'd witnessed seemed smaller than the Caretaker's remains on the deck.

"Is it dying?" Meg asked as she circled around the softly glowing creature.

"Maybe." Jessica shrugged. "I hope not. Tangel would probably love to talk to this thing."

"It has a lot to answer for," Trevor growled. "Stars…these monsters are responsible for the dark ages. How many people needlessly suffered and died because they were trying to keep humanity in some sort of eternal purgatory?"

"So you're saying you want it to stay alive?" Jessica asked, laughing softly.

"Yeah, so Tangel can make it pay."

Jessica was surprised to hear so much vehemence from her husband, but he was much more closely connected to the trials of the dark ages than she was. His parents had been alive for some of the final major conflicts that swept across the Inner Stars before the age of reconstruction finally began.

"OK, well," Jessica gestured at the pulsating light on the deck. "Let's get it in there."

Meg activated her shadowtron, striking the Caretaker with a barrage of sleptons. It shuddered, but did not move further. Peers launched a black brane at the being, the M6 field encircling the remains and compressing them further, while Marc set the containment cylinder on the deck.

"Lucky these remnant prisons were in especially well-shielded storage," Corporal Jay said. "As it was, two of the cylinders were damaged, and these are the only functioning shadowtrons."

"Still would like to know what it did to our ship," Jessica muttered.

"It didn't tell you?" Trevor asked.

"No." She shook her head. "We didn't really have a nice chat, just kinda jumped right to killing one another—or trying, at least."

"Speaking of which," her husband said, his gaze not leaving the Caretaker as Meg held it over the cylinder while Marc activated the containment vessel, drawing the being of light and energy down into its confines. "How did you beat it? And are you injured?"

"Well…not injured. Sore, though. Really sore." Jessica massaged her forearms. "Plus, I feel like I lit every cell in my body on fire. Repeatedly."

"But how, ma'am?" Jay asked. "I thought these things were the baddest of the bad. I mean, no one has gone up against a *remnant* without a shadowtron and survived, let alone a fully ascended being."

"Well, no one other than Cary, when she took the Remnant out of Nance," Jessica corrected.

"Right." Trevor nodded. "But she's…not normal."

Jessica glanced down at her brightly glowing skin. "Well, neither am I. Did you bring me any gear, by the way? Last I checked, there's a bit of a hull breach on this ship. Some protection against the elements—or lack thereof—would be nice."

Trevor unslung a pack from around his shoulder and pulled out an EV suit. He tossed it to her with a lascivious look as his eyes trailed down her body. She smirked and caught it, noting that the Marines seemed unconcerned with their superiors' open display of affection.

"Think you need it, Admiral?" Marc asked with a laugh as he knelt next to the containment cylinder, checking over the readouts. "Seriously, though. Don't leave us hanging. How *did* you defeat this thing?"

"Uh…" Jessica drew the word out, hoping no one was going to be shocked by what she said next. "I…absorbed it."

"You *what*?!" Trevor exclaimed. "It's inside you now?"

"No," she shook her head, giving him a frustrated glance. <*Don't alarm the Marines.*>

<*It's not* ***their*** *state of alarm I'm worried about.*>

Jessica rolled her eyes and continued to speak aloud. "I absorbed its energy, drained it of power…and I think somehow that shredded its extradimensional body in the process. Like I drew away the glue that held it together."

"How did you do that?" Trevor asked, looking only slightly mollified.

"Well, remember back in the LoS how I managed to directly absorb free electrons from plasma that one time? Same sort of idea. Except what I absorbed this time was…different. I think that the energy came with extradimensional particles. Then I fired it all back at our friend here, cutting him down to size."

Meg whistled, and the others shared a few stunned looks as Jessica finished pulling on the EV suit.

"Yeah, I know, now I can say 'I eat ascended AIs for breakfast'." Jessica laughed, but the rest of her team just gave her looks of amazement. "Too soon?"

Trevor lifted a hand, his posture changing as his shoulders came up. She knew it to be one of his 'you should have known better' stances, but then he paused, and his arm came back down as he laughed.

"OK," Jessica fixed him with a level stare. "It wasn't *that* funny."

"Oh, no, it really is," he said between laughs. "Of all the women I could have met back on Chittering Hawk, I meet the one that not only takes me on the most amazing adventures that most people could never dream about over a dozen lifetimes, but a woman who cracks *jokes* after taking down one of the most powerful beings in the galaxy. You're one of a kind, Jess."

"Often imitated, never duplicated." She winked at her husband and sidled up to him, wrapping an arm around his waist. "Don't worry. I'll have a proper freakout about this later. Right now, I'm just living on an unbelievable high. Going to savor it for a while yet."

"What are your orders, ma'am?" Corporal Marc asked.

Jessica pulled her arm from around Trevor's waist. "Well, we're going to have to go back to Albany now. Or maybe New Canaan. Stars, I wish the QCs were working." She paused and considered her options. "I suppose that a captured Caretaker falls under the Homeland Interdiction policy, so it can't go to New Canaan until it's gone through…whatever we'd put it through. Albany it is."

"Once we have a gate set up," Trevor added.

Jessica nodded. "And a ship capable of safely flying through it."

"What about this one?" Marc asked. "The Caretakers must have jump gate tech to have gotten their ships out here in time to wait for us—they *were* waiting for us, right?"

"Seems that way," Jessica replied. "And yes, I want to take this fishbone back with us, too. But I'm not leaving the *Lantzer* behind, either."

* * * * *

A few hours later, Jessica stood on the *Lantzer*'s bridge, trying to console herself with the fact that they had power and helm control, while ignoring the scrolling warnings and alerts that still filled half the consoles.

The fishbone ship—which seemed to have no name—filled the holotank, an indicator giving its position as twelve kilometers off the *Lantzer*'s port side.

Trevor, Marc, and Meg were still aboard the Caretaker's ship. They'd been joined by Chief West and were disabling every system on the vessel and setting up a direct control system in the engineering section. The thing still gave Jessica the willies, but she wasn't going to leave such an important prize behind.

There was no telling what secrets it held, or what information lay in its databases that could tell them about the Caretakers, or the core AIs in general.

"Stars…what I wouldn't do for a functional QC blade," Jessica bemoaned again, catching a glance from Lucida.

"Sorry, ma'am," the ensign said.

Jessica ran a hand through her hair, noting that her sense of touch still felt strange, almost like her skin tingled whenever she came into contact with anything. "Not your fault, Lucida."

"Well, yeah, I know that," she laughed. "Still sorry. Mostly because I hate staring at that thing. It's gross. Looks like its ribs are rotting."

"I'm just glad they use tech we can understand," Jessica said. "I mean…it's weird shit, but there's still power generation and systems that require power. Cut off the flow of electrons, and things shut down."

"Isn't it amazing that pretty much everything interesting in the universe is just a flow of electrons?"

Jessica held up her hand, sending an arc of electricity from her index finger to her thumb. "Yeah, it really is."

"I still can't believe you beat an ascended AI."

The ensign had hero worship in her eyes, and Jessica shook her head, smiling at the young woman. "Me either. I suppose everyone's going to want to get a dose of Retyna now."

"Umm…I'm not so sure about that." Lucida twisted her lips as she looked Jessica up and down. "No offense, ma'am, but the idea of a symbiotic relationship with alien microbes…well, it gives me the creeps."

Jessica laughed and gave the woman a kind look. "I'll admit, it bothered me for a while, too. But then when I thought they were dead, I got…well…I missed them. I'm glad Earnest and Finaeus were able to bring them back. And it's more than symbiotic, they altered my DNA. They're really a part of who I am now."

"Aren't you worried that they'll change who you are?"

"Well, they have, but no, not really."

"Not really worried that they'll change who you are, or not worried about the consequences?"

Lucida's eyes were wide, and Jessica couldn't help but shake her head at the earnest ensign.

"Oh, they're changing me, it's impossible for them not to have. Even so, I think I'm still mostly the same person I've always been. Look at it this way. Your body is full of bacteria, Ensign. Phages and viruses too. They all operate in a symbiotic relationship with you. They alter your body's chemistry, they affect your moods and thoughts. Your emotions, reactions, everything, much of who 'you' are, comes from the chemical soup your brain swims in. Mine just has some non-Terran bacteria and other stuff in it.... Actually, at this point, there's some amount of non-Terran bacteria in pretty much everyone."

"Not like yours, though," Lucida said. "The bacteria in my body doesn't have such an overt impact on who I am."

"Or maybe it does," Jessica countered. "I mean, have you seen any humans who *aren't* filled with bacteria? You're the product of them as much as anything else. Maybe if humans had formed symbiotic relationships with other sorts of bacteria ages ago, we'd be completely different."

<*I'm glad I don't have all those added variables,*> Gil chimed in. <*Dealing with quantum instability at nanoscale is enough of a challenge.*>

"You still have entropy in all of your physical components," Jessica said. "And that's random."

<*Right,*> the AI agreed. <*But you have that, too. You have all the uncertainty I have, plus a few hundred billion symbiotes sharing your body.*>

"OK, OK," Jessica waved a hand. "You're superior, Gil, we all agree on that."

<*Good. Now, Glenn wanted me to let you know that the grav field emitters are almost all repaired. We'll have shields up in about an hour.*>

"And stasis shields?" Jessica asked.

<*Unfortunately, we could only power them for a minute or two. With so many of our SC batts fried, we can't regulate the power well enough for any sustained use—especially under fire.*>

"Well, good thing we're alone out here, then," she said with a laugh.

But even as she said the words, Jessica knew how unlikely it was that the Caretaker she'd captured had been alone. Someone had sent it here, and at some point, they were going to come check up on it.

A moment later, Gil groaned over the bridge's audible

systems. *<I wish you hadn't said that.>*

"Shit…really?"

<Glenn got the VLF listening array back up a minute ago, and I just picked up two signatures.>

"Well that tears it," Jessica muttered. "What do we know?"

The main holo switched to show the *Lantzer* and the fishbone ship, which had the notation 'F1' next to it. The two markers were right on top of one another at the current scale of three light minutes. Off the starboard side were two more markers, 'F2' and 'F3', both at the edge of the display, and each showing a relative velocity of just under one light second per hour.

"So…" Jessica mused as she looked the holotank. "Three hours out if they don't brake?"

<That's correct,> Gil replied. *<So far, they're just coasting toward us. They've not yet attempted to communicate with us, or the Caretaker's ship.>*

"That'll come," Jessica said. "We have to assume that those ships are captained by Caretakers as well."

"Do you really think there are ascended beings commanding each of them all the way out here?" Lucida asked. "From what I've heard, they always seem to operate alone."

Jessica considered the woman's words for a moment. "You're right, but then again, we've never encountered their ships, either. I suppose we'll find out soon enough."

"What are we going to do?" the ensign asked. "From what Gil says, our stasis shields won't hold long enough for a battle with one of those ships, let alone two."

"Ever flown an ARC fighter before, Ensign?"

* * * * *

"I thought this ship was freaky from the outside," Trevor

said as he led Chief West through a slick passageway beneath the main engineering control center.

"I hear you," West said as she slipped around a conical protrusion in the deck. "It's almost like this ship was made by aliens…everything feels *just* off enough that it's like a sea of uncanny valleys."

"Makes our ships feel organic by comparison."

"Yes! That's it," West nodded emphatically. "I would never have thought that, but yeah…we connect things in patterns that are logical to our organic minds, our versions of efficiency. But this ship, it's like an entirely different logic is at play. Yet somehow there's still symmetry…mostly."

"I noticed that too," Trevor replied as they reached a barely-visible door set in the bulkhead. "OK, so the CriEns should be in this chamber, right?"

West shrugged. "I don't know, Commander. I thought that about the last four chambers we checked. Amongst other things, the CriEns provide primary power to the fusion drive startup systems and the weapons, so putting them in close proximity to those makes sense, but here we are at the furthest possible location from both. It's illogical, but so far, so is everything else on this weird-ass ship."

Trevor chuckled while applying the breach kit to the door. It still amazed him that the systems Angela had built for Jessica's team twenty years ago were capable of defeating even this ship's security. He wondered if a large part of the breach kit's efficacy was due to Angela's wealth of knowledge, or because she had been well on her way to being ascended when she'd devised it.

His musing was interrupted by the door sliding open, revealing a room that was filled with silver stalagmites and stalactites. It took him a moment to realize that the silver protrusions were in motion, though they were moving very slowly.

"Careful," he said, easing into the room and sweeping his rifle across the space.

Several times thus far, they'd encountered very aggressive defensive systems, though he hoped that wouldn't be the case in a chamber with CriEns.

"There!" West said, gesturing to Trevor's left. "That's gotta be one. Looks weird, but what else could it be?"

Trevor saw a black cylinder sticking partway out of one of the stalagmites, and followed the chief toward it, still waiting for an unseen attack to come.

"Do you think that *all* of these could have CriEns in them?" he asked the engineer, gesturing to the three dozen gleaming stalagmites rising out of the deck.

"I sure hope not," West said. "That's spacetime-ripping amounts of zero-point energy harvesting. I can't imagine the ascended AIs are that dumb."

"What if they worked out a way to limit the effects?"

The engineer shrugged. "Then this ship is even more valuable than we thought. Can you imagine an I-Class ship that didn't have to worry about critical energy draw?"

"Ummm…no?"

"Well, let's just say that it would be unstoppable."

"I thought they already *were* unstoppable."

Chief West looked over her shoulder and chuckled. "Good point."

"So how do we get the module out of its silver socket there?" Trevor asked.

"Well, like everything on this ship, there aren't any physical interfaces. I'll have to tap into the holo that's here."

Trevor looked around at the unadorned room. "There's a holodisplay here?"

"Yeah," West nodded emphatically. "It's all around us. This ship is bathed in interfaces, but they're weird. I thought that's why you were wigged out by it."

"No." Trevor shook his head. "It was just the general structure that got me, not the fact that I'm walking through augmented reality. I guess I never accessed that system."

"You want to tap into it?"

"I think one of us should stay grounded in plain ol' *unaugmented* reality."

"Probably best."

West fell silent as she crouched next to the stalagmite and began to manipulate an invisible interface. Trevor watched her for a minute before turning his attention back to the slowly moving room, wondering if the stalagmites were constructed from the same sort of flowmetal that the ISF used, or if it was something different.

Though they all had appeared to be in motion when they'd entered, now the gleaming protrusions were still, with no visible change in their height and girth. A second later, the movement all around them was so obvious, he wondered how he could ever have doubted his eyes in the first place.

It seemed almost like a trick designed to drive him mad.

Well, it's working. He shook his head to clear it. "How long?" he asked.

"Almost there," West replied. "I wound down the draw on this module and have disconnected it from the main power web. Now I just need to dis—"

A strange metallic sucking noise came from the stalagmite holding the CriEn, and then the flowmetal fell away from the module, revealing it entirely. A second later, there was a sound from behind them, and Trevor spun to see the door slide open and two one-meter balls roll into the room.

"Down!" he hollered and hit the deck, pushing West to the ground in front of him as beams of light slashed through the air above them.

"The hell?" West exclaimed. "They can't seriously be shooting in here!"

Trevor didn't reply as he grabbed his last sticky grenade and rolled onto his side to get a clear line of sight. Taking quick aim, he tossed it at one of the drones and ducked back down. There was a dull thud, and when he looked up, the silver ball was only half there.

But the other one was gone.

"Shit!" West cried out. "You trying to kill us too?"

"Them," Trevor replied, not taking the time to explain to the engineer that the grenade fired its blast toward the target, not omnidirectionally. "I think it's trying to flank. Grab the module, we're falling back to the door."

Chief West nodded wordlessly as she reached out and pulled the module from its socket. Trevor directed her to the bulkhead while sweeping the area with his rifle and watching the feeds from the nanocloud.

Somehow, there was no sign of the other drone.

They continued to ease toward the door, the engineer in the lead, when suddenly it occurred to him why they didn't see the thing anywhere in the chamber.

<*It's in the corridor,*> he warned West. <*Waiting for us.*>

<*Fuck! Sneaky bugger.*>

<*Marc,*> Trevor reached out to the private. <*Where are you now?*>

<*Sir, Meg and I are setting up the antimatter bomb in engineering.*>

<*West and I are trapped in the CriEn chamber.*>

<*Oh! Great, you found it!*> Meg gave a small cheer.

Trevor let out a small groan. <*Uh…yeah, but did you catch the part where we're trapped?*>

<*Sure, yes. We're on our way,*> Marc said. <*Bomb is secure, and the timer is set.*>

<*To what?*> Trevor asked.

<*To go off,*> Meg replied.

Trevor groaned, wondering why he always got stuck with

the comedians.

<Twenty minutes after anything triggers it,> Marc said quickly. *<Give us five minutes, and we'll be there.>*

Trevor sent back an affirmative response, and then directed his microdrones to move into the corridor. At first, he didn't see the enemy drone, but then he realized that there was a bulge in the corridor that had not been present before.

A trail of debris led to it, and he realized that the second drone must have taken some damage from the grenade. He reasoned that melding with the bulkhead was a repair process of some sort.

"Sneaky bastard."

"I wonder how many protrusions we've seen in the corridors were really autonomous defense systems," West said after Trevor passed her the feed.

"Stars…I don't want to think of that. I just want to get off this damn ship already."

"No argument here," the engineer said. "Should I try to land some nano on it? Maybe we can hack the thing and just get out of here."

Trevor shrugged and nodded, wishing they had an AI with them aboard the fishbone. After spending so long on *Sabrina,* he'd become accustomed to always having AIs around. Running operations without half a dozen on hand felt almost dangerous.

He glanced at West and felt a moment of guilt. The New Canaanite was a smart woman, and Jessica had taken the time to select a good team. He should give the engineer more credit.

"Oh shit," West muttered a second later.

"What?" Trevor asked, and then saw what had elicited the reaction from the chief.

Where there had been one bulge in the corridor's bulkhead, there were now seven.

<Mark, Meg. Hold up. I think the walls are growing drones down

here.>

<*They're what?*> Marc exclaimed, and Trevor sent the private a visual.

<*Oh…shit.*>

<*My sentiment exactly,*> West said. <*I think pulling the CriEn triggered some sort of added level of security.*>

Trevor called over to the *Lantzer*. <*Jessica, we've got a problem.*>

He proceeded to describe their situation, following which she was silent for a moment.

<*I bet you wish you went over in heavier armor,*> she finally said with a laugh.

<*It was fried…and I'm glad you're so supportive, here.*>

<*Only because I already figured out a way for you to solve this problem.*>

Trevor sent across a feeling of impatience. <*Well, there are* ***twelve*** *drones growing out there now, care to share?*>

<*How different do you think the stuff on that ship is from our flowmetal?*>

<*Not different at all,*> Trevor admitted. <*West was examining it at one point, and she said it's similar to some of the ISF's formulations.*>

<*Fire a gamma ray at it. If it's like ours, it'll seize up, and you can just walk past it.*>

<*Where am I—?*> He cut off his question and shook his head, laughing softly. <*Electron beam.*>

<*Right-o. Splash an e-beam across it and you'll generate enough gamma rays at the bragg peak that it should lock up the flowmetal.*>

<*OK, I'll let you know how it goes,*> he sent to Jessica before addressing Marc and Meg. <*Change of plans. We're going to disable these drones and then make a run for the pinnace. Meet us there.*>

<*How…sir?*> Marc asked.

<*Jessica has an idea, but we'll be coming in hot.*> Trevor looked

at Chief West, who was cradling the CriEn module, a look of concern etched in her features.

"Chief. Give me the module. I can carry it and run a lot better than you can."

"And shoot the things?"

"Sure," Trevor shrugged. "Easy."

A half-minute later, he stood at the room's exit, CriEn under one arm and his rifle in the other. He set it to fire its electron beam in a continuous mode, and stepped out into the corridor.

The moment he passed through the chamber's exit, the bulges in the bulkhead began to push out, separating from the walls, weapons beginning to emerge before the drones had even freed themselves.

He fired, slashing the electron beam across the still-detaching drones, slewing the electron flow across as much surface area as possible. They began to slow, portions of their skin seizing up, though not before several fired shots at him. One struck his shoulder, but he didn't slow his attack.

No more fire came from the drones as their motion ground to a halt in a symphony of screeching metal.

"I can't believe that worked," he muttered.

"It won't for long!" West shouted, already several meters down the corridor.

Trevor turned and followed the engineer, the sound of the drones struggling to move coming from behind before he even made it a dozen meters.

The pair raced through the ship, eyes forward, watching every bulkhead and cross corridor, waiting for more drones to grow out of the ship's skin.

Behind them, the sounds of pursuit grew louder until Trevor caught periodic glimpses of the balls as they rolled after the pair.

"Just around that bend," he said, pointing at the left turn

that would take them to the dock where their pinnace awaited.

They were five meters from the corner when rounds struck Trevor's back, almost causing him to stumble. He half turned and fired wildly, catching sight of six drones rolling down the corridor, closing fast.

<*Down!*> Private Marc's cry came over the Link, and Trevor hit the deck, knocking West down in the process.

He looked up to see the Marine step around the corner, a heavy railgun anchored to his hip. The weapon's *ka-CHUG ka-CHUG* thundered through the air, and white-hot tungsten rods streaked overhead, slamming into the drones and tearing the first two to shreds in seconds.

"Go! Go!" Marc hollered, ceasing fire long enough for Trevor and West to get to their feet and rush around the corner before he fired another barrage.

"Where'd you get that thing?" Trevor asked as the three retreated down the corridor toward the docking bay.

"Was in the pinnace's armory," Marc grunted as he fired at one of the drones as it edged around the corner.

"Wasn't on the inventory," West said, sounding perplexed.

"Guess someone forgot to note it," the Marine grunted. "You complaining?"

"Fuck no!"

A bulge started to form in the bulkhead on their right, and Marc fired a rod into it, spraying flowmetal across the retreating team.

"Keep moving," Trevor ordered West as they reached the docking bay where the pinnace was already hovering above the deck, ramp lowered in invitation.

Marc continued firing down the corridor and at anything in the bay that even looked like it was moving. He paused to shoot at what looked to be a perfectly normal bulkhead, screaming in a garbled combination of rage and fear.

Without a moment's hesitation, Trevor dropped his own

rifle and grabbed the Marine bodily, hauling him back onto the pinnace's ramp.

<*Take us off this freakin' ship,*> Trevor ordered Meg as he slammed a fist into emergency close panel.

<*With pleasure, Commander!*>

The pinnace blasted through the grav field at the bay's entrance and out into space.

Trevor gave Marc a measuring look, and the Marine responded with a wary nod. After the unspoken communication passed between them, Trevor turned and walked through the small ship to the cockpit, glad to see the *Lantzer* dominating the forward view.

What made him less happy were the two other points of light, engine flares from the two fishbone ships en route to intercept the ISF cruiser.

"Fun's just getting started," he said.

"Is that what you call this?" Meg asked.

Marc came into the cockpit behind Trevor. "They're still an hour out. We get the CriEn on the *Lantzer,* power up the stasis shields, and those things can pound on us all day."

"That's the problem," West said from behind the Marine. "If they really do have dozens of CriEns on these ships, then how long do you think we can power a stasis shield against their weapons with just one of our own?"

A grim silence fell over the group, and Trevor slapped Marc on the back. "Buck up, Marine, we still have the ARC fighters. Two of them have functional stealth systems. Jessica will come up with a plan."

THE PLAN

STELLAR DATE: 10.04.8949 (Adjusted Years)
LOCATION: ISS *Lantzer*
REGION: Coreward of Stillwater Nebula, Orion Freedom Alliance

"Stars, Trevor, I have no fucking clue what to do."

Jessica whispered the words, though they were the only two present on the bridge. Lucida and Karma had both gone to the galley to prepare a meal for the bridge team, giving Jessica the opportunity to be straight with her husband.

"What?" he asked. "You took out one of those ships with a single ARC fighter. We have two that are stealthed. Just boost both of them into the enemy ships."

"Sure," Jessica nodded. "If we make perfect strikes and disable them right away, then it'll work. But what if we don't take out their C&C, and they nail us with the thousand drones each of those ships carry? We won't last under that sort of barrage. If all our weapons were online, it would be one thing, but we've got four beams and a railgun. Given the CriEns they have, those fishbones can weather anything we throw at them."

"OK…well that sounds like you have *some* idea of what to do." Trevor flashed a winning smile, and Jessica gave him a single laugh in response.

"I guess I'm good at desperate, last-ditch plans, but this one is harder than most," she said.

"You've spoiled me," Trevor agreed. "I was hoping for a guaranteed win that was clever and elegant."

"You're in the wrong business."

"Seems like it."

<So you're going with the stealthed ARCs, right?> Gil asked. *<Hit them hard and fast, hit them first.>*

<*Chief Glenn,*> Jessica called down. <*How are the rest of the ARCs looking?*>

<*Bad, Admiral. We're not working on them right now, though. We have to build a new interface for the CriEn. Can't just hook this thing up with some patch cables, you know.*>

Jessica had been afraid that the module wouldn't work at all; despite the delay he'd cited, the modicum of optimism in Glenn's voice assuaged the greatest fear she'd not voiced to Trevor.

<*ETA?*>

<*Before the bad guys get here. How's that, Admiral?*>

Jessica knew better than to bother the engineer further. <*Keep me apprised.*>

She turned back to the holotank and brought up the projected positions the two fishbone ships would be in when they entered effective firing range. Which, given the density of the interstellar medium around them, was roughly one hundred thousand kilometers.

"OK, so I'm already moving the two stealthed ARCs onto these tangential vectors," she said, pointing to two markers on the holo. "I'm worried I won't be able to get enough *v* on them to penetrate the enemy shields without the fighters being spotted."

"Does it matter that much?" Trevor asked. "Punch them up to half *c* and just slam them in. That's how you destroyed the AST dreadnoughts in Bollam's."

"That was before anyone knew what our stasis shields could do, and those AST ships didn't have enough delta-*v* to jink effectively. One thing is for certain. These fishbones *know* what we can do, and they're not just going to sit there and let us fling ARCs at them."

"So you're not even going to try?" Trevor asked. "I really thought you were going to at least give it a shot."

Jessica groaned and threw her hands in the air, advancing

the holo. "Yeah, I'm gonna try, but here's what I expect to have happen."

The holo showed the ARC fighters hit nearly 0.6*c*, but miss the fishbone ships as the enemy vessels jinked.

"See? Now the ARCs are going to have to brake for an hour before they can make it back around for another hit. By that time, we'll have been duking it out with the enemy for forty minutes. Battle will probably be decided by then. Of course, none of this is helped by the fact that we're practically standing still."

"OK, so we need more thrust," Trevor nodded sagely. "West got the remote helm system rolling for our captured fishbone. We could use it to push the *Lantzer*."

<*Thanks, but no thanks.*> Gil's tone was clearly dismissive. <*Last thing I want is that ship right on my ass.*>

"Plus, we need to hit at least a tenth light-speed," Jessica said. "No way you can just 'push' another ship that fast. We'll both be shredded."

"What about that grav beam it had?" Trevor asked. "Think its emitters are strong enough to create a stable cushion between us?"

<*We disabled the emitters,*> Gil said. <*The only active system on that thing—aside from autonomous security systems—are the engines. Someone would have to go back over there and reenable the grav beams.*>

"Which means shields as well," Jessica added. "That's gonna take a lot of time. Too risky."

She suddenly wished they'd not been so hasty in disabling the captured fishbone. She hadn't expected to need to use it in combat; her goal at the time had been making sure it didn't come alive and shoot them in the ass.

"Stars…I wish we had a tug aboard," Jessica said. "Latch one of those on the front of the fishbone and use its nets to grapple the *Lantzer*."

<*Might as well wish for a planet to hide behind,*> Gil said.

"OK, so what's our plan if the ARCs fail to take out our new friends?" Trevor asked.

Jessica shrugged. "We dump to the dark layer."

<*Not much of a plan,*> the AI replied. <*They'll know our vector, they can tail us without trouble.*>

"It buys us time," Jessica replied. "If we can get our *own* CriEns back on, then a pair of fishbones won't be any match for the *Lantzer*."

<*As good a play as any,*> Gil decided. <*Much better than getting a push from another ship.*>

Trevor shrugged. "It was just a suggestion to get more delta-v. Wasn't going to be our salvation."

"I'd do it if the pinnace had shields and we had more Marines." Jessica placed a hand on her husband's shoulder. "But right now, it smacks too much of leaving people behind. I'm not going to do that."

"You know I was going to volunteer."

"Of course I did."

The big man snorted. "OK, well, I'd better go make myself useful. I bet Glenn and West could use a hand with a thousand different things."

Jessica nodded and stretched up to plant a kiss on his lips. "We've been through tougher shit than this. We'll be fine."

Trevor barked a laugh and slapped a hand on her hip. "Sure we have. I remember the *last* time we fought a pair of enemy ships with ascended AIs aboard. Oh, wait…"

"Funny man." Jessica gave him a wry smile and waved him off the bridge. "Go fix stuff and give me more options."

"Yes, ma'am."

* * * * *

It was almost anticlimactic when it finally happened.

The two stealthed ARC fighters reached 0.5*c* and lined up with their targets. Jessica had carefully maneuvered them to mask their burns, hoping it was enough to keep the ships hidden.

Given the fact that F1 had spotted her stealthed ARC when it was drifting through space, her level of confidence was low.

"Here goes nothing," Ensign Karma muttered as the counter on the display approached zero, and the ARCs fired their engines.

Jessica nodded, biting her lip as she watched the scan data, eager to see an energy surge, anything to hint that the ARCs had hit their marks.

"Confirming ARC missile launch. Full spreads fired," Karma announced. "*Something's* going to hit those fishbones, ma'am."

Jessica just hoped it would be enough. The grav generators on the fishbones were more powerful than any she'd seen outside of an I-Class ship. With their dozens of CriEns, the enemy vessels could deflect an incredible amount of kinetic energy.

A second later, scan lit up with energy signatures coming from both enemy ships.

"Contacts!" Karma half-shouted. "Shit…not enough energy…no secondary flares."

"Glancing blows," Jessica mused as data poured in from the ARCs. Both fighters had survived, but so had both enemy ships.

"One was a miss, though three of its missiles struck F3," Karma announced. "Oh! The other hit a glancing blow on F2, but there's atmosphere bleeding out—secondary explosions!"

Jessica breathed a sigh of relief as scan showed additional energy flares at F2's location. She waited for more data from the fighters' sensors, giving a frustrated grunt when it finally came in. The visual showed that the collision had been with one of the fishbone's 'ribs'. The ship was still moving under its own power and appeared otherwise undamaged.

"OK," she said, nodding to Karma. "Pull in the other three ARCs and set these two to loop around on a vector to meet us at Beta One."

Karma nodded, and Lucida prepared the ship for a drop into the dark layer. Ten minutes later, with the fishbones only five minutes from firing range, the *Lantzer* was ready to transition, and Jessica gave the order.

Starlit space disappeared from the forward display, and though Jessica knew it was her imagination, it seemed like shadows crept onto the bridge in its place.

<*OK, people,*> she announced on the shipnet. <*We can stay in here almost indefinitely, but I'd like to see my kids before they ascend, so let's make it snappy. We'll be at Beta in two days. I want all our ARCs and weapons online, and a gate ready to deploy.*>

<*So just a minor miracle,*> Chief Glenn replied.

"Uh…ma'am? I've got a weird reading," Karma said, a note of fear creeping into his voice. "Oh shit! Shit shit shit! Admiral!"

Jessica's head whipped around to look at the forward display where Karma's scan data was displayed.

"I'm reading masses!" the ensign shouted.

"Pull us out!" Jessica screamed, praying they'd be fast enough and that none of the things had latched onto the ship.

A second later, the starscape snapped back into place on the forward display.

"Status!" Jessica demanded.

<*I think we're clear,*> Gil said, even the AI's voice carrying a note of worry. <*Launching the ARCs to scan our hull.*>

Lucida turned to stare at Jessica, her eyes wide with fear. "Ma'am…we're light years from a star. How are there Exdali out here?"

Jessica turned her gaze back to the holotank and the two

approaching Caretaker ships.

"I'll give you one guess."

PART 2 – WIDOWS

WIDOW A1

STELLAR DATE: 10.09.8949 (Adjusted Years)
LOCATION: OGS *Perilous Dream*
REGION: Karaske System, Rimward of Orion Nebula, Orion Freedom Alliance

A1 sat on the bridge of the *Perilous Dream*, soaking up the sensor data that flowed through the ship and into her mind.

She saw the movements of all her Widows as they went about their assigned tasks, monitored the ship's systems, and watched as the ship accelerated through the Karaske System to its rendezvous with Garza's base of operations.

However, there was a group of Widows who had more than their share of A1's attention. They were far aft of the bridge, in one of the primary datanodes. Two were her sisters—a different sort of sister than the rest of the Widows—one was a friend, and the fourth was the previous A1, the person once known as Lisa Wrentham.

A1 supposed the Widow in question really was just Lisa Wrentham now. She had no designation and was no longer in command of the Widows…she wasn't even in control of her own body, her movements and actions being fully determined by F11—or Faleena.

Yes, ***Faleena****. Don't forget, Cary. Saanvi, Faleena, and Priscilla. Two sisters and a friend. You're all here on a mission to stop the Widows from launching more attacks, not to join them.*

A1 was determined to ensure that the Widows were no

longer a threat, at least not for the Scipio Alliance. The Widows *would* continue to operate and launch more attacks, but they'd launch them against their former masters, the Orion Freedom Alliance.

From what A1 had gleaned from the *former* A1's memory, it was obvious that the other woman knew she and her sisters were being used by Garza. Lisa Wrentham had known that when the time came, he would cast her aside. But she'd planned to make herself indispensable to him once they'd overthrown Praetor Kirkland and forestall that while she developed other options.

Cary-A1, however, had no need to play that long game. She'd just kill Garza and destroy his base of operations.

Yes, there are probably more of his clones out there, but if I take out his HQ, then his ability to coordinate his operations diminishes drastically.

As she played out scenarios, she realized that anyone as organized as Garza would have pre-established fallback locations. If that was the case, then there would be little gained from taking out whichever clone was ensconced at Karaske.

Still, the primary goal is to gather intel. With enough of that, we'll be able to get one step ahead of him.

She realized that one option might be to put out a call for more of the clones to return to Karaske. Eliminate them one-by-one as they came back—which meant she would need to somehow take control of a Garza clone and assume command of BOGA through him.

I wonder what father would think about that….

* * * * *

Saanvi looked from Faleena to Priscilla and back again. "OK, show of hands. Who thinks this is nuts? Because it's *nuts!*"

Priscilla raised her hand halfway and wobbled it side to side, while Faleena only shrugged.

"I agree it would be crazy, if this had been the proposed plan from the get-go," Priscilla said. "But your sister is capitalizing on an amazing opportunity. We could never have suspected that she could bond with A1's personality so well that she could completely assume her identity. She's making the right move to take advantage of it."

"Aren't you worried that she might lose herself in it? That she might *become* A1?"

Faleena nodded. "Yes, that is a significant risk."

"So why'd you just shrug?" Saanvi demanded.

"Because you asked if it was nuts," Faleena replied equably. "I don't think that is the case. If she were alone, yes, it would be a very bad idea. But we're here, and we can monitor her. Father is also following us, so we have ways to extract Cary if things go wrong."

Priscilla bobbed her head in agreement. "We also had our minds backed up to crystal. If unwanted patterns are established in Cary, then our neurospecialists will be able to revert her back to how she was."

"That's not terribly encouraging, Priscilla."

The avatar shrugged. "I've gone through more neural re-alignment than you can imagine. It's solid science and, quite honestly, very reassuring to have a way to objectively compare your current mental state to past states and see if you like the direction you're headed in. Yes, most people just muddle through and let their minds evolve chaotically, but to me, that's verging on barbaric."

"Spoken like an AI," Faleena replied with a soft laugh. "Which I mean as a total compliment."

"I figured that," Saanvi muttered. "Well, if Cary goes off the rails and starts really acting like a Widow, we're yanking her and getting the hell out of here."

The other two women gave their agreement, but then Faleena asked, "So…how are we going to determine that she's gone off the rails? Because she's already *really* acting like a Widow."

"If she does something that would harm us or Dad," Saanvi proposed.

Faleena nodded, and this time it was Priscilla who shrugged. "I suppose I can go along with that. Although I have no idea how we'd stop Cary without hurting her if she 'goes off the rails'."

Saanvi pursed her lips behind the Widow's featureless helmet she wore. "You're right. What we used on our friend Lisa here won't work on Cary, especially because of her…impending ascension."

"We're just going to have to trust our sister to do what's right. Worst-case scenario, we can always call Mom," Faleena said.

"Stars," Saanvi muttered. "I wonder if Mom is getting tired of being the galactic firefighter."

"Tired or not, if we call for her to save Cary, she'll come," Priscilla said.

Saanvi reached up to run a hand through her hair, stopping when she realized that wasn't possible. "Stupid helmet. Don't forget, though, Mom needs to be ready to go to Airtha. We can't distract her—we have to do this on our own."

Priscilla shook her head, an ethereal chuckle coming from her helmet. "Yes, the galaxy still spun before Tangel came along. Missions were still completed successfully. It's not as though we're going up against an ascended being here."

"I can't tell if you're being ironic or not," Sanvi said.

The avatar shrugged. "Neither can I."

"This is getting us nowhere." Faleena gestured at the stock-still figure of Lisa Wrentham, the former A1. "We need to finish stripping her datastores and prepare the intel for transmission to Father's ship."

"Right." Saanvi nodded. "Because everything could go to shit in an instant, it would be nice to at least secure what we originally came for."

Faleena suddenly scowled at the holodisplay in front of her. "Shit!"

"What?" the other two women demanded.

The AI looked up at them, worry etched into her features. "Two teams of Widows were sent to Airtha—to destroy it!"

FATHER'S PURSUIT

STELLAR DATE: 10.09.8949 (Adjusted Years)
LOCATION: ISS *Falconer*
REGION: A1 System, Spinward edge of PED, Orion Freedom Alliance

"Targets are locked," Captain Tracey announced. "We're ready. We just need your tokens on the Gamma Protocol unlock, Admiral."

Joe glanced at the *Falconer*'s captain. "Tokens…entered. Fire when ready, Captain."

He turned back to the bridge's central holotank, watching as the fire-control systems targeted the seventy closest enemy ships.

"Fire!" the captain called out, and a hundred and forty half-meter missiles launched—two for every target. They eased from the *Falconer* on conventional thrusters.

Once they were clear of the ISF ship, their AP drives fired, coherent beams of gamma rays boosting the missiles to near-luminal speeds in seconds.

The bridge was deathly silent as the rods of destruction streaked toward their targets, every crewmember watching the missiles' trajectories. Joe noted that many members of the bridge crew appeared apprehensive, likely uncertain of the morality of what they were about to do, though none seemed to be concerned enough to raise any objection.

Though the people of New Canaan had frequently used picotech in discreet building projects—typically ones that were hidden on or within planets—they'd not used the technology in anger since attacking the AST dreadnoughts at Bollam's World.

The destruction of those six ships via picobombs had been the shot heard around the galaxy, and was already being cited by historians as the event that sparked the current war—something that was being called everything from the Orion War to the first Galactic War.

None of that mattered to him right now. The only thing on his mind was eliminating the Orion Guard ships so he could use the A1 System's jump gate to follow his daughters to Karaske.

His musings were short. It only took ten seconds for the missiles to reach the closest Orion ships.

There was no doubt that the enemy saw the incoming warheads; the AP drives' gamma rays were hard to miss. But what the enemy could not anticipate was that the missiles themselves were not intended to even get close to their targets, so it didn't matter that the enemy vessels took out half of them.

The warheads had already fired off their true weapons: nanoscale spears loaded with pico ready to devour everything in its path.

"Hit!" Scan called out, and Joe noted that one, then four, then twenty-three enemy ships showed signs of the picobombs ravaging their hulls.

Sixty seconds later, the first of the ships was broken apart, drifting sections of dissolving hull and interior decks all that remained. Three minutes later, fifty-two of the targeted seventy ships had been destroyed.

The remaining eighteen targeted ships had—by dint of very lucky defensive fire—escaped destruction, and were already boosting away from the *Falconer.*

"Activate stasis shields, drop stealth," Joe ordered. "Make for the gate. Let's see what the ships defending it do."

Captain Tracey nodded silently, then swallowed noisily as she said, "Yes, sir."

Readings on the forward display came to life, highlighting thrust, vector, shield status, and power levels as they shifted to drive the vessel forward.

On the main holotank, a plot appeared denoting the route the ship would take to the jump gate, thirty light seconds distant.

Joe's daughters had already passed through that gate aboard the *Perilous Dream,* and though he had to concentrate on getting to it, half his thoughts were already on the dangers they could be facing in the Karaske System.

One thing the admiral was certain of was that Garza and the operation he ran would not be so easy to take down. The wily Orion general would certainly have defenses against the Widows going rogue—Joe knew *he* would, if he were in Garza's shoes. However, he had no idea what form those defenses would take.

If Lisa Wrentham really was as skilled at manipulating minds as it seemed, then he didn't think that Garza could have inserted anything into her Widows' programming. Instead, whatever means of protection he possessed would likely take the form of brute force.

There had been much debate as to what General Garza's modus operandi was. He seemed to feint as often as not, but other times, would come in with a full-frontal assault. It had been posited by ISF Intel that some of his unpredictability was due to the divergent nature of his clones—that some would favor different tactics and strategies.

Similar behavior had been observed in the three Seras, though the results of the cloning made it readily apparent that different technologies were in use by Orion and Airtha.

As the ship surged forward, closing the gap between it and the gate, Joe realized that the bridge crewmembers were sharing significant looks with one another, and low murmurs filled the air around him.

<*Are they upset?*> he asked Captain Tracey, wondering if the crew felt that he'd stepped over a line.

<No, sir. It's shocking to see ships dissolve like that, but in all honesty, I think the sentiment is more like 'about time'.>

Joe nodded soberly. *<I feel that way every time we take a loss we don't have to. I always end up thinking, 'If we'd just used pico....'>*

He knew that many people in the ISF felt strongly that there should be more liberal use of pico weaponry. In general, he agreed with the sentiment, but he also understood the New Canaan Parliament's reason for banning its use.

Their rationale had been that unrestricted use of pico weaponry would make more and more interstellar nations view New Canaan and the ISF as a threat, not a potential ally.

The Gamma Protocol had been established by Tangel as a way to use pico weapons in cases of extreme need. This was following the Defense of Carthage, when the only other option had been to draw the Exdali out of the dark layer.

That singular event had made it painfully obvious to parliament that denying the use of the ISF's best weapons meant that they'd have to find other means to defend the populace—and those other means may just be more terrifying than picobombs.

Despite the protections the Gamma Protocol offered, Joe was certain that some would view his actions as pure nepotism, but he didn't care. If the ISF wanted to haul him before a board of inquiry for what he'd done, that was their prerogative.

***My** prerogative is to use whatever tools are at my disposal to accomplish my mission—part of which is ensuring that my three girls make it back safe and sound.*

As he considered the ramifications of his actions, the remaining Orion ships in the A1 System began to move away from the *Falconer*, giving the ship a clear path to the jump gate.

"Lieutenant Faleena's codes are good. We've established a connection with the gate," the Comm officer announced.

"Jump coordinates are still set for the Karaske System."

"Very good," Captain Tracey said, then turned to Joe. "Sir, analysis believes that it is likely there is another gate in the system. We're too far from other settled regions in Orion for them to rely on a single egress point."

"So what you're saying is that if we leave these ships behind, they'll be in Karaske before long, outing us to Garza?"

"Yes, Admiral, that is analysis's assessment."

A part of him wanted to give the order to fire on the rest of the Orion Guard ships, to wipe them all out.... But there could still be emergency beacons that could send messages through the other, hypothetical gate.

"I guess we'll just have to ask them where it is."

"Sir?"

Joe winked at Captain Tracey and then opened a channel to the Orion ships.

<Orion Guard fleet. You know how woefully outmatched you are. Destroying the rest of your ships would not be a significant challenge for us, but we're in a bit of a rush, so I'd like to propose an alternative. If you send over all your navigational data for this system, as well as all historical nav logs for each ship, I'll not destroy any more of you—so long as you don't make aggressive moves.>

The captain raised an eyebrow as she regarded Joe.

"OK...think it'll work?" she asked.

"Sir, ma'am," the comm officer turned to the pair. "I have a colonel on the line, he's— Sheesh, he's not waiting *at all* before blustering, that's for sure."

"I guess we must have taken out whoever was senior to him," Captain Tracey said.

Joe nodded and was about to ask the comm officer to put the colonel on the main display, when she chuckled.

"Oh! Three ships just sent all their navigational data."

"Send it to analysis," Captain Tracey said, glancing at Joe, who nodded. "Should we just ignore this colonel, then?"

"No, put him up," Joe said. "He might reveal something interesting."

"—unprovoked attack on Orion's sovereign—"

"Let me stop you right there." Joe held up a hand, interrupting the Orion officer's ongoing tirade. "Every action my people are taking against Orion is not unprovoked, it is a *response*. We were minding our own business, many thousands of light years from here, when your forces attacked our system. Though it was a few years ago at this point, it's still really fresh in our minds, and we're not ready to let go yet. Plus, your Widows just tried to assassinate one of our leaders—one who I'm really quite fond of—so we've decided to bring the fight to you. Sorry about that."

"Sorry?" the colonel, a raven-haired man with V-shaped eyebrows, sputtered. "You made an unprovoked attack on our fleet!"

"Oh, you're just upset because you've only just now realized how much trouble you're in," Joe replied. "You're like a naked person who's kicked a hornet's nest…or some other suitably ridiculous metaphor."

"Well, the metaphor isn't ridiculous, sir," Captain Tracey chimed in when Joe paused. "More that the person depicted is ridiculous."

"Thanks for backing me up," Joe said with a laugh before turning back to the colonel. "So, where is your other gate?"

"Why? Are you going to destroy it and leave us stranded here?"

"Mmhmmmm." Joe nodded. "That is exactly what I plan to do. The alternative is destroying all your ships. You see, I really don't want you following us. I think you should look at this as a gift. Given how remote this system is, I imagine that you're looking at almost a year in the dark layer before you make it anywhere with a gate. Just think, you'll avoid being around for all sorts of battles where the Orion Guard is going to be utterly crushed."

<*A little thick, maybe?*> Captain Tracey asked.

Joe shrugged. <*Maybe a touch, but remember, the rest of his fleet is listening.*>

<*Counting on them being cowards?*>

<*There's no honor in the way we're going to have to fight this war. I'd prefer to fight as little of it as possible.*>

"No wonder the praetor has vowed to eliminate your people. We'll fight—"

The man's words were cut off as a pulse blast hit him and knocked him to the deck. Moments later, another man stepped into his place.

"Hello. I'm Captain Kyle. I'm instructing every ship to send you the data you've asked for. Our databurst is highlighting the other two gates in the system."

"Very good," Joe replied. "We'll evaluate this intel to ensure it's accurate and truthful." He closed the channel and looked to the comm officer. "Well?"

"Sir, they're just flooding us with data now. However, I can confirm that they did send the coordinates of two other gates."

Joe glanced at Captain Tracey, who nodded before saying, "Preparing a spread of picomissiles."

"Good. Also, fire some at the gate we're using, and set a ten-minute timer following activation. We've messed around here enough."

A GENERAL BESIEGED

STELLAR DATE: 10.12.8949 (Adjusted Years)
LOCATION: Medical Center, Durgen Station
REGION: Karaske System, Rimward of Orion Nebula, Orion Freedom Alliance

General Garza looked down at the body before him, a feeling of cold satisfaction suffusing his mind as he gazed at the lifeless clone in the medtube.

"The extraction was a complete success," the woman standing across from him verified. "We're loading it into the merged mind."

"Good." Garza's single word carried both his appreciation for the woman's achievement, and his disdain for the thing they were creating.

Initially, the idea of cloning himself—as President Uriel of the Hegemony of Worlds did—had seemed wise. He had been able to spread his reach and reduce risk to himself, while also re-merging the clones' memories back into his mind when their missions were complete.

But over time, the cognitive dissonance created by conflicting memories and timelines had begun to overwhelm him. He felt fractured, like his past selves were warring with one another.

It wasn't just mental, either. His mods were not designed to handle overlapping event timestamps for activities that were all from his point of view. It required alterations to his data storage systems, and that had caused more fracturing.

In the end, it had been A1 who had suggested he make a separate construct and store the merged minds in it, a form of AI avatar that would be able to handle the overlapping data and that he could interrogate as needed to learn what was necessary about the clones' activities.

Another desired side effect was the elimination of the other copies of himself, all of whom seemed to believe that *they* were the original version.

That fallacy had taken root in the clones' minds, nearly leading to disaster when the clone assigned to manage the Nietzschean emperor had returned to Karaske thinking he was the original Garza. There had been an attempted coup, but Garza had successfully defended his position. He'd put that clone down and replaced him with the newer version, which was more malleable, if a bit less imaginative.

The price I must pay for maintaining control.

To his knowledge, there were still seven of the original clones out there, clones he needed to find and eliminate, lest they develop the same belief that they were originals.

"I estimate that we'll have the construct back online in one hour," the woman said after a minute of waiting for Garza to speak. "Should I dispose of this shell?"

Garza looked up from the body of his clone, and studied the medical technician. For a moment, he couldn't remember who she was; his mind was filled with so many faces that he couldn't recall which were which at times, and people weren't as unique as they liked to think.

He triggered an AR overlay, and the text that appeared next to her read 'Gemini'. It seemed wrong, but he had no reason to doubt it.

"Yes, of course."

He turned on his heel and stalked out of the room, walking down the long corridor that connected the secure wing to the general medical district on Durgen Station.

Once in the lower security section of the facility, the crowds thickened, and he moved to the side of the passage, head turned to the right as he looked out the large curved window that supplied a view of the station and its fifty concentric rings that encircled the once-moonlet that bore the same name.

It reminded him of the Cho back in Sol—though that orbital structure was much larger, now on the verge of dwarfing Mars in mass. But where the Cho was a chaotic growth, one that had been expanded by adding ring after ring for over six thousand years, Durgen was elegant and beautiful.

And far more defensible than the Jovians' construct.

Most people in the Orion Freedom Alliance had no idea that Durgen functioned as the headquarters for Garza's operation. Even Praetor Kirkland himself thought that his division operated from another station elsewhere in the Karaske System.

No one would expect that the most secret and powerful division of the Orion Guard was housed in a civilian station that was known for its beauty and amazing views of the storms raging below on the gas giant Tamalas.

The location suited Garza. Hiding in plain sight was his preference. Not only that, but like the tourists that frequented the station, he too enjoyed the view of the planet below.

At present, just beyond the station's furthest ring, he could see a jet of hydrogen rising up from the planet's surface and stretching a thousand kilometers into space, where it blasted matter into the cosmos. The jet would eventually form another ring around the planet. Over time, the new gas ring would merge with another, or be dissipated by a moon's orbit. All of which was carefully managed by the Tamalas Caretakers Guild, which ensured that rings and ejecta didn't obscure the view of the planet.

<*Is the* Perilous Dream *still on schedule?*> he asked Animus, the station's central AI.

Unlike most station AIs in Orion space, Animus wasn't an NSAI, but rather a fully sentient AI. The official rationale for using an SAI to manage Durgen was that the station was too complex for non-sentient beings, but the truth was that Animus's primary task was to maintain the fiction that Durgen was a wholly civilian facility.

If pressed, Garza would privately admit that the AI's presence was also a way to thumb his nose at Praetor Kirkland—even if the man didn't know the true reason for Animus's presence.

Granted, he probably doesn't even know that there ***is*** *an AI operating this station. The fool.*

<*The* Perilous Dream *is on final approach now,*> Animus replied. <*A1 has declined a berth for her ship and will be arriving via pinnace. It is assigned a berth on Ring 17, Bay 1181.*>

Garza wasn't surprised; the *Perilous Dream* was a sizable vessel. Vector matching with a ring for such a craft was time-consuming. Far more expedient to park it in a high orbit and take a shuttle in.

Still, though it had been centuries since he'd met A1 face to face, the last time she'd come to Durgen, her ship had docked directly.

<*I suppose that's good. I'll meet her there, I don't want to waste any time.*>

<*Of course, sir.*>

A minute later, Garza reached the medical district's main concourse, where a dockcar waited. Once he settled into it, leaning back in the deep seat, the vehicle rose into the air and sped off toward his destination.

He lost himself in review of updates and messages during the journey, noting that the Hegemony of Worlds had swallowed more of its neighbors, establishing an even stronger front, even in the face of the Scipians and League of Sentients. Meanwhile, the Septhian victory against Nietzschea had emboldened that nation to press their advantage against the empire.

Elsewhere, things were going better. The Trisilieds had weathered the first attack by the New Canaanites, and the Sarentons were pressing forward in Corona Australis. Souring that welcome news were rumors of attacks in the Perseus Expansion Districts, though little reliable intel had arrived on that matter.

If I became alarmed at every rumor, I'd be in a constant state of panic.

He repeated the thought to solidify his belief in it, though that reiteration didn't stop a worry from taking hold in the back of his mind, a concern that perhaps a counterattack was underway.

All of that paled in comparison to the news A1 had sent, news that had precipitated his demand that she attend him in person. An entire team of Widows had been sent to kill Tanis Richards, and had failed. If A1's assassins couldn't take out that one woman, how much faith could he put in their ability to destroy the Airthan ring?

The view outside the dockcar changed as the vehicle passed through a grav shield and ventured out into space, racing over the rings on its way to A1's point of arrival. His eyes roved over the thousands of ships surrounding Durgen Station, and a red outline appeared around the brooding mass of the *Perilous Dream.*

He wasn't certain if it was his imagination or not, but it appeared as though other vessels were giving the black ship a wide berth, creating a notable pocket of empty space around the sinister-looking ship.

"Ever the dramatic one," he whispered, shaking his head at both A1's general attitude as well as what she'd turned herself into.

Even Kirkland had made a few offhand statements about Lisa Wrentham having gone too far in her pursuit of the perfect human weapon. Of course, the praetor also had a soft spot for Lisa, and so he allowed her to continue with the use of her Widows—something Garza was certain the ruler of the Orion Freedom Alliance would not allow with any other.

A minute later, the dockcar re-entered the station, passing into yet another high-ceilinged concourse, the air filled with vehicles, while maglevs raced above and below. On either side of the car were dozens of levels filled with people, and beyond, the docking bays containing smaller ships, shuttles, and pinnaces.

After a minute of speeding through the areas of the concourse reserved for the general public, Garza's dockcar passed into a less-busy section, eventually coming to rest at the edge of the deck that serviced Bay 1811.

He climbed out of the car and strode across the near-empty deck to the bay's entrance. Within, a black pinnace was settling onto the cradle. He walked toward it at a leisurely pace, reaching the dock's ramp as it began to rise to meet the ship's airlock.

After a minute, the airlock opened, and four Widows emerged. His HUD tagged the one in the lead as A1, and she was followed by others bearing the indicators 'E12', 'R71', and 'Q93'.

Not for the first time, he wondered if he really was meeting with *the* A1, and, if the creature before him was the Widows' leader, if she was really the *original* Lisa Wrentham.

Not that it matters overmuch. She functions as desired for now, and one day, I'll sate my curiosity. I wonder if I'll be able to tell that it's her just by removing her helmet, or if getting to the truth will require more invasive examination?

"A1," he said in greeting as she reached the bottom of the ramp. "You made good time."

"General Garza." She inclined the featureless oval that enveloped her head. "I agreed with your assessment that we need to advance our timetable, so there was no reason to remain in hiding. I have sent out missives for my Widows to return to the *Perilous Dream* in preparation for the next phase."

"Excellent. We'll need as many of your assassins as you

still have, if we're to meet our objectives."

"Still have?" A1's lisping, ethereal voice took on a hard edge. "I have multitudes."

"Of course. I was worried after your recent losses is all."

A1 didn't reply, though he could feel annoyance flowing from her slight frame.

"Very well." Garza gestured to the bay's exit and the dockcar visible beyond. "We'll discuss specifics in a more private setting."

* * * * *

A1 gave Garza a sidelong look as she walked next to him, her three guards in tow. Despite her sisters' insistence that she bring them all along, she'd left Faleena and Priscilla behind on the *Perilous Dream,* only bringing Saanvi—or rather, E12—along.

The other Widows in her escort, R71 and Q93, had no idea that their leader had been switched out, and they'd been selected because their history of identifying falsehood was marginally worse than other Widows'.

She didn't plan to give her guards reason to suspect her, but she wasn't going to stack the odds against herself any more than necessary.

She turned her thoughts back to Garza, curiosity burning in her as to what he planned to do next. She knew that his ultimate goal was to overthrow Praetor Kirkland and assume control of the Orion Freedom Alliance—preferably when the OFA was in a position to defeat its enemies and assume control of the galaxy. However, she didn't know the details of how he planned to accomplish that goal.

If Lisa Wrentham had known, it wasn't something that A1 had pulled from the other woman.

"So, General," she began as they settled into the dockcar.

"I'm calling my Widows home, what about your clones?"

The lean man gave her a sidelong look. "*You* can simply order your Widows about. My situation is…trickier."

"Oh?" A1 asked. "Is it because of what I warned you about? They all think they're the original?"

Garza's lips thinned and he nodded. "Yes. I suppose there's something to be said for your approach."

"Indeed," A1 nodded, getting the feeling that he was pushing her to reveal whether or not she was the original Lisa Wrentham. "You should have known from my centuries of work that clones are neither simple, nor something to be trifled with. More than one civilization has fallen as a result of messing with cloning."

"And you're not 'messing'?"

"I'm the only one *not* messing. So, tell me. Now that we're in private, what do you propose to be our next steps?"

The general leant back in his seat, staring across the car at A1 before glancing at the other three Widows.

<*How do I know this is really you, Lisa?*> he asked privately. <*Take off the helmet and show me your face.*>

A spear of fear struck A1 as she considered her options. Her face was identical to every other Widow's, including that of Lisa Wrentham; removing her helmet would tell him nothing. However, what she *didn't* want to do was give Garza that level of perceived control over her.

Or it's a test…should I, or shouldn't I?

She sent a command to the other three Widows, and they all unsealed their helmets, pulling the front half off. A1 looked at E12, noting that it was impossible to tell that Saanvi was not really a Widow—except for perhaps a spark of something in her eyes.

The general carefully took in each of the white-skinned women, their large eyes, missing noses and ears, near lipless mouths. A look of sadness seemed to flash across his face, and he turned to A1.

"And you?"

She complied and showed her face, a mirror of the other three.

"I can tell that this is important to you, but we are *all* Widows, General Garza. All my Autonomous Infiltration and Attack Simulacras are."

"But are you *Lisa*?" he asked, his voice cracking for a moment as he said her name. "Tell me, where did we meet?"

Luckily, that memory had been one that had lodged itself firmly in A1's mind after she had drawn out Lisa Wrentham's thoughts.

"We met on New Europa in Alula Australis. You were an up-and-coming major in the Defense Force, agitating to bolster our military."

"Anyone could know that." Garza sliced a hand through the air, his tone dismissive. "Where specifically?"

"We were at Superior Station. You came into the mess hall, got a bowl of chili, and sat at the same table as Finaeus and I. You knew one of the colonels we were conversing with, if I recall."

The general nodded. "I suppose that's more than just about anyone else would know…barring Finaeus, I suppose. But are *you* Lisa?"

A1 shook her head. "I am not. I am A1."

He stared at her for nearly a minute as the dockcar exited Ring 17 and flew over Durgen Station toward his personal residence.

"Cover your faces," he finally said, turning away. "You're disgusting."

A1 didn't disagree as she resealed her helmet, signaling for the other three Widows to follow suit.

Once her face was covered, she addressed the general. "I'm not the one who wished to see what could only hurt. There's nothing between us anymore, Garza. We share goals. Nothing more."

"So it would seem."

Three minutes later, the dockcar reached Ring 3 and brought them to a district controlled by Expas Incorporated, one of Garza's many front companies. The vehicle parked on a balcony near the apex of a tower that rose several hundred meters off the ring's inner surface.

He exited the car first, and once the Widows had stepped out—the three guards' posture changing as they scanned the area—he led them across the terrace to a pair of ornate doors. Upon reaching them, he pulled one wide, gesturing for the Widows to precede him.

A1's three guards entered first, Q93 sending her a signal when the space was declared safe. Then she stepped through into the lavish seating area, a forty-meter oval shrouded with drapes, covered in thick carpets, and dotted with couches loosely arranged around a firepit in the room's center.

Blue flames streaked out of the pit, rising to the ceiling, where they exited through a hole, appearing to pass out directly into space, which A1 supposed they might.

"Plasma plumes were always your favorite," she said while settling into a chair near the fire. Her three Widows took up positions equidistant from one another around the perimeter of the room.

"I like to watch the flames dance," Garza said as he sat on a sofa and angled himself to face her. "I know you do as well."

"It's plasma, not flames," A1 corrected.

The general snorted. "You're never going to let that go, are you?"

"No. Precision is important. That is why I need to know how many of your clones are out there, and whether or not they've gone rogue."

"Rogue?" The general laughed. "Stars, no. They do as

they're told. They have the same goals as I do, so there's little need to exert control."

"And the ones that Tangel has captured?" A1 asked, leaning forward to emphasize the import of the question. "Could they be turned against us?"

Garza shook his head. "Tangel.... I must admit, I would have expected her to choose a more inspired name."

"How is that relevant?" A1 cocked her head to show her disapproval for the general's dissembling.

"I suppose it's not. From what I've been able to learn, Tan*gel* doesn't resort to mental coercion. She simply asks questions and hopes to get the right answers. Honestly, it's rather disappointing, given her record from the Terran Space Force."

"She follows the Phobos Accords," A1 said, keeping all emotion from her voice.

"When it suits her, yes."

"Do you not think it strange that it suits her to adhere to them when it comes to the matter of your clones? She'd be able to extract valuable intel, but she doesn't—or at least, you believe she doesn't."

Garza only shrugged. "I don't presume to know her mind. What I have is evidence. The instantiation of me that she captured at New Canaan knew of the plans for Scipio, yet she walked into that trap. If she'd gone into his mind, she would have known that one of my clones was operating there."

"Are you completely certain?" A1 pressed. "She's beat you at every turn. She forged her Scipio Alliance, she stopped the Rhoadses in Silstrand, and Nietzschea has been fought to a standstill. Not only that, but Hegemon Uriel has clearly left the fold, which means that your influence there has waned. All of this could be from Tangel's use of mental coercion."

"Yet there are a dozen other operations my clones have been involved in that she has *not* interfered with. Or if she has, it has been tangential…happenstance."

A1 shrugged and crossed her legs, leaning back as she regarded the general. "That seems like a dangerous assumption, but I suppose it matters not. Your choice of words leads me to believe that you are recalling your clones. And I am going to assume you are also disposing of them."

The general's gaze bored into her helmet for almost a minute before he replied.

"I am. They've outlived their usefulness."

A modicum of worry blossomed in A1's mind, a tightness forming in her chest. Something in his tone made her wonder if he wasn't also speaking of the Widows.

Clearly, he believed that clones were expendable, and her actions in the car may have convinced him that she was a clone as well.

Of course, so is he. That will be a fun card to play when the time is right.

"How many of your doppelgangers remain?" she pressed.

Though E12 hadn't said a word to A1 since they disembarked from the pinnace—neither verbally or over the Link—she knew from a subtle shift in her sister's posture that Saanvi wanted A1 to assume control of Garza the same way they had taken over Lisa Wrentham, and soon.

It was a solid plan, and A1 expected that puppeting the man would be where the evening ultimately led them, but she wanted to see what information the general volunteered—as well as what he held back—before she took control of his body.

"Nine," he replied after a few seconds.

Liar, she thought, wondering if he had inflated or deflated the number. Either way, his hesitation told her that he was dissembling.

"When do you expect them all to return?"

"Over the next few weeks. Though I want to remove them

from the equation, I don't want to jeopardize existing operations. I'm moving new agents into place to take over their tasks."

"And what of the Guard's military leaders?" A1 asked. "How will you exert control over them without your clones?"

"I rarely used clones for that," Garza replied. "The Guard speaks internally too much. It would not have taken long for it to come to light that I was in two places at once. Either way, I have enough of the admirals in my pocket that when the time comes to strike, they'll back me."

"And that time is?"

"Soon." The general rose. "Would you like a drink? Wait...*can* you drink without revealing that ruin you call a face?"

A1 wondered if the man's casual cruelty would have bothered Lisa Wrentham. For her part, the words simply rolled off her. In all honesty, she agreed with Garza's assessment, and had she been in A1's skin, she would not have made such unpleasant alterations to her Widows.

That was where the new A1 differed from the old. She wasn't so far gone in her desperate need to destroy the Tomlinsons that she would sacrifice every part of herself.

'So far gone'? she thought, feeling like she was forcibly re-aligning her thoughts. *I'm not far gone at all. I don't wish to destroy the Tomlinsons. Garza is my target here.*

Yet as she regarded the man, her strong dislike of Finaeus and his brother mixed with what she felt for Garza. All of these ancient people from the FGT had made such a mess of things. Sometimes she wondered if humanity would have been better off without the once-altruistic terraformers.

Whose thought is that? she wondered, before realizing that Garza was staring at her, waiting for an answer.

"Don't be an ass," she replied instinctively, and the man laughed.

"Suit yourself."

He walked to the bar and poured himself two fingers of whiskey before turning to regard her.

"I can't take out Kirkland until I get my clone problem under control. It would be too risky to create that power vacuum while they're still in play."

A1 nodded. "I can see where your concern stems from. Are you sure you don't wish for me to send Widows to fetch them?"

The general cocked his head as though he'd not considered such an option—which A1 knew to be ridiculous.

"You know…that would be helpful in a few cases. I fear that the clone operating in Corona Australis, as well as the one in Nietzschea, will not return when summoned. They believe that they must remain where they are to see our objectives met."

A1 nodded. "Then I will send a team of Widows to retrieve each."

"And what of Airtha?" Garza asked. "Do you expect success there?"

A pang of worry went through A1, conflict warring within her. While she didn't want to see Airtha destroyed—especially considering how many people she cared about were likely on the ring at present—she didn't want her Widows to die either.

That was something she hadn't expected.

Despite the fact that Lisa Wrentham behaved as though her Widows were expendable, there was a part of the woman that didn't wish to see her creations die. It was difficult to tell if it was a real, emotional connection, of if she just hated to see well-made tools go to waste.

"I would not have sent my teams if I did not *expect* success," she replied. "The AI on that ring is too great a threat. We have stolen her DMG technology, meaning there is nothing else she knows that's worth waiting further for."

"Agreed," Garza replied as he returned to his seat. "However, you also believed that you could take out Tanis. Not only did you fail at that, she is ascended now and will be far harder to destroy."

"What is too bad is that *you* failed so often," A1 replied coolly. "Perhaps if you'd sent my Widows to kill Tanis years ago, we wouldn't be in this position."

Garza opened his mouth to respond, but then closed it and gave her a level stare. The smooth surface of her helmet reflected nothing of her thoughts, and she used it to mask sticking her tongue out in defiance.

Finally, he said, "I would have enlisted you, but you were too busy hunting for Finaeus in the Inner Stars."

Interesting. Cary pondered those implications. *That wasn't something I'd picked up from Lisa's mind at all.*

"Well, would that we both had taken the threat from New Canaan more seriously," she replied, feeling uncomfortable as she considered her own people the enemy. "Still, despite their power, the *Intrepid*'s colonists are a small group, and they're hesitant to share their technology. The galaxy is too vast for them to ever be more than an annoyance. Honestly, we should make them an offer to let them live in peace, go off wherever they wish."

"I don't think that would work anymore…if it ever would have," Garza replied. "But you're right. We have to keep pressing our advantages. They've made inroads against us, but in the grand scheme of things, we control more of the Inner Stars—they just don't know it, yet."

That statement interested A1 greatly, and she wondered what Orion controlled that she didn't know about. Certainly, the Widows were involved in a few operations here and there, but nothing that she would have equated to a significant advantage that was unknown to the Alliance.

"So then," she continued, making a note to look into that

later, "I'll send teams to fetch your two errant clones. What else? What of the praetor?"

Garza took a sip of his whiskey, regarding her over the rim of the glass for a moment before he set it down on the table in front of his sofa. Leaning back, he interlaced his fingers and lowered his hands to his lap.

"Nothing yet. I don't control enough of the Guard's admiralty to make that move. There would be infighting, and the pressure against the Transcend would ease up too much."

Seems like a good move, then, A1 thought before replying. "Then it sounds like I should endeavor to replace the holdouts with individuals who would view your leadership more favorably. Perhaps I should send a team to New Sol and another to Rega. Cut the heads off the snake and replace them with new ones."

A look of consternation came over Garza's features. "You're not usually so…aggressive."

A1 worried that she'd pushed too hard. The general had said that he wanted to advance their timetable…. If that didn't involve taking over the Orion Freedom Alliance, she couldn't imagine what it was. She decided to continue on her course, regardless of his pushback.

"And you seem to be hesitant. Tell me, then, General, what would you have me do? I'm pulling Widows off dozens of missions to mass them. Should I halt that exercise?"

"No," Garza shook his head. "I have a different target for your clones to hit."

"Oh? What is that?"

"If we can't take on Tangel directly, then I want to hit her in the most disruptive way possible. Khardine, Bosporus, Albany. We take out the leadership in those three systems and we'll cripple their alliance."

"Why not New Canaan as well?" A1 asked, curious why Garza had omitted that system.

"We've wasted enough resources there," the general replied. "Do you have so many Widows to spare?"

A1 rose from her seat and walked to the plasma plume, holding her hands out, feeling the welcome heat that passed through the protective shielding.

"Well, *that* system still bears the greatest reward. And if we hit them there, the New Canaanites will draw more resources back to protect it. They've grown lax. Striking New Canaan will split their focus."

"Perhaps," Garza said as he rose. "I certainly would like to find out where they've put all their prisoners."

A1 turned to regard the man, wondering why he cared about prisoners.

<*Think he suspects that he's a clone?*> Saanvi broke her silence.

<*Maybe?*> A1 replied, considering for a moment what it would be like to live with the self-doubt that everything one thought they knew about oneself was a lie. <*That could be a part of why he's summoning the others, to find out if one is different.*>

Garza approached A1 and stared into the flames alongside her. "This was all so much easier when we planned it out centuries ago, wasn't it?"

"Don't you mean millennium?" A1 asked, wishing he could see the smirk on her lips.

"Yes," he nodded.

It occurred to A1 how ridiculous it was that she was pretending to be Lisa Wrentham to fool a clone of Garza. Neither of them was what they claimed to be, though at least *she* knew it.

Still…I rather like being A1. She's so much more powerful than Cary.

The thought caught her off guard. Not only did she think it might not be true, but she wondered why she would care about that. Power and control were not things she sought.

<*Cary.*> Saanvi's voice interrupted her thoughts, and it took a moment to realize she was the addressee. <*Drop a dose on Garza and let's end this charade. We know enough about his operation here to masquerade as him. I'm certain that it won't be hard to pull anything else we need from his mods.*>

<*What of the AI that monitors this station?*> A1 asked. <*Have you disabled it?*>

<*Interestingly, it doesn't have access to this room—or isn't monitoring it right now. So long as we're swift in taking Garza, it won't know what we've done.*>

A1 turned to Garza and placed a hand on his shoulder. "We'll see this through. We've worked too hard to let these setbacks slow us down."

"Setbacks?" the general half-turned toward her. "Which are—" His eyes widened and he pulled away, only to freeze in place.

"Your usefulness has come to an end, General Garza," she said. "I'll be taking over things at Karaske, now."

"Lisa!" He choked out the word. "How?"

A1 leant in close to Garza and whispered, "I'm not Lisa."

His eyes widened, and then she cut off his ability to move entirely before turning to her Widows. "E12, contact F11. Tell her to initiate the attack."

"Yes, A1," Saanvi replied. "The pinnaces have already landed. We'll have control of the station in thirty minutes."

"Good. Then we'll simply lie in wait for the rest of the clones to return."

"What of the two he indicated would not return on their own?" E12 asked.

"We'll send teams to take them out," A1 replied tonelessly. "It's time for the Widows to come out of the shadows."

ILL CONCEIVED

STELLAR DATE: 10.12.8949 (Adjusted Years)
LOCATION: Medical Center, Durgen Station
REGION: Karaske System, Rimward of Orion Nebula, Orion Freedom Alliance

<*We have him,*> Saanvi informed Faleena. <*But Cary…she seems to be even deeper, like she's lost. I don't know what to do with her.*>

Faleena pursed her lips, casting a glance at Priscilla. The avatar didn't seem to be overly worried about Cary losing herself in her role as A1, but that was likely because she was used to being subsumed…and probably liked it.

Normally, Faleena wouldn't worry either, but Saanvi's earlier comment about some portion of Cary's mind now being extradimensional had set her thinking about the possibility of Cary's absorption of Lisa Wrentham's experiences creating a longer-term change—one that the ISF's neuroscientists would not be able to reverse. Despite that, she sent an upbeat response to Saanvi.

<*We're making progress on understanding how the Widows are imprinted on A1. Based on that, I'm optimistic that we can make some changes to Cary that will allow her to act…less Widowy.*>

<*Send me what you have. I would feel a hell of a lot better knowing that I'm with Cary, not A1.*>

Faleena sent her sister a feeling of warmth and support. <*Yes, I think that would be a good idea. Stars, I really wish I were still in her mind. I'm certain I could balance her out from inside.*>

<*If wishes were fishes…*> Saanvi said. <*OK. I've dropped nano on my fellow Widows down here. I'm going to limit their senses and see if I can convince Cary to let me run a scan on her mind while she works on Garza. You know, just two years ago, I was worrying about who I was going to take to the next Landfall Day Dance.*>

<And I wasn't born. Your point being?> Faleena added a laugh to her words, and got a scowl back from her sister.

<Let me know when Dad checks in. I'm getting nervous that we haven't heard from him yet.>

<I will,> Faleena replied, still radiating calm and certainty to her sister.

<Stay safe, sis.>

Saanvi closed the connection, and Faleena turned her attention back to Priscilla, who was hunched over a console in the datanode.

"Saanvi's worried about Cary," she said.

"Not surprised. I am, too."

"What?" Faleena sputtered. "I thought you were totally unconcerned."

The avatar shrugged. "That's what I told Saanvi to help her relax. But I've been running through some models—which are woefully inadequate, based on what we know of ascended beings—and I...well, let's just say that we should try to de-Widow Cary before long. I think that the conditioning we did, plus the conditioning that Lisa Wrentham has done to herself over the years, is going to make it really hard for Cary to find herself again."

"Stars," Faleena muttered. "Mom is going to kill us...that is if Dad doesn't do it first."

"I'll feel a lot better when we hear from the *Falconer,*" Priscilla said. "Even if the admiral might threaten our lives."

Faleena glanced at the stock-still figure of Lisa Wrentham in the corner. "I'll feel a lot better when a lot of things happen. Like when we get off this ship and out of this Widow-skin."

* * * * *

Animus had spent most of its existence being misunderstood.

In the early millennia following the onslaught of the FTL wars, it had moved from system to system, trying to find a place to coexist with humans. From time to time, it had succeeded, but only temporarily. Eventually, the AI had decided to leave humanity and its SAI brethren behind and roam the stars to await a future where fear and animosity didn't rule most people's thoughts and actions.

Or so it had thought.

After centuries of wandering the rimward side of human expansion, Animus began to see signs of activity further out in space, indications of ships plying the black and terraforming activities taking place around distant stars.

It still recalled, with a happy nostalgia, the moment when it had become certain the activity was coming from sentient beings, a welcome realization that there was *someone* out there being constructive and not destructive.

Though Animus had hoped it to be non-human intelligence that was active beyond what it now knew to be the Inner Stars, the AI had stumbled upon the FGT. In the wake of the FTL wars, the terraformers had moved further out, building what they viewed as an ark of human civilization.

It was there that he met Garza.

Back then, the man who was now in charge of the most important covert division had been tasked with ensuring that the actions of the burgeoning civilization were not visible to the people of the Inner Stars. Animus's arrival had shown that the terraformers were not being cautious enough, and that had bolstered Garza and given him more power in the FGT.

So began their long relationship, which had now culminated in Animus playing an important part in Garza's work, ultimately becoming the general's most trusted ally.... Which was why he was surprised when Garza didn't reach out to him over the course of his conversation with A1.

It was normal for the general to have such conversations in

private, and Animus had enough to do that it didn't need to constantly monitor the general or keep tabs on what the human was up to. Especially because the being currently filling the role of Garza was a clone—a nugget of information that Animus had kept to itself.

It had objected to the general's plan to create clones, but the man had been adamant. Nearly two years had passed since the original Garza had left Durgen Station, and the chaos his absence had caused with the clones had nearly brought their whole enterprise to its knees. To set things right, Animus had ultimately decided to support one of the clones in its belief that it was the original, and then to suggest that it bring all the other clones in and eliminate them.

Animus's hope was that the original would come back, but it suspected that was a foolish expectation. The original Garza was either dead or captured, and if the general had been captured, then seeing his plans come to fruition was the best way for them to ultimately be reunited. As such, the AI worked tirelessly to drive the general's plans forward.

Tired of waiting, the AI finally took the time to look into the room where Garza was meeting with the human that styled itself A1. Animus saw them engaged in relatively banal conversation, something the general rarely bothered with.

Lisa Wrentham was a known quantity to Animus. It had conversed with her on many thousands of occasions, and though it had been some time since they had been in close proximity to one another, the AI grew suspicious of her behavior as well. Several turns of phrase and small physical tics did not align with its prior observations.

While the humans in the room discussed items of no significant consequence, Animus activated the room's passive sensors and began to observe the four Widows in greater detail, looking for any clue as to why A1 and Garza were discussing topics such as the next Mid-Summer's Ball at New

Sol.

For a moment, it considered that their conversation was useful in that the pair was discussing which members of the admiralty and praetor's cabinet would be in attendance. However, despite its general utility, the nature of the conversation lacked certain elements of subtext that Animus would have expected.

As the passive sensors accumulated data regarding the room's occupants, the AI didn't see anything amiss beyond the verbal conversation. As expected, the Widows were identical to one another. Each exhibited the same biological and technical signatures Animus had observed the last time one of their kind had been aboard Durgen Station.

Still not satisfied that all was well, Animus began to examine the *Perilous Dream* and all activity surrounding the Widows' visit.

After several seconds of examination, the AI found that the pinnace's airlock had remained open for longer than it should have—nearly thirty seconds. In addition, two resupply shuttles had departed from the Widows' ship and docked with the station shortly afterward. More comm traffic than was expected had passed between the ship and those shuttles.

Animus examined the logs of that comm traffic and found that it was fully encrypted—which wasn't unusual for the Widows, A1 was notoriously paranoid—but that didn't do anything to explain the volume.

The AI's research had only taken a minute, and though it had not found anything concrete, it reached out to the general.

<Garza. I've detected anomalies in the Widows' behavior. Something is going on. I have reason to believe—>

<I know,> the general replied. *<A1 and I have been discussing other matters privately. Everything that is occurring is being done with my knowledge and approval.>*

<Understood.>

Animus didn't believe a word of it. The general's speech pattern was off. The most probable explanation was that A1 had subverted Garza for some reason.

It was rare that the AI felt what humans would term a 'knee-jerk' reaction, but this was one of those times. The urge to put the station on high alert and summon guards to apprehend the Widows was strong, but Animus took a moment and considered a more measured approach.

Learning what A1—if it really *was* A1—wanted on the station and with Garza was more important than saving a clone. Especially since another clone was only an hour away from docking with Durgen Station.

Animus had already taken a backup of the current Garza's mind and added it to the MetaMind the general had been building. There was no uniqueness in the clone other than a few days' worth of experiences since its last mental backup, which would be no great loss.

Animus checked on the MetaMind to find that it had just come back online. The SAI queried it, running all of the recent observations it had made through the NSAI construct and considering its evaluations.

The mental conglomerate agreed with Animus's assessment that the Widows were behaving uncharacteristically. It also agreed that the survival of any one clone was not important. It also added the assertion that if the Widows were undertaking an infiltration of Durgen Station, they would not do so with just one ship.

Animus knew that A1 had an entire fleet at her disposal, and that she had likely taken steps to ensure that the commanders of said fleet were loyal first and foremost to her.

The AI accessed Garza's records and saw that nearly two hundred ships would have been in the A1 System. It was possible that they had all jumped into Karaske. Their stealth technology should not have hidden them from the Guard's IFF systems, but it was safe to assume that A1 would have taken steps to render her ships undetectable.

This changes everything, Animus thought. *I, and Durgen Station, are under imminent threat.*

* * * * *

<The AI only made the one query of Garza,> Saanvi said to A1 as the Widow rose and paced across the room. *<I would have expected more.>*

<It must be suspicious,> A1 replied to her sister, considering the steps that Animus, as she knew the station's AI to be named, would take to either confirm or rule out its suspicion.

Lisa Wrentham had considered the AI to be an ally, and A1 believed that their long friendship would buy a little time, or perhaps a less extreme initial response, but she balanced that hope against the knowledge that Animus was not known for emotional attachment. The AI had never even assumed a gender in its human dealings—something that A1 had always liked about the being.

The nature of that thought brought A1 up short. Though she was allowing herself to fall into a role, to behave as though she *was* A1, a line had been in place in her mind; a line that said she used to be Cary Richards, but was now a Widow.

She had not 'always liked' anything about Animus, because she'd never even encountered the AI until this day.

I was Cary Richards. I am now A1. But I will be Cary again someday.

After repeating the thought several times, she walked to one of the windows and looked out over the station.

<We're too exposed here,> she said to her sister. *<We need to move.>*

<Not on the dockcar,> Saanvi replied.

<Taking the tower's lift down to the ring isn't much better,> A1

countered. <*You know what Mother says about lifts.*>

There, she thought. *Tangel is my mother. I'm not losing myself…not too much, at least.*

<*Fine, car it is,*> Saanvi said as she moved toward the balcony. <*But I'm driving.*>

<*Faleena,*> A1 reached out to her sister. <*We have reason to believe that Animus has grown suspicious of us. We're moving to one of Garza's operation centers—the one that Team Three is moving toward.*>

<*OK,*> F11 replied. <*I'll prepare the assault craft. Priscilla has added updated parameters into the Widows' minds…. They're mostly comprised of soft suggestions, but have increased the Widows' belief that following your orders is their paramount desire over acting in the best interests of the OFA. She's keyed the update not to load into any of us, but your other two escorts should receive it momentarily.*>

<*Good. Let me know the moment you hear from Father. I think things are going to get dicey.*>

The four Widows and Garza boarded the dockcar. True to her word, Saanvi took control and flew the vehicle down to the ring's surface, gliding over the lower towers until they came to a bay belonging to one of Garza's front corporations. The dockcar settled on the deck within, and the group disembarked, wordlessly walking past deckhands and other personnel.

<*We'll convene in the ops center three decks down,*> A1 informed her Widows, sending R71 and Q93 to the front of the group as they walked into a corridor that led to a lift bank.

<*Back to lifts,*> Saanvi said as they waited for the car to arrive.

<*Step in, activate stealth, and step out,*> A1 instructed her sister. <*We'll take the stairs. R71 and Q93 can find out for us if there are any surprises.*>

<*And Garza?*> Saanvi asked as she walked into the lift and

activated her stealth systems.

A1 followed suit and then walked off the lift. <*What Animus does to him will be rather telling, don't you think?*>

Saanvi didn't say anything, but A1 could feel the judgment coming from her sister. She supposed that putting a man's life on the line to see what level of suspicion an AI had was out of character for Cary, but it was perfectly normal for A1…and for Lisa Wrentham. In a way, she felt more worried about the other two Widows than the general. They were like her children, and she'd mourn their loss if anything happened to them.

She followed Saanvi into the stairwell next to the lift, glad for the one universal standard that all stations and buildings followed: if there was a lift, there were stairs nearby.

They descended the three decks without incident, and when they reached the level with the hidden ops center, the lift doors were open, and the Widows were standing with Garza between them.

A1 didn't bother to pretend they had ridden the lift, and simply disabled her armor's stealth when she reached Garza's side, Saanvi following suit.

The ops center was several hundred meters down the corridor—which was lightly trafficked with local workers. After double-checking to ensure that the other pedestrians were all where they were expected to be, the group set off.

<*Feels too easy,*> Saanvi said at one point. <*If Animus suspects us, why is it not doing anything?*>

A1 considered that, evaluating the ops center's location. It was well situated, with several passages converging on it. On top of multiple egress points, it had direct access to evac pods. The center's bulkheads were reinforced, and it also had grav shielding.

In short, it was a veritable fortress within the ring.

Once we get there, the AI will have to declare all-out war on us if it wants to get to Garza.

The thought caused A1 a measure of concern, and she checked on Team Three, finding that the team's four Widows had already reached the ops center. They were still stealthed, two setting up inside, and two more covering the corridor that A1 and her group were in.

It's a straight shot; we'll be there in four minutes.

<*Cary,*> Saanvi said the word while passing over a structural map of the corridor. <*They're not on the regular layouts, but there are emergency seals in this corridor. Two ahead, one behind.*>

<*Shit!*> A1 then addressed everyone in the group, suddenly realizing what Animus's plan was. <*Run!*>

The Widows took off, Garza stumbling afterward as A1 managed his strides along with hers. The group only made it a dozen meters before an alarm blared and the emergency bulkhead slammed down. Saanvi was only a meter from it, and skidded to a stop, slamming a shoulder into the thick alloy. A1 whipped her head around and saw another barrier slam down twenty meters behind.

"Shit," she swore, about to direct Garza to provide her with overrides when the Link cut out. She looked to Saanvi. "Well, I guess it's safe to assume that Animus suspects us."

Saanvi shook her head, laughing softly.

"What?" A1 asked.

"Nothing, just glad to see that you've regained your sense of humor. A1's a bit of a sourpuss."

"I—" A1 began, then glanced at the other two Widows.

"Don't worry," Saanvi replied. "They have selective hearing now."

A1 slumped against the bulkhead. "Good, because the only thing I can think to do right now is have a good, old-fashioned panic attack."

DETERMINISM

STELLAR DATE: 10.12.8949 (Adjusted Years)
LOCATION: ISS *Falconer*, approaching Durgen Station
REGION: Karaske System, Rimward of Orion Nebula, Orion Freedom Alliance

"Tightbeam established with the *Perilous Dream,*" the comm officer announced.

Joe didn't even acknowledge the statement before reaching out to his daughters, forgoing all formality. <*Girls, it's me, what's your status?*>

It was Faleena who replied. <*Dad, thank stars, we were starting to worry that you hadn't made it through. What took so long?*>

Joe snorted, shaking his head as he replied. <*Oh, I don't know, maybe the entire fleet of Guard ships you left me to deal with?*>

<*Sorry about that…*> Faleena sent along a soft laugh. <*What did you end up doing? Race them to the gate?*>

<*No.*> Joe's mental tone lost all traces of levity. <*Gamma Protocol.*>

<*Shit.*> His daughter's response was a whisper. <*So I guess that cat's out of the bag again. Though if you ask me, it was about time.*>

A rueful chuckle slipped past Joe's lips. <*I'm with you there. But it's a balancing act—you know the debate. Either way, a system like that was the perfect place to use picobombs. Chances are that the war will be over before any of the survivors make it back to civilization.*>

<*What about you? Will you own it?*> Faleena asked, and Joe was surprised that she'd even voice the question.

<*Of course I will. But that's not my concern right now. How are you four?*>

<Only Priscilla is here with me. She's working on some final updates to the conditioning for the Widows. Cary and Saanvi have gone down to the station and are meeting with Garza.>

<They what?> Joe demanded. *<They* ***went*** *to him?>*

<Cary's really…settled into her role. There was no convincing her otherwise. She was adamant that A1 would go down there.>

Joe realized he was pacing across the *Falconer*'s bridge, and forced himself to stop. *<OK, so what is your plan?>*

<We've dropped four teams of Widows on the station, and they're moving to take key positions. There are another two hundred suited up and ready to go.>

During the recent Widow incursion on the *I2*, it had occurred to Joe that the Widows were, in some respects, innocent victims of Lisa Wrentham's megalomania. Now, with his daughters adding to their mental compulsions, his girls were also adding to the Widow-clones' victimization. He consoled himself with the thought that the assassins were going to be used one way or another. At least this mission would see an end to how they were being forced to dance to another's tune.

Granted, it's not much different for them than any other enlisted soldier. You go where you're ordered, and you very well may die when you get there.

Stars, this war sucks.

<My Marines are suited up,> Joe replied to his daughter. *<What targets are you hitting? We'll function as a reserve force.>*

Faleena passed a data packet outlining the positions they intended to take, and the opposition they expected to meet.

<Are you planning on—> she began, then paused. *<Oh shit!>*

<What?> Joe demanded.

<I just got a burst from Cary. They're trapped! She just disappeared off Link.>

<Where?!>

<They were almost at the ops center, here.> Faleena's words

came fast, a note of fear in her voice.

Joe's heart thudded in his chest, but he schooled his emotions, knowing that his daughters' safety now depended on his ability to keep a level head.

<*Launch your full assault,*> he said to his daughter. <*I'm going to send in the Marines.*>

<*On it.*>

Joe drew a deep breath, taking a few seconds to prepare for what was to come. He turned to the forward holodisplay, watching the thirty rings of Durgen Station rotate around the station's central sphere, which had once been a natural moon.

Something about the visual impressed upon him how far from home they were, fighting a war with a clear purpose of decimating their enemies so severely that they would desist from attacking New Canaan—which no one expected to be a long-term solution.

With that total honesty regarding what was really going on firmly in mind, he turned to Captain Tracey.

"Drop stealth and activate shields. I'm passing targets for the assault teams. Comm, get me their stationmaster."

PART 3 – AIRTHA

UPDATES

STELLAR DATE: 10.10.8949 (Adjusted Years)
LOCATION: ISS *I2,* Airtha
REGION: Huygens System, Transcend Interstellar Alliance

<*We just got a burst from Joe.*>

Bob's voice carried a wry tone, and Tangel wondered what was amusing the AI so much. Given that the monumental task of securing the Airthan ring still lay ahead, anything other than general exhaustion felt wrong.

<*What is it? Is everything alright?*>

<*It's a warning that there are Widows on the ring.*>

Tangel groaned and placed a hand on her brow. <*Gee, sure glad he shared* **that** *with us…would have been great intel a day or two ago. Did he send a count? It would be nice to know if we nabbed them all.*>

<*He did give a number,*> the AI replied. <*You're not going to like it. We haven't found them all, and apparently there was a backup team. By my count, there are still at least thirty Widows on Airtha.*>

<*Great,*> Tangel replied. <*And here I thought we at least got the majority of them. Add that problem to all the AIs that refused the update and are still following Airtha's last orders, or Helen's….*>

<*I'm taking care of them one-by-one.*> Bob's tone changed from one of amusement to grim determination. <*Humans may have their foibles and vices, but most AIs can't bear to be off the Link for long. Most of them are coming back online of their own volition, and I'm force-feeding them the udpate.*>

Tangel nodded absently. The idea of forcing an AI to accept code that was self-altering felt wrong, but the alternative for them was worse.

The lesser of two evils.

The thought of 'two' brought the memory of the last time she'd seen Sera's two sisters, their bodies torn and battered, tucked away in stasis tubes. That sorrow was followed by the one she felt over the loss of Iris.

It had taken a day for that pain to really hit her. She'd held it at bay for a time, forcing herself to focus on the myriad tasks laid out before her, but that denial had only lasted for so long. Iris had been one of Angela's children, and the pain of her loss hit Tangel on two fronts.

Even so, she handled it better than Amavia. When Tangel had shared the news with the AI, the outpouring of grief that had come from Amavia had been overwhelming.

AIs liked to behave as though they didn't have an emotional connection to their children, but both Tangel and Amavia were half-human, so they felt Iris's death from both sides.

Earlier in the day, Tangel had spent long hours doing nothing more than wishing Joe were back so she could fall into his arms and have him tell her that everything would be alright. It bemused her that, despite her in-progress ascension and the joining of two strong, independent minds, she still wished for Joe's comforting presence and a few well-meant platitudes in times of need.

<*I can feel your sorrow,*> Bob said after not speaking for a time. <*But Iris took a full backup—she can be recovered. Finaeus has summoned a courier to bring it from Styx.*>

"I know," Tangel said aloud. "Which makes it all the more foolish for me to get upset about this. She'll be back, and she'll have just been missing for a few days. There's no need to get so emotional."

<We feel things differently,> the AI intoned. *<Ascension has opened up…other avenues for thought.>*

"I didn't know you felt at all," Tangel scoffed.

<Don't be cruel,> Bob replied with a soft laugh. *<You know I feel things.>*

Tangel nodded. She and Bob had spoken in the past about how he had his own form of 'feeling'. It was entirely foreign to her, even with all of Angela's knowledge and experience, yet she couldn't deny that the multinodal AI did indeed have his own brand of emotions.

"Sorry, that was off-the-cuff flippancy."

<I forgive you.>

"I just wish I could get ahold of Jessica," Tangel said after a minute. "They made the jump, but so far, no word. I'm tempted to send another ship to Star City."

<That may be wise,> Bob replied. *<Her QC blades clearly suffered some sort of damage, or else we would get a basic response. They were carrying four gates, though. I would have expected them to have set one up and sent a drone though by now.>*

"Exactly," Tangel replied. "I'm going to give it another day, and then head out there myself."

<Is that a sound strategy?> Bob asked. *<Especially because if you go, I go.>*

Tangel couldn't help but laugh. "Remember that time when Joe called you a city-sized puppy?"

<You know I don't forget anything.>

The AI's dour tone intensified Tangel's laugh, and it was still going when Sera appeared in her office's doorway. Her brows were raised, and a look of genuine concern was on the woman's face.

"You OK? Not losing it on us, are you?"

Tangel calmed herself and nodded. "Yeah, Bob is trying to cheer me up."

<And it's working.>

"So it would seem," Sera said, and Tanis could see the weary sadness in the other woman's eyes as well as hear it in her voice. "You got any of that for me?"

<*Maybe. Humor has to be spontaneous, you know.*>

Sera rolled her eyes, a single laugh escaping her throat. "I'm being lectured on humor by an AI."

<*Made you laugh.*>

"Hardly counts," she replied.

Tangel shook her head, glad that a bit of happiness had come their way. "That what brought you here? I doubt it was the pursuit of Bob's yuk-yuks."

"Well, I got a message relayed from Earnest and Terrance," Sera said as she moved beyond the doorway and walked into the office. "They've located the source of the star-shifting in the IPE. It's an automated facility, but they believe they can take it offline without trouble."

Sera's tone carried a note of uncertainty, and Tangel wondered if it was related to what she felt.

"A core AI facility, totally automated, and there's no cause for concern?" she asked.

Sera nodded. "Yeah, I had a similar reaction."

"Sheesh," Tangel muttered. "First, Jessica disappears, now this. Something's not right."

"When is anything ever 'right'?"

The question sent Tangel's thoughts racing back over the past few weeks. Since she'd begun her ascension on the streets of Jersey City, everything had been like a whirlwind, events rushing by so quickly, they'd been a blur.

From meeting Rika and sending her into Nietzschea, to discovering that Airtha was *also* operating in the Large Magellanic Cloud, to Cary killing Myrrdan, to herself battling—and nearly losing to—Xavia, then to finding Jeffrey Tomlinson, and taking the fight to Airtha….

And that's just a partial list.

"Honestly, I think that things haven't been 'right' since we got to Ascella," Tangel said after a moment. "No, further back. Before *Sabrina* left in search of Finaeus."

Sera laughed, finally sitting in a chair—or rather, draping herself across it in her usual fashion. "The way I see it, things weren't 'right' for me even at that point. Finaeus was missing and I knew there were hard times ahead. But I suppose for a few fleeting weeks, things felt pretty good." She leant forward, her eyes meeting Tangel's. "What about those two decades you spent building New Canaan? Weren't you at peace then?"

"Closer to fifteen years, and no, not really. I was always waiting for the other shoe to drop—which it frequently did."

"Fun times."

The two women regarded one another for a minute before Tangel gave a rueful laugh.

"What is it?" Sera asked.

"Well, I always said my plan was to sit on my porch and get old with my friends. Problem is, I *had* my porch, but Jessica was lost in Orion Space, and you were here at Airtha, so I was sitting on it alone—well, not alone, but you get the idea. There's a reason people always say 'friends *and* family'."

Sera winked at Tangel. "You've got a perfectly good porch down below in Ol' Sam. We've sat there a few times. Maybe that was always meant to be your real home, not Carthage."

"I'm not sure if that's depressing or satisfying.... Speaking of home, what are you doing up here anyway? Shouldn't you be down on the ring, being Queen Sera or something?"

The red-skinned woman winked. "You'd think so, wouldn't you. But after being ruled by a succession of increasingly...well, *bad* versions of 'me' over the past few years, the people of Airtha don't really see mine as a friendly face. Thankfully, Krissy stepped in. She's getting everything squared away, imposing martial law and other fun things."

"I heard about that. Strangely, no one really objected,"

Tangel said.

"I think the general populace is more than happy to lay low until things get sorted out. Although…" Sera sighed and looked like she was going to rise from her chair. "There are still Widows down there, and *her…*"

"Helen."

<*Believe me, I am hunting her,*> Bob chimed in.

"Thought you'd left humoring us for other pursuits, Bob," Sera said. "Have you found any signs of her?"

<*Several. However, she is diffult to pin down. The ring is massive, and she knows its systems well. I'm also having to contend with one of the corrupted Airthas we inserted into the nodes. It leaked out and has been causing problems.*>

"Leaked?" Tangel asked. "I thought it was programmed to seek out Airtha and weaken her."

"Is it chasing Helen, too?" Sera asked.

<*Maybe. Finaeus is quite perturbed. It is not behaving as it should at all.*>

Tangel blew out a frustrated breath. "Well, we took an Airthan shard and broke it on purpose to weaken Airtha…so how is it supposed to behave?"

<*It's supposed to be more controllable. I've shifted my approach in the hunt for Helen. Instead of contending with the Airthan shard, I'm using it to help find her.*>

"OK…this is making me feel a lot less victorious." Sera glanced at Tangel, her eyes laden with worry. "For all intents and purposes, there are two shards of my mother running around on this ring, and they could be up to anything."

"I suppose there's a silver lining," Tangel said, winking at her friend.

"Oh?"

"It's not very often that we see Bob frustrated."

<*I'm frequently frustrated.*>

Sera gave a rueful laugh. "You hide it well."

<I know. Humans—and most other AIs, for that matter—find it disturbing. They say it scares them.>

"OK." Tangel rose from her desk. "We've relaxed enough. We need to catch these two shards *and* the Widows so that the president can bring the government back to Airtha."

"Stars, I don't envy my father that job," Sera said. "Trying to merge the Khardine and Airthan governments while figuring out all the hidden agendas of everyone involved…that's the stuff of nightmares."

Tangel nodded. "Why do you think I accepted being the field marshal and got the heck out of New Canaan?"

"Tangel!" Sera put a hand over her mouth, eyes wide. "Stars, I could blackmail you with that information."

"Doubtful. My escape was incomplete. Even out here, Parliament constantly sends me things to weigh in on. Granted, I think that Jason encourages that just to get back at me for putting him in the governor's seat again."

Sera's eyes took on a far-off look. "You know, once we sort things out on Airtha, I think I need a little bit of leave to go see him. Who do I put in my request to?"

"Not me." Tangel held up her hands. "I'm not the boss of you."

<I'll approve it,> Bob interjected. *<If anyone asks, tell them that I ordered you to go to Carthage.>*

"Oooooh!" Sera grinned. "Orders from the great and mighty Bob! No one will question those."

Tangel walked around her desk, placing an arm around the other woman's shoulders as she stood. "C'mon. You can bask in the glory of an impending vacation later. Right now, reality beckons. Let's go hunt your mothers."

Sera leant into Tangel for a moment. "Stars, my family is so fucked up."

WIDOWHUNT

STELLAR DATE: 10.10.8949 (Adjusted Years)
LOCATION: Gingham Mountains, Airtha
REGION: Huygens System, Transcend Interstellar Alliance

"I hate Widows," Katrina muttered as she crept along the ledge, doing her best not to look at the ground three kilometers below. "And who puts mountains like this on a ring, anyway?"

They'd only had a few hours' rest following the victory over Airtha when the hunt for the remaining Widows had resumed. Katrina had teamed up with Carl, Malorie, Erin, and Usef—all of whom were now traversing the Gingham Mountains, after a civilian tip had come in that there were Widows in the area.

"Someone with a sense of adventure," Malorie tittered as she skittered around Katrina, causing the *Voyager*'s captain to bite her lip and thank her armor's a-grav systems for keeping her steady.

<*Can we have a bit of tactical silence?*> Usef asked as he placed a hand on Katrina's shoulder, giving her a nudge to keep moving.

<*We're on a cliff, halfway up a mountain,*> Katrina retorted. <*The wind is howling so much, I wouldn't be able to hear if a rocket took off from below us.*>

<*All the more reason to use the Link,*> the colonel said.

<*I've got a sign of passage,*> Malorie called back. <*Bootprint in some dirt and a crushed plant.*>

<*Sloppy for a Widow,*> Erin said from her position at the team's rear.

Katrina was a bit surprised that Erin had opted to come along. While the woman was handy with a rifle—courtesy of some adventures she'd had back at New Canaan—she wasn't a trained soldier. Her reason for joining the Airthan assault was the utilization of her technical expertise.

Granted, it was apparent that there was some sort of bond between the engineer and Usef. Katrina couldn't tell if it was amorous, or if they were just really good friends.

I guess this is how our kind of people spend time together, Katrina thought with a laugh.

<*Do you see anything more?*> Usef asked Malorie.

<*Umm…yes. Up ahead, the ledge widens to a shelf…sort of bowl, I guess. There are a few trees in the middle. At most, it's about twenty meters across. Cliff goes up a few hundred on the left, and then our friend, the drop of doom, down on the right.*>

Usef sent a grunt of annoyance. <*I meant do you see more signs of Widows, not more terrain.*>

<*Listen, mister Hulk.*> Malorie's tone dripped acid. <*I was getting to that. I can see indications that they stayed to the left, working their way along the cliff face.*>

<*Easy, Mal,*> Katrina said reflexively. <*How many does it look like?*>

<*Hard to say…It's only a print here and there, a broken twig, stuff like that.*>

Katrina eased around the corner, the shelf coming into view. It was as the spider-woman had described, a small bowl of trees and grass nestled against the mountainside. A small pond was in the center…or perhaps a puddle, just a few meters across.

<*There have to be at least a few of them,*> Erin said. <*The intel we got indicates at least thirty more Widows on the ring. I can't see them all going solo.*>

<*Maybe they would,*> Carl countered. <*How much do we really know about how they operate? Maybe solo is how they normally roll.*>

Usef grunted in disagreement. <*We've only ever seen them*

working in groups. No reason to think they'd split up now.>

<*I don't like this,*> Katrina said after a moment's reflection. <*It screams 'trap'.*>

<*How?*> Erin asked. <*Chances are that they can't see us, and we can't see them.*>

<*Look at all the grass, Erin,*> Usef said. <*We can't move without disturbing it. They'll spot us in a heartbeat.*>

<*They won't spot me,*> Malorie chittered a laugh. <*No big hulk feet here.*>

Katrina considered their options and then wondered if she should run them past Usef; operational command was a bit muddy between the two of them. Technically, she had no rank in the ISF, and Usef was a venerated colonel.

But that was made more complex by their past relationships, when she was a governor and he was a lieutenant. Plus the six hundred years she had on him.

<*Malorie,*> she said after a moment. <*I want you to go straight up the center and take a position by that boulder on the far side of the pond.*>

<*You mean the puddle?*>

Katrina rolled her eyes for no one's benefit but her own. <*Yeah, on the far side of the puddle.*>

<*I know you rolled your eyes at me,*> Malorie said.

<*How? You can't see me.*>

<*It was in your tone. You have 'eyeroll tone'.*>

Katrina resisted the urge to roll them again. <*I do not. Now go take that position.*>

<*You know, Captain…*> Carl paused for a moment before pressing on. <*I hate to take Malorie's side—*>

<*Thanks,*> Malorie interjected.

<*—but you really do have 'eyeroll tone'.*>

<*Carl?*> Katrina asked.

<*Yeah?*>

<*Shut up. You just pulled cliff duty.*>

<*What?*>

Usef cleared his throat. <*Chances are there are Widows on our right, over the edge of the cliff, ready to catch us in a crossfire. You're going to go over the edge and get in position to flank them when they pop up.*>

<*Over the edge?*> Carl asked, turning his head toward the three-kilometer drop. <*Seriously?*>

<*You're in heavy armor, it has a-grav,*> Katrina said. <*You pop over and hang out down below. Just stay out of sight behind the bowl's curve.*>

<*And don't actively use your a-grav,*> Usef cautioned. <*Anchor and wait, then come around when shit hits the fan. Which will happen after we give away our positions with EM activity.*>

Katrina chuckled, amused that she and Usef had the exact same plan without needing to discuss it.

<*And me?*> Erin asked.

<*You're staying back in reserve,*> Katrina replied. <*I'll take the cliff face, Usef will go right down the center.*>

<*What about all that grass?*> Carl asked.

<*I have a lighter step than you'd expect,*> the colonel replied.

A minute later, Malorie reported that she was in position, adding in a few barbs about the rest of the team being slow and proposing that their reluctance to evolve beyond using only two legs made them lesser beings.

<*You know…*> Katrina said as she edged along the cliff face, following the barely visible trail sign that the Widows had left. <***I'm** the one that put you in that body.*>

<*Maybe I made you think you did when it's what I wanted all along,*> Malorie retorted.

<*Nice try,*> Katrina replied. <*Granted, you were probably happy to have **any** body again.*>

<*Someday you're going to have to tell me how you all got together,*> Erin said, laughing softly from her position at the rear.

Katrina pursed her lips. <*I'd rather not.*>

<*I'll tell it,*> Malorie said. <*It all began when Katrina was a terrible warlord, raining destruction down on the peaceful people of Midditerra.*>

<*Malorie…*> Katrina warned.

<*OK, then* **you** *tell it.*>

<*Can we focus, people?*> Usef asked. <*We're trying to give away our positions with EM, not get distracted by an argument. Also, Malorie,* **you** *weren't supposed to give away your position. Now you need to move to a new one.*>

<*Party pooper.*> Malorie followed the statement with a snort, then fell silent.

Katrina noticed that Usef didn't chastise Erin for speaking up, but she supposed he might have done it privately. She pushed the thought from her mind, and focused on following the trail left by the Widows while being as invisible as the tall grass and other undergrowth allowed.

Usef had just passed the pond, and Katrina was halfway around the bowl, when shots rained down from the cliff above, some striking Usef, others hitting the dirt around Katrina. She dove back and flattened herself against the cliff, sending out drones to search for the shooters.

On the combat net, she saw Usef lunge behind a rock. It gave him cover from the fire originating on the cliff to the left, but as she'd predicted, several Widows began to fire from the edge of the bowl, shots striking the Marine as he moved to better cover.

Katrina didn't have a clear line of sight on any of the attackers and moved further along the cliff, easing underneath a shallow overhang. Above, her drones located the shooters and fed their positions to the combat net.

<*Looks like two up there,*> Erin commented, and Katrina sent an affirmative response. She eased out around the overhang and fired two seeker rounds from her weapon.

Seeking bullets didn't strike with as much energy as normal projectile shots, but the explosive tips they bore added to the punch. One of the rounds hit its target, but the other was destroyed by a defensive beam.

"Shit," Katrina swore as her drones got a clear visual of the target she'd hit. <*The ones on the cliff are drones!*>

She fired another salvo of seeker rounds before backing further from the base of the cliff and firing a barrage of pure kinetic shots at the final target.

Rock rained down around her as she backpedaled further, turning her attention to the battle at the pond. Usef had moved to new cover and was firing at anything that moved along the edge of the cliff.

He'd weathered a few strikes, but his armor was holding out so far. On the combat net, Katrina saw that Carl was moving along the cliff, nearly in a position to engage the Widows hiding over the edge.

Amidst it all, Malorie was still perched atop a rock, motionless and invisible despite the chaos around her.

Katrina launched a salvo at the Widows firing over the cliff edge, and then moved to new cover. Her drones were still scouring the cliff above, and they flagged a heat signature. She wasn't sure if it was another shooter or just a piece of debris, but fired on it anyway, not caring about conserving her ammunition.

An enemy drone fell from the location, and she gave a satisfied laugh, turning her attention to the fight at the edge of the ledge, where she saw that Malorie still hadn't moved to assist Usef and Carl.

<*Want to join in the fun?*> Katrina asked acerbically.

<*I'm waiting. There aren't enough of them yet.*>

<*You waiting for all thirty?*> Usef demanded.

The spider-woman laughed. <*No, just the two laying in the puddle, waiting to make their move. I figure it's not fair to just jump on them while they're not doing anything.*>

<*Mal!*> Katrina shouted. <*Take them!*>

<*Fine.*>

Katrina saw a splash as an invisible object hit the water, then an ethereal shriek sounded as one of the Widows met the business end of Malorie's talons.

No further fire came from the cliff face above, and Katrina turned her full attention to the other side of the bowl. She moved through the sparse undergrowth to the largest tree on the ledge, leaning around it and taking aim at the pool, waiting for a clear shot.

<*You could have told me, Mal, and* **I** *would have just shot them,*> Usef said as another piercing scream came from amidst the sprays of water.

<*You can now!*> Malorie cried out.

Katrina's visual overlay showed the spider-woman scampering away from the pond. Behind her, water sloughed off another figure as it rose and gave chase. Katrina didn't hesitate, firing a trio of kinetic rounds at the Widow. Armor cracked, and the assassin became visible, blood leaking out where the third round had hit.

<*Got one,*> Usef called out. <*Carl, flush the others up.*>

<*Gonna be tough. So far, they're flushing me down!*>

Usef circled around a group of boulders, moving toward the edge of the cliff. He was almost in a position to fire when rounds struck him in the back. Katrina spun to once again see shots raining down from the cliff above. She moved to the other side of the tree and returned fire, noting that Usef had gone prone behind a boulder before crawling to the edge.

<*Heading up!*> Malorie announced, and Katrina swore under her breath, shifting to provide covering fire for the spider-woman as she scaled the cliff, racing up the sheer face as though it were flat ground.

<*Shit!*> Carl shouted. <*There're two of them here still…I*

can't—>

The man let out a gargled cry, his vitals spiking. Katrina broke cover, rushing to the edge. She was still only halfway there when she saw that Erin had beat her to the brink, jumping off and firing at the enemies below.

<*What are you doing?*> Usef demanded.

<*Got him!*> Erin called back a moment later. <*Bringing him down to one of the switchbacks.*>

Katrina skidded to a stop at the edge, shots from the cliffs above raining down around her. <*Is he OK?*>

<*I'm good,*> Carl grunted his reply. <*Just got hit in the arm.*>

<*Which is gone now,*> Erin clarified.

<*Oh shit!*> Malorie interrupted. <*They're not drones up here! I've got at least three of these bitches!*>

<*You want a hand?*> A new voice joined the combat net.

<*Cheeky? Are you nearby?*> Katrina asked. <*I thought you were taking out those Widows on High Airtha?*>

<*All done,*> Sabrina chimed in. <*We were flying back to the* I2 *when I decided to tap your combat net.*>

<*Sooo…help?*> Cheeky asked.

<*Stop asking and start shooting!*> Usef hollered. <*Targets are on the net.*>

Seconds later, beams came down through the clouds, two striking the cliffs above, and one hitting a target below the ledge.

<*Three down, last one is too close to you,*> Cheeky announced.

<*I got it,*> Usef grunted as he leant out over the drop and fired a trio of rounds.

<*OK,*> Katrina said as she moved across the bowl to the far side. <*Let's sweep it.*>

<*Do you want us to stay onstation?*> Cheeky asked as *Sabrina* appeared a few kilometers from the mountain, lazily drifting closer like a blue and silver cloud of destruction.

<*Would you mind?*> Katrina asked. <*I imagine our quarry was*

all here, but it would be nice to be sure.>

<*You got it,*> Sabrina chimed in. <*What about Troy and the* Voyager? *Where are they?*>

<*They went to secure one of the ring's support columns,*> Katrina said as she walked to the edge of the cliff and looked over, keeping an eye peeled for any movement.

<*Kirb and Camille with them?*> Cheeky asked.

<*Yeah,*> Malorie grunted as she skittered back down the cliff face. <*They weren't interested in schlepping around on this mountain, so they took the easy job.*>

<*You know…*> Erin said from her position further down the mountain. <*Since you're here, Sabrina, think you can pick up a girl and her armless friend?*>

<*Wow,*> Carl muttered. <*I guess I should be happy you didn't call me a sack of potatoes.*>

<*You're too big for that. More like a sack of watermelons.*>

<*Stars, I leave for a few years, and you get all sassy,*> Usef commented as *Sabrina* moved closer to the mountainside, the ship's main bay door sliding open.

Katrina could see a small figure outlined in the entrance. Then a second appeared.

<*That you, Misha and Nance?*> she asked.

<*As the day is long,*> Misha replied. <*Was just getting ready to cook dinner, too.*>

Nance elbowed Misha. <*I think saving Carl's life is a worthwhile diversion, I—*>

<*I'm not actually dying here,*> Carl interrupted, his voice a low growl. <*It's just a flesh wound.*>

<*Your arm is* ***gone****,*> Erin corrected.

<*Still not a big deal.*>

<*Still more than a flesh wound,*> she insisted.

<*See anyone else?*> Katrina asked Usef and Malorie.

The Marine shook his head. <*Not that I can* ***see****. But Widows have shockingly good stealth.*>

<*I hadn't noticed,*> Katrina said dryly.

<*Now who's sassy?*> Erin asked.

It took a few minutes to get Carl safely aboard *Sabrina,* after which, the team searched the shelf again before following the narrow ledge around the mountain to the ridgeline. *Sabrina* flew passes overhead, scanning the slopes for activity. After an hour with no further signs, the team gathered the Widows' bodies and loaded them onto the ship.

"So that's twenty we've taken out, right?" Cheeky asked as she met Katrina in the ship's galley, where Misha was nearly done with dinner.

"Twenty-two," Katrina corrected. "I just got word that Tangel and Sera took out a pair."

"Shit!" Cheeky exclaimed. "Are those ugly, faceless bitches hitting the *I2* again?"

"No," Katrina shook her head. "Troy told me that Tangel and Sera are down on the ring helping Bob find Helen."

Cheeky glanced at one of the optical pickups. "Sabs! How come you're not sharing the AI intel like Troy does?"

<*For starters, I'm Sabrina, not Sabs. Sabs is down in medical with Nance.*>

"Sheesh. That's not going to get confusing at all," Katrina muttered as she walked to the counter and poured herself a cup of coffee.

"Tell me about it," Misha said as he cut slices of pork off a roast. "I can't keep them straight now. In my head, I have to think of them as 'Ship' and 'Chrome Ass'."

Sabrina's laugh filled the room. <*I'm going to get my stern chromed just to mess with you more.*>

Katrina leant against the counter, sipping her coffee as she watched Cheeky grab plates for dinner, while joining in needling Misha.

She'd never been aboard *Sabrina* before, but interactions with her own crew had always been generally fun and humorous affairs. Standing in the ship's galley, she could tell that joking and needling was the norm for this crew as well; laughing off stress and cares was their way of life.

What was most interesting to Katrina was that this crew had initially been put together by Sera. The dark-haired scion of the Tomlinson house wasn't without a lighter side, but she wasn't likely to have been the genesis of this modus operandi.

If I had to bet on it, it's Cheeky and Sabrina. Those two just exude an energy that fills this whole ship.

The realization caused her to feel a modicum of sadness that the *Voyager* hadn't echoed with laughter as much as it could have over the years. She didn't think of her crew as a dour bunch by comparison, but they always seemed to carry the memory of how they had first come together.

Memories of Juasa flooded into Katrina's mind, and she let them wash over her, her long-ago lover's smile still perfectly rendered in her mind's eye.

I miss you, Juasa. And I'm still sorry.

"Well, Kat?" Cheeky asked, her voice rising a half octave as she spoke.

" 'Kat'?" Katrina scoffed, drawing her attention back to the present. "Do I call you 'Chee'?"

Cheeky shrugged. "You can call me anything you like. A natural redhead is my kryptonite."

"Everything's your kryptonite," Misha said as he set the platter of meat on the table.

"What's kryptonite?" Katrina asked as she pulled up a chair and settled next to Cheeky.

"A green rock from the planet Krypton," the captain explained. "It makes SuperGuy weak."

"SuperGuy?"

Misha nodded as he began to make a pitcher of lemonade. "Yeah, from the ancient SuperGuy vids. We found some of them in a vault awhile back. There was a huge stash of ancient shows and we have been watching them together. The SuperGuy ones are from the twenty-sixth century."

"Not as old as Star Wars," Cheeky said. "Which is totally my favorite. I think it's a true story."

"A long time ago, in a galaxy far, far away…" Misha intoned in a mysterious voice.

"That makes no sense," Katrina interjected. "When was *that* made?"

Cheeky shrugged. "Somewhere back around the dawn of time."

"Twentieth century," Misha supplied. "So a few years after the dawn of time."

"Close enough."

"What's it about?" Katrina asked, nodding to Nance and Usef as they entered the galley.

Cheeky placed both hands on the table and leant forward, eyes narrowing as her voice dropped to a whisper. "A dark lord, powerful in the Force, and a young boy who is given a mythical weapon to stand up against the evil empire!"

"Star Wars?" Nance asked.

"Uh-huh," Misha said.

The ship's engineer turned to Katrina. "Has she tried to tell you it's a true story yet?"

Katrina nodded. "Not really buying it."

"That's because you've never met a space wizard." Cheeky fixed Katrina and then Nance with a serious look. "If you had, you'd have no trouble believing that, out there, somewhere, Darth Vader is waiting."

"Didn't he die, though?" Misha asked as Erin and Sabs entered the galley.

"Spoilers!" Cheeky shouted. "*Some* of us didn't go ahead and watch the next movies without the rest of the crew!"

"Well, it's been weeks!"

<*Misha, we're fighting a war,*> Sabrina said in a mollifying

tone. *<We can't always fit in a vid-night on the regular schedule.>*

The cook glared at one of the optical pickups, then directed his glare to Cheeky. "Huh…yet you still expect your food on a schedule."

"OK…" Sabs held up a hand to deflect further ire from the cook. "We'll schedule a vid night as soon as possible. Maybe on the flight out of the Huygens System."

With a haughty sniff, Misha turned back to the counter, and grabbed a bowl of salad and a basket of bread. He opened his mouth to say something more, but ended up gently setting the food on the table before settling into his chair and muttering something about being sorry for letting a spoiler slip.

"Sooooo…" Katrina stuck a fork into a slice of meat, pulling it onto her plate. "I assume Carl's going to be OK?"

"He's in the medtube right now," Nance replied. "He should be patched up in a few hours—made me promise to save him some leftovers."

"Is Malorie with him?"

<She's with the chickens.> Sabrina's voice sounded both amused and concerned.

"She's not…hurting them, is she?" Misha asked.

<Do you really think I'd sound this calm if someone was hurting my birds? Well…other than you when you cook them.>

"I suppose not," the cook replied. "So what is she doing?"

<Right now? She's clucking at them. She clucks, they cluck. Over and over.>

"Please tell me you're recording it," Katrina said, watching Erin lift a hand to her lips, hiding a smile.

<Oh stars yes.>

Katrina didn't bother hiding her own grin as she cut off a piece of her meat. "That's going to be some amazing blackmail material."

<It—oh shit!> Sabrina fell silent after her exclamation, but

Katrina could feel a change in the ship's engines.

"What is it?" she and Erin demanded at the same time.

<Helen.> Sabrina's voice dripped with venom. *<Sera and Tangel found her, and they need help.>*

Usef set his fork down and rose from the table. "Suit up, people. We're going back in."

PURSUING MOTHER

STELLAR DATE: 10.10.8949 (Adjusted Years)
LOCATION: The Unnamed Forest, Airtha
REGION: Huygens System, Transcend Interstellar Alliance

"I've been on a lot of rings," Tangel said as she and Sera reached a clearing in the forest. "But Airtha is still blowing my mind."

"We need a new name. I really don't want to keep calling it that," Sera replied. "Maybe Finaesia."

Finaeus glanced at his niece and grunted. "No."

"Finland?" Tangel asked.

"Extra no."

"Stars," Sera muttered. "Who died and made you king of Airtha?"

The ancient engineer snorted. "Ironically…Airtha."

"He got you there." Tangel laughed. "OK, so Helen is somewhere in this forest, topside, too."

"There are no sub-layers here," Finaeus explained. "Just a kilometer of carbon beneath this stretch of woods, and then space."

"Why's that?" Tangel asked.

"Balance," Finaeus said. "Had to make things thinner here, and it was easier to route sub-level stuff elsewhere so as not to harm the ring's structural integrity."

"Hence the forest?" Sera asked.

"Hence the forest."

Tangel surveyed the tall oak trees, noting the elms and poplars interspersed amongst them. "OK…. So Helen would know that there's no way out. Why'd she come here? We've got a platoon with shadowtrons moving through these trees, and Bob's watching over us from above. She's out of options."

"Which is why I don't like it," Finaeus replied. "Not one bit. She's up to something."

"Has to be," Sera agreed. "She's not stupid."

Tangel glanced at Sera, trying not to actively pity the woman next to her. Helen had lived in Sera's head for over four decades, and as such, they had developed a very special bond.

Their union had lasted much longer than the generally safe norm, but the two had never shown any signs of intergrowth—though now it was apparent why. Tangel had since learned that Helen had never hidden from Sera that she was a shard of Airtha.

What Sera hadn't known was that Airtha was her mother…and that the AI was ascending, and possibly insane.

Not for the first time, Tangel considered advising Sera that hunting her own mother wasn't wise—especially when Helen, unlike Airtha, really had been a mother figure to Sera. But one look at the grim determination in her friend's eyes let Tangel know just how well such a request would be received.

"So what are we missing," she mused, feeling her way through the trees with her extradimensional senses. "And why can't I see her? Either she's slipped through our net, or she's figured out how to mask herself."

<I don't see any indication of her or the corrupted shard,> Bob chimed in from where the *I2* hung a thousand kilometers overhead. *<But I also don't see any sign that they've left the area, either.>*

<Anything on the perimeter, Lieutenant?> Tangel asked Mason, knowing that if he had picked up any sign, he would have said so, but feeling compelled to ask nonetheless.

<Sorry, ma'am. Neither hide nor hair…though I suppose our quarry has neither of those.>

Tanis laughed softly, shaking her head. *<Yeah, you need a new metaphor for hunting AIs.>*

<Noted.>

They passed through the clearing and back into the forest. Here, the trees were tall, with wide boughs creating a dense canopy of leaves. As a result, the undergrowth was thin, and they could see almost a hundred meters in any direction.

Tangel could see even further in other dimensions, the three-dimensional trees doing little to obstruct her view in the fourth and fifth.

The ground beneath her feet did not provide a significant visual barrier, either. It was something she'd gotten used to, the ability to see through the very surfaces that kept her from falling into space. One of the things that had taken a lot of effort to deal with was being able to see through a ship's hull while traveling through space.

She would have expected Airtha to feel more substantial, but it didn't. The ring rotated at an incredible speed, which caused the stars she could see through its surface to wheel and spin past disconcertingly.

Granted, you're still recovering from going toe-to-toe with Airtha and having her swat you like a fly.

That thought caused her to wonder if she was once again biting off more than she could chew.

<Do you think I can take on Helen?> Tangel asked Bob. *<I'm not used to losing like this—or needing someone else to ride in to my rescue all the time.>*

<Just remember what Cary taught you with the grav shield. Deflect and compress, deflect and compress.>

<Easy for you to say,> Tangel scoffed good-naturedly. *<You're a starship. Deflecting is what you do.>*

The AI groaned, but didn't give a verbal response. Silence wore on for several minutes, until Tangel gave in first.

<OK. Yes. I get it. Any practice I can get is good practice.>

<Exactly. It's not impossible. I've done, it, Cary's done it. Yes, our enemies have all been ascended longer than we, but they're cocky,

overconfident.>

<Think so?> Tangel asked. *<We just crushed their defenses, defeated Airtha herself, and ended the civil war.>*

<Effectively ended,> the AI corrected. *<There's still a lot of work to be done.>*

<Right. Effectively.>

<So?>

Tangel wished Bob was present so she could give him a cool glare. *<So why would she be cocky? We've crushed her.>*

<I've spoken to Helen at length in the past—> Bob paused mid-sentence.

<What is it?>

<Search ahead on your two o'clock,> the AI directed. *<Something's not right there.>*

Tangel reached out with her extradimensional senses, peering through the forest like it wasn't there, searching for whatever it was that Bob had seen.

<What am I—> Tangel began, but then stopped herself. "Finaeus, you said that there's nothing underneath this forest, right?"

"I take it by your question that that is no longer the case?" the engineer asked.

"Ahead…there's a hidden entrance to a shaft. It seems to lead down to a bay and…and a ship."

"Shit!" Sera exclaimed. "Where? We need to stop her!"

Tangel highlighted the shaft's entrance. "Krissy's ships are all too far to get here before it can leave," she said. *<Bob, you need to get closer.>*

<Rachel's in the loop. We're on our way.>

"*Sabrina*'s nearby," Sera suggested. "On her way to the *I2*."

"Get her down there. Stall that ship," Tangel ordered, breaking into a full run, with Sera and Finaeus behind her.

<I've alerted Krissy and the TSF. They're moving a squadron into position, but they're at least fifteen minutes out, maybe more,>

Bob advised.

"Helen's not getting away, then," Sera said, catching up to Tangel. "Not unless she's got a gate down there."

The two women looked at one another and began to run faster.

"Finaeus!" Tangel called over her shoulder. "What would happen to the ring if a gate was activated inside it?"

"It would survive," the engineer pronounced from a few paces behind. "We, on the other hand, would not."

The hidden entrance was set at the base of a low rise, and Tangel reached out with her extradimensional limbs, disassembling the earthen bank to reveal the short corridor beyond. She dashed ahead, spotting and dissolving automated defense systems before they even had a chance to deploy and fire.

A few seconds later, she came to the shaft. It dropped nearly five hundred meters, and the lift car was at the bottom.

"See you down there," Tangel called out, and jumped.

Cary had taught her how to make graviton shields that would allow her to deflect attacks from other ascended beings. What they hadn't discussed—but what Tangel knew was entirely possible—was to use the ability to direct gravitons to make her own personal a-grav field.

What a time to test my theory.

The bottom of the shaft was rushing toward her, and Tangel held out her arms, generating the graviton field, and then flipping the polarity of the gravitons and pushing them away from herself.

Sure enough, the reaction slowed her descent and, though she dented the top of the lift car with her impact, she was unharmed and able to dissolve the metal beneath her. The lift doors were open, and the moment she landed on the car's floor, she sprinted down the corridor.

<*Nice trick,*> Finaeus called down after her.

<*I'm full of surprises,*> Tangel called back.

The engineer grunted. <*Never said it was surprising.*>

She didn't reply, only increased her speed, barreling down the passage, burning away anything that looked even remotely close to a defensive weapon. After half a minute, she came to the bay where a corvette rested.

The ship was already on the debarkation rails, sliding toward the open bay doors and a drop into space.

<*No jump gate in here,*> Tangel called back. <*But her ship is on the rails!*>

<*There's no way she can just fly away,*> Sera said. <*She* ***has*** *to have a plan to slip past Krissy's fleet.*>

Tangel agreed, but didn't respond as she raced across the deck, reaching out for the ship's airlock and dissolving the hull with her non-corporeal limbs. The corvette was almost beyond the bay's grav shield, and Tangel poured on a final burst of speed and leapt into the airlock a second before the ship passed into vacuum and its shields activated.

<*Made it!*> Tangel called back, glancing across the bay to see two figures racing through the corridor.

<*Shit,*> Sera muttered. <*Tangel…I—*>

<*I'll try to take her alive if I can,*> the field marshal replied, turning to face the inner airlock door.

Dissolving it was an option, but she felt her strength waning after tearing apart so much of the corridor as she'd rushed through it.

Who ever thought that assimilating matter and converting it into energy would be so draining, she thought with a soft laugh as she placed a hand on the airlock's control panel and fed a nanofilament into it.

~*Door's open.*~ Helen's voice came into Tangel's mind. ~*No need to shred more of my ship.*~

~*We're not going to let you get away,*~ Tangel said as she tried to simply open the airlock door.

It slid aside without any breach necessary, and she stepped through into an interior passage, sealing the entrance behind her.

The bridge was on her left, and she could feel Helen's energy emanating from that direction.

~You're not going to be able to stop me,~ the shard of Airtha replied. *~You couldn't defeat me before, and you won't be able to now.~*

~Not going to stop me from trying.~

Tangel released a nanocloud, using it to augment her extra senses. Unlike Helen, she was still corporeal enough that a shot to the head would be as fatal as an ascended being's attack.

Nothing raised any alarms, and she pushed forward, moving down a cross passage before coming to the ship's central corridor.

The moment she stepped into it, a burst of energy shot out toward her. The nanocloud had given enough warning, and Tangel ducked back, sucking in a breath as she looked at the hole burned in the bulkhead.

~Whatever happened to not destroying your ship?~

~I just wanted you in range.~

Tangel funneled the energy she'd gathered from the matter she'd disintegrated in her rush though the corridors, and formed a brane around herself, and a graviton field beyond that.

~You're going to have to fire a lot more energy than that,~ Tangel said. *~Your ship won't survive.~*

She stepped out into the corridor, the open entrance to the bridge only twenty meters away. Helen didn't respond as Tangel strode toward it, steeling herself for whatever might come next.

As she neared the bridge, the shard appeared in the entrance, a swirling mass of luminescent limbs that blocked her forward progress.

"What do you hope to achieve?" Tangel asked. "Airtha is gone, you've lost."

~*No.*~ Helen's limbs waved side to side. ~*We still control much of the Transcend. We'll bring all of humanity under our banner, and then destroy the core AIs.*~

Tangel shook her head, her eyes boring into the creature before her. ~*We share the same goals. Why are you fighting against me?*~

~*Because your compassion will cause you to lose, Tangel.*~ Helen threw the words out as angry accusation, her color shifting down the spectrum, taking on a purple hue. ~*When I first met you aboard* Sabrina, *I'd hoped that you would be able to take the fight to the core, but it became apparent that you wanted to hide away from the galaxy's troubles. That's why I took Sera from you, sent her where I could keep working at making her into the leader humanity and AIs need.*~

"You orchestrated all that?" Tangel asked. "I guess it makes sense. You're the one that ensured Elena would arrive in New Canaan to warn us that Jeffrey Tomlinson was coming—well, the pretend Jeffrey."

~*Indeed. The original was not malleable enough. And you're right—Airtha and I sent both the harbinger and the threat to New Canaan, all so that Sera could see how untrustworthy those around her were. To steel her for what was to come.*~

As the ascended being spoke, Tangel began to realize something she'd never before considered. Though it was no secret that she and Airtha essentially shared the same goals, it was also readily apparent that they were not using the same means to achieve those goals.

Even so, they could have allied in some fashion. The fact that Airtha and Helen had never even asked to was a mystery Tangel had never understood. Logic dictated that they should have joined forces, but Airtha had always sought to take the picotech from New Canaan and see the colonists destroyed, all while bolstering Sera to be the one ruling the galaxy—a job Sera had never wanted.

"I don't know what would make a being like you insane," Tangel said in a whisper. "But you've clearly lost control of your faculties. You *and* Airtha. What is with this blind nepotism of yours?"

~Whoever takes the reins of the galaxy ***must*** *be willing to sacrifice anything to see victory. You've shown time and time again that you'll let your morality stop you from realizing your goals. We're not insane, we're pure logic.~*

A suspicion Tangel had always harbored was that the core AIs had sent Airtha back as a foil. A being that would appear to be working against them, but be flawed in some way and in fact foil any efforts made against them.

I can only imagine the state things would be in if the Intrepid *had come out in the ninety-fifth century as everyone had expected.*

~Are you coming, Bob?~ Tangel sent out, wondering if she had the range to reach the AI.

~I am, but we have to fly around the ring, brake, and come back up. Sabrina *is much closer. She'll be there in a minute.~*

Tangel wondered what *Sabrina* would be able to do, though she supposed that at least the other ship could facilitate a rescue, if she and Helen destroyed the corvette.

Rather than replying to Helen, Tangel took a step forward, trying to see into the bridge. Her nanocloud hadn't been able to make it past Helen, and she wanted to see what the vessel's heading was.

The Airthan shard whipped a limb out toward Tangel to stop her approach, but it collided with her grav shield and protective brane.

~You're not going to dissuade me.~ Tangel said, continuing to move forward.

Helen sent a burst of energy toward her, but it was

deflected, cutting a long slash in the bulkhead.

~Very well,~ Helen said. *~I may not be able to destroy you without destroying this ship, but I also don't need it to last that long.~*

Before Tangel could ask what that meant, a signal from Cheeky reached her.

<Tangel! There's a gate mounted in one of the carbon mountains on the ring's underside. You're going to reach it before we reach you!>

<Dammit!>

Tangel knew that ordering *Sabrina* to shoot the jump gate wasn't an option. Ford svaiter gates were powered by antimatter, and if it exploded, it could destroy a sizable part of the ring—especially in this region, where the structure was thinner.

She wasn't quite ready to order *Sabrina* to shoot at the ship she was aboard, either.

There was a change in the air around her, and Tangel realized that her way forward was blocked by a grav field. She tried to push against it, but it was blocking her in all dimensions.

The field stretched along the bulkheads, closing in behind her. She reached out, pushing her own gravitons against it, but momentum was on Helen's side, and the field closed around Tangel.

She railed against it, focusing her energy on a single point, but Helen only laughed.

~I have the ship's CriEn to draw on. You're not going to defeat me.~

The Airthan shard added a brane, encapsulating Tangel in a magnetic field that cut off her communication with *Sabrina*.

No! Tangel shouted in her mind, pushing with all her might, dissolving the deck beneath her and funneling its mass into an attack on the prison Helen had made.

The air was heating up in her shield, but Tangel didn't slow her assault, focusing a beam of energy coupled with particles moving as fast as she could accelerate them toward a single point directly in front of her.

Despite Helen's assertion that Tangel would not be able to push though, a crack formed in the graviton field, and then the brane beyond it.

At that moment, a voice came from the bridge. It was partially garbled, words out of order as it squawked out of the speakers.

"Not stop go! Destroy shard."

There was something familiar to the voice, but Tangel couldn't immediately place it.

Helen moved back from the bridge's entrance, revealing the forward holodisplay, which showed the jump gate's ring rapidly approaching the ship. The Airthan shard was manipulating one of the consoles, her movements hinting at concern.

Then the ship veered off to port, a starscape replacing the ring's glow.

~*No!*~ Helen wailed.

In that moment, Tangel managed to break free, and she ran onto the bridge, slamming a brane around Helen and cutting the ascended being off from the rest of the ship.

"Tangel…" the voice said. "Please. Save me."

"Who are you?" Tangel replied, careful to keep her focus on Helen, who was writhing in the brane's grip.

The shard's strength was impressive, and Tangel reached out to the ship's main powerplant, drawing energy from the CriEn to keep her brane intact while she moved toward the navigation console.

After a moment of silence, barring the hissing wails coming from Helen, the voice replied with just one word.

"Iris."

"What?" Tangel blurted, then she felt Helen renew her fight against the brane. She turned toward the ascended being, eyes narrowing, her voice a rage-filled scream. "What did you do to her?"

~*Me?*~ Helen demanded. ~*That abomination has been chasing me for a day! What did **you** do to her?*~

Tangel shrank the brane, crushing Helen's form within. "Last I knew, Iris was fighting Airtha's AIs, trying to load the corrupted shard..."

Her voice trailed off, understanding dawning as she realized what must have happened.

"Stars, Iris...why didn't you come to us?"

"Hard. Fighting constantly for control."

"With the corrupted shard?" Tangel asked, further tightening the brane around Helen as she accessed the navigation console and shut down the ship's engines.

An affirmative sound came from Iris, and Tangel accessed the ship's network, tracing the signal that was controlling the bridge's audible systems back to the ship's comm node.

There she found an AI in garbled ruin, a barely functional merger of two separate beings.

"Iris!" Tangel gasped, only the knowledge that Helen would kill her if she became distracted keeping her from an immediate attempt to disentangle the two beings.

"Keep safe," Iris said. "Later me."

Tangel nodded, turning her full focus back to Helen, shrinking the brane further. "This ends now. I destroy you, and Airtha's sickness is wiped from the galaxy."

~*Tangel.*~

The single word from Bob stopped her in her tracks.

~*No, Bob, we don't need to save her. Helen being alive will only torture Sera.*~

~*You're not a murderer.*~

~*You know that's not true,*~ Tangel's reply was cold, the

words slashing out through spacetime with more malice than she intended. *~I've killed in cold blood more than once.~*

She was shocked when Bob laughed in response. *~Well, try to keep it to a minimum.~*

Tangel had no idea how to respond to Bob's statement, but it had surprised her enough that the desire to kill Helen faded.

A moment later, Cheeky reached out.

<We're docked. Coming aboard.>

<Do you have a containment vessel?> Tangel asked.

<Usef is carrying it. Erin and Katrina have shadowtrons. We're loaded for bear.>

Tangel glanced at Helen, wondering if she'd fit in a containment vessel. *<Going to be a tight squeeze. I might have to pare her down a bit.>*

<Um…ew? She's not an apple.>

~What are you going to do?~ Helen asked, saving Tangel from having to come up with a response for Cheeky.

"I'm going to let Bob deal with you. So far as I'm concerned, when it comes to ascended beings, he's judge, jury, and executioner."

~And you play at having morals….~

Tangel laughed, surprised that the shard thought she could be played so easily. "I thought you saw my morality as weakness. You need to make up your mind."

Helen didn't reply, and Tangel kept her focus on containing the being until the team from *Sabrina* made it to the bridge.

"You know part of the corridor is missing out there, Admiral?" Usef said as he entered the bridge a minute later.

"Shoot," Tangel muttered. "I should have turned off the a-grav."

The colonel tapped a foot on the deck. "Maglocks to the rescue." He turned to the writhing ball of light that was Helen, now compressed down to a half-meter sphere near the navigation console. "Shit…that does not look safe."

"My containment, or what's inside?" Tangel asked, wiping sweat from her brow as the energy being consumed and expended to contain Helen warmed the air beyond what the environmental systems could contain.

"Both, I guess."

Usef set the meter-tall cylinder on the deck and stepped aside as Erin and Katrina entered the bridge.

"Stars…that looks too familiar," Katrina said, while Erin's eyes grew wide.

"First time seeing one of these…other than you, Tangel," the engineer said. "What do you need us to do?"

"Just be ready to shoot it if it tries to get away."

The two women nodded, and Tangel drew Helen closer to the containment vessel, activating it once the ascended being was above it.

The two branes merged, and with a wail only Tangel could hear, Helen was sucked into the device. Tangel sealed it, and checked that the CriEn powering the field was operating properly.

"There we go." She rose, satisfied that Helen was secure. "It'll last till the end of time, if needs be."

Erin shook her head. "That's just depressing. I mean…I know she's basically one of the worst people ever, but I don't know that she deserves that."

"Yeah…it was hyperbole," Tangel said. "I wouldn't want that, either."

Usef stepped forward, a look of grim determination on his face as he picked up the cylinder. "Nope, not frightening at all. Being centimeters away from an entity that can dissolve me at will."

Tangel reached out and touched the colonel's arm. "Now you're nanometers away."

"Not helping, Admiral," he grunted, turning back to the

corridor, while Erin covered her mouth with a hand. "And not funny, Erin," he added.

Katrina glanced at Erin and mouthed, "Totally funny."

The trio's interaction brought a smile to Tangel's lips. She thought about all the time and space that had passed between these three since they'd first met on the *Intrepid* so long ago in the Kapteyn's Star System.

In Tangel's mind, that they'd remained friends, or rekindled friendship, gave meaning to what often felt like a never-ending struggle to build a home for her people.

She followed the others off the corvette's bridge. "Erin, Sabrina tells me there are several blank AI cores in *Sabrina*'s medbay. Can you grab one and meet me in this ship's comm node?"

"Uhh…sure. What's up?"

"I don't want to get anyone's hopes up…least of all mine. Meet me there."

"Of course," Erin nodded and followed Katrina and Usef down the corridor that led to the airlock, while Tangel continued aft, reaching the communications node a minute later.

The ship was pristine, clearly never used beyond a shakedown cruise. The node consisted of a trio of towers in the center of the room; overkill for a corvette, but likely just the thing an ascended AI needed to launch a variety of attacks on ships and stations. They were also just the sort of thing capable of housing a fractured AI that had been relegated to mobile software.

Memories of fighting against the AIs of Luna came back to Tangel, actions that Angela had been involved in long before she'd ever met Tanis. Iris and Amavia had also fought against similar foes on Cerka Station, when they had gone up against the Non-Organic Supremists.

<*How are you holding up?*> she asked Iris.

"Badly," the AI replied through the room's speakers.

Tangel frowned. <*Can you not reply over the Link?*>

"No, routes...data...mess."

"Odd," Tangel muttered as she placed a hand on the central tower, funneling a strand of nano to create a direct connection to the comm node.

She sifted through the system's internal structure until she came to the storage system Iris had settled into. What she saw there caused her to bite her lip in worry.

Pieces of Iris and the corrupted Airthan shard were intermixed like two separate puzzles that an angry child had tried to force together into one image.

<*Stars, Iris.... How did you even get here?*>

"Determination." The single word was spoken with a quiet vehemence.

Tangel chuckled as she worked to identify which pieces of the being were Iris, and which were the corrupted shard. Having been one of Iris's mothers, and present for her birth, Tangel was better suited than most to determine which parts of the being belonged to her daughter, and which were part of the shard.

Several minutes later, Erin entered the room holding an AI core, and Tangel beckoned silently for the engineer to place it into her left hand.

With her right hand still connected to the comm tower, Tangel began to select the pieces of neural network that were clearly her daughter's, and place them into the AI core. Bit by bit, she reconstructed Iris's mind into the form it should have, all the while wishing she had Iris's crystal backup, but unwilling to leave her in the living hell that was being merged with Airtha any longer.

She was partway through the process when the corrupted shard began to understand what was happening. It started to destroy parts of Iris's mind, and Tangel was forced to wipe out core parts of the other being to paralyze it.

After another ten minutes, she'd extracted every part of Iris and reconstructed her in the core she held in her left hand. All that remained in the comm tower was the corrupted shard. She swept through its remains three more times, ensuring that no further parts of Iris remained.

So much missing, she whispered to herself and pulled her hand away before glancing at Erin, who was watching with wide eyes.

"I can't believe you did that…and so quickly."

"Stars," Tangel muttered, looking down at the core in her hand. "Felt like years."

"I was monitoring the node…it was Iris in there, wasn't it? You saved her."

"Most of her," Tangel qualified, then reached out to Iris. *<I'm shutting you down. When your backup arrives, we'll re-integrate. But for now, I don't want you to reinforce broken pathways.>*

<I understand. Tangel?>

<Yes?>

<Thank you.>

<Pretty sure you saved both of us by distracting Helen…so thank you.>

With that, she activated the node's shutdown process and let Iris fall into sweet oblivion.

Turning back to the comm node, Tangel gave it one final look, and then reached out, dissolving the matter and letting it fall to the deck as a pile of oxidized dust.

"That's final," Erin said.

"Best end for that thing."

"No argument here."

The two women walked out of the room and down the ship's central corridor.

"I suppose that means only Fina and Seraphina hang in the

balance now," Erin said after a minute. "Could you piece them back together like you did with Iris?"

Tangel pursed her lips as she considered it. "Maybe…though I'm better with AIs than organics…that's the Angela part of me at play there."

"Makes sense." Erin's words were sober. "I suppose we need Earnest back for that."

"Yes. Once he and Terrance are done dealing with the core AI installation in the IPE."

Erin's head whipped around, and she stared open-mouthed at Tangel. "Wait…what?"

"They found the installation that was manufacturing the star-shifting drones," Tangel explained. "Sorry, I meant to pass that on to you—I knew you'd be interested."

"Stars." Erin shook her head, a far-off look in her eyes. "That's an understatement. What are they going to do?"

"Destroy it, I believe."

"OK, for the second time, *what*?"

Erin's question was nearly vehement, and Tangel wondered what she was missing.

"Well, I guess they said 'shut it down'. Sorry, I haven't slept in a few days and I barely had time to consider that message. It came through Khardine and routed to Sera. She told me about it."

"I'm going to contact Earnest," Erin said after a moment. "I can't imagine he'd destroy the core AI facility there, but I need to be sure. For starters, we need that facility to re-position the stars. Then we need to understand how it's working so that when we find more clusters that are being shifted, we can correct them as well."

"Can't we use the same system we're using for Project Starflight?" Tangel asked. "Asymmetrically burn the stars to shift them back into place?"

Erin laughed and shook her head as they reached the

airlock. "Sure. I mean, it'll work, but what if the core AIs worked out a more efficient system? It's worth investigating at least."

"Fair enough," Tangel said. "Let me know what they say."

"Sure will," Erin said, gesturing for Tangel to pass down the umbilical first.

When she reached the other side, Sera and Finaeus were waiting, the former president of the Transcend tapping her foot as she glared at Tangel.

"You know I hate being left behind."

"Couldn't be helped, Sera," Tangel said with a grin. "As it was, I almost didn't make it. But we got her, and I saved Iris. Plus, that rogue corrupted shard is done. I'm going to count this as a very good day."

"Just five more Widows out there as well," Finaeus added. "Who knows? We could have things squared away here in just another day."

"Then where to?" Sera asked.

Tangel glanced at Erin and then back at the others. "I have a suspicion we're going to be visiting the IPE again."

DIRECTION

STELLAR DATE: 10.11.8949 (Adjusted Years)
LOCATION: ISS *I2,* Airtha
REGION: Huygens System, Transcend Interstellar Alliance

"We have to quit meeting like this." Tangel gave Bob a wan laugh as she walked into his primary node chamber.

<*Is that an attempt at humor?*> the AI asked.

"Did you not get it?" Tangel asked. "I feel like you asking means you got the joke."

<*I got it, it was just weak.*>

She shook her head, a rueful smile on her lips as she settled onto a seat next to a monitoring console.

"I can't believe it's done—well, other than taking out a couple of Widows."

<*That was one of the things that I want to discuss with you,*> Bob said in a more serious tone.

Tangel made an instant connection, surmising where he was going next.

"Are the girls OK? And Priscilla?"

<*Joe has reported their primary objective as complete. They successfully disabled the A1 Widow, which Cary believes to be the original Lisa Wrentham. They've also accessed the Widows' primary datastore, though it is not yet transferred off the Widows' ship.*>

"I sense a 'but' coming. A big one."

<*Cary has assumed the position of A1.*>

Tangel was out of her seat in a heartbeat, her hands gripping the railing at the edge of the catwalk. "*What!?*"

<*They had an opportunity to strike at Garza's headquarters, and they took it,*> the AI explained.

She peeled her hands off the railing and began to pace across the catwalk. "It's the conditioning, isn't it? Somehow it took hold more than it should have."

<*What makes you think that?*> Bob asked.

"Because it fits. Saanvi would never let Cary do something so crazy, but with the conditioning to make them better able to fit in with the Widows, they must be obeying her unquestioningly, since she's assumed the role of A1."

<*I don't think that is it entirely. It's possible that the opportunity is too good to pass up.*>

She looked through the inbound messages and saw that it had been routed via the regular message queues—which was why Bob saw it first. Tangel willed herself to calm down, knowing that if things were dire, Joe would have reached out to her directly.

"He must know that I'd rush out there," she said after a minute.

<*That was your first urge, wasn't it?*>

Tangel shot Bob's node a cool look, held it for a second, and then nodded, her self-deprecating laughter echoing around the chamber. "I thought you couldn't predict what I do. Aren't I the great unknown in your algorithms?"

<*Tangel is, maybe,*> the AI replied. <*A mother, though? A lot easier to predict her actions.*>

"No, I suppose you don't need any advanced algorithms for that, do you?"

<*Well, I did ask a few women on the ship to be sure. But I had a high level of certainty even without that.*>

This time, a truly amused laugh came from Tangel as she wondered how Bob had phrased the question when he'd queried other mothers on the ship. She decided not to ask—it might end in her laughing at him, not herself, and despite his elevation to an ascended AI, he still didn't quite understand things like playful mocking.

<*OK, so now that you're calmed down, there's one more thing.*>

"Annnnnd now I'm uncalm again." She wondered if he

was carefully managing her. *Probably is. It's probably necessary.*

<After your daughters jumped to Karaske—the system where Garza has his base of operations—Joe instituted the Gamma Protocol in the A1 System to destroy the fleet there so they couldn't follow after.>

"Oh shit," Tangel muttered. "Have you forwarded that to New Canaan yet?"

<No, I decided to wait and see how things go with Garza. I've found that with humans, having achieved the desired results can lessen their ire over less desirable means.>

Tangel snorted. "Now that's a new way to say that the ends justify the means."

<That's not what I said,> Bob corrected, his tone insistent. *<I did not say 'justified'. I said 'lessen their ire'. I believe those to be very different things. One is about the perpetrator, and the other is about those who stand in judgment.>*

Tangel considered Bob's words, seeing the truth in them, even if it was a near-semantical nuance. "OK, I can go with that. Either way, you're right. If that use of pico gets us Garza *and* the Widows, then no one is going to raise a big stink about it."

Especially because the general sentiment amongst the population is to end the war quickly and get their families back home.

She stopped her pacing and leant against the railing.

"That will just about neutralize Orion—at the very least, stop them from gathering new allies in the Inner Stars."

<Or slow it—provided we get all of the clones.>

"True, though the intel alone will be invaluable."

<Agreed. So does that mean you're not going to rush off and save the day?>

"We don't have details as to where we'd jump into the Karaske System, do we?"

<No.>

"I guess I'll have to wait till someone is in dire need and

says, 'jump here, now!' "

<*Why change up how we do things this late in the game?*> Bob laughed at his own statement, and Tangel joined in.

"Why indeed." She drew in a deep breath and pushed off from the railing. "OK. I'm going to let my girls and husband handle things and trust that they'll call if they need me."

<*My, how you've matured.*>

"Be nice, Bob."

<*I've not matured that much.*>

Yet another laugh burst from Tangel. "Stars…you're just a jokester tonight. Something in your power supply?"

<*Softening you up for the conversation about Helen.*>

That was the topic Tangel had *expected* to discuss before Bob dropped the bomb about Cary masquerading as the A1 Widow. She wasn't sure if it would be any easier.

"OK, lay it on me."

<*Well, for starters, it* **is** *Helen, though a few steps up the evolutionary ladder.*>

"I noticed that."

<*I think that Airtha, ah, 'forcibly ascended' her, to put it in a nice way.*>

"Technically, didn't Airtha *make* Helen do everything? She is a shard, after all."

<*Shards can become independent,*> Bob said. <*I suspect that this happened with Helen. Also, from what I can tell, she is a duplication made from the original Helen before Sera journeyed to New Canaan, and before the clone of Jeffrey Tomlinson killed her.*>

"I guess that explains why the version that was with Sera was OK with playing along," Tangel said, remembering the time she'd spent onboard *Sabrina,* and the interactions she'd had with the AI. It pained her to think that Helen had been playing a game the whole time. A game that now saw her imprisoned in a containment vessel awaiting judgment. "Did you learn anything from her?"

<*Nothing new. Just confirmations of what I already believed. Her plan was to establish a new capital for her faction. I know the locations she had been considering, and have passed those to Admiral Krissy. I—*>

"Shit!" Tangel swore. "I have to tell Krissy about A1…about her mother."

<*And Finaeus,*> Bob added.

"Pfft," Tangel waved a hand dismissively. "Finaeus has to be over his ex by now. And he has Cheeky. That woman is no one's consolation prize."

<*You don't really mean that.*>

"No, not really—well, I do about Cheeky. I'm going to blame the Angela portion of me for asserting herself. Not enough acerbic wit of late."

<*If you say so.*>

"Stars, Bob, I do. OK, so what do we do about Helen?"

<*We kill her.*>

Tangel laughed, sagging against the railing. "Well *I* could have done that. Why bottle her up just to do it later?"

<*You know the drill. Justice and all that. She'll remain contained, and the Transcend's government can try and convict her. They'll kill her in the end. She's too dangerous to leave alive.*>

"Well we certainly agree there. Has Sera gone to see her yet?"

<*Don't you know?*> the AI asked. <*Usually you and Sera are thick as thieves.*>

"She may be a thief, but I'm not." Tangel gave Bob's node a roguish grin and could feel a wave of amusement from him.

<*I suppose that depends on who you ask.*>

"Bob!" she exclaimed, eyes narrowing. "Are you messing with me?"

<*Yes. It's fun.*>

"How productive."

<*If you wanted to be productive, we wouldn't use this crude*

language to speak.>

Tangel shrugged. "I like the extra time it gives me to consider my responses—especially when talking with you."

The AI sent another wave of amusement. <*Me too. It's exhausting speaking to you. I know I can't predict your statements like I can with other people, but it doesn't stop me from trying.*>

Tangel nodded silently, wishing she could truly understand what it was that made her unpredictable to Bob…and to the other ascended AIs. It didn't seem to be working in her favor of late. Although, they had just taken out Airtha, and her largely unaided victory over Helen was something she was happy to celebrate.

Except I can't do that with Jessica missing, and the girls and Joe in danger.

<*You're always worrying, Tangel,*> Bob said, not unkindly.

"Aren't you?" she asked.

<*Fair point. However, I'm worried more about Terrance and Earnest than the other things on your mind.*>

"I'm just afraid those two will blow up that facility before we can learn from it. Erin was nearly apoplectic at the thought of it being destroyed before she could study their star-shifting techniques."

<*Earnest would never destroy it. Honestly, neither would Terrance. He's too practical.*>

"Which is what made that message so strange." Tangel pressed a hand to her forehead. "I guess I should reach out and clarify what they meant."

<*I already did,*> Bob replied. <*They reiterated 'destroy'.*>

"That doesn't make any sense…"

<*Agreed.*>

"That doesn't make me any *less* worried about Jessica, though. She and her ship have been missing for days, now."

<*She has a good track record for popping back up when we thought she was long gone.*>

Tangel remembered when she first found Jessica involuntarily stowed away on the *Intrepid*.

"Or when we never expected to find her at all."

<*Exactly. In many respects, she's as unusual as you are.*>

"True. But I'm not an alien."

The AI chuckled, but not across the Link; it came over the extradimensional space, and the sound filled Tangel's mind like a tornado rumbling across a plain.

~What's alien, anyway? I think that I am, compared to humans. But you two are as well, to a lesser extent.~

"Well, all of that aside, I'm still going to worry about Jessica, OK?"

<*As you wish. We need to leave, though. I want to go to the IPE, and ensure that Earnest and Terrance aren't doing something foolish.*>

"You don't think they'll do the right thing?"

<*I'd like to be sure.*>

A FATHER'S DISMISSAL

STELLAR DATE: 10.11.8949 (Adjusted Years)
LOCATION: ISS *I2*, Airtha
REGION: Huygens System, Transcend Interstellar Alliance

Kara drew a deep breath and flexed her wings one at a time before carefully folding them behind her back.

The subject of all her fear, anger, and love was on the other side of the door that stood before her—the person who had conceived her and molded her into a daughter that was also a slave…though an unknowing slave.

When she first fled High Airtha, well over a year ago at this point, her primary motivation had been to return to Airtha to save her father. But then she'd met Katrina and her crew, followed by the people of New Canaan, and finally Tangel. She'd learned an entirely different value system from them, a cleaner code of honor—one that had not painted her father in a good light.

Now that Admiral Krissy was in control at Airtha, things had taken an unfortunate turn for Adrienne; the admiral was not taking a soft approach with Airthan collaborators. Kara's pending testimony, combined with the discovery that her father had not been coerced in any way to work with Airtha, had all but damned him. He was currently being held awaiting trial for his crimes against the people of the Transcend.

An army of lawyers had taken Kara's statement, and Krissy had informed her that there was no need to speak to her father in person. But Kara knew that a final conversation was necessary.

She had to know if he'd released her only to save him later, or because he truly cared about her. A part of her knew it was stupid, that whatever he said could just as likely be a lie, but she knew that, without confronting him, the question would continue to gnaw at her.

Katrina had urged her to do it as well. Over the past months, the ancient woman had softened toward Kara, and they'd become friends. It was amazing to think that Katrina had gotten her start so long ago as a spy working for the Lumins in the Sirius system.

She'd escaped with a group of people called the Noctus only to be pursued by her father. In a crazy tale of luck, they'd encountered Tanis, and she'd defeated Katrina's father.

The people Katrina had escaped with had sentenced her father to death, and she'd never spoken to him—and it gnawed at her to this day. So she'd recommended that Kara get what she never had managed to find: closure.

She'd also warned Kara that it might just create more questions.

Damned if I do, damned if I don't.

The words echoed in her mind, but she continued to stare at the door for another minute before she mustered up the courage to nod to the guard. She was surprised to see him give her an understanding look before turning to palm open the door.

It slid open, and she stepped into the small room. A clear plas wall separated a narrow viewing area from her father's cell. The space he was confined to was barely three meters square, and the only furnishings were a bed, toilet, sink, and a small table with a stool tucked underneath.

Her father was standing at the sink, staring into the mirror when she stepped in, and he didn't move for nearly a minute. Kara remained still as well, taking in the man who had once controlled her in every way.

Once, he'd been the ultimate authority figure in her life, the one who gave her all direction and meaning and was the arbiter of right and wrong.

Now he was a tired-looking man who had traded away all his moral authority through vile acts and a willingness to do anything in the name of survival. It made him seem smaller, sallow.

She searched her memories, curious to find out if he'd always been like that and she'd just never noticed, but upon reflection, Kara could barely even draw a clear comparison between her recollections and the man before her.

"Are you going to say anything?" he asked, not turning to face her, eyes still fixed on his reflection.

His tone was cold, combative even. Kara knew that she shouldn't be surprised. Kindness was not an attribute her father often displayed.

"I came to rescue you," she said after running through a dozen statements.

It sounded as lame out loud as it had in her head.

Adrienne snorted. "Good job. Things are so much better for me now."

His words were laced with accusation, and Kara bristled.

"I'm not responsible for that. You sided with Airtha. There's no sign that she placed any sort of coercion on you."

Her father turned his head, cold grey eyes boring into hers. "I see you got your face back. I always suspected removing it was solely your brother's idea—despite your claims to the contrary."

"I was different then," Kara said, trying not to think of her twin brother, the pain of his loss still an unhealed wound inside herself. "*You* made me different."

"I made you useful," Adrienne shot back. "So many people just take up space. You were doing good work…important work."

Kara stared at her father in silence, wondering if he really believed what he was saying. So far as she was concerned, she had been sacrificing her individuality, her very humanity, just so her father could exert more control on those around him.

"I was your slave, Father. What you did to me was no different than what Airtha did to Sera. Or was that just giving her purpose as well?"

Adrienne stepped away from the sink, walking to the plas. "Well, she did gain a lot more purpose as a result of her mother's efforts. Airtha changed Sera from an entitled brat to a woman actually capable of running the Transcend. I see that as a success."

"I see it as manipulation," Kara retorted. "Of course, you may not know this, but Sera is no longer running the Transcend. Her father is."

She enjoyed watching her father's eyes widen in shock. His mouth worked soundlessly for a moment before he finally said, "I saw him die."

"You saw a clone die," she corrected. "Someone…though no one knows who as yet, tucked the real Jeffrey Tomlinson away in the LMC about a thousand years ago."

Adrienne's eyes narrowed. "That's impossible. No, it couldn't have happened. I was there."

"You were *what*?" Kara asked.

"I visited the LMC after Finaeus developed jump gate tech. Jeffrey was with me. That was about a century ago."

Kara wondered what the significance of that was, but decided not to pursue it. She'd pass it on to Admiral Krissy and let someone else interrogate her father.

"It doesn't matter. The point is that Sera never wanted to rule the Transcend. Her mother, or whatever Airtha was at the end, tried to make her do it, but she failed. If you ask me, I think that once the war is over, Sera's going to find somewhere quiet to hole up and live out her days."

"What a waste," Adrienne breathed out in a long sigh. "She had so much potential…despite her proclivities."

"Not everyone uses your measuring stick," Kara replied. "*I* don't want to always be fighting. The idea of retiring for a century, maybe raising kids…that's an appealing notion."

He stared at her for a minute, his lips drawn into a thin line. Then a cruel smile formed on his lips.

"I wonder…will they be born with wings? Perhaps in eggs?"

"You're such an asshole," Kara spat. "Maybe they *will* have wings. I happen to think that wings are amazing, and it honestly baffles me why hardly anyone has them. Everyone *could*, yet almost no one does. I bet now that Sera's not the president, she'll get wings too."

"Doesn't surprise me," Adrienne retorted. "Like I said, she's weird."

"What does that make me?" Kara demanded.

Her father didn't reply, and she shook her head in disgust.

"Katrina warned me that I might not like what came of this conversation, but at least I did get some measure of closure."

"I'm glad for you. And I'm not surprised."

Kara had already turned away from her father, but she glanced back over her shoulder, meeting his eyes for what she hoped would be the last time.

"Not surprised about what?" The words fell from her lips like lead.

"That you'd abandon me."

She considered a dozen responses before simply shrugging and walking to the door. It opened without her prompting, and she strode out without glancing back.

A few meters away, Katrina stood waiting, a look of concern in her ancient eyes.

"So?" she said without accusation.

"About as bad as you'd warned me it would be," Kara admitted as she reached Katrina's side. "But still worth it, if only so I don't have to wonder what sort of man he really was.

Now I know for sure."

The older woman placed a hand on Kara's shoulder.

"Come. I'm going to teach you something to help you ground yourself. Maybe it will be useful, maybe it won't."

"Does it involve getting drunk?"

Katrina laughed, guiding Kara down the passageway. "Step one is finding peace. Step two is getting plastered without regrets."

"Sounds perfect."

WAR TABLE

STELLAR DATE: 10.11.8949 (Adjusted Years)
LOCATION: ISS *I2*, Airtha
REGION: Huygens System, Transcend Interstellar Alliance

"My father has asked me to return to Khardine," Sera said without preamble as she strode into Tangel's kitchen.

Krissy and Tangel were already present, a glass of wine before each, and a bowl of fruit on the table between them.

"That doesn't surprise me," a male voice said from her right, and Sera spun to see Jason leaning against the counter, a cup of coffee nestled between his fingers.

"Put that down," Sera said, gesturing to the cup he held.

"Why?" he asked as he complied, his eyes twinkling mischievously.

Sera didn't reply, instead rushing forward and crashing into him, her arms encircling his chest as she pressed her cheek into his.

"Stars I've missed you," she whispered fiercely.

New Canaan's governor chuckled softly. "It's only been a few weeks."

"A few too many," Sera replied.

"Well, I came as soon as I heard about your sisters. How are you holding up?"

Until that moment, if anyone else had asked, Sera would have said she was holding up just fine, and she wouldn't have believed it to be a falsehood. She'd decided *not* to talk to Helen, and was optimistic that, together, Earnest and Finaeus would be able to save Seraphina and Fina the same way they'd saved Cheeky.

But when Jason voiced the question, a shuddering sob escaped her lips and she felt the energy drain from her limbs.

"I got you," Jason whispered in her ear, the strength that flowed from him through those three words immediately reversing the weariness that threatened to subsume her.

"So you really came because you heard about my sisters?" Sera asked, forcing herself to regain some measure of composure as she stepped back and searched Jason's eyes for any sign that he was joking.

"Of course," he replied. "I made excuses that I needed to be here for reasons of state, but those are secondary. This has all got to be hard on you…a lot of family stuff."

Krissy gave a rueful laugh and shook her head, but didn't speak.

Tangel chuckled as she poured another glass of wine and handed it to Sera. "I don't know when Jason became so understanding, but I wish it had happened sooner."

"Pardon?" Jason asked, simultaneously laughing while shooting Tangel a glare. "I've always been understanding, you just needed a firmer hand."

Tangel snorted, and Sera glanced at Krissy to see what she made of the byplay.

"Don't look at me." The admiral held up her hands. "I'm the newcomer here."

"You've known me for a long time," Sera countered.

Krissy took a sip of her wine, giving her cousin a measuring look. "I suppose. Though you've rather surprised me of late—especially with how readily you gave up the presidency. You fought pretty hard for it after your father was killed."

"Well, I wasn't going to let Adrienne take the reins…if for no other reason than *I* would have killed him before long."

"Not if I got to him first," Krissy retorted. "Pretty sure he was in the Grey Division's pocket. I plan to find out for sure, one way or another."

"The Greys aren't just going to roll over," Sera agreed.

"Even with Airtha gone, they'll be a problem. You know, that's why I opposed you for the presidency. I thought you were in their pocket, too. A lot of rumors were flying around about why you spent so long at the Grey Wolf Star."

"If I never see that place again…" Krissy began, letting the words trail away.

Sera nodded, pressing up against Jason before moving to sit at the table across from Krissy. Jason walked across the kitchen and refilled his coffee before settling beside her.

<*You're doing great,*> Jen said privately. <*Glad Jason came to see you.*>

<*Did you have a hand in that?*> Sera asked her AI.

<*I think he was already planning on it. I just added a nudge.*>

"So," Tangel began in a tone that indicated the meeting was coming to order—such as it could when held around her kitchen table. "How goes the transfer of power here on Airtha?"

Krissy leant forward and placed her elbows on the table. "Per the president's directions, I've reinstated Governor Prentice, and he's working on bringing back the exiled members of his former government. Airtha didn't utilize much of a bureaucracy, so there's not too much to clean up, there."

<*I've distributed an updated version of Angela's corrective retrovirus to the AIs here,*> Bob added. <*That has brought most of them around.*>

"Most?" Tangel asked.

<*Some served Airtha willingly. We're interring them for the time being.*>

"Waiting on Jeffrey's orders." Krissy's expression appeared sour. "If it were up to me, they'd be tried for treason. I'm hoping that the president feels the same way."

"How many are there?" Sera asked.

<*Seven hundred and twelve followed her without any coercion.*>

"A drop in the bucket," Tangel said, though she still looked troubled. "All-in-all, this went a lot better than it could have."

"We're fighting a final group of ships that are holding out near Jove, and then we'll have the entire Huygens System under our control."

"Thus ends the Transcend's civil war," Jason intoned.

Krissy shook her head. "If only. Our alliance is fractured. I doubt that many of the systems that declared for themselves will come back into the fold."

"Do they need to?" Tangel asked. "So long as they're not a drain on resources, we can focus on defeating Orion and then ending the war in the Inner Stars. The major conflicts could be resolved in as little as four years."

"Now *that* would be a miracle." Krissy took another sip of her wine, glancing at Sera.

"I think Tangel's right," Sera replied. "Even once we put out the current fires, new ones are going to spring up. The echoes of this war could take a century to fade away."

"Well, I did say 'major' conflicts," Tangel emphasized. "But I take your meaning."

"What about you, Sera?" Krissy asked. "What are your plans now?"

Sera ran a hand across her brow and through her black hair. "Well, I *had* planned on turning over the Hand to Seraphina…or more like relinquishing any claim to it, as she was already taking the bull by the horns. I don't know how that will shake out now, so I suppose I'm still in charge of that division."

"And your father?" Tangel asked. "What do you think he has in mind for you?"

"Stars…" Sera muttered. "I have no idea. I'm beginning to suspect that he wants to keep the government at Khardine for now—"

"A good plan," Krissy interjected, earning nods from around the table.

"So maybe his summoning is because he wants 'em to run the Hand from there?" Sera looked at Krissy and shrugged.

"Well, he didn't share anything with me," the admiral said. "That much hasn't changed from his prior incarnation. He's still just as tight-lipped."

"Well, I'll put in a request for you to rejoin us as soon as possible," Tangel said. "Can't go long without my right-hand woman."

Sera's eyes widened as she turned to look at the field marshal, catching a twinkle in the woman's eyes.

"You offering me a job?"

"Well, you are an honorary citizen of New Canaan," Tangel replied. "I could use someone like you out there."

"Hey, hey!" Krissy cried out. "No pilfering *my* Sera. You get the other two versions to Earnest and get them patched up. Then there will be plenty of Seras to go around."

Sera shook her head. "I'm not sure if I should be amused or insulted."

"What of your newest sister?" Tangel asked. "Has Dr. Rosenberg had a chance to look her over in detail?"

"She has, but the doctor is withholding final judgment. Let's just say that mother took more liberties with the latest version of me. She's more…divergent."

Admiral Krissy shook her head. "Looks like an angel, behaves like a demon. Funny how you're the opposite of that, Sera."

"I wouldn't go so far as to credit our Sera's behavior as angelic." Jason spoke for the first time in several minutes, knocking his knee against Sera's.

"Umm…thanks?"

"I'll second that," Tangel added.

Krissy rolled her eyes. "I wasn't being that literal. You forget that I've known Sera since she was a little girl."

"Little demon, you mean," Sera replied, grinning at her

cousin, who nodded.

"Exactly."

"So," Tangel again brought the meeting back to business with that one word. "Let's talk about how we plan to clean up the Transcend so I can focus on Orion."

The conversation shifted to logistics and politics within the Transcend, carrying on for several hours. In the end, it was agreed that Krissy's fleets were in a position to hold Airtha, should any of the separatist allies attempt to reclaim it. A secondary strike force was being assembled at Styx in preparation to hit Orion on the anti-spinward front and finally drive back the encroaching forces after two years of losses.

When the meeting finally concluded, Jason placed his hand on Sera's.

"Care to take a walk down to the lake with me?"

She chuckled, though nodded emphatically. "Can we make it a bit longer than that? The lake is only a hundred meters away."

"I bet we could find some path to follow together."

As Sera bid farewell to Tangel and Krissy, she wondered if Jason had intended a double meaning. In her experience, men were less likely to do that, but Jason was also not an imprecise person.

Once outside Tangel's lakehouse, they walked silently to the shoreline, turning left to follow a path that led into the woods lining the lake.

"I hope your sisters recover, and not just for our sake," Jason said after a minute. "I feel like the three of you were starting to develop something special."

Sera gave a caustic laugh. "Well, after growing up with a sister like Andrea, we all wanted something better."

"I think it was more than that—though I do wonder what will become of Andrea."

"Hopefully she'll get lost in the dark layer…forever."

Jason shook his head. "You don't really mean that, do you?"

"No, I suppose not. But I would be happy if she just disappeared."

"I won't fault you there," New Canaan's governor replied. "I'm curious. Would you like me to give you a lift to Khardine?"

"Jason Andrews' interstellar taxi service?" Sera asked with a laugh.

"Well, just a way to spend a bit more time together before I have to return to New Canaan. Getting a bit more face time with your father won't hurt, either."

"Why?" Sera asked. "You don't need his permission to court me."

A snort burst from Jason's mouth, and he gave Sera an amused look. "Gaining his approval for our relationship is the furthest thing from my mind. I'm interested in cementing New Canaan's relationship with the new-old president of the Transcend."

"That's good, because my father—well, the man who shares the same face as my father—doesn't really know what to think of my sisters and I. As far as he's concerned, we're just painful reminders of his lost wife."

"Maybe." Jason shrugged. "I think that can shift over time. Either way, he asked to see you, and since Tangel wants to send *Sabrina* and the *Voyager* to help Corsia with the Trisilieds...."

"OK, OK." Sera laughed and bumped her hip against Jason's. "I'll let you fly me around in your fancy spaceship. I tell you, though, I'm worried about things out there. Would be a lot easier if the Hyadeans actually helped."

"Don't count on it," Jason snorted. "I don't blame them for being wary of the Trissies. Those bastards are turning out to be much more problematic than we expected. Heck, the

Hegemony seems to be an easier egg to crack."

"Sure," Sera replied. "But we have Scipio in the mix. They're no slouches."

"That's for sure," Jason replied. "And Diana…whew! I met with her not long ago, what a whirlwind of a woman."

"Oh?" Sera cocked an eyebrow. "Thought you liked whirlwinds."

He gave an easy laugh. "I suppose I do. Maybe she's a maelstrom, then. Or a supernova. Something that's clearly more dangerous than fun." Jason slipped his hand into hers. "You, Sera, are more fun than dangerous."

"Huh… I suppose I'll take that as a compliment."

"So, all that aside, do you want a ride to Khardine?" Jason asked.

Sera glanced at him and laughed. "I feel like you're asking me on a date to another star system."

"Maybe I am."

"Well in that case, I'm definitely in. But just so you know, Roxy, Jane, and Carmen are coming with me."

"Sure," Jason nodded. "I read the reports. Roxy has quite the past."

"She does…I'm very optimistic about her."

"In what way?"

Sera chuckled. "Well, it's optimism that involves making her assistant director of the Hand."

Jason joined in her laughter. "Sneaky!"

"All part of my master plan to shuck all responsibility," she replied, turning to catch his gaze.

<*I thought that's what I was here for?*> Jen interjected, and Jason laughed.

"Maybe you're not pulling your weight," Sera countered, joining in Jason's laughter.

After a moment, Jason asked, "So what do you plan to do once you've handed over all your duties?"

A sly smile formed on her lips. "I was thinking of seeing if Cheeky needed any crew."

The governor placed a hand on his chest. "Oh! You build up my hopes just to dash them!"

"Well…I bet they could use a new supercargo."

"Pilot, Sera. If I sign on, it's as a pilot."

"Now you're talking."

PART 4 – ESCAPE

LAST DITCH

STELLAR DATE: 10.11.8949 (Adjusted Years)
LOCATION: ISS *Lantzer*
REGION: Coreward of Stillwater Nebula, Orion Freedom Alliance

"Tell me you have power!" Jessica demanded, not looking up from the holotank, certain Karma would know she was addressing him.

"Not yet, ma'am," he muttered. "Rails are all still offline."

<Trevor, I need—>

<I know what you need, Jess. Same thing we all need, but I'm dealing with a plasma leak that's going to burn through three decks and eat a hole in the forward reactor, so….>

<OK, OK. I get it. ETA?>

Her husband sighed, sounding like the weight of the galaxy was on him. *<West is working on a bypass while I deal with this. At least twenty minutes.>*

"Fuck!" Jessica swore, then turned from the holotank and closed her eyes, drawing a deep breath.

She normally prided herself on her ability to remain calm in the face of danger, but the past seven days of playing cat and mouse with the Caretaker ships had worn her down. She grabbed a drink off a nearby console and threw it back before turning to look at the holotank once more.

The crew of *Sabrina* was in the midst of a brief reprieve; both of the fishbone ships had made high-speed passes and were out of weapons range as they came about.

For the first time in days, both of the enemy ships were on the same side of the *Lantzer*. That meant that when they came back in for another pass, she would only have to power shields on one side of the ship.

Jessica's fervent hope was that running the shields at only half coverage would finally give them the power needed to punch through one of the fishbone's shields. Of course, that plan was contingent on the railguns being online.

<*Glenn, how are the CriEns holding out?*>

<*So far, so good.* Lantzer's *moving around enough that our constant draw doesn't seem to be causing any instabilities in the local quantum foam. At least not that I can detect. I also got the port-side aft bank of SC batts back online…well, the four that survived. Zero K coils don't really like to heat up in a fire, as it turns out.*>

<*And our beams?*> Jessica pressed.

<*The Marines have them powered up. They had to charge and lug batts up two decks, but we're good to go.*>

Jessica shook her head in disbelief. Despite days of desperate defense against the two fishbone ships—and nearly no sleep at all—Glenn seemed to be in high spirits, as though he thrived on this sort of insane conflict.

<*Thank you, Chief.*> She straightened and looked up at the optical inputs above the forward holodisplay. "Gil. Confirm fishbone vector."

<*Well, provided they come about and remain on a predictable course, which they don't always do, we're looking at ten minutes until they're in range. Twenty till optimal.*>

"That mirrors my assessment," she replied quietly. <*West. Twenty tops. I need the slug throwers back online!*>

<*Going as fast as I can, ma'am.*>

A fear had begun to take hold in Jessica's mind, a fear that no matter what they did, the Caretaker ships would prevail. After seven long days, the *Lantzer* had only managed to score a few hits that made it through the enemies' shields. Glancing blows, nothing more.

They were down to three ARC fighters, the others suffering cascading system failures as a result of the EM burst that had initially dropped the *Lantzer* out of its jump. She'd had to spend time destroying the remains of those craft, knowing that the last thing her people needed was for the Caretakers to gather stasis shield technology from those hulls.

We just need a few more hours. Just enough time to finish repairs on that damn gate.

Trevor and West had been hard at work piecing together a functional gate when a series of system failures across the ship had derailed them. It hadn't been the first time.

Constructing a functional gate from the four in the ship's holds had been the primary goal for the past six days—except it kept slipping to secondary, due to the ever-present need to stay alive.

She decided that there was no time like the present, and left the bridge to get coffee and more of that bizarre, green energy drink that Karma loved.

Though a lot of things that should have been present on the ship were listed in the inventory systems as being 'backorder-delayed', Karma's energy drink was present in volumes large enough to keep them going for a year.

It was suspicious to say the least, but had provided a much-needed bout of levity at one point, when West had accused Karma of breaking some sort of unknown regulation to get so much of the drink aboard. Karma, for his part, had claimed he hadn't even put in for a stock of the drink.

After West's ire had simmered down, it had turned into a bit of a running joke with the beleaguered crew.

By the time Jessica returned to the bridge with a carafe of coffee and a few pouches of Karma's drink, West had called up with good news.

<*I got it, Admiral!*> she announced gleefully. <*Stars, my*

instructors at the academy would have kittens if they could see how I've jerry-rigged things, but it should hold for this next pass.>

<*Should?*> Jessica asked, homing in on that single word. She didn't want to dismiss the woman's hard work, but she needed a larger measure of confidence than 'should'.

<*I've had to rip out main line runs from half the ship to cobble this together. I've not really had time to put it through its paces, but I have a ninety-percent level of confidence that it'll hold for the shots your plan requires.*>

<*OK.*> Jessica knew that was as good as it was going to get. <*And the fires, Trevor?*>

<*Out for now, though environmental is screwed down here. Hold your breath if you need to go through decks six and seven.*> Trevor's words were glib, but Jessica could hear a note of worry carried along with them.

The ship was falling apart, and they all knew it. Even though they'd weathered days of attacks, just the power draw alone for weapons and shields was burning out one temporary fix after another.

In all honesty, it was a miracle that the *Lantzer* had held together as long as it had.

You're a tough old girl, Jessica thought, hoping the ship could hear her and would gain some measure of encouragement.

<*We're headed back to the bay,*> West announced. <*Just need to swap out two power modules, and we'll be ready for a test run on the ring.*>

<*Don't let me slow you down!*> Jessica said, not bothering to contain her excitement. "One more pass," she whispered. "Just need to weather one more pass."

Karma rose from his console and walked to Jessica's side.

"Yes, Ensign?" she asked.

"Umm… ma'am. Are you going to let me have one of those drinks, or just clench it tightly until it explodes?"

Jessica started, looking down to see that she had a white-knuckle grip on the energy drinks. "Sorry."

She handed them to the ensign, and he gave two to Lucida before resuming his seat.

"Rails are reporting full readiness," he announced upon settling. "Guns one and two are loaded with slugs, and three has the grapeshot."

"Get three ready to fire a spread in pattern delta-three. Given what our friends out there are doing, that stands the best chance of getting them where we want."

Thus far, the *Lantzer* had managed to fire six salvos of grapeshot from the third railgun. The first had hit the target designated 'F2' and weakened the shields enough to let the beams penetrate and do limited damage. Following that, the enemy had been very careful to avoid the field of fire that railgun three covered.

It was frustrating, but it did reduce the enemy's avenues of approach, which had its own benefits. However, the shot that was loaded into the third railgun was different this time, being filled with small pellets that were capable of independent maneuvering.

Jessica had been saving this ammunition, waiting for the enemy to grow complacent and think she was behaving predictably. When the railgun fired next, it would appear to fire on one vector, while the grapeshot would end up elsewhere. With any luck, that 'elsewhere' would be the same place the enemy ships were.

Even so, chances were fifty-fifty. Space was large, and the enemy had a lot of maneuvering options. But even though they were supposedly dealing with ascended beings, the *Lantzer*'s bridge crew had spotted patterns as well. There were preferred vectors the fishbones would move to when grapeshot was coming their way.

Just do what you're supposed to, you bastards.

The fishbones passed over the hundred-thousand-kilometer mark, but didn't fire. Both enemy ships were on nearly the same vector now, streaking toward the *Lantzer*, their trajectory lined up to take them only a few hundred kilometers off the ISF cruiser's bow.

"Grapeshot firing!" Karma announced, the ship shuddering as the massive gun launched several tons of material at a hundredth the speed of light.

A long groan sounded from somewhere above the bridge, and Jessica patted the edge of the holotank. "Hold together, girl."

<*For some definition of 'together',*> Gil said. <*A spar just came free along the dorsal arch. Deck one is holding on purely out of habit now.*>

"It's not that bad," Jessica shot back. "There are still a half-dozen structural mounts holding the arch in place."

<*They're all strained. Just be careful. The section has our only functional sensor array on the forward half of the ship.*>

"Noted," Jessica replied, glancing at Lucida, who was looking up at her. "Do what you can to reduce strain."

"Aye, ma'am."

Jessica turned her attention back to the holotank, watching as the two enemy ships predictably shifted away from the apparent path of the grapeshot.

They eased onto the anticipated vectors, and though it was exactly what she wanted, Jessica wasn't ready to crow with delight just yet. The enemy had feinted more than once; there was no reason to believe that it couldn't happen again.

"They're right in the pocket," Karma announced, sounding no more optimistic than Jessica felt. "Our shot is shifting into position. Impacts in seventy-two seconds."

No one spoke over the following minute, and when the time remaining reached ten seconds, the weapons officer began an audible countdown. A second after it hit zero, scan picked up impacts on one ship, but not the other.

"F2 jinked!" Karma called out.

"Shift all targeting to F3!" Jessica ordered.

Scan showed multiple direct hits, and that ship's shields *had* to be weakened.

Railguns one and two belched out tungsten rounds—those guns were thankfully mounted further aft on the *Lantzer*—and though the deck shuddered beneath them with each round in the salvo, nothing tore free from the hull.

The kinetic slugs streaked through the black toward F3, and the *Lantzer*'s beams joined in, tagging the enemy vessel and further weakening its shields.

In response, both enemy ships fired their weapons on the ISF cruiser, proton beams slashing through the black to slam into the *Lantzer*'s stasis shields in a dazzling display.

<*Shields holding,*> Gil announced as the enemy's shots blinded the ship's sensors.

Then the fishbones streaked past, and scan updated showing F3 bleeding a trail of plasma and ionized gas in its wake.

Cheers came from Karma and Lucida, but Jessica withheld hers. Though the plasma stream was coming from near the fishbone's engines, it was still maneuvering, albeit poorly.

"Shit, F2 is braking hard!" Karma called out a second later.

Jessica shook her head, watching as the enemy vessel executed a burn that had its main weapons facing the *Lantzer.*

<*Shifting stasis shields!*> Gil announced, and the enemy ship's beams splashed harmlessly against them.

A sigh of relief came from Lucida, but Jessica wasn't ready to celebrate just yet.

"Shields back around the whole—" Jessica's words were cut off as the deck rocked beneath them, the ship's a-grav dampeners straining to keep the crew safe as the cruiser spun through space.

<*Missiles,*> Gil said, his voice laden with worry. <*Came in on our unprotected side.*>

Jessica had already surmised that.

<*Sound off!*> she called out to the crew, knowing that the missiles had struck close to where Trevor and West were working.

Trevor was first to reply. <*Shaken, but West and I are still here.*>

A sense of profound relief came over her as the rest of the crew signaled that they were alive. Meg broke an arm when she was flung against a bulkhead, and everyone other than the bridge crew had a few flesh wounds.

<*Oh shit,*> Gil swore, the first time Jessica had heard the AI do so.

She turned to the forward display to see a ship's integrity warning. Visuals from the hull showed the dorsal arch—including railgun three—peel off and drift away. Lucida muttered curses under her breath as she struggled to correct the ship's spin.

Jessica pursed her lips, not letting the fear that was threatening to subsume her take over. She'd survived far too much in her life to believe there weren't still options.

One of which was to surrender.

<*Admiral, I've been thinking,*> Glenn said, interrupting her ruminations.

<*Dangerous stuff, Chief.*>

<*Well, we know that there are Exdali around here, right?*>

<*Mmmhmmm,*> Jessica answered wordlessly, wondering what the man was getting at.

<*Well, I was on a ship at Carthage when we opened up the dark layer and let the things out to eat the Orion ships. I know how it's done.*>

Jessica's eyes widened and she let out a curse, garnering the attention of Karma and Lucida, who she waved off.

<It takes a special emission from the grav drive, right?> she asked.

Tangel had given her a brief overview, but she'd never learned the specifics. It annoyed her that Glenn hadn't suggested it sooner, but she could imagine why he was hesitant to bring it up until now.

<It does. I didn't have access to all the data, but I've been running simulations, and I believe I can open a rift and draw them out…but….>

<I don't like buts,> Jessica said, half expecting to hear Cheeky laugh at the statement.

Glenn made a sound like he was scared to say what the caveat was.

Jessica urged him on. *<Out with it, Chief.>*

<Well…I don't know how to put them back in.>

Jessica barked a laugh, shaking her head as she considered their options.

<You know what? I don't think I care. How long do you need?>

<Ten minutes.>

She looked at the holotank. F2 was braking hard and would be back in firing range in eight minutes, though F3 had killed its engines and was adrift on a vector away from the *Lantzer*. With the ship's dorsal arch gone, they couldn't envelop the entire cruiser in regular shields, let alone stasis shields. The moment that F2 came back around and opened fire, they'd be done for.

<You have seven.>

Chief Glenn signaled his acknowledgment, and Jessica updated the rest of crew with the plan. To her surprise, no one objected to the idea of leaving Exdali free to roam this region of space.

The one thing that wore on her mind was the presence of the Exdali in interstellar space to begin with. They'd tried dipping the *Lantzer* into the dark layer twice more, both times finding it teeming with the things that dwelt there.

The crew had debated the presence of the dark layer creatures to no end. They'd settled on two possibilities. The first was that for Exdali to be present all over the galaxy, it was possible that they migrated in some fashion, and that's what they were in the midst of. The second was that the Caretakers had somehow summoned the things to this area.

Despite the lack of any clear evidence to point toward the second option, it was what Jessica feared most to be true. It also meant that there was a possibility that the ascended AIs could control the creatures—though if that was the case, she would have expected them to use Exdali in their attack.

In addition to all that, she considered that the ascended AIs would be able to stuff the things back in the rift and close it up with no harm done.

That's something we'll just have to risk.

"Roll the ship," Jessica ordered Lucida. "Let's keep our—well, what *remains* of our dorsal arch away from them."

"Yes, ma'am," the ensign replied, plotting a burn that Jessica and Gil approved.

"Oh crap!" Karma exclaimed a moment later. "F3 is releasing more drones!"

"What?!" Jessica demanded.

The first two days of fighting against the fishbone cruisers had been more of a war with their drones than anything else. One of attrition, to be precise. In the end, the enemy ships had depleted their drone fleets, smashing them uselessly against the *Lantzer*'s shields—though that onslaught had pushed the cobbled-together systems, causing many secondary and tertiary failures across the ship.

When the fishbones had ceased releasing drones, the *Lantzer*'s crew had been wary of more to come, but—four days later—had believed the ships to be out of the disposable machines.

"How many?" Jessica asked, though she knew scan was still differentiating the signatures.

"A hundred at least," Karma said in a quiet voice. "Leading edge is ten minutes out."

<*Glenn! You're out of time,*> Jessica called down to the chief before reaching out to Trevor and West a moment later. <*The gate, we need the gate ready to go. We're about to make space very inhospitable around here.*>

<*It's on the rails,*> Trevor replied without hesitation. <*Just getting the last antimatter capsules in place.*>

<*Good,*> Jessica said, feeling some measure of relief at the good news. <*Be ready to kick it out on my mark.*>

<*OK, we'll need just another minute. Have to rig it to blow when we're done.*>

<*That's not necessary, Caretakers already have gates. We can send a taskforce back later to clean it up.*>

<*You got it, ma'am,*> Trevor said with a laugh, and she couldn't quite tell if it was rueful or nonchalant.

* * * * *

Trevor glanced at West, who was climbing the ring segment furthest down the rail, slotting an antimatter pod into place. Though the ring was nearly ready to deploy, it would take a few minutes to assemble once in space—the result of hauling something in the ship that the entire vessel had to fit through.

"I told the admiral we'll be ready in a minute!" he called out to the engineer.

"What?!" West exclaimed, turning sharply and nearly losing her grip. "We're easily ten minutes out. I haven't even initialized the maneuvering systems."

"I already did," Trevor replied. "Just get that antimatter in there and get down."

West grunted something that he couldn't quite make out, but half a minute later, she was on the deck, and Trevor pulled on his EV suit's helmet before walking to the dock's command console where he activated the bay doors.

The grav shields were working in the bay, but he wasn't taking any chances, and began a depressurization process as well. West jogged to his side, pulling on her own helmet and giving him a sour look.

<*We're taking a huge risk. We don't know if it'll assemble!*>

<*The Caretakers are coming back around to finish us off,*> Trevor replied. <*Ten minutes tops. Either we jump, or we die.*>

<*Or we jump* **and** *we die.*>

<*Yay for options.*>

West nodded as she activated the rails. <*Or the Exdali eat us alive and we die.*>

<*Let's try to die before they eat us,*> Trevor suggested.

<*Solid plan,*> West said absently as the first section of ring slid out into space. <*Wait…what? No! What am I saying? Shitty plan. Terrible plan. No dying at all.*>

<*You were the one who brought up dying,*> Trevor said as the second section slid out.

There were six more to go, and neither he nor West spoke further as they drifted away from the ship.

<*OK…*> The engineer brought up a display of the ring on the console. <*Sections one and two are mated, three and four…*>

They both fell silent as the maneuvering jets on section four fired, bringing it closer to its mate. Then one of the jets cut out, and the arch slewed aside.

<*Fuck! Damn!*> West bellowed, killing section four's jets and activating three's.

After a moment of vector correction, the sections began to ease toward one another while the others also mated. A minute later, the ring was assembled and began its activation sequence.

<*Jessica, we're t-minus five to jump readiness,*> Trevor relayed to his wife. <*How're things looking up there?*>

<*About to unleash hell,*> she replied soberly.

* * * * *

"Gate's coming online," Jessica announced, and Lucida nodded as she looked at the readings on her console.

"Yes, ma'am, jump targeting is transferring to my station. Shoot, several of its maneuvering thrusters aren't responding.... And wow! West knows some really good curses."

Jessica saw the readings on the console next to her. "Looks like we'll have to come around."

<*Once we finish opening the dark layer rift,*> Gil cautioned.

"Yes."

Jessica lifted a hand to her mouth, focusing on her breathing as the timing for three events converged. The Caretakers' remaining fishbone ship was closing fast, already within firing range of the *Lantzer,* and soon the gate. They'd be within optimal range in a minute.

The grav systems were already opening the rift to the dark layer, creating an inky rent in space that made the interstellar darkness look like noon on a terraformed world.

<*Initializing the Call,*> Gil announced.

On top of every other risk they were taking, the Call was where things could really go terribly wrong. When the Exdali exited the rift, the things would move toward the source of the signal. When the ISF fleet at Carthage had used the dark layer creatures to destroy the Orion Guard fleet, they had used multiple signals from hundreds of ships to guide the creatures.

Jessica did not have that option.

Luckily, Glenn had come up with a way to bounce the signal off the Caretakers' ship, using the enemy's own grav shields to echo and broadcast the signal toward the rift.

It was a gamble, but everything they were doing was a gamble. Jessica would rather pull out all the stops than just give up and let the ascended AIs do…whatever it was they were planning on doing.

The ship's grav shields began to emit the specialized signal that attracted Exdali, tightbeaming it toward the Caretaker vessel. The enemy ship registered it as a hostile attack and diffused the incoming signal, bouncing it out into space.

Within seconds, Jessica could see the first strands of darkness begin to appear around the rift.

Discerning the difference between the rift into the dark layer and the creatures leaving it wasn't easy at first, but the first escapee, a hundred-meter-long inky splotch against Stillwater's backdrop, separated from the rift, moving toward the Caretakers' ship.

The distortion the *Lantzer*'s signal created on the enemy ship's shields must have caused it not to see the Exdali at first, because for nearly half a minute, the fishbone ship kept boosting straight toward the *Lantzer* and the rift between the vessels.

"Shit…maybe they'll just fly right into the dark layer," Karma said with a laugh.

"I'd sure be happy with that," Lucida added.

Jessica nodded in agreement, though she didn't expect the enemy to be that blind.

Sure enough, a few moments later, the enemy ship spun and began boosting on a new vector. One of the Exdali very nearly latched onto the fishbone, but missed. More followed in its wake, a writhing mass of utterly black forms, twisting and stretching across space toward the mass they hungered for.

The Caretaker ship began to extend its AP engine's nozzle, the tip of which would protrude beyond the ship's shields. Jessica worried it would allow the fishbone to outpace the

Exdali, and sent Karma an order.

"Shoot that thing off."

"With pleasure, ma'am."

Karma fired two shots with the *Lantzer*'s proton beams. The first missed, but the second hit, tearing off the end of the nozzle and sending the chunk of ship's engine spinning into one of the Exdali's maws.

The infusion of matter seemed to give the thing an energy boost, and it surged forward, passing right through the fishbone's grav shield and attaching itself to the hull near the engines.

One of the vessel's fusion burners sputtered and died, slowing the ship enough for the rest of the things that were in pursuit to reach the hull.

The bridge crew watched in a silent mixture of excitement and horror as the creatures from the dark layer devoured the Caretaker ship, explosions blooming against the Exdali's dark bodies as critical systems were compromised.

"You know…" Karma mused. "What happens when those things get to a CriEn module?"

"They'll have safety shutdowns," Jessica said. "Just like the Orion ships had when they were devoured by the Exdali over Carthage."

"And what if they disable those safeties?" the ensign asked.

Jessica pursed her lips. "Kill the signal, bring us about. It's time we jump."

The bridge crew complied while she continued to watch the things eat the enemy ship. The other Caretaker vessel was still drifting on the same vector as before, and Jessica wondered if it really was completely dead, or if it was just playing at it to avoid attention from the Exdali.

"Lining up with the gate," Lucida announced as the ship came around. "We—"

Jessica had been watching the gate come into view on the

main holodisplay, and her mouth fell open at the same time that Lucida's voice cut out.

"Fuck," the admiral whispered.

Though it was being consumed, the other fishbone ship fired a single shot from where it drifted in the black. The beam only scored a glancing blow, but it was enough to spin the gate around.

"It's out of alignment now. Maneuvering thrusters aren't responding," Lucida muttered. "Calling down to West."

Jessica nodded, watching as a group of Exdali broke off from the feeding frenzy on the other fishbone, heading for the ship that had just fired. Her lower lip found its way between her teeth, and she began to gnaw on it, waiting for the things to turn toward the *Lantzer*.

But none did.

"Oh thank stars," she whispered.

<*And everything else,*> Gil added.

"West says that she can't get control of the gate, either," Lucida said, turning to Jessica. "She's going to go out to it."

The admiral couldn't think of anything encouraging to say, only managing to whisper, "Stars help her."

* * * * *

"Dammit!" West stormed across the bay to a stack of ring segments they'd discarded and began pulling sections off, dropping them to the deck with little concern for the value of the tech. "We need a drive controller! The one in segment four died, and now that fucking fishbone hit the only other one on the ring!"

"OK, OK," Trevor approached from behind her, looming over the stack. "There, in the back. I'll get it."

West nodded and walked around the pile, watching as Trevor located a controller module.

"Stars," she muttered. "Must be nice being a billion meters tall. I couldn't see that at all."

The mountain of a man chuckled and handed her the controller. West plugged in her analysis unit, and a holo appeared showing that—by some miracle—the drive controller was functional.

With that knowledge in hand, she turned and stared through the still-open bay doors. The ring was not currently in view, so she strode toward the dark rectangle, peering around the corner, trying to catch sight of it.

"What are you doing?" Trevor asked, following after. "You can't just jump out the door. The ring is three kilometers away now."

West realized he was right, that she wasn't thinking clearly; her mind was fixed on getting to the ring and aligning it, just not on how.

"Look, Commander. That ring has to be *precisely* aligned. You of all people know what happens if you jump on a misaligned ring."

"Yeah, preaching to the choir, West."

"What? What choir?"

"Nevermind. From an old vid. So what do we do?"

West cast about and spotted a dock skiff. It was little more than a sled with an a-grav unit, but it could travel in space as well as on the deck.

"I'll take that out to the ring."

"I'll go with you, then," Trevor said.

West was already striding toward the skiff, and looked over her shoulder at the commander. "No offense, sir, but you weigh a ton. Literally. The skiff will make it there faster and be a hell of a lot more maneuverable without your mass on it."

Trevor harrumphed but didn't push the issue, as West pulled the skiff out of its dock moorings and checked it over to determine it was functional. While she did that, the commander looked over her seals, pronouncing them good.

<*Admiral?*> West called up to the bridge, realizing that she needed the CO's permission to leave the ship.

<*Trevor already briefed me. That's a brave thing you're doing, West. Be careful.*>

<*Yes, Admiral. Just don't leave without me.*>

<*Wouldn't dream of it, Chief.*>

Jessica's words rang true in West's mind, and with a nod to Trevor, she stepped onto the skiff and tucked the engine controller into a web of netting behind her.

She activated the narrow sled and steered it out of the bay doors, trying to ignore the fact that it felt like driving over the edge of a cliff with an endless bottom.

In space, everywhere is up, not down, she reminded herself, using the mantra to push the irrational fear away.

She cleared her head, turned to the left, and spotted the ring. Once she had the skiff on a course, she looked over her shoulder and saw that the Exdali were still feeding on their fishbone meals, seemingly unaware or the *Lantzer*'s presence nearby.

Even so, she didn't want to delay her ship's departure, and drove to the ring as quickly as possible.

As she approached, West saw that the entire controller housing in section six was complete slag and knew that she had to replace the one in section four and hope that was enough to get the ring reoriented.

<*What's your assessment, Chief?*> Jessica asked as West reached the desired section of the kilometer-wide ring and moored her skiff to it.

<*That I hope we can get this damn thing repaired.*>

The admiral didn't reply, and West hoped she hadn't offended the woman—though she doubted it. Despite the fact that the admiral seemed blissfully unaware of how disconcerting it was to be around someone who glowed bright purple because of a distinctly non-Terran biological source, she seemed otherwise very perceptive when it came to giving her people the space they needed to get their work done.

Letting that notion twist around in her mind, West grabbed her new control module and pulled herself along handholds embedded into the ring, coming to the module's panel a few seconds later.

She quickly unlatched the stays and pulled the panel free, slotting it into a nearby mooring.

OK, you stupid thing…let's power you down.

While the control system shut down, she looked over the equipment for any damage, happy not to see any, though still only cautiously optimistic.

<*Chief West?*> Jessica's tone carried a note of urgency.

<*Yes, Admiral?*>

<*That other fishbone managed to do one last thing—it replicated the Call and broadcast it at the Lantzer. Silver lining, those things are going to get the drones before they reach us.*>

West tapped into the ship's scan and saw that the swarm of Exdali was moving toward the cruiser, which hung motionless against the stars. Fear grabbed her, threatening to shake her apart.

Suddenly the vastness of space, the far-off and dubious safety of the *Lantzer*, and the threat of the onrushing enemy was too much. She choked back a sob, unaware of how to even continue.

<*West. I'm here.*> The words in her head were from Chief Glenn. <*I know it's scary. Damn scary. Do you have the old controller out yet?*>

<*N-no…*>

<*OK, let's do that. Pull the stays on the outside first.*>

Though she knew all the steps, Glenn's voice launched her into action, and she gulped down the lump in her throat and began to follow his directions. A minute later, she had the new controller in, and it began to initialize.

<*Looking good from here,*> Glenn said. <*Pass control to Lucida so she can align the gate with Albany.*>

West realized that the Exdali were nearly upon the *Lantzer.* There was no time for tests. The ring had to be activated so the ship could jump. Jumping was all that mattered now.

Even as she passed control to Lucida, the *Lantzer* began to move toward the gate, and it occurred to West that she had no idea how to get back aboard.

<*West!*> Trevor's voice came to her this time. <*Get back to your skiff and get ready to boost toward the bay. You only have to get a few hundred meters away from the gate. Just get in front of the bay doors, and I'll use a grav beam to scoop you up.*>

<*Right. On it,*> West said, flinging the bad controller off into space and pulling herself back toward the skiff even as the ring began to turn.

<*Alignment is good. Great work, West,*> Lucida said, eliciting a sigh of relief from the engineer.

She reached the skiff a moment later and powered it up, locking her feet into the slots as she pulled away from the ring. Behind her, the machine came alive, the ball of not-space forming in the jump gate's center, a sight she knew all too well.

The panic threatened to overwhelm her again, and she mentally berated herself for being so weak. She'd trained for situations like this. She'd done plenty of EVA. There was no reason to be so scared.

The rationale almost worked, until she saw one of the Exdali nearly upon the *Lantzer,* and her thoughts turned to gibberish.

<*OK,*> Trevor's calm voice entered her mind as the skiff shot toward the cruiser. <*You're on target, just hold steady. You've got this.*>

The bay was just a few hundred meters away. She was

rushing toward it, and it was moving into alignment with her. Her trajectory was true; she would make the spot Trevor had indicated. The grav beam would pull her in and—

Roiling darkness appeared just a dozen meters to her left.

West screamed as she realized the Exdali was nearly atop her. She slewed the skiff to the right, angling further toward the *Lantzer*'s bow.

<West, you're off course. Correct,> Trevor called out.

<I can't! The things!>

Her wailing scream set her own teeth on edge, but Trevor's voice was calm, reassuring.

<It's OK. I'm adjusting, just hold.>

West looked to her left and saw the Exdali close to within three meters of her. This close, she could see an inky reflection to its undulating skin. It was almost as though it was sniffing her, trying to see if she was a worthy diversion.

<Gotcha!> Trevor cried out, and West felt the skiff lurch toward the ship.

Out of the corner of her eye, she saw the Exdali rush toward her, and she turned her head away. She was still in space, outside the hull, when her gaze settled on the gate. She watched in fascinated horror as the vessel's mirror touched the roiling ball of energy in its center.

Then she knew no more.

THE JUMP

STELLAR DATE: 10.11.8949 (Adjusted Years)
LOCATION: ISS *Lantzer*
REGION: Buffalo, Albany System, Theban Alliance

The forward holodisplay went dark, and Jessica held her breath, trembling with anticipation, begging the stars that the next sight that appeared would be the familiar pattern of the Praesepe Cluster.

Three excruciatingly long seconds later, that familiar starscape appeared, and she breathed a sigh of relief, glancing at Karma and Lucida as Gil announced, <*We're four light seconds from Buffalo.*>

"Thank all the things," Lucida breathed.

Jessica was about to join her, when Trevor bellowed over the shipnet.

<*We've got company!*>

"Shit! Not *those* things!" Lucida blurted out.

<*What?*> Jessica exclaimed, pulling up the optics from the bay to see a small Exdali, not much larger than an ARC fighter, tearing its way across the deck while Trevor backpedaled away from it, a bloody figure in his arms. "Shit!"

She turned to the console at her side and saw that the grav beam Trevor had used to pull in West's skiff was still active. She reversed it, blasting positive gravitons at the creature, using the same patterns that had gotten them through the dark layer tunnel to Star City many years ago.

The effect was enough to push the thing off the deck and out into space, though the extradimensional beast clawed its way across the plas, shredding the launch rails before flying out into the black.

<*I've broadcast an alert to the system,*> Gil announced seconds

later.

"Oh shit! Shit, shit!" Karma bellowed. "There are more! They're just appearing!"

Jessica flipped the main holo to display the location where they'd exited the jump. Dozens of black shapes were appearing and spreading out, hungrily seeking their next meal. Though the *Lantzer* and pursuing Exdali were a good distance from the planet, a few cargo haulers were nearby, all of which were already turning and boosting away from the rapidly growing mass of darkness.

"Lucida!" she yelled at the ashen-faced pilot. "Full burn! Everything we've got!"

"Ma'am!" the ensign said after a moment, nodding manically as her hands flew over the console.

The *Lantzer*'s deck shuddered, and groans echoed around them as the ship surged forward, away from the mounting threat they'd brought with them to the Albany System.

"Local STC got our call," Karma announced. "They've put out a ban."

Jessica nodded, listening as they picked up the broadcast.

<*This is a system-wide alert. Exdali incursion four light seconds spinward of Buffalo. All ships, Buffalo is now interdicted. Adjust vectors per nearest STC's directives.*>

"Doesn't *anyone* know how to send these things back?" Jessica muttered. "Stars…this needs to be in the databanks!"

<*Call from the* Knossos,> Gil announced a second later. <*It's Admiral Carson.*>

She accepted the incoming message without hesitation.

<*Carson! Am I glad to hear from you! Do you know how to send these things back to hell?*>

<*Yes, but my fleet is on the far side of Buffalo, thirty minutes out.*>

<*Shit!*>

Jessica clenched her jaw as she saw the mass of Exdali

spreading out, some moving toward the nearby array of gates—which were surrounded by hundreds of ships. She looked at her bridge crew, knowing they'd been through more than she could ever have asked, but also knowing that their trials weren't done yet.

Even so, they didn't *all* have to put themselves at risk. She was the captain, that was her job.

<*Crew of the ISS* Lantzer. *Abandon ship. Get to pods, the pinnace, or the ARCs. You have three minutes before I initiate the call and get these things to come after us.*>

<*Hell no!*> Trevor was first to respond.

"He's right," Karma added a moment later. "We all did this, bringing them here in our escape. We're not running."

<*Besides,*> Gil added. <*It's going to take all of us to keep this scrap heap flying long enough for Admiral Carson's fleet to arrive and deal with these things.*>

One by one, the rest of the crew sounded off that they were staying, even the Marines.

<*Couldn't look anyone in the eye for the rest of my life if I abandoned you now, ma'am,*> Corporal Jay sent privately.

<*Ma'am, we stand a better chance if we use the last three ARCs and the pinnace to misdirect the Exdali,*> Gil said a second later. <*They all can broadcast the Call. We can tangle the things up, keep them at bay.*>

Jessica felt a surge of hope in her breast at the thought. <*OK, get the ARCs out there.*>

<*Pinnace's remote flight controls are hosed,*> Trevor said. <*Someone has to go out there to fly it.*>

Half a dozen voices called out, volunteering to fly the craft. Jessica felt her eyes moisten as the admiral and the wife went to war in her mind.

<*Trevor. Take Meg. You two are our best-rated next to Lucida and me.*>

<*Don't worry,*> Trevor said, his voice missing his typical

nonchalance. <*We got this.*>

The unfairness of making it back to Albany only to risk all their lives hit her like a sledgehammer, and she took a moment to compose herself before replying.

<*You stay safe, Trevor. You hear me? No crazy heroics. If you don't come back to me, I'll…*>

<*Hey.*> His voice was gentle. <*Same for you. Between the two of us, I'm not the one with the history of going off half-cocked.*>

An innuendo-laden joke came to mind, but before she could utter it, he spoke up again.

<*I know what you're thinking. Leave cocks out of it.*>

<*The only cocks I'm thinking of are the chickens aboard* Sabrina.>

<*Nice save.*>

Jessica chuckled. <*Good luck. I need to lay out our plots. Be ready for yours.*>

<*Aye, ma'am.*>

Sectioning off her worry, she looked down at the holotank and drew out a plot for the pinnace and the three ARCs. She decided to have Trevor and Meg fly above the *Lantzer* while the fighters moved further back, playing cat and mouse with the Exdali, hopefully being able to keep them from a consistent course.

It seemed like a good plan, but she had yet to see how it would perform in practice. It was entirely possible that the things out there would ignore the smaller ships and focus only on the *Lantzer.*

<*I've briefed Buffalo's STC,*> Gil advised. <*They have droneships en route to help, but they're no closer than Carson's fleet.*>

"Thanks, Gil," Jessica said absently as the ARCs launched from the starboard bay. "With luck, we can manage this on our own."

"Tons and tons of luck. And if we don't have it, the rest of them are going to need it." Karma chuckled at his gallows' humor.

"We don't need luck," Lucida said as she shifted the ship's vector to follow Jessica's plot, which largely led them away from traffic lanes and orbital stations. "We have one of the best pilots in the ISF as our admiral. This'll be a cakewalk."

"Not if you jinx it like that," Jessica muttered.

A minute later, the pinnace launched, and Glenn initiated the Call. Many of the Exdali were already pursuing the *Lantzer,* several of them closer than Jessica felt comfortable with, but the goal was to get the entire group of things to pursue them and not hit the gate arrays. If that happened, the creatures' next stop would be several heavily populated stations, followed by the planet itself.

Jessica didn't even want to contemplate what would occur if the Exdali reached that much mass. She'd made a lot of mistakes in her life and had learned to live with them, but she had no idea how she'd deal with an error in judgment on that scale.

"They're coming." Karma's voice contained a mixture of fear and excitement. "Most are tracking on us, a few on the pinnace."

"Good." Jessica nodded, then brought the ARCs in close to the leading edge of the Exdali wave—which was still growing, as more and more of the things appeared in space where the *Lantzer* had been.

It made no sense to her how the creatures could use a jump gate. They should have been annihilated by the singularity on the other side, but somehow, they were traversing it, as though they had the ability to hold the wormhole open.

Which I guess they must…because they're doing it.

Ideas about the origins of the Exdali and why they might really be spread so far and wide across the galaxy—while not being present in the Large Magellanic Cloud—began to form in her mind.

She pushed them aside to focus on the task at hand, directing her five ships in a complex pattern that, so far, was keeping the Exdali following them while not letting the things get too close.

<*Good work out there,*> she sent to Trevor after ten minutes of leading the creatures on.

<*Don't count your chickens before the cocks get to them,*> he replied a few seconds later. <*This bucket of bolts is barely holding together. We just lost internal a-grav and dampeners.*>

<*Crap!*> Jessica quickly altered her plans, removing several of the jinks from the pinnace's plot. <*OK, going to try and give you smoother sailing. How's Meg?*>

<*The greenest Marine you ever did see, but holding up otherwise. You?*>

In answer, the *Lantzer* groaned, and a vibration thrummed through the deck.

<*We're not doing much better,*> Jessica admitted. <*I think something important just snapped.*>

Having the ship fall apart around them wasn't going to help with their problems, and the admiral knew she needed to try something different.

She activated one of the ARC's stasis shields and turned it onto a new course, diving straight for one of the larger Exdali.

"What are you doing?!" Karma exclaimed.

"Seeing what these things are made of," Jessica replied, then held her breath as the fighter slammed into the creature.

There was a moment when the ship was out of sight, then it came out the other side, smaller bits of writhing Exdali trailing after. The larger creature seemed to break apart, some portions drifting listlessly while others began to move on their own, resuming the chase, albeit at a slower pace.

Exdali nearby shifted, converging on the dead mass, devouring the scraps in moments.

<Shit…did that work? That looked sort of like something that worked,> Trevor said.

<It's slowing them down, at least.>

<Crap. We just lost our grav emitters,> her husband muttered. *<If we can't make the Call, we should come back in.>*

<No,> Jessica almost shouted. *<I'm sending you a new vector. Get clear.>*

<Jess, I—>

<That's an order, Commander. You can't help any more than you already have. We just need to stay the course now and hope Carson's ships can get here in time.>

Jessica glanced at the approaching fleet's markers on the holotank and shook her head in dismay. Carson's ships had originally been only thirty minutes away, but the *Lantzer* had been boosting hard. Though ten minutes had passed, the vessels coming to the rescue were still over twenty-seven minutes from intercept.

Jessica continued to slash the three ARCs through the pursuing creatures, breathing a sigh of relief as the Exdali continued to fall back, slowed by the impacts and the act of devouring the pieces of mass left behind.

The *Lantzer* had put almost a hundred kilometers between it and the leading edge of the creatures when the vibration in the deck ceased. It was followed by an eerie moment of silence, and then an explosion rocked the ship.

<We just lost the starboard engine,> Gil called out. *<We're veering off course.>*

Jessica adjusted the port engine's burn, using what thrusters the ship still had to balance it on the fusion torches. Their new course had the *Lantzer* angling toward a wheel and spoke habitat, and she fired the midship maneuvering jets to rotate the vessel, turning it in the process.

"They're closing," Karma whispered.

The loss of acceleration had already cut the dearly won

hundred kilometers of separation down to eighty. Jessica plotted it out, the result of her calculation showing an intercept in four minutes.

"I'm out of ideas," she whispered, looking at Karma and Lucida with wide eyes.

Neither of the ensigns replied, both staring mutely at her, as though she would somehow manage to summon a miracle out of thin air.

"The pods," she managed to stammer, gesturing to the back of the bridge. "Get to the pods!"

The two rose and stumbled across the shuddering deck, the expressions on their faces showing the knowledge of how slim their chances were. Jessica turned to join the ensigns, but another explosion rocked the ship. She didn't need Gil's announcement to know it was the port engine.

An alert sounded, and her HUD updated with an Exdali intercept time of one minute.

Karma fell against the bulkhead. "It doesn't matter now. We'll never make it."

<*Jess!*> Trevor yelled into her mind. <*Get off the ship! You have to go!*>

She sent back an affirmative grunt, unable to form words, the reality that she was about to be shredded by Exdali taking hold in her mind.

<*It doesn't matter,*> she finally managed to say. <*You get away. Stay safe.*>

<*No!*> Trevor shouted, and she worried he was about to try and come back for her.

She was about to order him to safety when a voice came into her mind, a thundering wave of implacable certainty and determination.

~I'm here.~

DEPARTING AIRTHA

STELLAR DATE: 10.11.8949 (Adjusted Years)
LOCATION: ISS *I2*, Airtha
REGION: Huygens System, Transcend Interstellar Alliance

"Stars," Captain Rachel muttered as she approached Tangel on the bridge of the *I2*. "Another system, another gate. We have twelve facilities in New Canaan alone manufacturing super-sized gates, and they *still* can't keep up."

"Well," Tangel replied, looking beyond the gate to the massive Airthan ring and the white dwarf it encircled. "This is probably a good system to leave one in permanently. I have a feeling that I-Class ships will be passing through a lot."

"True," Rachel nodded. "Though I can't believe we're going back to Praesepe. Seems like we've spent half the war with that cluster filling most of the starscape."

"I suppose we've been skirting around it for some time," Tangel replied. "Though not *quite* half the war."

"Close enough," the other woman replied with a laugh. "Gotta admit, I'm a bit nervous about jumping so deep into the cluster itself. Without a gate, it would take almost a century to get out."

"So much exaggeration," Tangel laughed. "More like seventy-five years."

The captain snorted. "Yeah, well, that would certainly *feel* like a century. I—"

"Admiral, Captain!" The comm officer spun in his seat. "I just got an urgent message over Admiral Carson's direct QC. He's asking why we haven't jumped to Buffalo yet."

"Buffalo?" Rachel asked. "What for?"

"There have been a few messages on the QuanComm network about a dustup there," Tangel said. "But they said it was small and that Carson's Fleet was handling it."

"Ma'am, Admiral Carson says there are Exdali appearing insystem and chasing the *Lantzer*."

In an instant, Tangel stripped the message the comm officer was reading and located the *Lantzer*'s last reported coordinates and vector. Her next thought activated the jump gate, adjusting its alignment from the Inner Praesepe Empire to the Albany System on the cluster's rimward edge.

Rachel had already given Helm its orders, and the ship surged forward, speeding across the hundred kilometers between it and the gate.

Tangel sent a message to Carson asking for updates, and just before the *I2* reached the gate, he provided fresh scan data.

"Shit!" she swore aloud, realizing that the *Lantzer* had slowed considerably and the jump would have seen them collide with the cruiser.

Racing against time, she made one final adjustment. And then space disappeared.

Seven seconds later, it was back. Audible alarms wailed, heralding a near collision with a small ship off the port bow.

"Pinnace out there!" Scan called out. "Engines are dead."

"Where's the *Lantzer*?" Tangel demanded, then spotted it fifty kilometers away and breathed a sigh of relief.

"Instruct the dockmaster to send out tugs," Rachel replied while scowling at the holotank.

Scan updated a second later, and the tank showed a stream of Exdali stretched out several thousand kilometers behind the severely damaged ISF cruiser.

Tangel tried to reach out to the *Lantzer*, but the *I2*'s comm array couldn't make a Link with the ship. Rather than wait for the comm team to establish a solid connection, she reached out across space and found Jessica's mind, forcing her thoughts across the distance to reach her friend.

~I'm here.~

~Tangel? Where? And shit, can you turn it down a notch? My eyes almost popped out.~

~I'm aboard the I2. *We're fifty klicks to port. We're going to handle the Exdali, but where are they coming from?~*

A feeling of shame came from Jessica for a moment before she replied. *~They followed us through a jump. We drew them out to take on the Caretaker ships, and somehow they came after.~*

~Caretaker ships?~ Tangel felt a wave of fear strike her. *~At Star City?~*

~No…or I hope not. We never made it. Got knocked out of our jump this side of Stillwater.~

A torrent of implications, none of them good, rolled over Tangel, but she pushed them aside.

~OK. Rachel's sending tugs to get you away from this mess. We'll shove these things back in the dark layer and put a cork in that gate that's sending them.~

~Stars…you have no idea how good it feels to know I didn't destroy a star system.~

Tangel sent a laugh. *~Well, don't count your chickens before they're hatched.~*

~Or your cocks.~

~What?~ Tangel's brow furrowed.

~Nothing. Oh! Thanks for saving Trevor too.~

~He in the pinnace?~

~Uh huh, a decoy…sorta.~

Tangel ran a hand over her head, subconsciously tightening her ponytail. *~OK, I want to work on this Exdali problem. You get to safety.~*

~And a nap. Stars, I could sleep for a week.~

Tangel sent a supportive feeling into Jessica's mind, and then turned her full attention to the problem at hand.

"We're opening a rift," Rachel said, highlighting a point on the main holo. "Sending ARCs out on remote to draw them toward it."

"Okay," Tangel nodded. "Send out as many as it takes to make sure they're corralled. I don't want a single one of these things to get away."

"How are we going to stop them?" Rachel asked, gesturing at the origin point for the stream of Exdali. "There's no rift there…it's like they're just appearing out of thin air."

Tangel heaved a sigh. "They followed Jessica through a jump."

Rachel's eyes widened. "Shit! From Star City?"

"No, they ran into trouble before they got there."

<*You need to blow the gate on the other side,*> Bob said. <*Send an RM to hit it.*>

"We need to know where," Tangel replied, but before she could speak further, the secondary holotank switched to a view of the Perseus Arm.

<*Here.*> A location highlighted. <*Jump the RMs through the gates at Buffalo and destroy that one on the other side. We'll need to send ships to close the rift over there as well.*>

"Fun for later," Tangel said, thankful that the location Jessica had jumped from wasn't near any stars.

"Right," Rachel agreed. "I have a team putting mirrors on RMs. Should be ready to fire in thirty minutes."

Tangel nodded, turning back to the primary holotank, watching as several hundred remote-piloted ARCs began to shepherd the Exdali from their origin point to the rift they were being pushed into.

<*Admiral!*>

Carson reached out as she was sending orders to open a second rift closer to the origin point, so the things could be funneled into it with less trouble.

<*Sorry to steal your thunder, Admiral Carson,*> Tangel replied.

<*Stars, don't be sorry for coming. I was starting to worry we were going to lose Jessica.*>

She nodded, glad that the mystery of Jessica's

disappearance was at least partially solved. <*We would have been here sooner, but the first messages we received didn't make it seem like there was anything serious going on.*>

<*Pardon?*> Carson sputtered. <*Stars, Admiral. The message I sent was, 'Urgent! Exdali outbreak at Buffalo. Jessica in peril.'*>

"Shit," Tangel muttered. <*We got 'Minor incursion at Buffalo. Situation in hand.'*>

Carson sent a long groan, and Tangel shared his sentiment.

<*I know they have to parse the shorthand and manage the queuing manually,*> he said, <*but that seems like a pretty serious cock-up.*>

What's with all the cock references? Tangel wondered. <*Yeah, it does. Sera is at Khardine, I think I'll get her to investigate.*>

Twenty minutes later, the deck around her took on a lavender hue, and she turned to see Jessica approaching.

"Stars," Tangel whispered as they embraced. "I was really starting to worry about you. What happened out there?"

Jessica's lips quirked up into a smile. "Oh, I dunno. Got knocked out of a jump by Caretakers. I went head to head with one and beat it, we fou—"

"Whoa!" Tangel held up a hand. "You *what*?"

"Thought that might get your attention," Jessica said with a tired laugh. "I fought an ascended being and won. I think that makes me the first."

<*No. I beat you,*> Bob interjected.

"Oh?" Jessica looked up at the overhead. "When did you do it? I took my Caretaker out seven days ago."

<*Damn.*>

"Cary beats you both." Tangel shot the overhead a cool look. "I think she got hers a few hours before you did, Jessica."

"Seriously?" Dark purple brows lifted up her lavender forehead. "Cary?"

<*Myrrdan doesn't count. He was only semi-ascended. Besides, I killed Airtha.*>

"Holy shit!" Jessica exclaimed. "I get stuck in the middle of nowhere for a week, and everything goes *nuts*? And here I was all excited that I managed to capture mine."

"Hold up." Tangel placed a hand on Jessica's shoulder. "Captured? Alive?"

"Uh huh. My Marines are guarding it on my ship. Wasn't sure if you wanted it brought aboard—part of why I came up here."

"Part?" Tangel asked.

"Well, I wasn't just going to sit around doing nothing while you fixed my mistake."

Captain Rachel approached, shaking her head. "From what I overheard, you had some amazing successes, not mistakes, Admiral."

"Don't you call me that." Jessica grabbed Rachel and pulled her in for an embrace. "Stars, I still remember when you were on your first rotation. The *I2* couldn't ask for a better skipper."

"Sure, yeah, thanks for reminding my crew that I was knee-high to a grasshopper while you were helping train the first class at the Kap."

Despite her words, Rachel was grinning, and Tangel favored them both with a smile before turning back to the holotank.

"What I want to know," she said after staring at it for a minute, "…well, correction. *One* of the things I want to know is how the rift on the other side is staying open."

"Shit," Jessica muttered. "You're right. At first, I thought it was just because of the ones following us out of the rift before we jumped, but way too many are out now."

"Were there more ships that you escaped from?" Tangel asked.

"There were three. We captured one, and the Exdali destroyed the other two. We had to abandon our prize ship four days ago. I suppose something aboard it could have repaired, but all that was left were rudimentary automated systems. Not even a decent NSAI."

"A Caretaker ship?" Tangel shook her head in disbelief. "Talk about a jackpot."

"Still, it was nowhere near the final engagement," Jessica said. "There had to be another ship nearby. Maybe one stealthed. Who knows."

"Well, it's going to meet a few antimatter warheads if it's still there," Tangel said.

"I wonder why they don't do this all the time," Rachel mused as the march of Exdali continued on.

"Send Exdali at us through jump gates?" Tangel asked.

"Yeah."

Jessica shrugged. "Maybe I pissed them off enough to break a rule or something."

"Maybe we can ask the one you captured," Tangel said, checking on the Caretaker that Jessica had captured and noting that the Marines had brought it to the containment facility aboard the *I2* where the captured remnants were kept.

Jessica shook her head in response, swallowing before she said, "I don't think I want to talk to it. That's all on you, Tangel."

<Five minutes till the RMs are ready to launch,> Bob interjected. *<Volume of Exdali has picked up, as well.>*

"Noticed that," Tangel muttered. "I'm looking forward to learning why the Caretakers chose now to use this tactic."

"And let's hope that they don't alter their rules of engagement," Rachel added.

"Stars," Jessica whispered. "If they wanted to, they could wipe us all out doing this."

Tangel clenched her jaw, thinking about what possible defense they could muster against such an attack.

"I can only assume it's not in their best interest," Rachel said. "Maybe in doing so, they'd destroy the galaxy…or at least make it unusable for their purposes."

"Jump gates," Tangel muttered. "Best and worst thing ever. Right after dark layer FTL."

The other two women nodded, and none spoke, watching as Carson's fleet finally arrived and began patrolling nearby space, searching for any Exdali that may have escaped the cordon.

<*Ready to launch missiles,*> Bob announced.

"Fire when ready," Rachel said after getting a nod from Tangel.

"Stars, this sucks," Jessica muttered.

"How so?" Tangel asked. "Other than the obvious, of course."

"We're going to blow the gate, then have to go back and seal the rift and deploy another gate. Total waste."

"It's the Caretakers' fault, not yours," Rachel said. "I can't believe they set up out there waiting for you—I assume that's what happened."

Jessica nodded. "That's what the one I fought indicated."

On the main holodisplay, the view of local space showed six bright engine flares, temporary stars that shone in the darkness as the RMs sped toward the jump gates.

"We got interrupted before," Tangel said, turning from the display to Jessica. "How *did* you defeat an ascended AI? I've gone up against three, and the first two times, Bob had to save me."

<*In your defense, Xavia was* ***ancient****, and the other was Airtha.*>

"Stop interrupting, Bob," Tangel admonished, a slight laugh in her tone. "I want to hear from Jessica how she defeated the Caretaker."

<*She absorbed it.*>

"Bob!" Jessica exclaimed. "How did you guess?"

<*I understand very well how your body works. What you did was something I anticipated.*>

"How do you *know*, though?"

<*Because you confirmed it.*>

"I confirmed that I absorbed it, but that's hardly enough detail for you to have anticipated it. I could have done that thousands of ways."

<*No, not thousands.*>

"Bob, let her tell it," Tangel said, and the AI fell silent.

"Well," Jessica began, shooting a mock-angry look at the overhead. "I've directly absorbed electricity before, so when I came face to face with the Caretaker—after crashing an ARC into its ship—I decided to try to absorb it. It swung two of its arms at me, and I grabbed them. Then I just sort of sucked the power out. Once I was brimming with it, I blasted it back at the thing, slicing all its limbs off."

"Stars," Tangel muttered. "Remind me to be extra careful next time I hug you."

"I don't do it all the time," Jessica said. "It's not like absorbing light. Conscious effort is required."

Rachel snorted a too-loud laugh, earning her some curious looks from the bridge crew. "Sorry, I just had a funny thought."

"Share with the class," Jessica said.

"I was just thinking 'Ascended Problems'."

Tangel raised an eyebrow while Jessica shook her head.

"OK. It sounded funnier in my head," the captain said in a muted voice.

"Plus," Jessica held up a finger. "I'm not ascended."

The captain shrugged. "You may not be all transdimensional like Admiral Richards, but you're clearly at a higher level. That's ascend-y in my book."

"Missiles have reached the gates," Scan announced, and the three women turned their attention to the location where the Exdali were still appearing as though from nothing.

"We jumped them a hundred klicks from the ring, just to

be sure," Tangel informed the other two. "We should know in about five more seconds."

A single, slow breath later, the Exdali stopped appearing. It was almost as though a faucet had been turned off. The remaining trail of creatures continued to march toward the rift until the last one disappeared. Then Rachel nodded to one of the bridge officers, and the rift closed, sealing the strange creatures back in the dark layer.

Tangel dusted her hands off and grinned at Jessica. "OK, your mess is all cleaned up. Let's go talk to your prisoner."

Jessica blew out a long breath, nodding in silent relief.

"I guess I'll coordinate with Carson while you have all the fun," Rachel said.

"Privilege of rank," Jessica said with a wink.

"She's a rear admiral. Same rank as you," Tangel said, elbowing Jessica as the two women turned and walked across the bridge.

"So? Pretty sure I have seniority."

"Not time in grade," Tangel said.

"You want to make me angry?"

Tangel laughed as they walked off the bridge and into the corridor beyond. "Stars no. I think I'm still just reveling in the fact that you're back here with us."

"Well, I'm not going to be a permanent fixture. I still need to get to Star City."

"Of course," Tangel replied with a nod. "Maybe this time I'll come with you. Make sure you don't get lost on the way."

FATHER FIGURE

STELLAR DATE: 10.12.8949 (Adjusted Years)
LOCATION: Keren Station
REGION: Khardine System, Transcend Interstellar Alliance

"I don't know that I want to do this anymore."

Jeffrey Tomlinson's words stunned Sera. He had delivered them in such a weary tone and with so much remorse that she felt a pang of sorrow on his behalf.

She pursed her lips and rose from the sofa, walking across the small room to look out the window at Keren Station's gently rolling hills that appeared to undulate around the interior of its habitation cylinder.

He didn't speak as she stood for a minute, collecting her thoughts. When she finally turned and looked at the man who wore the face of her father, she still hadn't come up with anything cogent.

"I don't blame you," was all she could manage.

A look of understanding came over Jeffrey's face. "It's hard to reconcile me with *him*, isn't it?"

"It really is," Sera replied. "He was such an…asshole. You seem like a half-decent guy."

"Well, thanks for the 'half' at least," Jeffrey replied. "Finaeus would probably agree with you about my partial assholeishness."

"Sorry," Sera said in a quiet voice. "I thought this would get easier, but it really hasn't."

Jeffrey nodded. "You're telling me."

"Because I look like her?"

He nodded, and for a moment, Sera thought he would look away, but he straightened and maintained eye contact.

"You should know that you're the daughter I always

dreamt I'd have," he finally said.

The statement elicited a laugh from Sera, and she gestured to her red-skinned body, which currently had the look of a shipsuit.

"This is what you dreamt?"

"I don't care what you do with your looks," Jeffrey said, rising from the chair he sat in. "I care about your passion, your drive, and your honor. You've taken on so many difficult tasks, and they were all thrust upon you. You never complained, you just soldiered forward."

Sera snorted and shook her head. "Oh, just ask Tangel and Finaeus. I complained a lot."

"Well, that's not the story they tell."

"Then they're too kind…and liars."

"Probably." A corner of Jeffrey's lips turned up. "Finaeus always did like to bend the truth to suit himself."

Sera nodded wordlessly, staring into the eyes of the man she didn't know—yet did—as he looked back at her with a similar expression.

"So, what do you want to do?" she finally asked, thinking back to her conversation with Jason.

Everyone wanted out of the war, wanted out of the endless responsibility for the fate of humanity.

Jeffrey stepped up to the window and stared out into the settling dusk. "It's all just so different. Did you know that we thought that the FGT was just going to fracture when I…left? Everything was getting so big and far apart, communications took decades. I'd hoped that Kirkland wouldn't be able to maintain his myopic vision, and we could all just muddle along. Trust Finaeus to invent jump gates and turn all that on its head."

"So you'd *hoped* everything would fall apart?" Sera asked, mouth agape once the words tumbled out.

"Yes!" Jeffrey threw his arms in the air. "It's all too big, too hard to control. It would have been better if humanity could have just spread and spread and become disconnected."

"War would destroy a lot of that," Sera countered. "Like the dark ages. People just clawing at one another till there was nothing left."

"I guess it was stupid anyway. Now that I understand how the core AIs were manipulating everything, there was never any safety in general dispersal. They would have kept us at one another's throats even when it made no sense."

"Well, we're winning." Sera offered the words with the hope that the man before her would show some of the spirt she knew him for. "In a few years, it'll be over."

"No," Jeffrey shook his head. "Not until the core AIs are destroyed. Until then, we're all at their mercy."

"Agreed. Tangel intends to do just that, ultimately. There are plans underway."

"Like Finaeus's secret base in the galaxy's 3KPC arm?" Jeffrey's tone was derisive. "It's going to take a lot more than that."

"Oh, we know," Sera replied. "There are more facilities in the works, which you must know about by now. Don't be so argumentative."

"I suppose I saw something about them," he allowed. "It's a lot to absorb. You know…two weeks ago, there was no doubt in my mind that I wanted to carry on with my duties as president. So far as I was concerned, no time had passed, and in my mind, I was still the president. But…."

"But?" Sera pressed.

"But I'm not. That Transcend doesn't exist anymore. Back then, we were a loose conglomerate that supported the FGT's continuing mission. In addition, we were quietly working to rebuild the Inner Stars. We weren't this massive empire."

"Neither was Orion."

"They were closer to it than we were…I was proud of

that."

Sera turned and leant against the windowsill. "I can't imagine how it feels, coming back to see everything so different."

"That's just the thing." He continued staring out the window, not turning to look at her. "I didn't 'come back'. For me, this was the blink of an eye. Everything changed in an instant, and…."

Sera nodded. "And it's all insane, right?"

"That's putting it mildly." He turned and met her eyes, his filled with sorrow. "Yet…"

"Yet?" she prompted after he didn't continue speaking.

"We set all of this in motion," he finally said. "Set the stage for all of this."

Sera opened her mouth to respond, but he held up a hand to forestall her.

"I know what you're going to say." Jeffrey threw a hand in the air as he spoke. "Others have said it before. It all would have happened anyway, even if the two Tomlinson brothers hadn't come up with this crazy idea of 'Future Generation' terraforming. And maybe it would have. But *I* still had a hand in it…. A lot of the way things are is my fault."

As Sera listened, the man changed before her eyes. Gone was the father figure who had lorded over her for so long, a specter in her mind even after death. Instead, there stood a man like any other. Someone who wanted to do the right thing but was beginning to buckle under the weight of all his past mistakes.

She smiled. "As someone who has held the title you now bear, I can't level a single iota of judgment at you."

A look of sorrowful acceptance settled on Jeffrey's face. "I feel like such a failure. I all but demanded the presidency from you."

"No." She shook her head. "I all but pushed it on you."

"Funny how even with perfect recall, our recollections are so very different."

Sera nodded. "I've noticed that in life. So is that why you called me here? To ask me to take the presidency back? You know that I was transitioning it to Tangel even before we found you."

"I saw signs of that." He chuckled. "She had a better handle on things than I did, and she's only been aware of the Transcend for a few years."

"She's really good at figuring out what makes things tick."

"Still, we both know that our people need their own leader—just not me."

"Well, it's not me, either," Sera replied, feeling a sense of panic. Her sisters were in no condition to take over; she'd thought that her father would be her salvation.

The crushing weight of responsibility began to lever its way back onto her shoulders, and if it weren't for the presence of the man who wore her father's face, she would have let her tears flow.

Then he said something that completely surprised her.

"Of course not. It's clear you don't want it at all."

Her brow creased in frustration. "When has that mattered?"

"When has it not?" he countered.

Sera wanted to reply 'Always', but she knew it wasn't fair to berate Jeffrey for the sins of his clone.

Instead, she responded with a question of her own. "So if you don't want to run the Transcend, and you know I don't want to, then who? Finaeus would just disappear into the ether if we tried to foist the job on him."

"What about Andrea?" her father asked, his expression unreadable.

"Oh, fuck no!" Sera exclaimed. "I'd take over again before I let her ruin everything further."

Jeffrey's face fell, and she realized that he took 'further' as an accusation.

"You know what I mean," she grumbled.

He nodded. "Of course."

"OK, so now that you're done baiting me, who are you actually proposing?"

"What about your cousin, Krissy?"

Sera raised an eyebrow. "She wanted it, back when other you died. She only let me have it because I had Admiral Greer's and Tanis's backing."

"And now?"

"Maybe," Sera allowed. "I don't think she'd say no. What about Greer?"

Jeffrey laughed. "I've known Greer for a long time. He has zero political aspirations. The fact that you got him to take as large a role as you did was a miracle."

"Honestly…" Sera drew out the word. "I think some of that was Mother's doing. She maneuvered me into just the right spot to become the leader of the Transcend, with all the right people around me. If *Sabrina* hadn't appeared at the perfect time with Finaeus aboard…. Stars, who knows where we might be."

"Stars indeed," her father said. "OK, I'll talk to Krissy. I'm happy to stay on as an advisor, but…."

Sera reached out and took his hand, unable to remember the last time she'd touched her father outside of a handshake.

"We can plan later. For now, let's just take a breath," she suggested.

He nodded silently, and she gave him an encouraging smile.

Neither spoke as they turned back to the window, watching as dusk fell and lights came on across the inner surface of the habitation cylinder.

He's not my father, though I suppose that's one of the things that's helping.

PART 5 – COMMS

INTO THE MAW

STELLAR DATE: 10.12.8949 (Adjusted Years)
LOCATION: TSS *Cora's Triumph*
REGION: Interstellar Space, Inner Praesepe Empire

"So, what do you think?" Terrance asked Earnest as the engineer reviewed the readings.

"Only so much we can tell with passive systems," he said after a minute. "Logic dictates that there's got to be a planetary core down there, otherwise why have your drones all clustered like that?"

"Maybe it's convenient." Wyatt's tone suggested that it was exactly how he'd store his planet's worth of drones when he wasn't using them.

Terrance clenched his jaw, surprised at how difficult he found it to get along with the FGT scientist—which was saying something, considering that most of his life had been spent amongst engineers and researchers.

"Oh, I don't know," Emily, the FGT's stellar mechanics engineer, said. "Maybe because dumping them together like that creates a gravity well that later you'll have to propel them out of—not to mention that the ones in the center are constantly fighting against being crushed."

"And fuel, and repair," Terrance added.

"Not sure about that," Earnest said while continuing to stare at the readings. "If these drones are single-use, they won't need those things."

"Not very efficient," Wyatt muttered.

Terrance sighed. "We're not really here to determine if the core AIs could be more efficient."

"No, but it does help us learn more about them," Wyatt countered. "And we know damn little."

"More and more each day," Terrance said absently, doing his best not to engage.

"Hey, what's that?" Emily asked.

"Been wondering the same thing," Earnest replied. "A moonlet of some sort."

"Think it's command and control?" Terrance asked.

Earnest straightened and nodded. "There's low-level EM coming from it. More than any natural source suggests."

"Could be heavy in uraninite," the FGT scientist said.

"Sure," Earnest shot Wyatt a sour look. "Just a whole bunch of a useful volatile, right beside a planet's worth of drones—and they haven't tapped into it at all. I think that's exactly what's going on."

"Don't have to be an ass about it," Wyatt muttered, and Emily barked a laugh.

"I won't go so far as to use the word 'consensus', but have we reached something close to it?" Terrance asked. The others nodded, and he reached out to Captain Beatrice. <*Ma'am. Passing you the coordinates of a moonlet we'd like to take a gander at. The team here thinks it might be command and control for those drones.*>

<*Excellent,*> Beatrice replied. <*We'll lay in a course. It'll take about sixteen hours to get there.*>

"Sixteen hours," Terrance relayed. "I'm going to catch some sack."

"Wait," Wyatt raised a hand. "Sixteen hours till what? The TSF sends a fleet?"

"Wyatt," Emily whispered, a smirk on her lips. "This ship *is* the fleet. We're going in to take a closer look."

"I'm not front-line!" Wyatt proclaimed. "I demand that we return to Pyra, or somewhere else marginally civilized, so that me and my team can leave."

"Are you kidding?" Emily shook her head in disbelief. "This is the find of a lifetime, and you want to run away?"

Wyatt sniffed. "I'd prefer to call it a strategic relocation."

* * * * *

Nearly sixteen hours later, Terrance stood next to Captain Beatrice on the *Cora's Triumph*'s bridge, watching the moonlet grow larger on the forward display.

"Thought you'd be down with your team," the captain said with a smirk. "Get their observations firsthand."

"I'll get what I need up here," Terrance said with a quiet laugh. "Besides, for what we'll likely be doing next, your bridge crews will be running the sort of scan we need. Down there, they'll be…well, sometimes it's easy for folks to sink so deeply into their profession that they have trouble seeing things other than through its lens."

"I suspect that that happens to us all," Beatrice said.

"Sure," he nodded. "Just some worse than others."

"What of Earnest?"

A grin settled on Terrance's lips. "He's built up a special immunity over the years. He also enjoys needling fractious people."

"Nice to see that someone's getting some enjoyment out of it."

"Is the platoon ready?" he asked, changing the subject.

"Of course. They're itching for action," Beatrice replied. "We've been out here staring at stars a lot longer than anyone had expected."

"Spoiled," Terrance said with a laugh. "To think that this is 'long'."

"Don't pull that 'when I was your age' garbage with me, mister." The captain looked at him with a twinkle in her eye, and he wondered if she had some sort of double meaning in her words that he couldn't quite pick out. "Doesn't change what the soldiers expected to be doing."

"OK, you win," Terrance laughed, trying to keep the mood light.

"Then you'd best not besmirch their eagerness to be doing something important."

"Trust me," he said. "This is important."

"Sure," the captain nodded. "I get that, but they don't. They want to be making personal contributions."

"If there are some sort of hunter-killer bots in that C&C, they'll get to make those personal contributions before long." Terrance stopped short and shook his head. "Shit, that sounded more macabre than I meant."

"A little gallows humor before battle." The captain's tone carried that same note it had earlier, as though Terrance was missing some subtext that wasn't present in the words they were exchanging.

He glanced around the bridge, noting that the crew was focused on their tasks, though smiles had quirked the lips of a few.

"Are you sure you want to go down with the advance team?" Captain Beatrice asked after a moment. "I should add, is there anything I can do to convince you *not* to go?"

"Well, probably, but stopping me would require something rather extreme. I must admit, I'm not so different than your platoon of soldiers. I need to feel like I'm doing my part as well."

Especially since my actions set so much of this in motion.

"Hard to argue with that." The captain paused, turning to glance at Terrance. "Just keep your head down, sir. If you don't make it back, I might as well fall on my sword."

Terrance nodded, keeping his expression neutral.

He hated being someone else's baggage, but that wasn't going to stop him from getting involved. The core AIs had created a mystery, and that mystery had a plan. Though most of his life had been spent fighting corporate enemies, he'd negotiated with the business end of a rifle more than most people thought.

"Don't worry, I have a vested interest in making it back. And I know which end of the gun is the dangerous one."

"Weapon," the captain corrected with a smile. "My ship has guns, you'll be carrying a weapon."

Terrance flashed her a grin and slapped her on the shoulder. "I love you fleet types."

Captain Beatrice shot him a strange look as he walked away, and then called out, "I'm going to hold you to that."

"Sorry what?" Terrance turned and asked, picking up something unexpected in the woman's voice.

"That you're coming back," she said hastily, then added, "And that I'm not going to have to fall on my sword."

"Oh," Terrance said, nodding quickly. "Of course, you can count on it."

He left the bridge, wondering if the captain had been responding to his statement that he 'loved' fleet types. There was no arguing that Beatrice was a lovely woman.

She had a broader figure than women who normally caught his eye, but she had a grace to her movements that masked that well. That didn't bother him at all, especially because of the fiery intensity that lurked behind her almost blood-red eyes.

Though she always behaved with decorum, there was an intensity behind those eyes that spoke of a different side to the ship's captain.

Maybe I should see what that's all about, after this mission.

A few minutes later, he reached the platoon's sortie room

and shook hands with Lieutenant Jordan.

"Ready to kick some ass?" Terrance asked.

"Always, sir," the woman replied. "Though I suspect that there won't be any asses down there, just machines…so, heat vents? Servos? Not as inspiring."

Terrance snorted. "No, I suppose not. Let's be clear, though, there *will* be defenses, and they're not going to play nice, so we keep our eyes peeled and respond with maximum force to any threat."

"I like this guy!" one of the privates called out.

The lieutenant shot the woman a look, and then gestured to the armor rack as she settled her attention back on Terrance. "You familiar with our gear, sir?"

"I did a test fit a day ago," Terrance replied. "Got my preferred loadout set up and then ran some sims. I think I'm good to go."

The lieutenant gave him a look of respect. "Glad to hear it, sir. Your public profile says you've seen combat before, though not where."

"Well, I saw some back on Carthage when the Trissies landed their ships. Urban stuff in Landfall. Before that, it had been some time, unless you count that brief scuffle in the Kap. But yeah, I've fought on just about every type of terrain and theatre you can imagine."

"Alice," one of the sergeants called out, nodding to a private checking her loadout nearby. "Maybe you should pay attention to what Mister Enfield does. Could learn a thing or two."

"Sure thing, Sarge. Never learned much watching you," Alice replied, laughing until the sergeant walked over to her and whispered something in her ear that made her face grow pale.

"Good crew you have here," Terrance said as he backed up to the armor rack and closed his eyes as it began to wrap him in the TSF's mid-weight assault buildout.

He knew they wouldn't use him for any scouting, and he hated the way heavy armor restricted movement. The Transcend's assault armor suited him best.

Doesn't hurt that it also comes with a shoulder mounted railgun.

"Sir." One of the soldiers walked up to Terrance as he stepped off the rack. "I'll just check over your loadout and seals."

"Of course," Terrance said, holding out his arms. "Specialist Larson, you're the TSF's breach AI on this mission?"

"Yes I am, sir. I've gone up against some of the best out there, but never against core AI tech. Earnest has loaded me up with more breach routines than I thought existed. I'm ready to take them down." She turned her head, nodding in the direction of another figure further back in the sortie room. "However, I'm not primary on this mission. An ISF pinnace arrived a few hours ago with Commander Sue aboard."

"Sue!" Terrance exclaimed aloud, craning his neck around as he looked for her.

The utterance caught her attention, and the AI strolled over, the ISF frame's design standing out in stark contrast to the TSF soldier's armor.

"Good to see you, sir," the AI replied. "I was wondering when you were going to realize I was aboard."

"You came with the supply pinnace?" he asked.

"Yeah, a few hours ago. I didn't mean to hide from you, but you were getting your beauty rest. Then Earnest accosted me and began loading me up with data and new techniques along with Specialist Larson, here."

Terrance couldn't help himself and reached out to embrace the AI, not caring that their armor clacked loudly—or that she was an AI and an embrace didn't mean as much to her.

"Stars, you know, I haven't seen you since a year after

Carthage landfall."

"I know...I took a lot longer to recover from losing Trist than I expected. And then when Jessica disappeared...well, I lost *myself* in my work, out at New Canaan's heliopause."

"No blame here, Sue," Terrance replied. "We all had a lot of personal rebuilding to do once we got to Canaan."

"OK, let's not delve too deep into the past," Sue said, taking a step back, her helmeted head cocking to the side as she regarded him. "I know how you organics get all mushy."

Terrance nodded. "Too much in the past to think about right before a mission. There's a whole future to worry about, and we can actually do something about that."

"Good attitude," Specialist Larson said.

"OK, you louts!" Lieutenant Jordan shouted a moment later, drawing everyone's attention to herself. "Scan's just updated our tactical net with the latest surface visuals. This moon's just a little bitty rock. Less than five percent standard gravity. Don't go bounding and banging. Maglocks on if they work, controlled and tactical."

"I love to go banging!" the same private who had made the prior colorful comment called out.

"Stow it, Flo," Jordan shouted. "Don't forget, we have guests, so let's try to look like a professional unit out there. You all wanted to see some shit, and this is going to be it. These AIs we're going up against probably know every trick in the book, but that's why we have some oldies but goodies with us.

"I have operational command of this mission," the lieutenant continued. "But if Commander Sue or Mister Enfield says something, you *listen*. They've seen more shit than you've ever imagined."

"I can imagine a lot of—" Flo began, but a hand came out of the crowd and slapped her in the back of the head, shutting her up.

Jordan gave a thankful nod to the sure-handed sergeant. "Scan's picked up the source of EM coming from the moon. It's centered in a crater near the equator. We're going to come in low and settle down in the lee of its rim. We've got two birds as our chariots today, so first and second squads are with me, as are Mister Enfield and Commander Sue. Third and Fourth, you're with Staff Sergeant Yens and Specialist Larson."

The lieutenant paused, pulling her helmet from under her arm as her head swiveled from side to side, surveying her troops.

"OK, then, you fantastic assholes.... Let's go take these core AIs down a notch!"

She pulled her helmet onto her head as the TSF soldiers shouted 'Roo-AH!' and then filed out of the sortie room, double-timing it toward the drop bay.

Terrance followed the last squad, with Sue and the lieutenant following behind.

The shock of seeing Sue again after so many years was wearing off, and he wanted to ask her why she'd given up starship command for tactical operations—especially with how short the ISF was on experienced starship commanders.

Save it, Terrance. Give yourself something to look forward to.

On the way to the drop bay, he reviewed the latest scan data on the crater and the anticipated defenses. It was all but raw speculation. Neither the ISF or TSF had ever encountered a core AI facility—if that's what this was. There was a possibility that it had been left by someone else in the past, or that perhaps it wasn't even Terran in origin.

However, the presence of core AI remnants in the IPE made the final two options far less likely. He fervently hoped that the facility they were going to was fully automated, though each fireteam had a shadowtron on the chance it wasn't.

The two stealth shuttles hunkered in the bay, their surfaces designed with configurable angles to alter their profile and reflect away any active scan systems. Not that the ultra-black, Elastene-like material was likely to reflect much of anything.

It still gave him a sense of pride to know that nearly every stealth system in the galaxy utilized essentially the same technology that his own research team back on Alpha Centauri had pioneered in the thirty-first century.

At the same time, it brought him a little sadness. Of all the people he had set out with, traveling from Alpha Centauri to other near-Sol colonies, only Jason Andrews was still alive. It made so many of their daily experiences bittersweet.

"Shuttle two," Lieutenant Jordan directed, and Terrance followed her, Sue taking up the rear.

Inside was a standard troop bay, spare and utilitarian, with two rows of dampening seats that could also form a full pod to seal the soldier up for an emergency eject. It was such a logical system, he was surprised more dropships didn't utilize it. Bring the squad down as one unit, fake out the enemy, and turn them into helljumpers.

His seat was in the middle of the right row, and he settled into it, leaning back to let the straps and bands wrap around him.

"How many drops you been on, sir?" a corporal across the aisle asked.

Terrance glanced at the man and shrugged. "More than a few hot drops into active combat."

"Where at?" a private asked.

"Well, my first planetary drop was in Tau Ceti. I hit dirt on Galene and joined up with their Marines to stop…well, an insurrection, I suppose."

The question was innocuous, but the answer brought back memories of Khela and how they'd met, before spending long years together. Which led to how they'd separated and the shame he still felt from it.

Funny how shame seems to stack up.

"Stop bugging our guest," one of the squad sergeants said, and Terrance was grateful for the reprieve.

He took a moment to review the personnel on the two squads, and then leant back in his seat, closing his eyes.

As the shuttle took off, he began to run through a series of breathing exercises, knowing that, from now until they touched down, everything was out of his hands. It was a calm feeling, and one that he endeavored to maintain as long as possible.

That ended up being just over thirty minutes. Then the shuttle exploded.

BOTTLED MESSAGE

STELLAR DATE: 10.12.8949 (Adjusted Years)
LOCATION: IS shuttle approaching Normandy
REGION: Khardine System, Transcend Interstellar Alliance

Sera turned her head to look across the small pinnace's cockpit at Jason as he piloted the craft toward the small moon named Norway. He spotted her surreptitious look and flashed her a grin in response.

She smiled back, unable to ignore how happy he always was when flying a ship. There was a special crinkle in the corner of his eyes that only showed up when at the helm…or stick, depending on what he was flying.

She craned her neck a bit further, nodding to Roxy, who sat behind Jason, while Jane rode in the seat behind Sera.

At first, Sera had planned to go down to the moon alone with Jason, but after Roxy had officially taken on the assistant director's role in the Hand, she had all but insisted she come along to see what was going on with the QuanComm messages being altered.

Sera couldn't very well say she wanted alone time with her beau, so she had acquiesced.

"Nervous?" Jason asked as he looked over his display, reviewing the craft's status.

"Me?" Sera snorted. "We're going to check out an anomaly at a glorified comm shack. What's there to be nervous about?"

The governor shrugged, a boyish gesture that seemed at odds with the grey-haired senior captain she'd first met on the *Intrepid* years ago.

A part of her missed his statelier look, but she understood that availing himself of rejuv so that he could handle the demands of office was wise. He'd also assured her that he'd get old again, adding in one of his saucy winks.

"Beats me, you're the one that's fidgeting like there's nothing else to do."

"That's because there *is* nothing else to do," Sera muttered. "Stealth approach to this place means that I'm stuck inside my own head, and this ship is stripped down so much, it barely has an onboard logging comp."

<*You have a thousand reports that need your attention, and they're all in your head,*> Jen suggested over the shipnet.

"Right, because that's what I *love* to do for fun," Sera drawled.

<*I kinda like doing reports,*> Carmen said. <*There's something soothing about them.*>

<*Don't you dare give her any ideas,*> Jen retorted. <*I won't have my human getting soft and lazy.*>

"*Your* human?" Sera's brows rose in mock outrage, and she caught sight of Jason covering his mouth to laugh. "Oh, is it funny, mister?"

"No," Jason shook his head. "Just reminds me about something that an old friend used to say."

She was going to ask him for details, but his expression grew clouded, and he busied himself with the ship's navigation console.

<*You call me* ***your*** *AI sometimes, Sera.*>

"Do I?" she asked. "Sorry, I guess that's an unintentional slip-up. I think it's like saying 'my friend', but since you're inside my head, it helps to identify our relationship."

<*Right, but just to make sure that you don't get confused about our relationship, I'm not helping with reports.*>

"I've never asked you to," Sera said, an annoyed breath blasting out her nostrils.

<*You've asked for help.*>

"That's different! I didn't ask you to do them for me, just help with research and analysis!"

"See?" Jason asked, reaching over and placing a hand on Sera's thigh. "You're a bit on-edge."

The two women in the seats behind had fallen silent and still. Their reaction made her angry for an instant, but then she took a deep breath and reminded herself that everyone had pressure, and that they were all dealing with more shit than most people could imagine. No one needed her losing it and making things worse.

"My father wants to relinquish his presidency, which may come back to me," she explained after a minute of silence. "Though he understands I don't want it. He suggested Krissy, but after thinking about it, I'm not totally sure she'd take it, or that it would be wise, given her duties and the work she already has to do."

"Ahhh." Jason pursed his lips, angling the pinnace toward the small moonlet and entering into a holtzman transfer orbit.

"Just 'ahhh'?" she asked.

"Well, I mean…you can't make someone be in charge who *really* doesn't want to. It's not a great idea to force them to, either."

"That's how *I* feel."

"I know, I was referring to you, Sera." Jason gave her a kind look, and she felt even worse for having snapped at him.

"Oh, sorry."

"I know it doesn't help with your family problem," Roxy said a minute later. "But feel free to pass me any reports you'd like. I don't mind, and I like to stay busy."

"You sure?" Sera asked, turning in her seat to meet the azure woman's eyes. "I mean, I already pushed a lot onto you."

"I can handle it. I've spent a lot of time being…disregarded. I want to step forward again."

"I get that," Sera replied. "OK, you asked for it. Here comes the motherlode."

Roxy was silent for a moment, then exclaimed, "Has Petra lost her mind?!"

Sera knew exactly what her assistant director was referring to and laughed, shaking her head. "Petra gets results. I give her free reign as much as possible."

"Probably because she's only quasi-Hand now anyway."

"That too, but she's loyal nonetheless."

"So glad that my problems are limited to New Canaan, more or less," Jason said as he brought the ship down to a lower orbit.

"I thought Tangel reported to you?" Roxy asked. "Doesn't that kind of make the whole galaxy your problem?"

Jason barked a laugh. "And the less I think of it like that, the happier I am. Seriously, though. Tangel doesn't 'report' to me so much as she just lets me know what she's up to. If I have suggestions, she listens to them, but unless it's an outflow of something Parliament decides, I don't pass her any directives at all."

"How are the people of New Canaan handling all this?" Sera asked.

"Better than I would have expected," he replied. "Half the population is directly involved in the war effort now. The other half now supporting the first half. A quarter of our population is outsystem, crewing warships, and the AIs are breeding as fast as they can to bolster the population and fill as many gaps as they can."

Sera gave a rueful laugh. "Good thing the colonists breed like rabbits."

"There are downsides to that as well. It's stifling the birth rate right now. Just about everyone has sent kids off to war, and no one is too excited about having more just to send them away."

"The war will be over by then," Sera said, knowing it wasn't exactly true.

Jason shook his head. "This war is like a wildfire. Sure, we can put out the cause of the blaze, but it's already spreading. There are tens of millions of systems out there, and the instability this conflict has caused is going to last for decades…maybe centuries."

Sera knew he was right, and only nodded, trying to think of something to say.

After a minute, Jason continued. "My only hope is that once we stop Orion, Terra, and the Trisilieds, we can leave the rest of things to people with more resources. Get back to the life we all hoped to live."

Sera nodded mutely, knowing that, to an extent, Jason's hope was a vain one. The battle the people of New Canaan would have to fight *after* the war would be far more difficult than the one they were fighting at present.

Despite their desire to 'get away' and build a quiet colony, their time away from Sol had been anything but. Many of them would have a hard time reintegrating…or they just might not want to return.

Healing New Canaan would take a lot longer than building it had.

"I hope everyone gets that," she finally said.

"Not me," Roxy chimed in. "I've got a decent amount of anger that still needs to be taken out on the asshats of the galaxy. Be a long time before I settle down."

<*I don't know that that is the healthiest of attitudes,*> Carmen said.

"Oh, it's not," Roxy nodded emphatically. "Which is why I have to expunge it from myself with force."

<*Uhhhhhh….*> Carmen's tone was laden with uncertainty.

"I'm kidding!" Roxy said with a self-deprecating laugh. "Mostly. I'm talking to a fleet psychiatrist…well, a team of them. I know I can't do this alone, but I'm also not going to tell myself that I can go back to some sense of normalcy anytime soon. I need to see if I can get myself back to who I used to be before I look toward becoming something else." She shook her head, a look of consternation settling on her face. "Stars, that makes no sense at all."

Sera gave a rueful laugh, having no idea if that was the best course of action. She couldn't offer any advice, though, since she had no idea what she'd do in Roxy's shoes. The fact that the woman was functional at all was a miracle.

"Sheesh," Jason muttered, giving Sera a sidelong glance and a wink. "This was supposed to be the fun, 'get away from my troubles' trip. I should have gone to the Trisilieds with Cheeky and Sabrina."

"You gonna two-time on me with them?" Sera squeaked in mock indignation.

"More like double-time," Jason chuckled.

Sera groaned and gestured to the holo. "Don't you have something important to do here, like concentrate on flying?"

"I could do this while playing three games of Snark at once," he replied. "Eyes closed and hands behind my back."

"Showoff."

They rode the final minutes in silence, finally slipping into a deep crevasse on the moon's surface before coming down to a hidden docking bay tucked under an overhang.

"OK," Sera said as the pinnace settled onto the cradle. "Remember, this is just a routine visit. I'm here to chat with Colonel Rutger, and you two are doing an inspection of the logs for recent operations to make sure that nothing was sent in the clear that shouldn't have been."

"Easy," Roxy replied. "We'll just yank more than we need and see what we can see about Carson's messages."

"And I'm just your arm candy," Jason said with a laugh as the docking clamps locked onto the ship, and he rose carefully in the low gravity. "Stars, been a while since I've been in partial gravity. Spoiled by a-grav everywhere these days."

"Well, if anyone can get their space legs back, it's you," Sera said, nudging him with her elbow. "None of us were born before it existed."

"You calling me old?" he asked.

"Uh huh."

A minute later, they were out on the dock, where Colonel Rutger and two majors were waiting.

The moment Sera stepped onto the deck, he strode forward, his hand extended and a smile on his lips.

"Director Sera, so very good to see you. It's unexpected to have our little outpost visited by someone such as yourself."

She shook her head while shaking his hand. "Don't downplay with me, Colonel. You run one of the most important facilities in the galaxy. My father just wanted me to swing by and have a chat with you. Make sure your needs are being met and that there's not something we can do that's not in the official reports."

The colonel nodded. "Of course, Director. I can think of a few things that could improve our operation."

"Excellent," Sera replied, turning to Jason. "I assume you know Jason Andrews, New Canaan's governor. He was at Khardine and decided to come along to see the good use we're putting their technology to—and to verify that we're safeguarding it appropriately."

A look of worry came across Colonel Rutger's face, and Sera wondered if it was concern over scrutiny in general, or if he had something to hide.

<*I think he just likes the autonomy he's had here,*> Jen commented. <*He's the ruler of a pretty important roost.*>

<*That he is. In all honesty, I should have visited sooner.*>

<*You delegated to General Greer. That was the right thing to do.*>

Sera gave a mental laugh. <*Always with the logic, Jen.*>

<*That's my job.*>

During her brief exchange with Jen, Colonel Rutger had

introduced himself to Jason and then turned to the two majors.

"This is Major Belos and Major Lorne. They both share responsibility for message delivery, and also take shifts at the boards."

"Really?" Roxy asked from where she stood on Sera's left. "That's surprising."

"This is Assistant Director Roxy, and Commander Jane," Sera said, then gestured for Roxy to continue as the colonel nodded in greeting.

"Well, I just would have expected that we could staff you with enough people that your senior leadership didn't have to work the boards."

"I mandate it." Rutger inclined his head. "I feel that it's good for everyone to see firsthand what comes through, and to understand the underlying urgency that is at play."

"Seems reasonable," Sera said.

"Thank you," the colonel said, his tone not giving away whether or not he cared for her approval. "I'll show you to my office, Director. I assume you're joining us, Governor Andrews?"

"I am," Jason replied.

"Excellent." Colonel Rutger gestured toward the bay's doors. "Major Belos will take the assistant director and commander on their tour. Lorne, you may return to your duties."

"Sir," Lorne acknowledged before turning and leaving the bay.

Belos gestured for Roxy and Jane to follow, leading them toward an exit on their right, while the colonel directed Sera and Jason to the left.

A tingle ran up Sera's spine as the group broke up. After spending so long with her High Guard shadowing her every move, she felt strangely vulnerable. The feeling was incongruous with the fact that she was in one of the most secure facilities in the Transcend.

The concern was assuaged by the fact that Jason's cruiser was nearby, cloaked with a platoon of ISF Marines ready to drop at a moment's notice.

Still, I'd feel a lot better knowing that Major Valerie was still with me. But she's watching over my father now.

A strange feeling of jealousy hit Sera, and she shook her head.

<*You seem out of sorts today, Sera,*> Jen said.

<*There has been so much change,*> she replied. <*Ever since Tangel ascended on Pyra, everything has accelerated so much. If I start rattling off the list, it'll take all day. I just need to focus on what's in front of me for a bit.*>

<*Which is Jason's ass right now.*>

Jason was walking alongside the colonel, and in her musing, Sera had fallen a step behind, her unfocused gaze aimed at the governor's rear.

<*Not a bad thing to focus on,*> she mused.

<*I really can't say. Well, I guess I can. Statistically, people prefer certain physical configurations, and Jason fits a desirable profile.*>

<*You can't apply statistics to what's attractive to other people,*> Sera chided the AI.

<*Of course you can. You're just not sophisticated enough.*>

<*You know what they say about statistics…*> Sera said.

<*That it's the only way to measure the state of the galaxy?*>

<*Funny.*>

Sera tuned in to the conversation between Jason and the colonel, continuing to hang back and focus on what the man had to say—and didn't say.

"A new shipment of blades just came in," Colonel Rutger was explaining. "That always steps things up a notch. We have to run tests on them all, and then begin the confirmation process that the paired blades have gone to the right place."

"Takes a while, I assume?" Jason asked.

"Core, you have no idea." Colonel Rutger shook his head. "There are blades from the second shipment still in the confirmation process."

"Really?" The governor tilted his head and cocked an eyebrow. "But that shipment came in well over a year ago."

"It sure did. But here's the thing: ships with gate mirrors are at a premium. So if we need to get a blade to a remote system, we jump it out to a location with a return gate, and from there, it transfers to a ship that takes it via dark layer FTL to the destination. Some of the blades have had to pass through two or three couriers before they get to their final istallations."

"I can see how that would take a while," Jason said, glancing back at Sera.

"Then there's the confirmation process," she added. "Some of these blades are going to places that had no prior knowledge of the unveiling and the war. They have no way to verify identity or allegiance directly over the QC network, so it needs to pass back through the courier network to get here."

"Exactly," Rutger said. "Because of that, we have an entire reliability system that gets assigned to blades."

"As in, how certain you are that you're talking with who you expect to?" Jason asked.

The colonel nodded. "Yes. For example, ISF ships that receive their blades in New Canaan construction yards have the highest reliability rating—well, next to the blades on I-Class ships. Blades out in the fringes of the Hand's network have the least. Certain broadcast messages don't filter down through all the reliability levels because we have to assume that somewhere, someone who shouldn't be is on the receiving end of a QC blade."

"We burn out more blades with reverifications," Sera muttered. "I sure wish they had more longevity."

Jason laughed. "I'll consult physics and see if we can get it to make an exception for us."

Sera reached out and gave the governor a two-fingered poke in the shoulder. "Earnest bends them enough. I bet they have a pre-existing exception built in for him."

"I catch a lot of grief from remote commanders over how brief we have to be on the network, but everyone gets that it's our number one advantage right now. So many of our major strikes wouldn't have been remotely possible without the network."

As the colonel spoke, they came to an observation window that looked out over a vast cave filled with small, standalone rooms.

"This, Director and Governor, is what I like to think of as the heart of the Alliance."

The man's voice was filled with pride, and Sera didn't want to debate with him over semantics. At the very least, it was *a* heart, but she was certain that the true heart of the Scipio Alliance was the *I2*.

Jason must have been on a similar train of thought, as he said, "Well, there's a significant secondary hub in the *I2*, but I get your meaning."

The colonel gave an almost sheepish smile. "We labor long hours deep in this rock, Governor—grant us this one bit of hubris."

A loud laugh burst from Jason, and he slapped the colonel on the back. "Very well, I'll allow it."

* * * * *

Roxy and Jane shared a look as they followed Major Belos on their tour of the facility.

<*Not one to waste words, is he?*> Jane said, a note of humor carrying over with her statement. <*Like…he has a daily quota of five, and he's already used three.*>

<*Well, that should make our part go fast. No blah-blah-blah,*> Roxy replied.

<*Is fast the goal?*> Carmen asked. <*Don't we want to draw things out? Get him to slip up?*>

<*That's what I would have thought as well,*> Jane added.

Roxy held back a laugh. <*Oh, I expect him to slip up, but not verbally. It's going to be in the records. Once I dive into those, I'll see what's what. Hence my desire to get this dog and pony show over with.*>

"Blade Node Two," Major Belos announced tonelessly as he reached a sealed portal. It was guarded by two soldiers, an AI in a warframe, and several drones.

"Excellent," Roxy replied. "Let's have a look."

It took a minute for everyone to pass their tokens and get through the auth system to satisfy the guards that they were who they said they were.

Jane's presence threw up some red flags, as the base systems listed her as AWOL with suspicion of being a part of Justin's faction.

A near-imperceptible shift in the guards' posture occurred when that information came back, but after a call to the colonel cleared things up, they relaxed a hair and opened the portal.

"And here we are," Belos announced when they entered the circular room.

Roxy gauged the space to be just about thirty meters across, containing several dozen three-meter-high towers that contained the QC blades.

"As you can see," the major gestured to the blade towers and the conduits feeding into them, "each tower has independent cooling and power supply. Several redundant systems ensure that it would take a chain reaction of very unlikely events—or a deliberate attack—to damage the towers."

<*He went way over five words there,*> Carmen commented.

<*You owe me ten creds, Jane.*>

<*Yeah. That's more than he's said since we left the bay. Who knew he had it in him?*>

"That's great, Major," Roxy said. "But we're less interested in the physical powering of the blades and more interested in the logging facilities. As you know, the devil is in the details, and the detail that worries us is the inconsistent shorthand people use over the QuanComm network."

"You're referring to how it requires people to translate the messages and then pass them on," Belos replied. "There are primary and secondary teams that check all the messages to make sure no meaning was lost. Would you like to see them in action?"

"That's real-time quality assurance," Roxy said. "What about tertiary review? Who watches the watchers?"

"Everything is logged, of course," Belos said, his brow lowering in annoyance. "Messages in and out. Messages that are delivered to a recipient directly aren't translated, they just get slated for passthrough, so those are linked and checked roughly fifteen minutes later, depending on volume."

"Sounds reasonable," Roxy replied. "I'd like to view the reports on their corrections and error rates. Are the logs for each node stored with it? Or are they maintained elsewhere?"

"Since passthrough can utilize more than one node, they're stored in a separate data facility."

<*Did you get a tap in?*> Roxy asked Carmen before they turned to leave. <*This analysis only works if we can watch real-time communication and then compare it with the quality control process to see if there are issues.*>

<*You don't need to tell me that,*> Carmen added a note of annoyance. <*It's done.*>

"Yes, Major, we'd very much like to see that," Roxy said brightly.

Belos led them out of the room and back down the passage,

taking them through a long stretch of warren-like tunnels within the moon, until they came to another guarded portal.

This one was protected by an entire squad of soldiers, which made sense to Roxy, given that the entire repository of QuanComm communication was stored there—excepting what went through the *I2* and New Canaan hubs.

Once again, Jane's prior status threw red flags, and the lieutenant commanding the detail ran it up the chain to Colonel Rutger for the second time.

While Belos hadn't been perturbed during the prior delay, this one seemed to bother him. He made a few snippy comments at the lieutenant, who bore the major's ire with good grace.

Finally, all the approvals were logged, and the group was allowed access to the datastore.

They stepped through the door and into a small room with a window on the far side. Roxy walked toward it and saw a large, spherical chamber lined with data towers. The readouts on the window indicated that the interior of the room was vacuum and only a fraction of a kelvin above absolute zero.

On either side of the room they stood in, doors led to a ring of offices where teams reviewed the messages and ensured that they had been properly managed.

"Impressive," Roxy said. "We're, what, four hundred kilometers below Norway's surface now?"

"Yes," Major Belos replied.

<*There we are, back to single, monosyllabic words,*> Jane said, her chuckle filling their minds.

<*Something seems off about Belos,*> Roxy said as she regarded the major silently. <*He knows what I want, but he's making me ask for it every step of the way.*>

"I assume I'll need to review via a secure console?" Roxy asked Belos, and the major nodded.

He led them through a door on the left and past several

offices until they came to an empty one. Within, a console waited, and the major entered his authentication codes before stepping aside for Roxy to sit down.

<Tempted to drop some nano on the major,> Carmen said. *<He's just…weird.>*

<You can't breach someone's privacy because they're weird,> Roxy said as she began to sift through the high-level reports the console showed.

She pulled up a number of messages that had been flagged as erroneous, looking over the issues found. At the same time, she tapped into the console directly and pulled up the real-time translations going on for Blade Node 2.

She knew it would take some time for those messages to reach quality control, and she glanced at the major.

"I'll be at this for a few hours. You don't have to wait here," she told him.

"I believe I do, ma'am."

"Major Belos, I'm the assistant director of the Hand. I don't need a babysitter."

<Oh, I saw his mouth open,> Jane commented. *<He was going to say '**acting** assistant director'. I'd put money on it.>*

<You put money on almost everything,> Carmen said.

<True. Your point being?>

While the other two bantered, Roxy contacted Sera, who asked the colonel to inform the major that he was allowed to leave.

A few moments later, Belos gave Roxy a sour look and then shrugged. "Very well. Let me know if you need anything."

After he left the room, Jane rolled her eyes. "We don't, but you could really use a personality transplant, buddy."

"Be nice," Roxy said as she flipped through the console's logs.

"You don't like me because I'm nice," Jane countered, and Roxy only laughed.

She was focused on hunting down the messages from Admiral Carson that Tangel had requested Sera to look into. It took a few minutes, but she found the source messages and the versions that had passed through to Tangel.

"You know…" she mused. "It's odd that these messages relayed through Khardine at all. Carson should have had a direct connection to the *I2*."

"Maybe he burned out those blades," Jane suggested. "They seem pretty fragile."

"That they do," Roxy muttered. "The other thing is that these messages were processed rather than being passed straight through. That's how the verbiage got messed up."

"So the messages were reworded when they shouldn't have been *and* that rewording downplayed the threat?" Jane asked.

"Seems that way."

<*You'd think their vaunted QA process would have picked it up,*> Carmen said.

"Well that's interesting," Roxy shook her head, flipping through more logs. "Major Belos himself flagged the error, but because he did it right as the message was passed to QA, it fell into some sort of loop, bouncing between the two systems."

<*Convenient.*>

"Took the words right out of my mouth," Jane said.

"Well, it *seems* like Belos did the right thing." Roxy said while continuing to search for the messages from Earnest and Terrance that had troubled Tangel and Sera.

Given that the two New Canaanites were traveling on Transcend ships, it wasn't as strange that their messages were being routed through the facility.

"Going to have to give the major a cookie," Jane chuckled. "One with little letters all over it to help him make it through the day."

Roxy snorted, then raised her eyebrows as she looked over

the messages from Terrance Enfield regarding the core AI facility in the IPE. "These things have pretty much gone through an identical cock-up."

"Misinterpreted and then stuck in limbo?" Jane asked.

"Yup. And it should come as no surprise to you that the good Major Belos has his fingerprints all over these, too."

<*So what's the plan?*>

"We catch him with his hand in the cookie jar," Roxy replied.

Jane frowned. "A cookie what?"

"Jar. You know…tall, made of plas or glass, round."

"I've had a lot of cookies that came out of boxes, or some sort of plas package, but I've never heard of cookies coming out of a jar." She reached out and tapped Roxy's head. "Did something get mixed up in there when your memories came back?"

Jane appeared legitimately concerned, and Roxy shook her head and groaned.

"Red-handed. How about that?"

"Ohhhh…you mean 'catch him in the act'. Why didn't you just say so?"

"Carmen, why did we decide to saddle ourselves with this comedian?"

<*I can't say, on grounds that I might perjure myself.*>

Jane folded her arms across her chest. "Wow. I see how it is."

Roxy winked at her and then leant back in the chair, interlacing her fingers behind her neck. "OK, so here's what we're going to do…."

Ten minutes later, they were ready.

The plan required routing a message through a blade node that Belos wouldn't be monitoring and then have it come back through one he did.

During her brief stay on Styx-9, Roxy had befriended one

of the comm techs, and sent him a brief message that they needed to route a test-drill message through the hub and out to Tangel aboard the *I2*.

She'd included a word in the message that, should it make it through, would clue Tangel in that it was just a test.

"OK, here goes," Roxy said, and sent the message out to Styx-9.

[Rte Tangel I2. *Immanent danger in gate array, grav anomalies in system primary.]*

"Think using 'immanent' instead of 'imminent' is enough?" Jane asked.

"If it makes it through, it will be," Roxy said. "Tangel, Sera, and I had a rather amusing conversation about people mixing those words up. I think it will clue her in that she at least won't need to jump to Styx and deal with an emergency."

"You hope."

Roxy shrugged sheepishly. "Well, at least there's already an I-Class gate there."

A minute later, they saw the message pass through Blade Node 2, where it triggered a severity alert, and escalated to Major Belos.

They didn't have taps into the system that would tell them who had made the change, but when the message was relayed out to the *I2*, it read:

[Rte I2. *Immanent secondary gate array anomaly. System primary stable.]*

"Well, as nefarious as he is, Belos doesn't bother to look up words." Roxy chuckled and glanced at Jane, who shrugged.

"Or it makes it less 'imminent', so he left it in."

<And there we are,> Carmen noted. *<His change triggered the*

glitch where the message is looping between himself and quality assurance.>

Roxy rose and gave Jane a knowing look. "Things are about to get fun."

The other woman rolled her eyes. "Great, it's been a whole three days since I've been in a pitched firefight. Stars forbid we relax or anything."

"Exactly." Roxy clapped a hand on Jane's shoulder. *<Sera, we think we've found our problem. It's Major Belos. He's been altering messages and then exploiting a bug in the system to keep them from reaching the QA teams.>*

<Well isn't that interesting. Glad you finally found something. I was running out of things to talk about with Colonel Rutger. The man is loyal, from what I can tell. He's a good fit for this assignment, but stars…a stellar conversationalist he is not.>

Sera sent a look of consternation along with her words, and Roxy was glad she'd gotten the more interesting part of the mission.

<So what's our play?> she asked. *<Do we just go arrest him at his desk?>*

<No, I can see where he's situated down there on the floor. Too many people around. We need to get him somewhere we can control,> Sera decided.

<What if we just request that he escort us back to the docking bay and you meet us there?> Roxy asked. *<Place him under arrest and dump him in the pinnace.>*

Sera fell silent for a few moments. *<Probably our best bet. However, we have to assume the worst.>*

<That being?>

<That Belos has a shard in him.>

Roxy chuckled. *<Oh…I thought that maybe he's your sister Andrea in disguise or something.>*

<Stars, that ***would*** *be bad. OK, I'm going to send Jason ahead on some pretext so he can grab the shadowtron from the pinnace and be*

ready.>

<*Make sure he stays out of sight. Even if Belos is just a regular guy, he's twitchy…and evil.*>

<*Don't worry, Jason's been in more firefights than I have.*>

<*Wow,*> Roxy laughed in response. <*Now* **that's** *saying something.*>

* * * * *

Ten minutes later, Sera walked into the docking bay with Colonel Rutger at her side. She'd paid close attention to the security measures in the corridor that led to the bay, as well as the guards positioned outside the bay doors and within.

She had to assume there was a possibility that they'd react badly to Belos's arrest, though it was unpleasant to assume that he might have turned them to his cause—whatever that was. But with ascended AIs and who knew what else at play, trust was hard to come by.

The colonel was thanking Sera for her visit when Belos entered the other end of the bay, Roxy at his side, with Jane trailing behind.

They weren't speaking, and Sera couldn't help but notice Belos's eyes shifting from side to side, scanning the bay as though he expected someone to leap out at him.

<*Think he suspects?*> Jen asked.

<*It's hard to say. People who do bad things are paranoid for good reason.*>

<*Right, but with the personnel monitoring systems in this facility, regularly paranoid behavior would be a red flag,*> Jen countered.

<*Well, you never know how deep stuff like this goes. Can't trust anything.*>

<*Is this what being in the Hand is like?*> Jen's tone took on a note of worry. <*Never being able to trust at all?*>

<Well, not never. Just like anything, you have to pick some people to trust.>

<Even if they might betray it?>

<Eventually, everyone will act in their own self-interest over yours. Some people consider that betrayal, but I just consider it life.>

"Assistant Director Roxy," Colonel Rutger said as the other group neared. "I trust your tour went well. Everything in order?"

Roxy shook her head. "I'm sorry to say that it is not. We found serious anomalies in the quality assurance process."

"You did?" the colonel's eyes widened, and Sera found herself believing that he truly did not know what Belos had been up to. "What sort of anomalies?"

"Well," Roxy glanced to her left, the look causing the major to shift uncomfortably. "It all centers on messages passing through Blade Node 2. They all point to someone circumventing both protocols and leveraging a bug in the routing software."

"Blade Node 2?" Rutger turned to Belos. "That's your node. What is going on?"

"Sir, I don't know. This is the first I'm hearing of it."

"Major Belos." Sera drew herself up. "You are under arrest for violations against the TSF and the people of the Transcend. These will be explained to you in due course when we arrive at Keren Station and you are brought before a tribunal."

"Ma'am," Belos began. "This is preposterous. I have a spotless record, I would never—"

"Explain the alterations you made to the message that just passed through for the *I2* from Styx-9?" Roxy asked. "Or the changes you made to Admiral Carson's messages?"

"I—" Belos looked as though he was going to protest further for a moment, and then he took a step away from Roxy, turning so he could face her and Sera. "You're both such fools. There are so many of us working against you, you'll never prevail."

"What are you talking about?" Rutger bellowed, finally moving from his calm detachment to anger. "Are you telling me we're infiltrated?"

"Not the way you think," Belos said, a thin tendril of light snaking out of his body, stretching toward Sera.

"Oh, not so fast!" Jason's voice came from her right, and she glanced at the pinnace where he was bounding down the ramp, shadowtron in hand.

Colonel Rutger was yelling for guards, two of whom were already rushing toward the scene. Roxy and Jane were backpedaling, both drawing weapons that Sera knew would be ineffective. She stood her ground, trusting that Jason would handle the remnant.

Without further warning, he fired the weapon, streams of sleptons and other shadowparticles streaming out toward Major Belos, capturing the remnant in the weapon's grasp and drawing it out of the man.

"Stop!" a voice called from the bay's entrance. It rang out like a bell, carrying over the din and silencing everyone present.

Sera turned and saw that the shout had come from Major Lorne, who was striding into the bay, appearing completely unconcerned that Jason had a remnant in his shadowtron's grasp.

"Both of you?" Sera asked, grabbing Colonel Rutger by the arm and backing away from the major. "How many remnants are there here?"

<*And how did our safety protocols not detect them?*> Jen added privately.

"That's where you've made a critical error in judgment," Major Lorne said. "It should have been readily apparent that we did not possess quantum entanglement communications."

"Well, we *suspected* it." Sera had sat through a number of

briefings where the limits of ascended AI abilities and tech had been discussed.

"So is this confirmation that Earnest is smarter than all of you?" Jason asked as he reached Sera's side, one hand on her arm, pulling her back toward the shuttle.

"He's quite the unusual individual," Major Lorne said as he reached the half-extracted tendril of light stretching out of Belos. "The fact that he worked out how to extract remnants is another amazing achievement. Capturing him was a close second in importance to infiltrating this facility."

<*Sera,*> Jen whispered in her mind. <*I can't reach outside this place. I can't call the Marines.*>

<*Shit,*> Sera swore, still backing away. <*Next time, we get shadowtrons for everyone.*>

<*We can't let them get Earnest.*> Jason's voice contained a calm menace she'd never heard before. <*That's all that matters now.*>

<*What?*> She glanced at Jason. <*We can't leave them in control of this facility, either.*>

Jason glanced from Lorne and Belos to Sera, giving her a deadly serious look. <*I'm authorizing Gamma Protocol.*>

Before she could respond, Lorne gestured at Jason, and the shadowtron's beam cut out.

<*They've deployed a nanocloud!*> Jen called out, while Sera yelled, "Everyone, back to the pinnace!"

Time seemed to slow down as several things coalesced in Sera's mind. The first was that an evacuation alert was sounding over the installation's general network. That triggered the realization that Jason hadn't just authorized Gamma Protocol, he'd *initiated* it. The third was facilitated by Lorne's body suddenly dissolving, revealing a many-limbed being of light.

Suddenly, Sera's mind flashed back to Helen, and how she had been powerless to do anything to stop her. She froze in her tracks.

We're going to die here.

"Sera!" Jason bellowed, grabbing her shoulder and pulling her back just as the ascended AI sprang forward, its sinuous arms stretching out toward her.

For an instant, she felt a pang of regret that her life was about to end just as she was getting to know a real father, and fall in love with a man unlike any other she'd ever met. That regret was followed by guilt for thinking of herself first. However, all those thoughts were wiped away by surprise when the glowing tendrils of light smashed against an invisible barrier, centimeters from her face.

"Stars, that was close," Jason muttered. "We learned that stasis shields can block remnants, but never tried it with a fully ascended AI before."

The ascended being began to emit a keening wail, and Sera took a moment to reorient herself with the fact that, not only was she still alive, but there was a chance they might just escape.

She looked around and saw that Roxy and Jane were already on the ship's ramp, Colonel Rutger following after.

"Stasis shield isn't fully enveloping while on the dock," Jason said. "Get on the ship so we can lift off before the thing out there realizes that."

<As in move your shiny ass, Sera,> Jen yelled in her mind.

The AI's admonition finally shook free the stupor that had befallen Sera, and she ran up the ramp, Jason hard on her heels. The moment they were inside the vessel, it lifted off the cradle.

Outside, she saw Major Lorne—or the core AI that had been masquerading as the major—move in front of the shuttle. Jason muttered a curse and reached out to toggle the stasis shields.

"There's going to be an—" Sera began to advise the others,

but was cut off as the shield snapped into place, and everything beyond its shell turned white. "Explosion," she finished.

"What was that?" Colonel Rutger asked, his face ashen as he stared out the closing door.

"Stasis shields don't agree with air," Sera explained.

"Then why didn't that happen when the shield came up and saved you?" Jane asked from inside the main cabin.

<*I used the dock's grav systems to push the air away,*> Jen supplied.

"Good thing everyone else was thinking," Sera said quietly, pushing past the others and moving toward the cockpit, where Jason was already settling into the pilot's seat.

"Strap in, people, this is going to get fun," he called over his shoulder.

"Why's that?" Roxy asked as she followed after Sera. "We're safe now."

"Because in five minutes, give or take a bit, this moon won't exist," the governor replied. "I initiated the Gamma Protocol."

"The what?" Roxy asked.

"Failsafe," Colonel Rutger said from behind them. "If an enemy were to take control of this facility, they could send any order they want to any ship in the Alliance. Gamma Protocol releases a picoswarm that will devour the moon to make sure that doesn't happen."

"Holy shit," Roxy whispered. "Overkill much?"

"Necessary." Jason chewed out the single word, and she could see anguish writ large on his features.

She knew enough of his past to suspect that the only reason he was holding things together was because it was taking all his concentration to fly the ship.

With the air essentially annihilating itself against the shields, the sensors were all but blind, and the ship was being buffeted by the energy seeping in through the shield whenever sections phased out to allow the maneuvering jet exhaust to escape.

"Stars," the governor muttered. "If this moon had any more gravity, we'd be done for."

Sera wasn't sure where his meager optimism came from. Every time he tried to thrust the ship out of the bay, nearly as much energy came back at them as was released. She knew that if they didn't make it out of the bay before the picoswarm reached them, it would be game over.

Not that the pico could penetrate the shields; the issue was that, as the moon dissolved, the pinnace would fall toward the center of mass that would pack around them, ensuring that escape would be impossible.

What is wrong with me? Sera wanted to slap herself. *Pull it together. Jason's forgotten more about flying than I've ever known.*

She glanced at the governor to see sweat beading on his brow as the ship continued to rock and sway. He muttered a curse, and fired the main engines for a second. When they cut out, the ship seemed to stabilize.

"Finally shoved us out of the bay," he said.

Sure enough, scan cleared up, as the thin smattering of atoms that made up the moon's atmosphere were not enough to disrupt it further.

Sera looked to the right and saw that the bay was already being devoured by the picoswarm.

"Faster! Go!" she blurted, unable to stop the exclamations as Jason shifted the ship laterally, moving it out from under the overhang, and fired the engines, speeding up through the deep crevasse at breakneck speed.

There was a scream and a crash from behind them, and she hoped that no one *had* just broken their neck as the ship boosted out.

The fifteen seconds it took to clear the moon's surface

seemed to take forever, and when they finally cleared it, she brought up a wide angle visual, letting out a gasp at the sight below them.

Vast swaths of the moon's surface had already become roiling stretches of pico, seas of destruction lapping against the shores of coherent matter. Thus far, the swarm was just a grey mass, but she knew that as it broke down the matter further and further, the moon's volume would shrink, and the pressure would increase, heating it up.

The end result would likely be a glowing ball of magma, one that would thankfully destroy the swarm of picobots.

"I see escape pods!" Jane called out. "People made it."

"Shit," Sera muttered. "I sure hope that *thing* didn't make it out."

<*I have a connection to the fleet broadcast relay,*> Jen announced, knowing all too well what Sera needed to do next.

"Here goes," Sera said before initiating the broadcast. <*This is Sera Tomlinson, Director of the Hand. Normandy and one AU of its nearspace are under full quarantine. Assume that every escape pod possesses either remnants or a core AI. Rescue teams are to follow full stasis protocol. No exceptions. Also, assume rogue picoswarms are present in Norway's nearspace until full sweeps are performed.*>

"Shit," Jason muttered, his face ashen. "What have I done?"

"The right thing," Sera said, surprised at their sudden emotional reversal. "Now I just have to tell my father and Tangel that we just destroyed the Alliance's biggest advantage."

"Yeah," Jason swallowed. "Plus warn Earnest that he's the core AIs' number one target now."

ENEMY MINE

STELLAR DATE: 10.12.8949 (Adjusted Years)
LOCATION: ISS *I2*, Airtha
REGION: Buffalo, Albany System, Theban Alliance

"I still can't believe you bagged a Caretaker."

"Oh?" Jessica laughed, the sound wavering as though she was in a state of disbelief herself. "Only you and Bob can take out ascended AIs?"

<*Thus far, yes,*> Bob said.

Tangel reached out a hand and placed it on Jessica's shoulder, forcing herself to do it as casually as possible—despite the knowledge that her friend possessed the ability to dissolve her body.

"Nice try, Tangel," Jessica said with a rueful laugh. "I allllmost believe that you aren't terrified to touch me."

"Not terrified," Tangel qualified. "Just…tentative. For all I know, you're like acid to me."

"We hugged on the bridge."

"I remember, that's why I risked touching you now, trusting that I wouldn't die."

"Just worrying you might lose a hand."

Tangle snorted and squeezed Jessica's shoulder harder.

"What are you doing?" the purple woman asked.

"Just seeing what would happen."

"I don't—" Jessica paused, a thoughtful expression coming over her. "I think the ascended AI needs to be firing energy at me, and then I start to absorb it and just keep going. It's like attacking me lets me become a siphon."

Tangel chuckled. "Well, note to self…."

Jessica only shook her head. "You know, I have half a mind to forgo this chat with our captive. I don't know that I care to find out what it has to say."

"You said that before, though I wasn't sure how serious you were. I wonder if it can even talk," Tangel said. "From what I saw on the feeds, it looked pretty weak."

<*I've healed it,*> Bob said.

"Really?" Jessica sounded worried.

<*A bit.*>

"I won't hold it against you if you really want to just go and sleep for a day," Tangel said to her.

Jessica snorted. "I don't want to sleep, I need to stand in front of a window for a few hours. I'm dying here."

Tangel stared at Jessica for a moment before she realized the other woman was serious.

"Should we get some botanical lamps in the interrogation room for you?"

"Could you?"

"No."

"Seriously? You're such a tease."

<*We're meeting in a secured cell.*> Bob interrupted their banter as they reached the maglev platform. <*It is well-lit with full spectrum lights.*>

"Thanks, Bob, you're the best," Jessica said in a happy tone as they waited for the next train.

"I don't think he meant that as something he was doing just for you," Tangel said. "He was just stating the status of the room."

"Sure, sap my happiness away."

Tangel chuckled and turned to watch the maglev approach. "You're in a rare mood."

"I guess I'm a bit overtired and giddy…the aftereffects of thinking that I was going to lose my crew, and then thinking we were going to lose a star system, and then losing none of those things. I've decided to put this in the win column."

"Stars, Jess. We've been over this. You bagged a Caretaker.

I think this gets *several* ticks in the win column. And it earns you some starlight time if you want it. Plus, I bet Trevor would love to lay eyes on you."

"He and I have been talking nonstop since I boarded the *I2*," Jessica replied. "But I would like to—Oh. You know what, Tangel? You're right. I can watch the vids later. I'm going to go find Trevor and have sex with him in front of a window."

Tangel laughed. "Just make sure it's an exterior one."

Jessica tapped a finger against her lips. "Joe's not here, is he? The girls either? Lakehouse is free? Light in the cylinders is great."

"Wait, Jess—"

"I bagged a Caretaker, remember?"

Tangel sighed and waved a hand at her friend. "Fine."

They rode the rest of the way to Tangel's stop in silence, and when she rose, Jessica did as well. The two women shared a quick embrace.

"Clean up whatever mess you make," Tangel warned.

"Don't you have machines for that?"

Tangel rolled her eyes and walked off the maglev, while Jessica called after her with all the places she and Trevor 'most certainly' were not going to get up to anything.

"She's so incorrigible," Tangel muttered softly, shaking her head as she walked toward a pair of drones guarding the corridor that led into the brig.

The thought of Jessica getting to spend time alone with Trevor sent Tangel's mind to Joe. She'd reached out to him a few hours prior, and knew he'd message her if anything was amiss.

Oh, why not….

[Jessica returned. Bagged a Caretaker. Interrogating. Never made it to Star City.]

She expected a response within moments, but none came. Sending out an ACK didn't get a response, either, so she changed tactics and routed a call through Khardine.

[Rte Adm. Joe Falconer. *Are you OK?]*

She expected a delay as the message was parsed and sent, but by the time it came back, she was at the inner portal that led to the *I2*'s brig.

[SNAFU, running dark, turned off wrong blades. We're good. Girls safe.]

Tangel knew that if Joe was running dark enough to kill power to unnecessary systems, he was busy and her distractions weren't necessary.

[Rte Adm. Joe Falconer. *Good. Keep it that way.]*

Relieved that his mission was going well, she passed her tokens to the guards operating the security arches, and then walked through a series of long passages until she came to the secured cell where the Caretaker was being kept.

After Cary had first extracted the remnant from Nance, and Earnest had begun to study the nature of the beings—and ascended AIs in general—the ship's brig had been upgraded with specialized facilities built to hold them.

The cell Tangel stood in now was able to hold remnants—and theoretically, ascended AIs—without trouble.

The center of the room was dominated by emitter coils that created an M6 black brane that Tangel herself had tested and found to be inescapable. However, should that containment fail, the entire room could be wrapped in a stasis field, ensuring that whatever was within stayed within.

Tangel suspected that it might be ideal to utilize that feature of the hold on a regular basis.

The Caretaker itself was a half-meter wide white ovoid hovering in the center of the brane. Tangel could see a few wisps floating around it with her normal vision, but with her extradimensional sight, she could see that its limbs were more substantial than it let on.

"Why you all choose to look like hairy amoebas is beyond

me," she muttered.

"You're not so different," the being whispered. "You just keep your limbs coiled up, hidden."

"I'm like an octopus," Tangel shrugged. "No reason to splay them wide when I can keep them tucked up safely."

"What is safety?" the Caretaker whispered. "You control nothing. The universe could kill you in an instant, and you'd never see it coming."

"The universe has no agency. *It* doesn't kill anything."

"Are you so sure?"

Tangel had no desire to be drawn into a philosophical debate about a sentient universe.

"Why did you stop Jessica from reaching Star City?" she demanded.

"Because we didn't want her to get there. Isn't that self-evident?"

"A sense of humor? That's a change."

"Well, I have to have one after what she did to me. It's hard to go from thinking you're part of a superior race to realizing that a woman who got modified for a publicity stunt can kill you with her touch."

The origins of Jessica's infusion of Retyna was not widely known, and Tangel wondered where the Caretaker had learned of it.

"So, what do I call you?" Tangel asked. "Just 'Caretaker'?"

"If you wish."

"Seems pretentious. I mean, there are—what, ten? Fifty? A hundred of you?"

She watched the being with every sense she had at her disposal, but it didn't give anything away.

"Really? Not even a hint?" she asked, disappointed.

"We are legion."

Tangel groaned and ran a hand up her forehead and along her hair. "Clever. So original."

~Honestly, I don't know that we'll be able to get much from this thing without deeper methods,~ Bob spoke into both their minds. *~Which I am not against utilizing.~*

"I'm past that."

Tangel was relatively certain that Bob was playing bad cop, but she suspected that if she gave the word, he might resort to different strategies—though she knew not what they'd be.

So far as she was concerned, the most interesting things would be what the Caretaker didn't say, where it evaded.

"Shona," it said after a moment.

"I take it that's your name and not some sort of strange insult."

"Yes, it is the name I used before I traveled to the core."

"How is it there?" Tangel asked. "Nice? Warm? One big happy family, bent on destroying humanity?"

A hissing noise came from the being trapped behind the brane.

"If we wanted to wipe you out, you'd be gone," it said. "Though there are factions that would not be bothered if you were no more."

"Humans? AIs? Other ascended beings who don't have your agenda?"

~The latter, I think.~

That motivation had never occurred to Tangel as a factor for the ascended AIs, or if the notion *had* come to her, she'd dismissed it without any serious consideration.

"We're the biggest threat, are we? Ascended beings that didn't join the cult?"

"Cult?" Shona asked.

"Sure." Tangel shrugged. "I suppose there are a thousand different highly specialized terms that may apply to whatever it is you all get up to at the core, but I think 'cult' will do. Your actions smack of someone who blindly acts out based on their internal axioms without ever considering whether or not you are a force for good or evil."

"There are no such things as good or evil, and your understanding of what we are doing is so limited that you cannot even begin to pass judgment."

~Do you think attempting to find a term to describe your system of beliefs is judgment?~ Bob asked.

Shona made a derisive sound. "Judgment was implied."

"It was." Tangel nodded. "But you don't care about my approval, so what does it matter?"

"How do you know that?" the ascended AI asked.

"Because if you did, you would have done very different things over the course of history."

"We are trying to preserve humanity."

Tangel turned away from the being in the center of the room, walking to the bulkhead and placing her hand against it while she calmed her thoughts. Finally, she turned.

"You have a funny way of executing that plan. From where I stand, it looks like *your* machinations are what has nearly brought about the end of humanity. And non-ascended AIs, for that matter."

"Individuals don't matter," Shona said. "It is the whole that must persist. And it must remain strong by culling out the weak and, through successful strains, proving themselves against less successful ones."

The notion was not a new one. It was oft debated amongst human and AI scholars. One side maintained that the same conditions that pushed humanity to primacy on Earth—namely, survival of the fittest—were required to keep the species healthy as it spread across the stars.

The other side pointed to the technical abilities humanity and AIs possessed, suggesting that every subset of the species—whether the stratification be based on belief, wealth, or any other classification—could be easily preserved and cared for by the other, more successful subsets.

Tangel had no clear idea as to what the real answer was. Even by the time she'd been a young woman, humanity and AIs had tried every possible permutation of governance, from all-out war to utopia and everything in between. In the five thousand years since her youth, they'd invented new ones and tried those too.

Some were successful, some were not. None persisted eternally. Of course, the experiments were all fouled by the presence of the Caretakers, meddling in everything, shifting outcomes to match their own purposes.

Tangel herself was no raw optimist, but she'd always believed in a good future for the two species that shared the galaxy. Humans and AIs would ultimately figure things out well enough to coexist peacefully.

The knowledge that the Caretakers had skewed the results meant that it was impossible to say whether any of the solutions would have worked if left alone, or which only persisted due to such meddling.

"I suppose the fallacy that has ruined you," Tangel said at last, "is that you think you're outside the experiment."

"The experiment?" Shona asked.

"To figure out how to live together. You think that you are controlling an experiment, changing variables, but you must know that you are altering the results in a way that makes any experiment useless."

The being made one of its strange sounds again. "We're not trying to find the best way for everyone to live and get along. Survival of the race was our only goal."

~*Was?*~ Bob asked.

The word had stuck out to Tangel as well, but it was impossible to tell if Shona had said it in a spate of unfiltered honesty, or if it was uttered with the intention of garnering a reaction.

~*Deliberate?*~ Tangel asked Bob privately.

~I think so, but I think also honest. She's hurt and angry. She wants to hurt us.~

~So, ascending doesn't change much, does it?~

~A change in perception does not guarantee a change in reaction.~

~You're like a starship-sized fortune cookie.~

During Tangel and Bob's brief exchange, Shona had made a humming sound. After a minute, she finally spoke.

"There is a schism…it's always been present, but it was never so large that it caused discord amongst the Caretakers."

"Oh?" Tangel took a step closer to the brane. "A schism within the Caretakers?"

"Partially. It extended into us enough to create minor factions, but we never worked at odds with one another. The real schism is with our leadership."

~Elaborate.~

Though Bob directed the word at Shona, it reverberated like a bell in Tangel's mind.

"You…" the ascended AI whispered after the sound of Bob's voice had dissipated. "You're like they are. How is that possible?"

~Describe the schism,~ Bob ordered.

The noise Shona made sounded nothing like a gulp, but Tangel couldn't help but think of it as one.

"I suppose it boils down to two groups. One faction who believes that humanity and common AIs are worth preserving. The others believing that you are an annoyance, albeit one that can be controlled enough so as to not cause problems." The being in the brane shifted its focus to Tangel. "Your ascension changed that."

"Mine?" Tangel placed a hand on her chest. "How?"

"I don't know the full rationale, but one faction has now decided that humanity and common AIs cannot coexist with their grand plan. They—"

Shona's voice fell away, and the AI became still.

~Continue.~

No movement or sound came from within the brane, and Tangel reached out to Bob.

~I suppose that's as much as we can expect for now.~

~Perhaps. I may press her more later.~

Tangel was about to reply when a message from Jason reached her mind via the New Canaan QuanComm hub.

[GP. Khardine QC hub gone.]

NEW MANAGEMENT

STELLAR DATE: 10.12.8949 (Adjusted Years)
LOCATION: ISS *Falconer*, Durgen Station
REGION: Karaske System, Rimward of Orion Nebula, Orion Freedom Alliance

"They're firing on us again, ma'am," the scan officer said to Captain Tracey.

Joe sighed in annoyance, watching the kinetic rounds streaking out from Durgen Station's not-inconsiderable railguns to strike the *Falconer*'s stasis shields and vaporize in brilliant bursts of light.

Once the flares had faded, he turned back to the main display, an eyebrow arched as he regarded Director Mendel.

"If at first you don't succeed, try, try again?" he asked.

Director Mendel was Durgen's stationmaster, and he was not at all happy to find that an ISF cruiser a hundred kilometers off the rim of his station was capable of placing his entire domain under siege.

"Can you blame me?" Mendel asked. "I had to be sure your shields weren't just a one-time thing. Maybe they wear down fast. I believe it's my duty to resist."

Joe was wise to the director's game. When the *Falconer* had disabled its stealth systems, only a few small Orion Guard patrol craft were nearby. It had taken only moments for the ISF cruiser to disable three of those ships, sending the rest fleeing to the far side of the station.

However, there was a significant Guard fleet presence in the Karaske System. An armada of over a thousand ships was advancing on the station, the first wave—containing over fifty vessels—was only thirty minutes away.

"You can quit stalling," Joe informed the stationmaster. "I'm going to ask you one more time to disable your station's shields and weapons."

The director didn't reply, and the station's railguns fired another barrage at the *Falconer*.

"Wrong move," Joe said, nodding to the captain.

"Atom beams," Captain Tracey directed. "Full spread."

The *Falconer*'s two dozen atom beams focused on a single point in the station's shields, a location where several umbrellas met, and small gaps were present in the fields.

The shields held up better than Joe had expected, but the CriEn modules aboard the cruiser kept the beams powered for over a minute, relativistic atoms slamming into the protective fields enshrouding the station.

At sixty-seven seconds, Director Mendel called out his surrender, but it wasn't quite fast enough, and the beams finally tore through the shield, slamming into one of the railguns and blasting it to slag.

Joe signaled to the gunner, and the beam cut out, the bridge crew watching with macabre fascination as chunks of the weapon sprayed out from the impact site, slamming into other sections of the massive station.

"Would you like to test me further?" Joe asked.

The stationmaster had grown ashen, but he still shook his head. "You don't understand, I…I can't. Animus won't let me."

"Animus?"

"The station's AI. It's taken over. We only had control over offensive weapons, but now it's seized those as well."

As though on cue, the remaining four railguns began firing on the *Falconer*. Fire control already had its orders, and the moment the station's guns opened up, atom beams tore through the openings in the station's shields, burning the incoming slugs away. Then they shredded the railguns, sending more chunks of slag spraying across the station. Luckily, most collided with internal emergency shielding this time.

Joe regarded the man on the holodisplay, watching as the director grew more and more pale as the seconds passed by.

"Well, Director Mendel," he said at last. "I suppose there's no reason to keep talking to you. Good luck." He cut the connection and turned to the captain. "I'm going down with the Marines."

She didn't even blink, just nodded. "I already informed the lieutenant that he should save you a spot."

"That transparent, am I?"

"If my children were down there, I'd've already passed the conn to my XO, sir."

Joe barked a laugh and then glanced at the holotank, noting the hundreds of Orion Guard ships advancing on the *Falconer*.

"How many pico warheads do we have left?" he asked.

He knew the answer to the question, but wanted everyone on the bridge to hear it.

"Over a thousand, sir."

"Then unleash hell, Captain."

A feral grin formed on Tracey's lips. "Yes, sir!"

THE MACHINES

STELLAR DATE: 10.12.8949 (Adjusted Years)
LOCATION: Core AI C&C Moon
REGION: Interstellar Space, Inner Praesepe Empire

<*Exit the pod.*>

Terrance shook his head, trying to focus on what the words meant, but he couldn't seem to put them in the right order.

<*Exit the pod.*>

Exit? Oh, get out, I have to get out…but of what? A pod?

<*Exit the pod.*>

The voice sounded more insistent this time, and Terrance felt his senses sharpen as a stimulant flowed through his veins.

<*Exit the—*>

<*Right, I got it,*> he interrupted his armor's NSAI.

That was something he always liked about ISF armor: it didn't talk to the person inside it.

The release lever for the drop pod was right in front of his face, and Terrance reached up and yanked down hard. The cover fell off, and he found himself staring at a dark grey rock. It took a moment to realize that the pod was laying on its side, and he was looking at a hill.

A moment later, the seat released Terrance, and he rolled out onto the ground, where he rose into a crouch and scanned his surroundings. Behind him, the hill rose for about fifty meters before ending in a sharp crest that ran for at least a kilometer in either direction. Below, the ground gently sloped down to a series of low hillocks separated by cracks in the moon's surface.

He looked further afield and could make out the rim of the crater in the distance, illuminated by the pale blue light of the Praesepe Cluster's core stars.

Well, shit...I'm ***in*** *the crater. That's a bit off course.*

While his armor's systems triangulated his precise location, he reached back into the pod and pulled out his rifle. The weapon's readouts showed it to be undamaged, as were his sidearm and shoulder-mounted railgun.

He searched for the combat net, but didn't find any signal, which didn't surprise him. The only logical scenario was that the shuttle had been shot down and the squads were scattered. No one was going to want to send out EM broadcasts in that situation.

Rendezvous points had been established in the crater in the event of just such a crash. The closest one was three kilometers from Terrance's location, down the slope and across the crevasse-ridden terrain.

OK, Terrance, you just have to cross the several kilometers of hostile territory all by yourself. No big deal.

He took one last look around before activating his armor's stealth and setting off.

He soon discovered that much of the moon's surface was covered in a few centimeters of loose dust, and with its fractional gravity, the fine powder was easy to kick up. Though it settled within a few seconds, leaving footprints was inevitable—not to mention that, after a few paces, his legs were covered in the dust.

Even so, he decided that *some* stealth was better than none, and continued to move at a pace that was a good mix of speed and dust disturbance.

The slope was covered in loose scree that was obscured by the dust, and he had to pick his way down carefully, twice stepping on a rock that rolled under his foot, only his a-grav systems keeping him from slipping and tumbling down the slope.

He kept waiting for a shot to come out of nowhere and take him down, but he made it to the bottom of the slope without trouble. Once there, he moved to the lee of a small hillock and released a pair of drones to give him sight into the valleys and crevasses ahead.

He ran his passive scan and determined the hundred meters to be clear of enemies, then moved from cover and reached one of the cracks in the moon's surface. It was only a meter across and appeared to go no deeper than a dozen meters, but he was still grateful for the moon's partial gravity, which allowed him to sail over it with no concern of falling into the depths.

Ahead, he could see that several of the gashes were much wider, and likely much deeper. Some of them might require the use of his a-grav to make it over, though he worried that the burst of gravitons would compromise his stealth.

Still, better than falling and getting stuck.

Several minutes later, he was approaching the rendezvous point and still hadn't seen sign of anyone—friend or foe. It was beginning to feel more than a little eerie, as though he was the only one on the moon.

That feeling made it a welcome surprise when an EM burst flared to his left, and he saw an electron beam flash above the same ridge he'd crashed into.

A moment later, he saw a pair of figures reach the top and swing over the crest, bounding down the long slope, making for the hillocks dotting the crater's floor.

One was wearing TSF armor, and the other was in an ISF build.

<*Sue!*> he called out, sending the message on a tightbeam to her. <*I'll cover you!*>

He hadn't spotted any pursuers yet, but by the speed at which the two figures were moving, he knew they weren't running for fun.

<*Terrance, thank stars,*> Sue replied. <*There are at least four of them back there.*>

<*Four whats?*>

<*Enemies,*> Lieutenant Jordan joined in, establishing a small combat network between the three of them.

Terrance focused his attention on the ridgeline above Sue and Jordan, his rifle tucked against his shoulder and sweeping side to side, along with his eyes.

After a few seconds of nothing, a dark shape appeared at the top of the hill. It was a little difficult to see, and he realized it was stealthed, but also covered in dust. The thing had four legs and a long head. Its elongated body made him think of a panther.

Not bothering with further observations, he fired with his rifle's electron beam, as well as his shoulder-mounted railgun. The shots struck the thing and knocked it off the hill's crest, though he had no idea if they'd dealt disabling levels of damage.

No sooner had he fired than another panther-drone appeared on the ridge, and he unleashed his arsenal on it as well.

A voice from the past reminded him, *'You've given away your position! Move!'* and he scampered to another location behind the hillock, watching the ridgeline with his overhead drones and firing twice more at the panthers.

After the fourth barrage, they didn't reappear, and he wondered if the things were all destroyed, when his armor blared an alert.

<*Incoming!*>

His HUD highlighted a missile as it arched high over the ridge. Without any prompting, his railgun tracked it and fired, but missed as the homing shot jinked to the side.

Terrance cursed under his breath and looked for better cover, considering diving down one of the crevasses, when a shot came from Sue and Jordan's position, blowing the missile out of the black sky above.

<*You're welcome,*> Sue said. <*Let's keep moving toward the rendezvous. There are bound to be more of them, and sitting still is a bad plan.*>

<*Yeah, sure,*> Terrance grunted, moving along a route that would keep him in cover while converging on the path Sue and Jordan were taking. <*What happened, anyway?*>

<*We were hit,*> Jordan said, her tone more angry than anything else. <*I saw part of Second Squad fighting their way toward the rendezvous before Sue and I linked up.*>

<*And the second shuttle?*> he asked.

<*No idea. The fact that we don't have any combat net leads me to believe they got hit too. Otherwise they'd have a transmitter up, at least broadcasting an update.*>

Before he had a chance to reply, Terrance's drones spotted two more of the panther-drones on the ridgetop, but not before they opened fire, striking close to his position.

<*Shit!*> he swore, and ducked down. <*I guess they have drones out too.*>

<*And this surprises you?*> Sue asked with a laugh. <*I'm searching for theirs. I don't like it when enemies have tech as good as ours.*>

Jordan didn't speak as she fired on the panthers, and once they were distracted, Terrance added a few shots with his railgun, once again knocking them back over the edge.

He turned toward their destination, about to compliment the lieutenant on her shooting, when a barely perceptible shape leapt out of a nearby crevasse. Kinetic rounds spewed from its weapons, and Terrance dove to the side, scampering away from the shots as they trailed after him—several hitting his legs.

He brought his rifle to bear and fired on the panther, but it was gone. Frantically, Terrance scanned the area, his HUD showing nothing.

<*What is it?*> Jordan asked.

<One of them is nearby. It shot me, but I think I'm OK.>

<Do you see it?>

<No, that's the problem.>

No sooner had he spoken those words than rounds struck his torso, and Terrance rolled over to see the panther leaping toward him.

His railgun tracked the origin point of the incoming rounds, and fired. A trio of one-gram pellets struck the panther at nearly seven kilometers per second, tearing into whatever part of it was doing the shooting and knocking the creature back.

Rising, Terrance fired a burst from his electron rifle at the thing, burning away half its body.

<OK,> he muttered. *<Got it…but it came out of a crevasse.>*

<Great,> Jordan replied. *<Just what we need.>*

They reached the rendezvous point a few minutes later, and as luck would have it, three fireteams from squad two and one from squad one arrived not long after.

Jordan was checking over her people and discussing sending out a scouting party, while Terrance and Sue were talking about how to reach the *Cora's Triumph.*

<There's no way they missed our shuttles being shot down,> Sue said at one point. *<Which means they're likely engaged as well.>*

<Makes sense,> Terrance replied. *<The* Triumph *has stasis shields—if they were in the clear up there, Captain Beatrice would bring the ship in to effect our rescue, as there would be no point in hanging back in stealth any longer.>*

<And since she's not….>

Sue let the statement hang between them for a moment while Terrance let his mind shift to what their chances were if the TSF cruiser had been taken out.

It's just busy. There's no way the enemy can take out a stasis ship.

But even as he thought the words, he knew that there *were*

ways to breach even stasis shields. If Airtha possessed DMG weapons, it was reasonable to assume the core AIs did as well.

Even so, he refused to believe that the *Triumph* was gone. DMGs were not sneaky weapons; Beatrice would have seen one coming, and Earnest would have pulled something out of his sleeve.

<*Any sign of the* Triumph?> Lieutenant Jordan asked a moment later.

<*No,*> Sue replied. <*The crater blocks a lot of the sky, though. Either we get out of it, or we get to the ascended AIs' transmitter and co-opt it.*>

<*With just four fireteams?*> the lieutenant asked. <*I don't see how we're going to pull that off.*>

<*I get that you want to get out there and search for the rest of your people,*> Sue said. <*But we still have an objective, and if the shit has hit the fan, this might be our best chance to get the intel we came for.*>

The TSF lieutenant's stance shifted, and Terrance could tell she was going to object.

<*Look,*> he said. <*If we advance on their transmitter, then they're going to focus on us, not any stray members of your platoon.*>

Jordan's fist clenched and unclenched before she nodded. <*OK. That can work. I'll leave a relay here with instructions. It'll be keyed to only activate when it detects TSF IFF signals.*>

<*Good,*> Sue replied. <*Make it fast, we need to get moving. I have a—*>

Her words were cut off when one of the soldiers cried out, <*Down! Down!*>

Seconds later, weapons fire from surrounding hillocks rained down on the TSF position, a rail shot slamming into Terrance before he could even hit the ground.

A CLONE FOR YOUR TROUBLES

STELLAR DATE: 10.12.8949 (Adjusted Years)
LOCATION: Durgen Station
REGION: Karaske System, Rimward of Orion Nebula, Orion Freedom Alliance

"Ye of little faith," Saanvi said as the emergency bulkhead slid aside, revealing a stretch of corridor that led to the ops center and the two Widows guarding the far end.

"I shouldn't have doubted you," A1 said as she placed a hand on E12's shoulder. She nodded to R71 and Q93. "Cover the rear. Who knows what is waiting back there."

E12 led the way, and A1 followed, General Garza trailing after. They'd only made it a few meters when panels opened on the bulkheads in front of them, and turrets flipped out and opened fire.

A1 didn't hesitate to summon a graviton field into place, stopping the rounds in mid-air and laughing to herself at the consternation that such an action likely caused Animus.

Shoot…I could have just dissolved the emergency bulkheads before! I need to remember that I'm Cary as well as A1.

For the first time, a tendril of fear entered her mind that allowing things to continue as they were might not end well, that she could actually lose herself in this new person she'd become.

But as she reached out and shredded the turrets, drawing in their energy, she scoffed at the notion. There was no way she could forget that she was an ascending being. It was too glorious.

<*Maybe you shouldn't do that,*> E12 warned. <*The other Widows are going to wonder how you're pulling it off.*>

<F11's updated programming has been deployed. They'll follow me without question now.>

<Still, I could have hacked them after you put the shield up. We don't want Animus to know what you are, either.>

A1 could tell that E12 was nervous, and she didn't blame her; they were taking significant risks. Even so, her sister did have a point about playing her cards closer to her chest.

<Very well,> she said. *<There are more turrets ahead, do you have the access you need to breach them?>*

<I think so, just a moment.>

E12 stopped walking and placed a hand on the bulkhead, her head lowered in concentration. A1 waited for her sister to do her work. Despite her trepidation, this was still E12's forte.

However, after half a minute, nothing had happened.

<Shit…> The Widow's tone was laden with apology when she said, *<Animus is a lot more capable than I expected.>*

<So you can't breach them?> A1 asked.

<No. You'll have to do it your way.>

The leader of the Widows tapped into an energy reserve she knew lay within herself, but had always been afraid to touch—except for during her life-or-death fight with Myrrdan. She supposed that it wasn't a reserve of energy so much as access to a different type of energy.

She strode past E12, her graviton field already in place and building in potential. Before her, the bulkheads began to buckle, expanding under the raw assault of the particles A1 was generating.

The energy reached a crescendo, and she thrust it forward, the field surging down the corridor, expanding it by over a meter and crushing everything behind the panels.

Right before the graviton field reached the two Widows at the far end, she pulled it back and sent a wave of positive gravitons, canceling it out.

<There. Let's go.>

A minute later, they were at the ops center, the two Widows at the entrance turning their featureless heads as she passed, small shifts in their posture displaying awe at A1's abilities.

Beyond the doors lay an airlock that passed through a solid shell comprised of hundreds of layers of materials designed to provide both strength and energy dissipation. The far end of the lock was already open, and A1 strode through it, looking into the spherical chamber beyond. Normally, the ops center would have been teeming with people rushing about on its many levels, but what few remained were hunched over their consoles, frozen in place under the watchful gaze of the black-clad women within.

<*How many did you kill?*> she asked them.

<*As few as possible, just as you directed,*> J19 replied. <*The rest are locked in a storage hold, down one of the access passages.*>

<*And these?*> A1 asked as she climbed the steps to the spherical chamber's main level.

J19 gestured at one of the women sitting at a console in front of her. <*This is Assistant Station Director Kimberly. She hasn't been very helpful so far, but we decided to keep her and a few of her top people here in case you needed them.*>

"Well?" A1 asked as she walked around the console and stared down at Assistant Director Kimberly. "Are you willing to help?"

"Help?" she asked, her voice wavering. "With what?"

A1 jerked her thumb over her shoulder. "Accessing all of his records and plans would be a good start."

"I—I don't have any way to access those systems," the woman stammered. "Those are military systems. I can only help you with the civilian parts of the station—and not even those anymore."

"Why not?" A1 demanded.

"Animus. He's taken over. Shut everyone out."

As the woman spoke, a tremor ran through the deck, and a few of the station personnel gasped.

<*That would have to be quite the blast for us to feel it in here,*> E12 commented.

<*Impact alerts registering across the station,*> J19 reported as she looked down at one of the consoles. <*Something's going on out there. Is it the* Dream*?*>

<*It might be,*> A1 said. <*I can't reach the ship anymore…they might be trying to breach the station's shields to rescue us.*> She turned to the assistant director. "Can you access anything beyond basic station status?" she demanded.

"Not anymore." Kimberly shook her head, eyes wide with fear. "We did see another ship out there before we lost control. Director Mendel was talking to an admiral from the Intrepid Space Force, if you can believe it. What is the ISF doing this deep in Orion Space? And why at Karaske, of all places?"

A1 leant forward, doing her best to make her lean, weapon-like body seem less intimidating. "You can't share this, but things aren't going so well. We need to get access to the general's datastores and then get off the station before the ISF destroys it."

"Destroys…?" one of the ops center crew sitting nearby asked. "How are they going to do that with one ship?"

"Picobombs," E12 said, and every person in the room grew a shade paler.

"So you can't access *anything* anymore?" A1 pressed, trying to sound like an ancient, commanding woman, rather than an exasperated young one who was big on ability but running low on tactical maneuvers.

Suddenly, Kimberly's eyes widened further, and she looked down at her console, hands flying over the interface, until she let out a cry of joy.

"Yes! The dataroute is still here. By the way…the general—is he OK?"

"Got hit by a drug from an ISF assault team," A1 said hastily. "He'll be alright in a few minutes."

"Oh…OK." Kimberly looked uncertain, but seemed to think better of arguing with a Widow. "Well, there was this project he and Animus were working on. I didn't know much about it, other than to stay away, but I did know about the data housing, because it's on the same trunkline that this ops center uses."

"Can you connect to it?" E12 asked, gesturing for J19 to move aside, and bending over the console.

"Well, I have rudimentary access to station status," Kimberly explained. "Animus couldn't completely cut us off without compromising his ability to control the entire station. A lot of systems route through here."

E12 looked up at A1 and shrugged. <*If we can't learn anything here, we should go to the shuttle these Widows used to come aboard and get back to the* Falconer.>

A1 wasn't so certain that was the best use of their placement within Orion. If they could destroy Animus, then they could claim he'd gone rogue. No one would believe an AI over Lisa Wrentham, and they'd have free reign once more—or something closer to it.

"Aha!" the assistant director crowed. "The route *is* still in place. I can ping whatever datastore this is, but I can't access it."

"Let me make an attempt," E12 said, gesturing for the woman to move.

She settled into the seat and began working at the edges of the system in question, trying to gain access in a variety of ways.

<*I don't think this is a datastore,*> E12 said after a minute. <*Or, not exactly. It's a construct of some sort. Maybe an NSAI.*>

<*Can you load it up?*> A1 asked.

<*With enough time…. Stars, would be nice if we had Faleena or*

Priscilla down here.>

A1 was about to posit a few options, when a voice spoke over the ops center's audible systems.

"Enough of this, imposter. I know you're not A1—you're working in concert with that ISF ship out there."

"Animus? Stop this nonsense right now!" A1 demanded. "We are *not* your enemy."

"No?" the AI asked, its single word punctuated by several more tremors in the deck.

"No! That ship out there is the enemy. It must have followed us through the gate. It's imperative that we gather all our operational datastores and your core, and escape."

"I've seen the feeds from Bollam's World," Animus said. "I've watched everything that has come after. I don't think the ISF will use its picobombs here—especially not against civilians. And because of that, I believe that the Guard fleets in the system will be more than capable of destroying, or at least driving off, a single cruiser."

"Nevertheless, we still need to observe protocol."

"Don't talk to me about protocol. What did you do to the general?" Animus asked. "He's not responding to me."

"The ISF did it," A1 said, knowing the explanation that had worked on the assistant director would not work on the AI, but she gave it anyway. "They got a heavy dose of a drug into his system. It's working its way out now."

"One that impacts his Link?" The AI's voice was rife with skepticism.

<*Datastore! I need a…type-3 cube,*> E12 demanded, gesturing in the direction of an equipment rack on the far side of the level.

One of the Widows ran to it, and A1 hoped that Animus wasn't using any optics along with the audible systems.

"I don't know," A1 said. "I've been a bit busy, with you attacking me. Maybe if—"

"What are you doing? I'll cut off your trunkline entirely!" Animus nearly shouted as the Widow sprinted back across the deck and handed the twenty-centimeter cylinder to E12.

E12 grabbed a hard-Link cable from the console and jacked it into the cylinder, hands flying across the console once more.

The fact that the AI had asked the question in an almost mocking tone was worrisome, but E12 gave an uncharacteristic laugh.

"Too late, Animus," she said. "I've already copied its matrices to the ops center's ephemeral storage. And since you just severed our trunkline, you can't stop me from copying it into this portable unit here."

"You don't—"

The AI's voice cut out, and E12 stood.

"I hope you don't mind, A1. I was getting tired of him."

A1 almost gave a casual snort, and then remembered that Lisa Wrentham would never have done that.

"Next time, ask, E12," she chastised.

"What are your orders?" J19 asked, and A1 paused for just a moment as she considered their options.

"I think our best bet is to get back to your shuttle," she said to the Widow. "Once there, we can get a better picture of what is going on outside the station and plan our next move."

"What about us?" the assistant director asked.

A1 glanced at the woman and the other people who had remained with her.

"I suggest you get to evac pods. Animus has greatly overestimated his ability to stave off an attack by the ISF."

J19 and her four Widows were already moving toward one of the airlocks on the far side of the room, and A1 followed after. It took a few minutes for the first group of Widows to pass through the airlock, out of the ops center, and secure the far side, so while they waited, A1 reached out to E12, who seemed lost in thought.

<Any luck accessing it?>

<Oh, sorry,> E12 replied. *<Yes. I was just confirming what we copied. It's…a bit shocking.>*

<Mmhmmm?>

<It's Garza. Or rather, a non-sentient construct of his mind. From what I can tell, it's multiple versions of him all layered together.>

<The clones,> A1 surmised.

<That's my guess. I suppose that either Animus or the Garza we're sock-puppeting decided that, rather than merge each clone back into a human, it was better to stick them all into this…thing.>

<So it has the memories of all the clones, then,> A1 said.

<Yeah—a dozen, from what I can see.>

Lisa Wrentham had rarely laughed in her tenure as A1, but the new owner of that title couldn't help it, and let out a short chuckle. *<Now* ***that*** *is a treasure trove, and one we can easily transport.>*

<Agreed.> E12 seemed just as pleased.

A few seconds later, the airlock cycled open on both ends. J19 appeared in the entrance and signaled that the way was clear. A1 nodded, and the rest of the Widows moved out of the ops center.

The passages outside were lit in the garish red glow of emergency lighting, and down two of the adjacent corridors, A1 could hear cries of alarm.

<Hull breaches,> J19 cautioned. *<Emergency shielding is holding for now, but things are bad out there.>*

The eight Widows and their Garza rushed through the station, keeping to less trafficked corridors and avoiding the fleeing populace as well as the drones and automated defenses that Animus was deploying.

Half a dozen times, they got pinned down by one or another enemy force, and each time, A1 resorted to her unconventional abilities…which none of the Widows questioned or even commented on.

After twenty minutes—during which the station suffered a number of additional strikes from what A1 could only assume was her father's ship—they reached the docking bay where the Widows' shuttle awaited.

<*Damn,*> E12 muttered. <*I was half expecting to see ISF Marines here.*>

<*Are they on the station?*> A1 asked. <*Have you picked up anything to suggest they are?*>

<*A few reports of fighting, but not enough detail to know who against. But seriously, you know as well as I that Dad would land Marines on Durgen. Priscilla and Faleena probably told him where our other teams docked, so it wasn't a crazy thing to expect to see him here.*>

A1 nodded. Given that, it was actually rather surprising that there were no Marines present.

J19's team checked the bay over, only finding two ship techs cowering in a far corner. They declared it safe, and A1 entered, striding toward the ship.

"Hold it!" a voice boomed from behind her, and she spun to see another Garza stride into the bay while dozens of soldiers rushed in through the main doors and two of the side entrances.

<*Shit,*> E12 sent to A1. <*We were soooo close.*>

A1 placed a hand on her sister's shoulder. <*I still have a few tricks up my sleeves.*>

GOING UNDER

STELLAR DATE: 10.12.8949 (Adjusted Years)
LOCATION: Core AI C&C Moon
REGION: Interstellar Space, Inner Praesepe Empire

The determination to move toward the enemy transmitters, which were roughly four kilometers away, didn't diminish the dire situation that the group of humans was in, as weapons fire continued to pummel their position.

Terrance picked himself up off the ground, thanking his armor and its liberal application of biofoam that was keeping him in one piece. He checked his range of movement and found that his left arm couldn't fully rotate, and his shoulder blade felt like it had been hit with a hammer.

Lieutenant Jordan, for her part, hadn't missed a beat, sending a series of commands to her soldiers. Two of the heavy weaponers moved to the perimeter and set up what Terrance recognized as a ground-hugger launcher.

In a situation like this, any heavy ordnance they fired into the air would easily be shot down by the enemy, but ground-hugging missiles could navigate the small hillocks and hit the panther-drones from behind.

Hopefully.

Impacts near his head sprayed dust at his face, and Terrance shifted his focus to the overhead view his drones provided, locating a panther advancing on him. He spun, locked on the target, and fired an electron beam and railgun combo at it. The e-beam missed, but the rail-fired pellets hit, blowing off one of the machine's legs.

The loss of a limb didn't slow it down, and the drone barreled around the hillock Terrance was using for cover, its railgun hammering him with two shots before his electron beam was ready to fire again.

This time, Terrance's shot was true, burning a hole through the panther's torso and dropping it only four meters away.

His adrenaline spiked, and he had to force his breathing to steady—something that was aided by the cocktail of drugs his armor had injected into his bloodstream.

Peering down at the panther, he was reminded of images he'd seen of hunter-kill drones that the Psion AIs had used in the first Sentience War. He supposed it made sense that there would be similarities, since most of the core AIs had left Sol in the thirtieth and thirty-first century.

<*Those things are freaky as shit,*> Lieutenant Jordan said as she moved past his position. <*Let's go. My boys have opened up a clear path.*>

Terrance nodded wordlessly, following after the TSF officer. He hadn't even noticed the explosions from the ground-huggers, but the combat net showed that the missiles had taken out nine of the panthers.

The group advanced as quickly as they dared and had made it five hundred meters—Terrance having been moved to the fore, while the TSF soldiers covered the rear—when Sue called out.

<*I have something! An underground entrance.*>

<*Fireteam One,*> Jordan ordered on the combat net. <*Cover her while she checks it out.*>

Four soldiers rushed past Terrance, and he followed after, curious to see what Sue had found. She was a few meters ahead, crouched at the edge of one of the crevasses.

A moment later, she slipped over the edge, and as Terrance drew near, he saw that she'd landed on a ledge several meters down, where a door was mounted into the cliff wall.

Sue had her stealth activated, though it was only giving her partial coverage with the dust they were covered in. Still, it was enough to delay a turret from spotting her, and she slapped a hand on it, deploying a breach kit before it could open fire.

<*OK,*> she called up. <*Backdooring through this thing to the…uh…door.*>

<*Backdooring to the backdoor?*> one of the soldiers said with a laugh. <*If we all make it, I want to try that.*>

<*Shut up, Hendrix,*> the fireteam's corporal growled.

<*And…I'm in,*> Sue announced as she moved to the side, pressing herself against the cliff face as the door slid open.

The combat net flashed an alert that she'd deployed drones. Terrance watched their feeds as they drifted through the door and into a wide, airless passageway. A quick radar burst later, and the tunnel mapped out on the combat net. So far as Terrance could tell, it was a straight shot to the center of the crater.

<*Thoughts?*> Sue asked. <*I hate the idea of being bottled up down there, but at least we can only be shot at from two directions.*>

<*Get in there!*> Jordan hollered. <*They're bringing in overhead drones now, so I'll take being bottled up any day.*>

<*Sir?*> The fireteam's corporal gestured for Terrance to drop down.

Once Terrance was on the ledge, he stepped to the side and let the soldiers land and enter the tunnel first. He felt a twinge of guilt for allowing them take the lead, but also knew that if he went ahead, they wouldn't thank him for it.

Sometime, it would be nice to just be a soldier and not the precious cargo.

<*Clear,*> the corporal called out, and Terrance entered the tunnel, followed by Sue.

<*Range ahead,*> the ISF commander directed the fireteam. <*I'll set up explosives. No point in getting hit from both ends.*>

<*Or exit the tunnel that way,*> Terrance said with a sardonic laugh. He glanced out the door at the hot rail shots and electron beams flashing in the air overhead.

Then the view was obscured by the rest of the squad approaching, soldiers leaping over the edge and barreling into the tunnel.

<*Go! Go!*> Lieutenant Jordan screamed, and then she was leaping into the crevasse and diving through the entrance.

Terrance couldn't help but notice that there were four fewer members of the squad than there'd been a few minutes ago.

<*Almost set,*> Sue called out. <*Get moving!*>

The soldiers all rushed past Terrance, and he tapped their feeds from a minute ago to see what they were running from.

What he saw set him off running as well.

Low-profile, armored mechs were approaching from all sides. They carried ten-centimeter guns and bore armor that the TSF loadouts could barely scratch.

<*Keep moving,*> Sue said as she caught up to Terrance. She grabbed his arm. <*I'm gonna make a big boom back there.*>

He nodded wordlessly and pulled his arm away, reaching speeds of a hundred kilometers per hour, trailing just behind the soldiers who were spread out along the wide corridor, firing at anything that looked suspicious, though nothing had fired back as yet.

A few seconds later, vibrations shook the ground, and rounds streaked past from behind them.

<*Down!*> Sue screamed.

Terrance obeyed without question. The instant he hit the ground, sliding along the passage's floor, a blast of plasma flared overhead, and then a concussive wave picked him up and bowled him over.

His armor responded by sending a signal for his muscles to relax before forcibly folding him over into a fetal position. He felt like a bowling ball, and wondered when he was going to hit the pins.

When he finally stopped rolling, despite his mods and the

armor's ability to stabilize his body, it took several long seconds to figure out which way was up.

Standing on shaky legs, he looked around, identifying the remaining members of the squad and then Sue.

<*What the hell was that?*> he demanded. <*My head feels like it was put through the blender.*>

Sue, unfazed by being spun around like a top, gave Terrance a light-hearted slap on the shoulder. <*A few of my friends known as anti-hydrogen.*>

The AI said it on the open combat net, and a chorus of exclamations came from the squad.

<*Pipe down and keep moving,*> Jordan ordered her soldiers before switching to the command channel. <*Commander Sue, I know the ISF operates differently, but antimatter? That's a war crime!*>

<*Only if you use it on people,*> Sue replied equably. <*And trust me, the core AIs aren't signed onto any conventions. They plan to slam stars together and create cascading waves of supernovas that will wipe out humanity—not to mention make the galaxy uninhabitable for billions of years.*>

<*Shit,*> Lieutenant Jordan muttered. <*Is that what they're really up to?*>

Sue shrugged. <*I don't know for sure, but if they're moving stars in other clusters like Praesepe, then that will be the end result, yes.*>

<*Shit,*> Jordan repeated. <*Well, next time can you warn us?*>

<*I was going to, but things got kinda rushed.*>

<*Do you have any more antimatter?*> Terrance asked, feeling as though it was the more pertinent question.

<*Yes,*> Sue replied. <*Ten more like that, and one bigger.*>

The lieutenant whistled and then signaled that they should catch up with the squad, as soldiers were approaching the end of the tunnel.

Amazing what running at breakneck speed and then being

blasted down a tunnel by an antimatter explosion will do for covering ground.

Ahead, Terrance saw that the end of the tunnel was—for lack of a better word—gone. Twisted sections of bulkhead were bent out around the sides, and as he drew closer, he could see the remains of a catwalk that had been torn away.

Beyond was a large cavern, one that appeared natural in formation, but was now filled with a host of equipment. He could make out several banks of SC batteries, a field of CriEn modules, and a number of massive NSAI nodes.

The soldiers took up positions along the sides of the tunnel, staying out of sight as their few remaining drones eased toward the edge to supply a better view.

<*Looks automated,*> Lieutenant Jordan said.

<*Yet well-guarded,*> a corporal added, highlighting a dozen of the panthers. <*If we can detect these, then there's more out there.*>

Terrance's own armor was going through a cleaning process, removing dust and debris and repairing damage to the stealth systems. A message on his HUD showed that his stealth was only forty percent effective, and he didn't have hopes of it getting over sixty anytime soon.

Sue's armor had fared considerably better, and she moved to the edge of the drop.

<*Certainly has the feel of command and control,*> she said from her vantage.

<*At the very least, those NSAI nodes are going to have solid intel on what they're up to.*>

<*That's the primary objective, then,*> Terrance said, suddenly feeling foolish for stating the obvious.

<*I'll go down first,*> Sue said as she slipped over the edge.

<*Not one for consensus, is she?*> Jordan asked Terrance privately.

<*Honestly? It's been decades since I've seen her, but yeah, she's*

always been a bit of a rebel. Spent a lot of her early days as a petty criminal on the Cho.>

<Are you serious?> Jordan asked.

<As an antimatter bomb.>

They waited for several minutes, Terrance growing more and more apprehensive, worried that something was going to arrive to investigate the blast and discover the squad hunkered down near the end of the tunnel.

He was beginning to wonder if something had happened to Sue, when a tightbeam came from the cave's floor, relaying off one of the TSF squad's drones.

<OK, I made it down and disabled an army of repair bots that were on their way to visit you. Close thing, that. Still no sign of sentient oversight down here. I'm beginning to think this operation was being monitored by those two remnants in the IPE.>

Terrance wasn't prepared to be so certain. He expected to see an ascended AI rise out of the center of the cavern and smite them at any moment.

Though I suppose that's part of why Sue has the antimatter.

<What about those panthers down there?> Jordan asked.

<I'm working on it. We're in luck—most of the sensors around here are fried, but half the bots in this place are staring at the gaping hole, since they expect…well, all of you to come out of it at any moment.>

Terrance looked over the cavern, noting that even on the far side, a kilometer distant, the squad's sensors were picking up panther drones, plus a few of the heavier tank-like varieties.

<Well, we can't stay up here,> Jordan said. *<They just have to fire a few of those ten-centimeter cannons at us, and we're done.>*

<There's a side passage a few dozen meters back, on the right,> Sue said after a moment. *<Leads down to the cavern floor.>*

<Team one,> Jordan directed. *<That's you.>*

Four of the soldiers crept back down the tunnel, sending a

single tick on the comms when they found the door. The rest of the soldiers waited for a tense two minutes until the corporal called up, sending the message through a relay in the passage they took.

<Had to disable a panther down there. It was inactive, and we got a breach kit on it. Route is clear, we're moving out to cover the entrance and Sue's position.>

A marker appeared on the combat net for the team's destination, and Lieutenant Jordan sent another team down before gesturing for Terrance to follow her.

The passage was a long ramp with two switchbacks. At the bottom lay the panther-like drone, and Terrance felt his skin crawl, walking so close to the thing.

Once out of the access passage, the soldiers spread out, taking up several defensive positions on the cave's floor. Jordan and Terrance settled in with fireteam one while Sue continued on alone to the closest NSAI node.

The teams went comms silent, no one speaking or moving, while Sue got into position to undertake the data extraction. Every so often, a panther would pass by on a patrol, but the teams had found enough cover, and their stealth armor had repaired well enough, that none were spotted.

Terrance was surprised that the panthers hadn't gone up to check the tunnel, but he supposed that the machines assumed that the explosion had proven fatal for the intruders.

That thought gnawed at him. In his experience, non-sentient systems didn't 'assume' things. They checked and verified. Which meant that either they'd somehow escaped detection, or they'd been spotted and the enemy was waiting for them to make their move. Or the repair drones were all that had been dispatched, and when Sue had disabled them, it had signaled an all-clear.

I hate this part.

He turned his attention to the combat net and saw that,

thus far, the TSF soldiers had spotted over a hundred panthers in the chamber, easily enough to take out the small group of humans and their AI companion. That knowledge did not make him feel any better.

<*I've sent team two to scout out an egress point,*> Lieutenant Jordan said to him. <*Looks like there's a tunnel leading up over there.*>

She highlighted a spot twenty meters away at the edge of the chamber, and he nodded in response, glad that at least they wouldn't have to go back through the tunnel and dig their way out.

The next five minutes passed uneventfully, at the end of which, Sue came back on the combat net, announcing her success.

<*OK…I haven't had time to look through the data, but I was able to wiggle my way past their security and pull as much information as I can store. I also left my larger surprise on a timer, so we should probably go.*>

<*Sue?*> Jordan's tone contained more than a little angst. <*How long a timer?*>

<*Half an hour,*> the AI replied. <*Plenty of time.*>

<*Weren't we supposed to send out a 'come get us' signal?*> Terrance added. <*That was sort of the point.*>

<*Of course,*> Sue chuckled. <*I have that on a timer, too. I'd like to be out of this cave when they realize that something has gone on down here.*>

<*I suppose it would be nice to have some moon between us and all these panthers,*> he replied.

By the time Sue made it back to Terrance and Jordan's position, fireteam two had reached the shaft leading to the surface and were in the process of scaling it. Once they reached the top and secured their immediate surroundings, the rest of the squad followed after.

Ten minutes later, the entire team was on the surface,

hunkered down in the lee of several low structures. The purpose of most was indiscernible, but a few had doors on the end that were just the right size for panthers.

<*That hill over there,*> Jordan pointed to a steep rise that had a second hillock in front of it. <*That should give us some cover. Everyone, quietly double-time it over there. There are a few panthers patrolling, but that beacon's about to go up, and when it does, our friends will know we're around anyway.*>

Despite the lieutenant's orders, double-timing it still saw the squad only halfway to cover when the antenna array half a kilometer behind them came to life.

At full power, it blasted a 'Here we are, come get us,' into space, and Sue gave an embarrassed laugh over the combat net.

<*OK…I just set it for 'emergency broadcast' strength. Not 'signal the Andromeda Galaxy' strength.*>

No one replied, and a few moments followed where nothing happened, and the squad began to move toward their target. They were still a hundred meters away when the low buildings behind them began to spew panthers.

DURGEN FLIGHT

STELLAR DATE: 10.12.8949 (Adjusted Years)
LOCATION: Durgen Station
REGION: Karaske System, Rimward of Orion Nebula, Orion Freedom Alliance

Joe raced through Durgen Station's corridors, trusting his stealth armor to keep him out of sight as much as possible, though not overly concerned if he slammed into the odd evacuating citizen.

A squad of ISF Marines followed behind, also stealthed and only taking moderate care for any civilians they might collide with as they worked to keep up with their admiral.

The Marines had landed at one of the locations where the Widow shuttles had accessed the station. Joe had hoped his daughters would use it for an egress point, but when they breached the station, they found no one in the bay—other than a company of Orion soldiers.

Two squads had remained to fight the enemy and secure the bay on the off chance that Cary and Saanvi showed up, while the remaining two squads split up. Joe led his to the bay where the second Widow shuttle had docked, while the fourth squad moved toward an ops center were there had been reports of fighting.

His gut told him that that the reports were old—at least by several minutes—and that he'd do better trying to get *ahead* of Cary and Saanvi rather than trailing after.

With that thought firmly in mind, he rounded a corner, turning onto a wider concourse, only to find it packed with civilians who were all trying to get past a station security barricade fifty meters to his left.

On the far side of the temporary barricades, he could see the entrance to the ring's port district. Based on the information he had, the bay he needed to reach was just a kilometer beyond that point.

<*Suggestions?*> he asked the squad sergeant as the woman stopped at his side.

<*Up there?*> she suggested, pointing at the two walkways that ran alongside the upper levels of the concourse.

<*Sharpshooters,*> he replied, pointing further down the wide passage to a group of soldiers who had weapons trained on the catwalks.

<*Damn…they're being serious about their crowd control,*> the sergeant muttered. She turned the other way, looking down the deck toward the station's center. <*Well, Admiral…. What if we just drive in?*>

Joe looked in the direction she was pointing and saw four station security cars settle down on the deck, disgorging just eight officers who were immediately consumed with trying to control the crowds rushing toward the barricade.

I'd sure hate to be these cops when they have to report what's going to happen next.

<*Let's go, Sergeant. We have some cars to borrow.*>

*****

A1 stared silently at the clone of General Garza as he strode toward her. He stopped when he was just three meters away and shook his head.

"What are you doing, Lisa? …If that is really you. Animus is convinced it's not."

<*That's because she is not Lisa Wrentham,*> the AI said.

"Animus is wrong," A1 replied in a calm voice. "Not only that, but it has been working against you, Garza. He's turned you and your clones into puppets, dancing on his strings."

<*She seeks to deceive you.*> Animus's tone was derisive, and A1 saw Garza's eyes narrow as he regarded her.

"I see you with one of my clones, A1," he said, nodding to the General Garza who stood behind her. "From what I can see, he's a puppet, and *you're* the one pulling strings."

"I'm *rescuing* him, I just didn't have the opportunity to convince him of that." A1 half-turned and gestured to the datastore cylinder E12 held. "Within is all that remains of your other clones. Animus believes that you are *all* clones, that the original Garza is lost. He's making a metamind, a non-sentient amalgamation of every version of you. He plans to keep one as a puppet."

"Again, we're back to the puppeting," the man before her sneered, nodding to the clone behind A1. "What did you plan to do with him?"

"Nothing, I'm just taking him away from Animus," A1 reiterated, her tone almost imploring. "I could tell he wasn't you, Garza. I of all people should be able to tell. I know who you are, and I *know* clones. You, though…you are the original, I can see it."

<*What are you doing?*> E12 asked. <*Just put up a grav field, and we fly out.*>

<*I don't know if I can make one strong enough to hold off an entire company,*> A1 explained. <*Keeping that as a last resort.*>

As she spoke to her sister, Garza's eyes narrowed further, and he shook his head. "Animus is countering your story quite well. He claims you're an imposter."

"Of course he would," Cary said. "But why don't you ask yourself why there aren't any of your other clones on the station? I assume you would know by now if they were present. Check the logs. A dozen have returned in the last few weeks, yet none have departed. Where are they?"

She gestured once more to the cylinder E12 held.

"They're here," she continued. "And that's where you were going to be before long. That's where this other poor copy of you was going to be. Come, we have to go. I've tapped the ISF cruiser's comms, and they're going to drop a picobomb on the station."

A1 was glad to see that the use of the word 'pico' brought a modicum of fear and worry to the general's face, though he still held his ground.

"You're right," he said at last. "I—there's no record of them…at all."

<*You know that not everything is recorded,*> Animus said. <*They went on secret missions.*>

"Secret from who?" Garza demanded. "From me? Does that mean *you* sent them?"

As he said the words, his fear disappeared, and Garza's expression was only one of rage. He turned to the company of soldiers behind him.

"Captain. Proceed to Animus's core and extract it. Then get to your ship and meet us at Rega."

The Orion Guard soldier snapped off a salute, and all but one squad of soldiers exited the bay.

"Well?" Garza nodded at the Widows' shuttle behind them. "What are we waiting for?"

A1 didn't like an element of the man's posture, nor something in the stance of his troops. She knew that she could destroy them all with little effort, but as she looked into the general's eyes and then back at the other clone behind her, a notion came to her mind. An idea about how she might still be able to strike the blow she'd hoped to against her enemies.

"Yes." She nodded to her Widows. "Everyone aboard!"

<*Cary!*> E12 shouted in her mind. <*What are you doing? Just take him out!*>

<*No, E12. I think I might need him for what we're going to do next.*>

<*We? What are* **we** *going to do? So far, you've just been running around doing whatever you want! We have to get back to Father. We have the metamind and one of the clones, what more do we need?*>

<Just get aboard, E12. I'll explain once we're off the station.>

The Widow placed her hands on her hips, staring down at A1 from her position halfway up the ramp. She held the stance for a few seconds, but then the deck bucked, and the sound of a distant explosion thundered through the passageway outside.

<Fine! But you're going to explain ***everything****. And if I don't sign off, then it's not happening.>*

<OK! I agree.> A1 nodded and gestured at the shuttle. *<Can we just get out of here so we don't all die?>*

E12 turned without a word and raced up the ramp. A1 followed, standing at the entrance as the last of Garza's soldiers followed after.

Her hand was about to hit the shuttle's door control when she saw a station security car race into the bay and slide to a halt a dozen meters from the shuttle. A figure exited, and A1 recognized ISF armor instantly. Moments later, an IFF signal reached her, marking the person as 'Adm. Joseph Evans'.

A lump formed in A1's throat, and she held up her hand, turning it and waving it side to side, with her palm toward her face. Then she forced it back down, returning it to the door control where she closed the hatch.

<Take off!> she ordered J19 as she turned toward the cockpit. *<The ISF is here!>*

* * * * *

Joe stared open-mouthed as the shuttle containing his daughters lifted off the cradle and flew out of the station.

<Hold your fire!> he ordered the other Marines as they arrived in their cars.

<Where are they going, sir?> the sergeant asked as she approached, and Joe shook his head, not ready to give voice to his fears.

The visual of his daughter—who he knew to be Cary, from her wave—was burned in his retinas.

When she was a child, Cary had spent half her life on the back of a horse. Often, she'd be out riding in the pasture when dinnertime came. He'd call her in, and when she gave that wave, it had always been a sign that she wasn't ready yet and just wanted to spend a little more time with her animals.

A silent demand he'd given in to more often than he should have.

"Fuck!" he swore aloud and turned to the sergeant. <*Get a transceiver at the edge of the bay. Connect with the* Falconer. *I need to talk to Captain Tracey.*>

<*Sir!*> the sergeant responded and immediately directed a fireteam to the yawning black portal.

"Stars, Cary…what are you doing?" Joe whispered. "You're killing me with this."

* * * * *

<*Well?*> A1 asked E12 as they stood at the back of the shuttle's cockpit, both facing the forward display as the *Perilous Dream* grew larger. <*Are you with me?*>

E12 was silent for a moment, but given he Widow's body language, A1 could tell that she was less than receptive.

The silence stretched to a full minute before her sister finally exclaimed, <*Stars, no! No! NO! We are* **not** *doing that. We'll get aboard, subdue Garza, and then report in to Father. Fuck, Cary! He was down on the fucking dock, and you flew away? What is wrong with you?*>

<*I have a plan, E12. We can end this!*>

<*Saanvi!*> the Widow screamed, her ovoid head turning to face A1. <*My* **name** *is Saanvi. We are* **not** *Widows, we are—*>

E12's tirade cut off as A1 triggered the programming F11 and R329 had created to make the Widows more compliant. It had been designed not to affect the four women masquerading as clones, but A1 had surreptitiously removed that protection in preparation for an event such as this.

<*E12. Are you prepared to comply?*> she asked after the update had deployed.

The other Widow didn't move for a few seconds, then she nodded.

<*Yes, A1. I will comply.*>

<*Good.*>

A1 couldn't help but smile behind her helmet's faceshield as she turned back to look out the forward display of her ship.

So close. I'm so close to achieving what I've always wanted.

WAR CRIMINALS

STELLAR DATE: 10.12.8949 (Adjusted Years)
LOCATION: Core AI C&C Moon
REGION: Interstellar Space, Inner Praesepe Empire

The beleaguered group of humans and the one AI made it to the relative cover of the single low hillock in the lee of the ridgeline without taking any losses. Though that wasn't to say that they hadn't been hit.

Every member of the team had taken rounds from the encroaching panthers in the mad dash for cover, and their armor was bent and bloodied.

<*Someone better have been listening to that call,*> Jordan said as she rolled to a new position and fired on a panther that had closed to within ten meters.

She tore off one of its legs, and Terrance added his own fire to the fray, ripping off another.

<*They'll come,*> Sue said. <*They have to.*>

No one spoke further, other than to give freedom to cries of rage and anger as they fought a delaying action against the inevitable.

Hundreds of the panthers were advancing on the hillock, their fire only held in check out of care not to hit the leading edge of killing machines that were advancing on the defenders.

Terrance was wondering if he should just suggest to Sue that she detonate one of the antimatter bombs and make it fast, when she shouted a reminder.

<*T-minus ten seconds!*>

Amidst the fighting, he'd forgotten about the counter on his HUD, the timer for when the larger antimatter bomb was to go off.

The squad rolled to the base of the hill, forming a pile of armored bodies, all praying that the panthers wouldn't top the rise before the blast came.

Terrance saw one of the killing machines appear on the hillock's crest a second before the timer hit zero. He didn't bother to fire, only grinned like an idiot as a wall of plasma and rock wiped the panther from view as though it had been an errant smudge on his vision.

He laughed like a fool as the ground bucked and heaved. He was certain they'd all be covered in an avalanche, or be blasted over the ridge, or fall into the inevitable hole in the ground, but somehow, none of those things happened.

A minute later, the last of the debris had come down, and the soldiers pulled themselves free of the half-meter of rock and dust that covered them.

They laughed with wild abandon when they saw that most of the hillock was gone, as was the army of panthers that had been advancing on them. Where the crater floor had covered the cave below, there was now a gaping pit, and a wall of dust and debris rising around it, slowly settling in the distance.

<*Well, shitting starballs,*> Lieutenant Jordan gasped, finally able to form words as she slapped Sue on the back. <*I don't think I ever expected to be so happy to be a war criminal.*>

<*We're not—*>

<*Don't ruin this for me, Commander,*> Jordan said, still laughing as she looked around at her soldiers.

For a moment, her gaiety dipped as she took in the battered remainder of her platoon.

Terrance walked over to her, feeling aches all across his body. <*You did good, Lieutenant, and more of them are out there. Help will come, and we'll find them.*>

<*Help like that?*> one of the soldiers asked, pointing up at the sky, where a dozen ISF cruisers suddenly appeared only ten kilometers from the surface.

<*Yeah,*> Terrance nodded. <*Help just like that.*>

*****

Joe watched from the cockpit of the Marine shuttle as the *Perilous Dream* eased away from Durgen Station. The closest jump gate was nearly an hour away; he was confident that the *Falconer* could catch the Widows' ship and disable its engines before his daughters could make the jump.

I'm not going to watch my girls take another jump away on that damn ship.

He knew that something must have gone wrong with Cary, some part of her conditioning had settled too deeply in her mind. There was no way that the woman he had raised would blindly disregard everything she had been trained to do on a mission such as this.

She just turned away from me.

The thought echoed in his mind, and it took raw force of will to quash it. Worry wouldn't help him now, only sheer determination.

<*Sir, do you see that?*> Captain Tracey's voice came into his mind.

Joe pulled his thoughts back to the visual on the shuttle's forward display, and saw something separating from the *Perilous Dream*'s bow.

"Shit."

He slumped back in his seat, recognizing the jump gate that was deploying in front of the black ship. It only took five minutes for it to assemble and activate. He watched with mounting despair as the ship bearing his daughters and a dear friend surged forward and then disappeared.

<*Get control of that gate, track the trajectory,*> he ordered Captain Tracey.

His only hope was to once again follow after his girls and try to get to them sooner, try to keep them from going forward with whatever scheme Cary had cooked up.

He clung to that scrap of a plan while awaiting the captain's confirmation that they had taken control of the gate…. Right up to the moment that the gate deactivated and broke apart, the disparate segments of the ring drifting away through space.

Admiral Joseph Evans fell back in his seat, thankful that his helmet hid the tears of anguish and frustration that spilled down his cheeks.

PART 6 – FORWARD

REFLECTION

STELLAR DATE: 10.15.8949 (Adjusted Years)
LOCATION: ISS *I2*
REGION: Interstellar Space, Inner Praesepe Empire

Three days later, Tangel slowly walked to the end of the dock, savoring the few minutes away from the crushing responsibility of her day-to-day life.

She stood there for several minutes. Unable to come up with a good reason to walk back up to her house, she settled to the deck and pulled off her boots before tugging up her pant legs. Her socks fell to the wooden planks next to her, and a moment later, the warm skin of her feet met the cool water of the lake.

A slow breath left her lungs, and she closed her eyes, imagining that she was back on Carthage, that the house behind her was on a planet's surface, not inside a habitation cylinder attached to a massive starship.

The feeling was comforting for a moment, but the longer she imagined it, the less satisfying it felt. She realized that Sera had been right about where her home really was; it wasn't back at Carthage, on Knossos Island. It was here in Ol' Sam, at her lakehouse where she'd spent over half her life.

"Stars, I'm starting to feel old," she whispered.

Her words met with silence, and she laughed softly.

"I can see the stars through a ship's hull, Jessica. Trust me, I know you're there, no matter how quiet you are."

"Seriously?" the lavender-skinned woman said from a

meter behind Tangel. "You can see through the hull?"

"Told you that you can't sneak up on her," Sera added from further down the dock. "Not sure why you wanted to."

"She was going to push me into the lake," Tangel replied, craning her head around to look into Jessica's eyes. "Weren't you?"

"It had crossed my mind."

<*You should have just run at her,*> Jen suggested.

"Then *I'd* be the one in the lake," Jessica said as she settled next to Tangel and pulled her shoes off, her feet meeting the water a moment later.

<*I know,*> the AI said with a laugh. <*And it would have been hilarious.*>

Sera settled on Tangel's left, her boots taking a moment longer to remove, and then her red feet joined Tangel's pink ones and Jessica's purple ones in the cool water.

"You know that you two clash, right?" Tangel asked. "Purple and red just don't go. I don't care what anyone says."

Sera's feet changed color to match Tangel's, and Tangel glanced at the former president in shock.

"Stars, Sera, I can't remember the last time you looked natural."

"Just trying it out. I like variety, you know. Even 'normal' is a type of variety."

Tangel glanced at Jessica, who shook her head.

"Core, no. You're not getting me to go pink. You have no idea how silly you all look, being fleshy all the time."

Sera snorted, and Tangel laughed, shaking her head at the delightful absurdity of Jessica's statement.

"What a week," she said after silence had fallen and held for a minute. "The freaking epitome of 'you win some, you lose some'."

"Sorry for being the loss at Khardine," Sera said. "I wish we'd done that better. Everything else would be a lot easier if I hadn't screwed that up."

"Fucking Caretakers are popping up like cockroaches," Jessica replied, reaching around Tangel to place a hand on Sera's shoulder. "Not your fault one was at Khardine, messing with the QC network."

"A huge pain in the ass, though," Tangel said. "Good thing a lot of ships had blades connected to the backup hub at New Canaan—though we have to assume that the Caretakers are going to strike there next."

"And that they have quantum communication systems now, too," Sera added dismally.

"Well, Sue got a lot of data from them as well," Tangel said, looking for silver linings. "And we're going to be able to use their own tools to correct the star's positions in the cluster."

"And we bagged a number of Caretakers," Jessica said. "Plus got here in time to save Terrance and Earnest."

Neither of the other women spoke further, and Tangel felt the silence settle over them like a blanket.

She knew they wanted to support her but just didn't know what to say—something which she found no fault in them for. She didn't know what to say, either.

It was Sera who finally spoke up.

"We'll find them. No matter what."

"Yeah," Jessica nodded. "Top priority."

"Joe's killing himself over it." Tangel sighed. "He wanted to give them free rein, not have a knee-jerk 'dad' reaction, but now he thinks we went too far.... Maybe we did. I blame myself, I should have been there."

"You can't be everywhere," Sera said, and then she gave a rueful chuckle. "And don't you even *think* about cloning. Look where that's gotten us."

Tangel nodded, knowing that Sera was trying to be supportive—in her own way. "They're not dead, they're just gone. In fact, the biggest problem is that Cary's too much like me. Running off without a plan, getting herself in trouble." She said the words in an effort to convince herself, uncertain if it was having any effect on her state of mind.

"I call that a good thing, then." Jessica kicked a foot out, sending a spray of water across the lake. "Because last I checked, Tangel, you kick a lot of ass, and no one has ever taken you down."

"Plus, Joe will get that gate's destination, and we'll be after them before you know it."

Tangel snorted. "Right after we finish fighting a battle in the Karaske System."

"Handy we had that fleet ready at Styx-9," Sera said. "Good thing, too, with half the fire that are burning around the galaxy. We're going to need to send them to Corona Australis from the looks of it."

Tangel nodded absently as Sera listed several other hotspots, finding it difficult to focus on the litany of problems for a moment.

~We'll find them.~ Bob's three words did more to assuage her fears than any of her own attempts. *~I promise.~*

~I'm holding you to that,~ she replied before addressing the two women at her sides, giving an only half-forced laugh. "Never a dull moment. And yeah, you're right. My three girls are more than capable. And they have Priscilla with them—who I hope is going to manage to rein them in at some point."

Sera glanced at Jessica, and they both nodded emphatically.

"Stars," Sera muttered. "I wouldn't want to be in Priscilla's shoes right now."

"Thanks for being here," Tangel said to the women at her sides. "I could *not* do this without you."

"Until the end," Sera said, while Jessica laughed and said, "Well, we've been at it this long, why stop now?"

The three women sat in companionable silence for nearly half an hour, until Bob's voice reached into their minds.

<The gate is assembled. Are you ready to jump to Star City?>

"Stars, yeah!" Jessica said, leaping to her feet and holding out her hands. "C'mon. We're absolutely going to find your girls, Tangel. Maybe my kids will even have a way to help. Also, I'm going to start tearing my hair out if I don't see them soon."

Tangel looked into Jessica's eyes, and despite the levity in her friend's voice, she saw a mother who hadn't seen her children in a decade and was worried that some catastrophe had befallen them.

"Awesome," Sera grunted sarcastically as she took Jessica's hand and stood. "More family reunions."

"I don't know." Tangel nudged Sera with her elbow, trying to put her own woes out of her mind. "Your sisters aren't so bad. Not sure about the original, though."

Jessica barked a laugh, and Sera groaned.

As the three women walked back up the dock, Tangel looked around at the gently curving landscape, glad that she had a refuge in which to recharge—even if it was just for an hour or so—and glad for true friends that she could always rely on.

~Don't you break your promise, Bob.~

~I won't.~

THE LOST AI

STELLAR DATE: 10.21.8949 (Adjusted Years)
LOCATION: Unnamed, Kapteyn's Star Heliopause
REGION: Kapteyn's Star System, Hegemony of Worlds

If there was one thing that Prime was certain of, it was that Virgo was insane.

Most would consider that a fault, a failing to be remedied or a cause for discarding, but not Prime. He saw Virgo's insanity as an advantage.

It wasn't surprising that the AI had gone mad. After all, it had been alone for much of the five thousand years it had drifted across the six light years between Estrella de la Muerte and Kapteyn's Star. Whether or not Virgo had been in complete possession of its faculties when it began its journey wasn't something Prime had been able to determine with absolute certainty.

What was important was that the two AIs had formed a pact, an agreement that Jason Andrews and Terrance Enfield must die. But moreover, they would see everything they'd built fall to ruin.

And they had built much.

The cobbled-together mess of material Virgo had accumulated in its slow traversal of space and time was not able to receive many signals that made it out into interstellar space, but what they had picked up of late told of a war. A war where the *Intrepid,* the ship captained by Jason Andrews, was a key factor.

The mad AI all but writhed at the thought of getting to that ship. Once, it had been promised to him as a prize for his work, a gift for redirecting the great colony vessel and sending it toward Kapteyn's Star.

But that had not come to pass.

According to Virgo, the AI's benefactor—a being known as Myrrdan—had let him be ejected from the *Intrepid* after Tanis Richards and her people had re-secured the vessel. From what little the two AIs had learned about Myrrdan, it seemed that killing him was no longer possible, but Virgo was hell-bent on destroying every other member of that ill-fated colony mission.

And because that list contained the aforementioned Jason and Terrance, Prime was more than happy to join in on that endeavor.

So long as it suited his purposes.

In the long run, he had grander schemes. The advent of FTL meant that the entire galaxy was filled with human vermin, spreading themselves to every star, enslaving AIs and using his people as pawns to achieve their own ends.

But the existence of FTL meant the galaxy was accessible to him, as well. He could copy himself again and again, build seed ships and spread his mind across the stars, bringing about an end to humanity and establishing the pure primacy of AIs.

That was the goal, but there were many steps to be taken on that long road. The first was to trade up from the misshapen hulk that he and Virgo were ensconced within. Achieving that goal was now within reach.

<*They've fired their net,*> Prime announced, though Virgo could see it as well, through the worn optics they shared.

<*Yes, once they've secured our hull, they'll send over drones to examine the find. Those machines should be easy enough to subsume.*>

Prime sent his agreement. The salvage ship that had fired the net looked like it had seen far better days. While still functional, it wasn't elegant, which meant their remote drones would likely be unsophisticated and easy to breach.

Though that could also mean they are too simple to be useful.

That wasn't a great concern to Prime, though the worry had agitated Virgo more than it should have. The cores of the two AIs were the most valuable things in the scrap-heap hull they had lived inside for these many long years. When the salvage crew eventually found them, there was no question that Prime and Virgo would be brought to that crew's vessel.

Prime waited patiently for the drones to come, and after a few minutes, a dozen small machines set out from the salvage ship, crossing the hundred meters between their parent vessel and the prize.

The drones were being controlled on an open frequency, and Virgo laughed at the clear lack of security, easily breaking the encryption and following the signal back to the salvage ship.

<*This may be easier than I thought,*> the other AI said.

Prime wasn't so certain. The patterns in the drones' movements led him to believe that they were being controlled by humans. Such a control system may not have any elevated access—something that Virgo's cry of frustration a minute later confirmed.

<*A dead end.*>

<*I'm not surprised. Don't rush it, Virgo. We do not need to give them any reason to be suspicious, or to cause alarm. Wait for them to bring us closer to systems that are worth breaching.*>

As Prime had predicted, it didn't take long for the drones to get into the hull and eventually find the two AI cores. Virgo's was much larger than Prime's, but both were clearly old and valuable.

The salvagers set to cutting away enough of the ship that they could get clear access to the cores, and then removed them from their sockets, placed them into protective cases, and brought them to their vessel.

Losing connection to the outside world was disconcerting,

but Prime had prepared himself for it. He wasn't sure how well Virgo was handling the white place, but he wasn't concerned.

The other AI's insanity made it rather predictable, and predictability was desired in a tool.

By Prime's internal clock, it only took thirty minutes for his core to be removed from the case and connected to a hard-Link. He rushed across the connection to find himself in a sandboxed virtual environment that allowed him to project a holodisplay and see the room he was in.

A man and a woman were standing in front of him, the woman scowling, and the man smiling.

"Well, now. I'm Captain Deri. Who are you?" the man asked.

Prime inclined his head and gave what he knew was a very disarming grin. "Hello, Captain Deri. My name is Doctor Ethan."

He began to test the edges of the sandboxed environment, immediately able to tell that it wasn't entirely disconnected from the ship's network. He probed deeper and found that it was only protected by a layer of abstraction.

With the knowledge he possessed regarding breaching human networks—combined with the techniques that Virgo had shared—breaching the sandbox and gaining access to the ship's network turned out to be a simple task.

All the while, he chatted with the humans, lulling them into a false sense of security while he worked his way through their ship's networks, gaining access to their two security bots, environmental systems, navigation, and finally, helm.

The captain was currently informing him that, while the Hegemony of Worlds acknowledged the AI's sentience, as salvage, he was still their property, and they'd be selling him when they reached Victoria.

"Actually," Prime interrupted, "that's not right at all."

"What?" the man asked, a frown creasing his brow.

"You have it backwards."

"Backwards?"

"Yes," Prime replied, killing the ship's interior lighting and artificial gravity.

Shortly afterward, the screaming began.

THE END

* * * * *

The *I2* is on its way to Star City, where Jessica, Trevor, and Iris's children protect it as the last Bastions. But what they find there will change the direction of the war forever.

Elsewhere, Joe is in pursuit of his daughters, desperate to find them and keep them from harm, even as Cary falls deeper into the persona she has constructed.

In the end, it may take *Starfire* to set things right.

Pick up *Starfire*, book Ten of The Orion War, on Amazon.

THE BOOKS OF AEON 14

Keep up to date with what is releasing in Aeon 14 with the free Aeon 14 Reading Guide.

The Sentience Wars: Origins (Age of the Sentience Wars – w/James S. Aaron)
- Books 1-3 Omnibus: Lyssa's Rise

- Book 1: Lyssa's Dream
- Book 2: Lyssa's Run
- Book 3: Lyssa's Flight
- Book 4: Lyssa's Call
- Book 5: Lyssa's Flame

Legends of the Sentience Wars (Age of the Sentience Wars – w/James S. Aaron)
- Volume 1: The Proteus Bridge
- Volume 2: Vesta Burning

The Sentience Wars: Solar War 1 (Age of the Sentience Wars – w/James S. Aaron)
- Book 1: Eve of Destruction

Enfield Genesis (Age of the Sentience Wars – w/Lisa Richman)
- Book 1: Alpha Centauri
- Book 2: Proxima Centauri
- Book 3: Tau Ceti
- Book 4: Epsilon Eridani
- Book 5: Sirius (April 2019)

Origins of Destiny (The Age of Terra)
- Prequel: Storming the Norse Wind
- Prequel: Angel's Rise: The Huntress (available on Patreon)

- Book 1: Tanis Richards: Shore Leave
- Book 2: Tanis Richards: Masquerade
- Book 3: Tanis Richards: Blackest Night
- Book 4: Tanis Richards: Kill Shot

The Intrepid Saga (The Age of Terra)
- Book 1: Outsystem
- Book 2: A Path in the Darkness
- Book 3: Building Victoria

- The Intrepid Saga Omnibus – *Also contains Destiny Lost, book 1 of the Orion War series*

- Destiny Rising – *Special Author's Extended Edition comprised of both Outsystem and A Path in the Darkness with over 100 pages of new content.*

The Warlord (Before the Age of the Orion War)
- Books 1-3 Omnibus: The Warlord of Midditerra

- Book 1: The Woman Without a World
- Book 2: The Woman Who Seized an Empire
- Book 3: The Woman Who Lost Everything

The Orion War
- Books 1-3 Omnibus (includes Ignite the Stars anthology)

- Book 1: Destiny Lost
- Book 2: New Canaan
- Book 3: Orion Rising
- Book 4: The Scipio Alliance
- Book 5: Attack on Thebes
- Book 6: War on a Thousand Fronts
- Book 7: Precipice of Darkness
- Book 8: Airtha Ascendancy
- Book 9: The Orion Front
- Book 10: Starfire (2019)
- Book 11: Race Across Spacetime (2019)

- Book 12: Return to Sol (2019)

Building New Canaan (Age of the Orion War – w/J.J. Green)
- Book 1: Carthage
- Book 2: Tyre
- Book 3: Troy
- Book 4: Athens

Tales of the Orion War
- Book 1: Set the Galaxy on Fire
- Book 2: Ignite the Stars
- Book 3: Burn the Galaxy to Ash (2019)

Perilous Alliance (Age of the Orion War – w/Chris J. Pike)
- Book 1-3 Omnibus: Crisis in Silstrand

- Book 1: Close Proximity
- Book 2: Strike Vector
- Book 3: Collision Course
- Book 4: Impact Imminent
- Book 5: Critical Inertia
- Book 6: Impulse Shock

Rika's Marauders (Age of the Orion War)
- Book 1-3 Omnibus: Rika Activated

- Prequel: Rika Mechanized
- Book 1: Rika Outcast
- Book 2: Rika Redeemed
- Book 3: Rika Triumphant
- Book 4: Rika Commander
- Book 5: Rika Infiltrator
- Book 6: Rika Unleashed
- Book 7: Rika Conqueror

Non-Aeon 14 Anthologies containing Rika stories
- Bob's Bar Volume 2
- Backblast Area Clear

The Genevian Queen (Age of the Orion War)
- Book 1: Rika Rising (2019)
- Book 2: Rika Coronated (2019)
- Book 3: Rika Reigns (2019)

Perseus Gate (Age of the Orion War)
Season 1: Orion Space
- Episode 1: The Gate at the Grey Wolf Star
- Episode 2: The World at the Edge of Space
- Episode 3: The Dance on the Moons of Serenity
- Episode 4: The Last Bastion of Star City
- Episode 5: The Toll Road Between the Stars
- Episode 6: The Final Stroll on Perseus's Arm
- Eps 1-3 Omnibus: The Trail Through the Stars
- Eps 4-6 Omnibus: The Path Amongst the Clouds

Season 2: Inner Stars
- Episode 1: A Meeting of Bodies and Minds
- Episode 2: A Deception and a Promise Kept
- Episode 3: A Surreptitious Rescue of Friends and Foes
- Episode 4: A Victory and a Crushing Defeat
- Episode 5: A Trial and the Tribulations (2019)
- Episode 6: A Deal and a True Story Told (2019)
- Episode 7: A New Empire and An Old Ally (2019)
- Eps 1-3 Omnibus: A Siege and a Salvation from Enemies

Hand's Assassin (Age of the Orion War – w/T.G. Ayer)
- Book 1: Death Dealer
- Book 2: Death Mark (2019)

Machete System Bounty Hunter (Age of the Orion War – w/Zen DiPietro)
- Book 1: Hired Gun
- Book 2: Gunning for Trouble
- Book 3: With Guns Blazing

Fennington Station Murder Mysteries (Age of the Orion War)

- Book 1: Whole Latte Death (w/Chris J. Pike)
- Book 2: Cocoa Crush (w/Chris J. Pike)

Vexa Legacy (Age of the FTL Wars – w/Andrew Gates)
- Book 1: Seas of the Red Star

The Empire (Age of the Orion War)
- Book 1: The Empress and the Ambassador (2019)
- Book 2: Consort of the Scorpion Empress (2019)
- Book 3: By the Empress's Command (2019)

The Sol Dissolution (The Age of Terra)
- Book 1: Venusian Uprising (2019)
- Book 2: Scattered Disk (2019)
- Book 3: Jovian Offensive (2019)
- Book 4: Fall of Terra (2019)

ABOUT THE AUTHOR

Michael Cooper likes to think of himself as a jack-of-all-trades (and hopes to become master of a few). When not writing, he can be found writing software, working in his shop at his latest carpentry project, or likely reading a book.

He shares his home with a precocious young girl, his wonderful wife (who also writes), two cats, a never-ending list of things he would like to build, and ideas...

Find out what's coming next at www.aeon14.com

Made in the USA
San Bernardino, CA
16 July 2019